OUTSOURCED

OUTSOURCED

R J Hillhouse

A TOM DOHERTY ASSOCIATES BOOK • NEW YORK

This is a work of fiction. All of the characters, organizations, and events portrayed in this novel are either products of the author's imagination or are used fictitiously.

OUTSOURCED

Copyright © 2007 by Tasopé International, LLC

A Forge Book
Published by Tom Doherty Associates, LLC
175 Fifth Avenue
New York, NY 10010

www.tor-forge.com

Forge® is a registered trademark of Tom Doherty Associates, LLC.

ISBN-13: 978-0-7653-5481-5
ISBN-10: 0-7653-5481-0

First Edition: June 2007
First Mass Market Edition: May 2008

Printed in the United States of America

0 9 8 7 6 5 4 3 2 1

To Cynthia

ACKNOWLEDGMENTS

No spies or soldiers were harmed in the making of this book. Any revelation of classified national security information is purely coincidental and is the product of a rigorous analysis of open source materials coupled with a vivid imagination. I am indebted to the many fine journalists who have brought many of the inner workings of the War on Terror into the public domain. I am particularly grateful to the many professionals, including friends and family, who have shared their knowledge of unclassified matters with me.

Like countless other Americans, the War on Terror touched me personally, as friends and family were sent to Iraq. This novel was conceived during the long hours, and sometimes days, of waiting for an e-mail from a loved one who was in combat. My deepest thanks goes to LtGen James Mattis, LtGen Richard Natonski, and BGen Joseph Dunford, USMC, who keep bringing my cousin home safely.

My cousin, SSgt Grant Smillie, USMC, has been an inspiration and a teacher, without whom this book would not have been possible. A decorated marine, internationally ranked martial artist, and a true patriot, Grant has not only taught me rudimentary tactical, infantry, and combat skills, but has also given me a glimpse into the passion behind being a Devil Dog. From him I gained the highest admiration for the men and women of the US Marine Corps. There is truly *No Better Friend*.

My favorite bomb-maker, LCDR Jim Froneberger, USN (ret.), has kept my characters from blowing themselves up. LtCol Ben Fuata, Hawaii Army National Guard, and his staff generously shared their extensive knowledge of combat helicopters, as did CW4 Robert Nance, US Army (ret.), and CW4 Jeffrey Crandell, US Army/CA ARNG. My cousins LtCol Jerry "Rebel" Summerlin, USMC (ret.), and Pam Summerlin went to great efforts to help me understand the midair refueling process. Fellow thriller writer and former USAF C-5 pilot Cindy Dees provided additional flight assistance. Rob Krott, former Senior Foreign Correspondent for *Soldier of Fortune* magazine, author, and mercenary extraordinaire, helped sketch in the fine details about contract soldiering in Iraq. GySgt Scott Stutler, USMC, was the official armorer for Black Management, assisting with weapons choices, their functioning and limitations. My sister and medical advisor, Renée Walker, D.O., F.A.O.C.O.O., kept the characters alive, and me out of trouble. My father, Charles Hillhouse, has been to me what "Q" was to James Bond, creating and testing unusual approaches to escape, evasion, and sabotage, including some that actually worked and made it into these pages; I'm grateful to my mother, Donna Hillhouse, for keeping Dad from killing himself in the process, as well as for her constant encouragement.

I am grateful to the many others who have donated their technical assistance, including SrA Cecily Okimura, USAF; 1Lt Charles Newman, Hawaii Army National Guard; Reef Hardy, Ph.D., criminalist, LAPD Scientific Investigation Division; Keith Yamakawa, D.D.S.; Keith Shiigi; fellow writer Lauren Baratz-Logsted; ACO Sgt Kathy Wheeles; and Paul Wheeles. Bobby Carmichael is for the OR crews in Joplin.

Michael Lukson, my first reader, partner in crime, and Web guru has come to my rescue countless times. Leah Wilson's keen insight and suggestions helped the manuscript reach its full potential. Sarah Wang has provided outstanding legal counsel to me, as well as to Black Management, and her keen eye for detail has made this book a much smoother read.

My editor, Eric Raab, has worked diligently and tirelessly to champion this novel and to ensure it was not only the best book it could be, but that it was published well. Tom Doherty has my gratitude for his preserving belief in my work. The staff at Tor, including Linda Quinton, Kathleen Fogarty, Elena Stokes, Tom Espenscheid, AJ Murphy, Mike Rohrig, Patricia Johnson, Christine Jaeger, Patty Garcia, Edwin Chapman, and others behind the scenes, have done truly exceptional work.

Scott Miller, my literary agent, has a gift for making just the right observation at the right time, one of which was the springboard for the structure of this novel. He is golden. My thanks also go out to Holly Root and others at Trident who've worked diligently on the project. Maryann Palumbo and Sarah Self's enthusiasm and hard work are greatly appreciated.

This is the point where an author usually thanks a spouse for processing endless scenes, plot, and character ideas, but instead I have to thank my dogs LynnDy, Jordan, and Suzie-Q for listening to these ramblings—even if it did take many boxes of biscuits to ensure their rapt attention. I am so blessed that my partner gives me a book-free space, where I can get away from the shadowy world I'm writing about so I can focus on the people, things, and dogs that really matter. My deepest love and appreciation are for Cynthia Curatalo, who makes it all worthwhile.

CAST OF CHARACTERS

Individuals

Abdullah	leader of one of two al Qaeda factions; disputed successor to bin Laden
al-Zahrani	leader of one of two al Qaeda factions; disputed successor to bin Laden
Larry Ashland	an executive in Rubicon who is also a spy
Beach Dog	Both call sign and nickname of the Black Management helicopter pilot, a former Night Stalker; his call sign and nickname are the same
Camille Black	president of Black Management; an alias used by Stella Hawkins
Greg Bolton	an alias of Hunter Stone, created for him by Force Zulu to serve as his cover while he penetrated Rubicon
Bushmen	members of Force Zulu
Joe Chronister	CIA case officer
Genghis	Black Management operator, former Delta Force
Stella Hawkins	real name of Camille Black
Manuel "Iggy" Ignatius	Black Management's Chief Operations Officer
Lightning Six	Camille Black's call sign
Jackie Nelson	a geologist, wife of Brian Nelson
Brian Nelson	an executive in Rubicon's petroleum division

Sue "Pete" Peterson	Black Management deputy project manager for logistics for Baghdad; former personal assistant to Camille Black
Ray	an alias of Hunter Stone
Saber Tooth	Hunter Stone's call sign
Virgil Searcy	Black Management's Deputy Operations Officer
General Grant Smillie	Deputy Undersecretary of Defense for Intelligence; oversees the SSB, including Force Zulu
Hunter Stone	member of Force Zulu; his call sign is SABER TOOTH; aliases include Greg Bolton, Ray and Sergei
Tin Man	Iggy Ignatius' call sign
Zorro	alias of Joe Chronister

Companies and Organizations

AegeanA	British intelligence firm, specializing in signals intelligence (eavesdropping on communications)
Black Management	private military corporation founded by Camille Black
Blackwater USA	private military corporation founded by a former SEAL
CIA	Central Intelligence Agency, slang names include Other Government Agency (OGA), the Agency and Christians in Action
Delta Force	popular name for the Army's elite counterterrorism unit (SFO-D)
Force Zulu	a deep-cover espionage and covert action unit that combines elements of espionage along with commando tactics; part of the Pentagon's Strategic Support Branch (SSB); the

	real-life designation of the unit is highly classified and changes frequently; also referred to as Task Force Zulu
Gray Fox	a military spy organization; precursor to SSB and Force Zulu
Halliburton	multinational energy services and construction company whose subsidiary KBR is a major military contractor that provides the Pentagon with billions of dollars of outsourced services, including private military services
Lyon Group	private intelligence corporation
Rubicon Group	multinational energy services and construction company whose subsidiaries include a major military contractor that provides the Pentagon with billions of dollars of outsourced services, including private military services
Special Activities Division (SAD)	paramilitary unit of the CIA, composed primarily of former Special Forces operators
SSB	Strategic Support Branch, the Pentagon's new spy organization responsible for black units of Special Forces operators specially trained to collect human intelligence and run covert actions; the agency responsible for Force Zulu
Triple Canopy	private military corporation formed by former Delta Force noncommissioned officers
ZapataEngineering	private military corporation, services include bomb disposal

See pages 485–490 for a glossary of terms.

We are not simply a "private security company."
We are a turnkey solution provider for 4th generation warfare.
—Blackwater USA, LLC

Triple Canopy provides legal, moral, and ethical Special Operations services.

—Triple Canopy, Inc.

PROLOGUE

Aurora, Missouri
May 11th

Camille Black stared at the electric meter, pretending to read it, while across the street her aunts, uncles and cousins cried over the flower-draped casket. Her family plot at Maple Park Cemetery was close enough to the edge that she could see the tears flowing down Aunt Ethel's face—or at least she convinced herself that she was looking at streaks in her aunt's makeup so that she wasn't alone in her tears. Camille had made a fortune from the War on Terror, but she was starting to suspect she had sold her soul, damning herself to exile, a spook haunting cemeteries, reading meters and faking deliveries while she stole glances at her loved ones' coffins. Two years ago it had been her fiancé Hunter's homecoming from Iraq, a flag-draped casket and a Marine Corps honor guard. Today it was Granny Lusk. She turned Hunter's engagement ring on her finger, then scribbled a number on her clipboard before moving on to the next house, all the while scanning the area. A UPS truck circled through the neighborhood—for the third time.

Across the street, the UPS truck pulled over and parked at the side of the cemetery. A maple tree with the delicate light green leaves of spring was the only thing that shielded her from the driver's view as she studied the vehicle. It was definitely the same one that had been in the area for the past fifteen minutes, but something seemed different. For some reason the guy now had the doors closed, although it was a warm spring day. And there was something else that bothered her.

The driver now had dark wiry hair and a deep tan.

A blast of adrenaline jolted her body and her muscles tightened, hardening for battle. She was marked. He was either an old enemy or paparazzi trying to get another shot of the elusive CEO of Black Management, the only female player in the sexy shadows of private military and intelligence corporations. That novelty had already splashed her grainy image across tabloids around the world and she didn't want to give them any more fodder, particularly at the expense of her family's privacy.

She carried a USP Tactical pistol under her coveralls, but she knew a frontal assault would be too loud and too public and she also wanted a quiet chat with the driver. She melted to the ground. Like a sniper creeping into position, she inched herself along on her belly until she was behind a weathered barn, out of the driver's line of sight. She looked around for options. As she accidentally trampled a flat of tomatoes awaiting planting, she could almost hear the words her father had repeated over and over again as he had trained her: *Paint the picture you want him to see.*

A cottage with an attached carport stood a good forty feet across an overgrown vacant lot from the barn. She peeled off her coveralls and pulled off a baseball cap, freeing the shoulder-length hair of her wig. Then she picked up a plastic flat of wilting tomato plants. As much as she wanted to dash to the carport, she paced herself, plucking dead leaves from the plants as if she gave a damn.

The inside of the carport was old-lady tidy with little more than a silver 1979 Buick LeSabre, a clothes basket filled with canning jars and a cardboard box with bundles of tied-up newspapers inside. Whoever the occupant was, she wasn't giving her much to work with. The only potential weapon she spotted was an ancient screwdriver with a cracked wooden handle and hand-hewn metal shaft that was pitted with rust. It was too crude to wield smoothly. She chided herself for not going inside the barn, but now had no time to double back. In the past month she had personally neutralized over a dozen Iraqi insurgents and she had felt no more than a few fleeting pangs of fear. Now she was breathing hard and her arm wouldn't stop trembling. She closed her eyes for a second and took a long breath. When she opened them, she grabbed a mason jar and her arm stopped shaking.

Camille dumped the newspapers from the cardboard box, then wrapped an old rag around the jar for insulation. She hurried over to the hot water heater. The valve at the base didn't want to turn, but she forced it open and filled her mug with steaming water. *Perfect.*

Shielding her face with the cardboard box, she ran toward the UPS truck. Its height complicated things and a street scene was out of the question. She would have to strike high so that the driver didn't fall forward and onto the pavement. She banged on the passenger door. "Hey, so glad I caught you."

The driver slid the door open and she threw the scalding water into his face. With her gun pointing straight up, she sprang into the truck and jabbed his chest with the hard polymer grip, her body's inertia magnifying the blow. In the split second that he fell backwards, she aimed the weapon.

Camille saw his kick coming at her the same instant his sunglasses flew to the floor. The sight of his face made her pause for a moment, slowing her pivot. His foot struck her thigh hard.

"Stella!" he said using her old name—her real name. "Break off! It's me. Hunter." He put his hands on the pistol and she let him guide her aim away from his chest.

"Oh my god. Hunter?"

"It's me, honey. Alive and missing you like hell."

"Why?" She stared at him, stunned.

Her late fiancé, Hunter Stone, blinked hard as he moved

past her to close the door. Without a word, he took her in his arms. She pressed her body against his, yearning for the joy they'd once had, but she knew all too well that death had a way of changing people.

They left the funeral separately after agreeing to meet up in an hour south of town in the Mark Twain National Forest. Hunter had planned to camp for the night, but Camille insisted upon breaking into an empty fishing cabin outside of Shell Knob that she thought still belonged to her uncle Chuck. Over the years, she had learned to take advantage of creature comforts whenever the rare opportunity arose.

The cabin was perched on a bald limestone bluff over a hundred feet above wide, winding Table Rock Lake, which stretched for miles in front of them, then disappeared into the rolling hills. The sunlight sparkled on the water, diamonds bursting across the silver surface. High above it, gnarled cedars clung to the occasional patch of soil. She picked up some dry needles and rolled them between her fingers, pricking herself, then raised her hand to her nose. Nothing smelled more like home than red cedar. God, she missed the Ozarks. She was a creature of these rugged hills and deep hollows and she longed to return for good someday.

Hunter walked outside and set three shot glasses on the picnic table along with a box of matches. He filled all three, struck a match and lit the vodka in one glass.

"This is for Granny Lusk. It's a tradition among the guys that after we've come home from combat, we order a shot of vodka and let it burn for those who paid the ultimate price watching our backs on the front."

"I know," Camille said, reaching over for his hand, trying to touch the past. "I lit one for you once."

A huge redheaded woodpecker knocked on a nearby hickory and buzzards circled overhead. Camille and Hunter sat silently, each staring at the lake and distant hills until several ski boats roared by.

"You're going to have to come clean with me. What was so important that made you pull a stunt like this? We were almost married, for god's sake." Camille looked him in the eyes, but he was staring past her. "You know I broke into the funeral home in Springfield so I could see you one last time without the damn press hounding me. Your coffin was stainless steel, welded shut. I found the paperwork. The Marines' medical examiner claimed the explosion hadn't left much of you and what was there, the Iraqi heat had turned into a biohazard. The casket was ordered sealed before it was allowed into the country."

"I didn't ever mean for you to go through that."

"I sat there all night beside you, beside that empty tin can. I can still smell the formaldehyde." Her jaws clenched as she fingered the engagement ring. It was starting to feel like it had been on her finger for too long, two years too long.

"I'm so sorry. You've got to believe me. I thought I was doing the right thing." He reached for her hand, but she pulled it away. "Around that time, a couple of my teammates' wives and kids had suspicious accidents. There was a lot of talk about families getting targeted. I couldn't risk that happening to you."

"That's absurd. I make my living in the crosshairs and you know that. And if being with you puts me in so much danger, why in the hell did you decide to resurrect yourself now? The world suddenly became free of bad guys?" She filled the shot glasses and glanced over to the third one. The flame now had burned away half of the vodka.

"What I did was wrong. I made a mistake and I can see now that it hurt you. I'm trying to set it right and I had to break a lot of rules to slip away to come here. Besides, I couldn't stand it any longer without you. Forgive me."

He finally looked her in the eyes and she could tell he

was telling her the truth, part of it. "You joined one of the new counterterrorism units, didn't you?" she said.

"I'm just a cook from Springfield."

"Don't bullshit me. Meal service is outsourced—the cooks all work for Halliburton now and—"

"Remember that time when we stole my dad's plane and I flew us down to the horse races in Hot Springs?" He flashed her a smile, his eyes twinkling, distracting.

"You're not deflecting me. One of the Israelis who trained black units at Fort Bragg works for me out of Kandahar. I know the hunter-killer teams exist—5-25, 6-26, Omaha or whatever the hell they're calling them now."

"Stella. You know I'm a simple mud Marine—a bug eater."

Camille studied him, but didn't see the reaction she'd expected. "It's not them, is it?" She swatted a mosquito. "Oh god, don't tell me. It's Force Zulu, isn't it? You're one of the Pentagon's new secret squirrels, aren't you?"

"Stella, don't make me—"

"It's Camille. Camille Black." And it had been ever since she had won the battle with the CIA to leave the Agency *overt*, with it allowing her to be public about her experience in counterterrorism. But her real coup was securing permission to maintain her alias as Camille Black, a legend that was well known in military circles and one that gave her an instant boost when it came to marketing and branding her new company.

"You'll always be Stella to me."

"You're a spy, aren't you? That's why you came to Granny's funeral and why you couldn't approach me at any Black Management facilities, isn't it? You're undercover and there are too many eyes watching Black Management. Please don't tell me you're spying for the Pentagon. Those guys learned their tradecraft from *Get Smart*—it's a known fact."

"You've done an impressive job building up your outfit,

by the way." He couldn't look at her, but instead watched a heron fly low across the lake, its wings nearly dipping into the water. "Who would've ever thought my Stella would create one of the world's largest private military corporations. You're sure giving Blackwater and Rubicon a run for their money. Your daddy would be so proud."

"This isn't like the Hunter I knew. What are you hiding? Why the hell aren't you being straightforward with me?"

He reached for the bottle to pour another round, but she pulled it away and continued speaking. "Let's get things straight. You faked your death one week before our wedding and I've grieved for you ever since. It takes a lot of nerve to pop back into my life and dance around the truth. Kind of makes me want to see you dead again, so I can remember the good man I loved. Today's a truce because of Granny. Either you come completely clean with me or tomorrow we're at war."

"You're in the business. You know there are things I can't talk about," Hunter said, still avoiding eye contact. "Why don't we hotwire a boat and take a ride up toward Piney? You always wanted to hike in there and find the old Jordan homestead. The chiggers shouldn't be too bad yet."

Camille twisted off her engagement ring. She rolled it across the table as the blue flame flickered, then died out.

PART ONE
Private Wars

The worrisome thing isn't what Halliburton and other big contractors are supposedly doing behind the scenes. It's what
they're doing in plain sight. National defense, the blood-and-iron
burden of government, is increasingly becoming a province of the
private sector.

—THE NEW YORKER, January 12, 2004,
    contributed by James Surowiecki

ONE

Camp Tornado Point, Anbar Province, Iraq
Two months later

Her nose burned as she inhaled the dry air, heavy with diesel fumes that barely masked the stench of the burn pit and the overpowering fragrance of night-blooming jasmine. To Camille Black it was the sweet scent of life on the edge, the smell of money, the perfume of Iraq. She coughed dust and smiled as she circled her new mine-protected personnel carrier, a six-hundred-thousand-dollar Cougar, admiring it as if it were a Ferrari. In this part of Iraq, it was her Ferrari. Its V-shaped underbelly made it look more like a boxy boat than a small troop transport, but it could channel away blasts that would rip open an armored Humvee. As she watched several troops saying short prayers and kissing pictures of loved ones, she ran her hand along the vehicle's side and sent off her own lonely prayer. She felt a blister in the desert-tan paint and she pretended to care.

Without warning, Drowning Pool's "Bodies" blared over the Cougar's sound system, heavy metal shifting the mood. All at once, the men put away their photos and got in each other's faces, shouting the song's angry words about letting bodies hit the floor. "Three! Four!" They counted with the lyrics, laughing and smiling, pumping themselves up for the night's combat mission, a mission that she, too, was supposed to be part of, even though at the moment it didn't feel that way to her. When the song was over, the operators slapped each other on the back in a bravado of brotherhood—a brotherhood that Camille had grown up with.

She admired the men. Some of the operators wore the

short beards and moustaches favored by Force Zulu and Delta Force and others sported shaved heads typical of Navy SEALs. All but one had more wrinkles than their active-duty counterparts and they all had fatter paychecks, Black Management paychecks that she had signed. They were the rock stars of the Iraq War. And they were hers.

The men's bodies moved with the heavy metal rhythm of combat as they groomed one another, inspecting each other's equipment, cinching their buddies' gear and slapping duct tape over loose straps. None of them seemed to notice as she walked into the shadows on the other side of the Cougar, smiling. There she quietly sang "Bodies" to herself as she felt for her extra magazines of ammo to make sure everything was there and accessible. She touched her USP Tactical pistol, then her knife to confirm positions and she tightened her webbing. After she checked her XM8 assault rifle, she was geared up, ready for action. And she was amped.

She circled back around the vehicle. By then the men had already crammed themselves and their war gear into the back of the Cougar, ready for a preemptive raid on what Black Management intelligence suspected was an insurgent safe house. As Camille approached the crew door, one by one each man stopped inspecting his weapon and stared.

But no one spoke to her.

She grabbed a rung and started to climb aboard. Her body armor and gear weighed her down, but she was determined to board without assistance—not that any was offered to her. It stung. All of her life she had trained with Special Forces operators and she knew what they thought about women accompanying them into combat. No matter how many times she had proven herself in battle, they never quite trusted her. She remained an interloper in their shadowy male world, the very one that she was raised to inhabit. She hoisted herself up, barely able to get her center of gravity far enough inside.

The men were tightly packed on benches along the side-walls and they seemed to spread out a little more as she searched for space.

"Like it or not, boys, you need to make room for me."

"Put yourself down right here, sweetie." An operator grinned at her as he patted his thigh.

"You really want a lap dance from a woman with a Ka-Bar knife strapped to her ankle?" Camille smiled as she pointed to the Marine combat knife her father had given her for her sixteenth birthday. "I'm game if you are."

He elbowed his buddy and they scooted aside. Camille Black took her place among the operators, pleased with herself.

In the twenty minutes since they'd left the base, no one had spoken to Camille. The Cougar's air conditioning was fighting the summer heat, but it was a losing battle. The air was warm and stale and the ride hard. A man with a scar the entire length of his right forearm sat across from her, staring at her, calculating something. She looked him in the eyes and he wouldn't look away or even blink.

His dark eyes looked intelligent, the wrinkles around them, experienced. He was bald and most of his face was clean-shaven, but taunting the Black Management dress code by several inches was a long narrow moustache and a thin veil of a beard that outlined his jawbone and came to a point well below his chin. As she studied him, she realized he could only be the operator known as GENGHIS.

GENGHIS studied her weapon. The lightweight assault rifle was a next generation kinetic energy system that the Army had hoped would replace the Vietnam-era M4 and M16 carbines until Pentagon politics killed the program. Camille loved its sleek design, molded polymer casing and clear plastic magazine. To her the XM8 seemed more like something used to blast space aliens rather than Iraqi insurgents. It had outperformed her expectations on the firing range and she couldn't wait to field-test it, but more importantly, it was cool, jock-cool and it made her feel that way, too.

GENGHIS cleared his throat. "That's one sexy kit. Haven't seen that before here in the sandbox."

The men stopped talking among themselves and watched. Camille handed him the rifle. He weighed it in his right hand.

"Light enough for a girl, I see. So what's a little lady doing all dolled up with an XM8?"

"Accessorizing."

"I know who you are." His teeth were stained from chewing tobacco. He tossed her the carbine. "There's never been a finer warrior than your daddy. Everyone agrees the Malacca incident never would've happened if Charlie had still been with his team where he belonged. It was a helluva blow to the unit when your mommy died and he chose to leave the Corps to raise his little princess."

"He raised a warrior, not a princess."

"We'll see, won't we?" GENGHIS reached for an empty plastic water bottle and spat tobacco juice into it. Brown sludge oozed down the side of the container and she turned away.

A few kilometers ahead on the potholed highway through Ramadi, Hunter's body moved with the beat of Metallica's "One" blasting through the Ford Expedition. The country sucked. His employer sucked. The mission sucked. Expecting high-stakes action, Hunter had left his beloved Marine Corps and faked his death to join Force Zulu, the Pentagon's new elite espionage and counterterrorism unit, but instead of daring raids with the latest high-tech equipment, he was sitting in an up-armored Ford Expedition, a spy undercover as a common mercenary working for Rubicon. He was one of the government's most highly trained operators, now crammed into a SUV with a bunch of bomb guys on his way to do a job that a bunch of first-year grunts could've accomplished. He'd stepped on enough toes over the years that military politics had to catch up with him sooner or later and damn him to this crappy assignment, spying on a military contractor that might have gone bad. At least he was playing ball and he was jazzed, ready for the game. He scanned the road ahead of them and noticed a small shadow moving on the overpass.

"Change lanes!" Hunter said, as the Expedition sped underneath the overpass. Froneberger, the driver, hadn't been in theater long enough to understand the danger above them. Hunter leaned over him, grabbed the wheel and turned it. Froneberger stomped the brakes and the SUV spun out of control. As they whirled around, the concrete retaining wall blurred in front of them, then a split second later the vehicle behind them streaked by. Hunter fought the driver's foot for control of the brakes as he struggled to steer. His thoughts raced and the seconds stretched. Everything seemed to move in slow-mo, except him. This was his favorite part of combat—the feeling that he could step out of time and act faster than light.

On the other side of the overpass, the vehicle weaved like a drunk as it came out of the spin. Hunter thought he saw something dark falling from above, the grenade that he had anticipated. An orange flash and a starburst of sparks exploded in midair. His ears rang from the loud bang and the vehicle rocked from the concussion, but the armored door held.

"Get us outta here! Now Froneberger!" Hunter said. He slid back into his seat, grabbed his AK-102 and cracked the door open. He sprayed the overpass with bullets, even though he knew *haji* was probably plastered to the concrete, spending quality time with Allah. The gunfire would keep him pinned down while the two other trucks in the convoy passed underneath. Then Hunter shouted at the top of his lungs, "*Allahu akbar*! Allah is great!"

He loved playing with their minds.

Titcomb leaned forward from the backseat and said over the blaring heavy metal, "Don't you want to go after him—teach him a permanent lesson?"

"Nah, we've got to make sure we're first at the site. I'm determined to be there early. Black Management is muscling in on our turf and we need to kick ass and get out before they show. It wouldn't be pretty to run into Black Management— trust me." At least that was the party line at Rubicon, but Hunter didn't believe it for a second and he knew it was more like the opposite. There were insurgent nests all over the country and he still hadn't figured out why Rubicon kept assigning him to take down targets just ahead of Black Management teams. Stella's shop did seem to have better local intelligence networks than Rubicon and had an edge at locating big arms caches, but he couldn't come up with an explanation that made sense unless someone in charge of contracts at the Pentagon or CIA was watching and Rubicon was simply trying to make itself look good at Black Management's expense. He would analyze it later. Right now he had a job to do.

Hunter stopped the convoy one click from the target. He shined an invisible infrared commander's laser pointer onto a satellite image and read it using his night vision goggles. The insurgent compound had one small building inside and it was ringed by a concrete wall with a single iron gate. In the mission briefing, the project manager had claimed that intel indicated that they should expect only light resistance. Without an advance recon team on the deck, Hunter felt blind, but Rubicon had refused to issue him one, claiming their forces were stretched too thin. He knew of a half-dozen qualified operators who were back at the base on "rack ops," snoozing away, so he suspected there were some things Rubicon's management preferred that no one observe. Maybe he would finally get the dirt on them so he could finish the suck mission and get back to the real action with his fellow Bushmen at Force Zulu. He had little respect for the overpaid contract soldiers who had left their country's service to become corporate warriors, contracted to anyone with the money for a private army. He couldn't wait to get away from them and back with his own kind. Why Stella would become one of them, he had a hard time accepting, even though he understood that, as a woman, she could never see any real action any other way.

He punched a couple of buttons on his handheld GPS to confirm that they had reached the target. The last thing he wanted to do was take down some goat herder's mud shanty by mistake like another Rubicon team had done a few nights ago. The backlit LCD screen glowed and he squinted as his eyes adjusted to the brightness.

"Get the headlights off and pull over." Hunter turned off the music, then spoke into his headset, relaying to the other vehicles orders to go black out. He looked in the rearview mirror at his men. Given a choice, he would have hired only one or two of them. The best operators gravitated toward the quality shops like Triple Canopy, Black Management and Blackwater. Rubicon snarfed up the table scraps without even bothering to do background checks. More than once he had heard troops bragging of the criminal records that they had left behind, including a South African who boasted that he was a bona fide war criminal.

"You know the game plan," Hunter said to the seven men in the SUV. "I want to breech the compound from two points. Froneberger, Titcomb, you're placing charges on the gate. Cronan and Reeves, think you can arrange for a nice big hole in the back wall? Shooters, take your heavy gun, climb up that dune and keep an eye on them." The two would stay at the rally point and provide cover with the PKM machine gun in case they were pursued by tangos.

"Got it, boss," Froneberger said. The others nodded.

"Let's do it," Hunter said as he opened the door. His

body ached as he got out of the vehicle, pulling down the bottom of his flack jacket that had ridden up on him during the trip. The ceramic plate inserts made it hot and heavy, but comfort was not something he worried about in combat situations. He leaned against the SUV and popped a couple of Motrin—grunt candy. Since he'd been back in Iraq, it seemed he'd relied on that stuff even more than caffeine to keep him going.

He took his night vision goggles from his belt webbing. The Marine Corps always got the rest of the military's hand-me-downs and when even they were phasing out the PVS-7 NVGs Rubicon was issuing them. Cheap Russian weapons, old military surplus gear and rejects from the other players—Rubicon must have been raking in the dough because they sure weren't spending much of it on the frontline troops.

He placed the awkward night vision goggles onto his head and suddenly the dark veil of night was lifted to reveal a blurry green world. His peripheral vision blocked out, he felt like he was looking through toilet paper tubes.

Everything appeared in order—no signs of tangos. So far the terrorists seemed to be bedded down for the night. He watched his explosives team work its way toward the target, dashing between spindly trees and scrub as they tried to conceal themselves. They were sailors and even though the Navy EOD school did turn out the best trained bomb guys, they seemed to skip over lessons in stealth. Only one of them really seemed to know what he was doing. Hunter laughed to himself as three of them ran straight toward their target, not bothering to approach on the oblique.

Squid. No wonder the Marines always had the urge to beat them up—it was for their own good—survival training.

He took the night vision goggles off and rubbed his eyes. At first he wasn't sure, then he distinctly heard a truck engine coming from behind them. It sounded like the low growl of a tractor-trailer rig shifting gears. He hoped for a truckload of insurgents since he could easily ambush them and take them out, but his gut told him he wouldn't be that lucky. His greatest nightmare was Stella—the *legendary* Camille Black—riding along with her troops, nailing him as his Rubicon team poached Black Management's mission. Even though he had spent the past year on assignment infiltrating Rubicon, blowing his cover with them was the least he would have to worry about if she were along for the ride. He had stood her up a couple of weeks ago out of concern that Rubicon was becoming suspicious of him and the rendezvous might blow his cover. He knew she would still be fuming over it. The Marines might have coined the phrase *No better friend—No worse enemy*, but Stella was the one who really brought that to life.

The Black Management Cougar stopped behind the convoy. Camille was sure it was from Rubicon. For some bizarre reason, they had beaten Black Management to over a dozen job sites in just the past month. There were plenty of tango nests to go around and she couldn't imagine why they were doing it except to set her up at a time when both Black Management and Rubicon Solutions were trying to woo the CIA for another major no-bid contract. She waded through her troops, handed GENGHIS her XM8 and jumped out of the back. The extra pounds from her gear made her land hard and she felt the impact in her knees and hips. She really dreaded turning thirty.

A week earlier in a Herndon, Virginia boardroom, Rubicon executives in their thousand-dollar suits had denied ever muscling in on jobs assigned to Black Management, pointing out that there was ample work to spread among all of the private military corporations. That was true—and that was what made Rubicon's behavior all the more puzzling unless they were just trying to pull down her pants at a time she needed to look good. Then she had vowed that if she could ever prove Rubicon was poaching her sites, there would be war between the two private armies. Now she had caught them *in flagrante delicto* and she stomped across their first battlefield, ready to engage the enemy.

The Rubicon mission commander left the lead SUV and hurried toward her. She noted a familiar smooth gait, but couldn't see his face well enough to recognize him. Still, there was something about him—he walked like Hunter, she realized. She told herself it couldn't be him because his chest stuck out more than usual, but she knew ceramic plates in body armor could account for that. What the hell was he doing there, leading the Rubicon raiding party?

"Rubicon's not getting away with this anymore. I don't know what the hell you're up to, but stand down and get the fuck out of my way."

The commander now jogged toward her.

It couldn't be him, but it was. "You? I can't believe this."

"Quiet," Hunter said in a low voice. "We're in black-out."

"Noise discipline because of a flat tire? Right. Don't worry. We're upwind of the target," she said, lowering her voice just in case.

"We're transferring an HVT and one of our vehicles got a flat. This really isn't what it seems."

"Nothing with you is what it seems. You say you love me; we're getting married—then you stage your death. You say you love me; we'll meet in Dubai and you'll make things right—then you stood me up last weekend. And now—now you're working for the enemy, raiding my assignments, trying to ruin my company. I suppose you still love me?" Camille pulled her USP Tactical sidearm from its holster and pointed it at him. He had hurt her enough.

"Not now," Hunter said.

"And you're playing contract soldier now? I thought you despised us mercs. Guess you'll go to any lengths to screw me over, won't you?"

"Trust me. More than anything on this earth, I love you, Stella."

"And I love you, too." She squeezed the trigger and it felt good. Real good.

Hunter fell backwards and hit the ground. His troops piled out of the trucks, training their weapons on Camille. She holstered her gun, then held her clenched fist in the air, signaling her forces not to move.

He keyed his mike and spoke as he pushed himself up from the desert floor. "Stand down. Situation is under control. Repeat. Stand down. Situation is under control."

"The situation is not under control," Camille said.

"You bitch. It could've pierced the Kevlar if I didn't have the SAPI plates in. Did you ever think that it might've ricocheted off the plates and blown my fucking chin off?"

"Don't be such a girl. Besides, your chest looks like Mighty Mouse—I knew you were wearing them. Next time you can count on it that I won't be shooting at your ceramic plates."

"You blew my opsec."

"What operational security? I thought you said you were just changing a flat?"

"Stella," he whispered. "You have to trust me. It's not what it looks like. I am on your side. Please don't blow my cover. Make it look like this is only a turf war. Act like you don't know me."

"I *don't* know you." Camille shook her head. She was glad tears evaporated almost instantly in the arid desert.

A rapid pop of automatic gunfire erupted from the direction of the insurgents' compound.

"You have men down there?" Camille never let personal issues compromise her professionalism. When the shooting started, the private militaries were all on the same side.

Hunter nodded as he ordered his shooters on the dune to give them cover fire. The medium machine gun roared.

"You're rolling with me," Camille shouted. "I don't want you out of my sight. Radio your troops to fall in behind us." She turned and sprinted toward the Cougar. When she reached the back of the vehicle, three hands reached out to help her up.

GENGHIS handed Camille her carbine as she pushed her way to the front of the vehicle. She spoke to the shift leader, a bullet-headed ex-cop. "NOONER, inform Ops at Camp Raven that LIGHTNING SIX is now assuming command. Then move us into the tango compound." Camille looked back at Hunter and decided not to blow his cover. "Rubicon, order your troops to rescue your men, then assume positions outside the walls to provide backup. We'll call for them if needed." Camille pointed to the concrete wall encircling the compound. Green tracers came from all over the compound, crisscrossing as they fired at imaginary targets. "We're crashing their party. NOONER, take us in right there—about five meters to the right of the gate."

"I'm not sure what the vehicle can do—I don't know it well enough yet," NOONER said.

"It's got a Caterpillar 330 horsepower engine and Iraqis don't use rebar in their concrete. Do the math. As soon as we're in, I want a man at each firing port and one at each roof hatch. We're going to tour the compound and light it up before dismounting. Brace yourselves. Now!"

Camille plopped to the floor and bear-hugged the nearest legs. The Cougar's engine revved, then she heard a loud crash, then felt a jolt like a plane hitting sudden turbulence. The ride immediately smoothed out.

The troops opened the roof hatches and hot air rushed inside. She shoved in her earplugs as she scrambled to the nearest firing port. She turned the steel plug counterclockwise, then let it fall onto the seat. Bullets plinked against the fortified walls, then seconds later the sharp echo of her troops' automatic gunfire drowned everything out.

She shoved the XM8 through the firing port and looked outside through its night vision scope. A dozen insurgents scattered across the courtyard like ants swarming around a disturbed nest. They sprayed the Cougar with their AKs, but they might as well have been using squirt guns. The rounds didn't penetrate.

She aimed the XM8. A trickle of sweat rolled between her breasts and she itched underneath the bulky body armor. She slowly squeezed the trigger, then stopped before firing. She didn't feel even the slightest tinge of fear that she, the predator, could become prey and without that sense of danger, she didn't want to do it, not from the comfort of her air-conditioned Cougar. But she knew she couldn't risk her men sensing even a hint of compassion because it would be all over for her—even if she did pay them eight hundred bucks a day.

With only a few seconds delay, she targeted and fired, retargeted and fired, dropping one bad guy at a time. It was almost fun. Hell, it was fun. And the world was a better place without them, she told herself as she dropped out the empty mag and snapped in a full one. Just then something caught her eye. An insurgent dropped onto one knee and pointed a long tube toward them.

She shoved the XM8's barrel back through the port, acquired the target and fired. The shooter crumpled to the ground just as his weapon spat out a trail of flames and a small orange fireball.

"RPG!"

As she listened to the whistle of the incoming rocket-propelled grenade, she fired off a stray prayer to whatever god was listening and targeted rounds at the first tangos she could find. A clap of thunder rocked the vehicle. She steeled herself for a flash of heat, then searing pain.

She waited.

Nothing.

The tango must have aimed the RPG at Cougar's belly

since that was usually the most vulnerable point on a vehicle. The over-priced jitney actually lived up to Force Protection, Incorporated's sales promises and deflected the explosion.

She searched for additional targets, but didn't locate any. Bodies lay strewn across the courtyard and the house seemed lifeless, as if all the insurgents had dashed outside for action at the first sign of an assault. She lowered her weapon, careful to keep the hot muzzle from touching her leg, then shouted to NOONER. "Give me your best man to clear rooms. Use the others to secure the perimeter. I don't want anyone coming in and joining us."

"GENGHIS, you're with us," NOONER said, then gave orders to the others.

Camille pointed at Hunter. "You're going in with me. I'm going to find out what Rubicon is always trying to beat us to. We'll go in with a three-man stack. I'll take point."

"Three-man stack or three-man lift?" Hunter said as he got in position to quickly exit the vehicle.

The men laughed.

"Don't you fuck with me."

"Understood. Three-man stack, except I'll be the number one man."

"You think point's too dangerous for a woman?"

"I'd rather have a chick's gun pushing up against my backside than some ugly dude's." Hunter smiled, but this time the men seemed to know better than to even snicker.

"Okay," Camille said and continued, "but only because I know better than to trust you behind my back."

GENGHIS flashed a signal and they all burst from the Cougar, their weapons sweeping the compound.

At the entrance to the mud-brick structure, NOONER got into the breech position to kick the door down while the others formed a stack. Camille pushed up against Hunter's back as tightly as she could. Her body armor disguised the feel of his body pressing against hers, but she caught a whiff of his earthy scent and bit her lip to distract herself.

GENGHIS stacked himself against her back and squeezed her thigh just below her ass, signaling he was ready. She did the same to Hunter, much lower down his leg than she normally would.

Hunter struggled to focus on the task at hand, but with Stella plastered against his backside, it wasn't easy. Since he'd officially died two years ago, he'd dreamed of her spooning against him again every day. One wild fantasy even had them doing it, both jocked up in full combat gear, but not even in his worst nightmares was Stella sandwiched between him and another guy like they were at the moment. He already hated himself for what he had put her through and now she was more furious with him than ever. He would never forgive himself if he lost her.

He was afraid he already had.

Hunter felt Stella grab his leg and he flashed NOONER a hand signal. NOONER kicked in the door and they flooded inside. Hunter hugged the wall as best he could given the clutter and worked his way to the right corner of the room, sweeping his section. He knew that, only a second behind him, GENGHIS would buttonhole the door and neutralize any *muj* hiding behind it. As he moved to the back corner of the room, he saw a figure raise a weapon. He fired a burst, dropping the tango and continued on to his position in the corner.

Camille rounded the doorway and moved to the left. She pointed the XM8 toward the far left corner and fanned it toward the right corner.

"Surrender. Friend. Surrender." A man moved near the center of the room, shouting in heavily accented English and waving his empty hands in the air.

She targeted, but saw no weapon and didn't fire. Trusting

that GENGHIS and NOONER were in place behind her, she rushed toward the insurgent. "Tango down! Moving!"

She smacked her boot against his ankle and swung the butt of her weapon into his back. He tumbled down face first. She pushed her boot into his back and pointed her weapon at him.

"*Allahu akbar. Allahu akbar*," he said over and over. "Allah is great."

Although Hunter already knew it was lifeless, he kicked the body of the insurgent he'd shot just to be sure before he worked his way over to Stella. A jumble of tables, chairs and assorted junk blocked his way. He bulldozed a trail.

He patted down the prisoner and found a small sidearm and took it. The man continued to pray loudly, moving his head with the beat of his words. *"Is kut!"* Hunter shouted to shut him up as he pulled out a zip-tie. He was tightening it around the tango's wrists when Stella shined an infrared light into the man's face.

Hunter froze.

He was trained not to forget faces and this one had been etched into his mind—in Afghanistan where the man had been posing as a Taliban. At the time Hunter had understood from some of the other operators that the guy was some kind of an undercover operative.

Hunter wasn't sure who he worked for, but Hunter guessed the *Other Government Agency*—the CIA. He wasn't going to blow the spook's cover, not even with Stella, so he barked orders at him in Arabic and pulled him to his feet. The sound of gunfire in the courtyard had now slowed to only an occasional shot. In less than fifteen seconds after exiting the Cougar, the action was over.

Camille searched the room, moving quickly. GENGHIS walked behind her and muttered under his breath, just loud enough for her to hear. "Should've neutralized him. You're going to get someone killed someday."

She ignored him, turned the XM8 around and smashed its butt into a mirror. It shattered with a high-pitched ring and the shards fell. A stash of computer disks and papers were in a cavity in the wall behind it. She pulled them out and stuffed them into her cargo pockets. An oriental carpet hung on the wall and a kilim and pillows covered a sofa. She threw the pillows onto the floor and ripped away the tapestry, revealing a long wooden crate. The lid was not nailed shut, so she picked it up and moved it aside. Inside was a three-inch diameter tube, about a meter and a half long with Russian markings. Camille immediately recognized the SA-7, an old Soviet missile that could shoot down a low flying aircraft. Packed around it were slabs of plastic explosives and various types of detonators. She picked up several and looked them over. They had Chinese and Russian markings.

Quality.

Camille yelled at Hunter, who was hurrying outside with the prisoner. "Someone here's planning a big party, but then I guess you were already invited. So this crap is the big trophy Rubicon was trying to snatch away from me?" Camille motioned toward the crate. "What the hell does Rubicon want with a cache of Russian weapons?"

"I don't know what you're talking about," Hunter said as he stood at the side of the doorway with the prisoner.

"You've crossed about every line I have. Now get the hell out of here and take your men with you. I don't ever want to see you again unless you're in my crosshairs." Now she wished she had chosen a shotgun over the XM8; she wanted to pump it for the sound effect.

TWO

[S]ome critics say . . . that the US government employs private
security workers to skirt restrictions by Congress on what US
troops can do on the ground, as well as on troop numbers.
—THE CHRISTIAN SCIENCE MONITOR, April 2, 2004, as reported by
Ann Scott Tyson

Camp Tornado Point, Anbar Province
3:00 a.m., Two hours later

At a bend in the Euphrates River, a hodgepodge of hastily
constructed plywood structures, prefabricated metal buildings and one of Saddam's bombed-out palaces housed most
of the private military corporations and the command center of the Marines in that area of operation. Skirting political pressure not to deploy more troops to Iraq, the Pentagon
had quietly increased the number of boots on the ground
with soldiers from private military corporations. Other
companies were there, claiming to work for the State Department, even though everyone knew there were no diplo-
mats in Anbar. Like their Marine colleagues, most of the
contract soldiers in the camp were now returning from their
nightly PT, cleaning and stowing their war gear for the next
day. Hunter had already taken off his gear and only carried
a knife, his sidearm and a couple of extra mags. He walked
across the compound toward Rubicon's local corporate offices. He knew he should be thinking about why some corporate executive would want to meet with him in the
middle of the night, but he couldn't get the confrontation
with Stella out of his head.

His chest ached a little from where she had shot him. The
last thing he wanted was physical pain and a telltale bruise

to remind him of the pain of losing her. He was afraid things had gone too far this time—that she'd never forgive him even if he could explain that, technically, he hadn't really betrayed her. His gut told him that they'd hit the point where sorting out facts didn't matter.

But it did matter to him. Hunter Stone was the kind of guy who still believed in right and wrong, even if Stella didn't.

He yawned and hoped the meeting would be short because he still had to finish his report about the evening's raid before hitting the rack.

A civilian Hunter had never seen there before showed him into the office and introduced himself as Kyle. He was the type not seen very often in Iraq—slight build, meticulously groomed and with a certain metrosexual air about him that told Hunter he would never be seen wearing khaki, let alone carrying a gun. But Hunter knew better than to believe the image Kyle projected. He was probably a hardened operative who could kill someone with a Twinkie.

"You mind telling me what this is all about?" Hunter said as he crossed his arms.

"Wait here and Mr. Ashland will join us in a moment."

"Who's Ashland?"

"Someone at a higher pay grade than you."

Mr. Ashland backed into the room, still talking to someone in the hallway. He wore tan Royal Robbins 5.11s that gave no indication of his rank, but made it easy to blend in with fifty thousand other contractors in Iraq. Ashland closed the door and turned around and Hunter knew why he was being called to the meeting—or at least what had prompted it. The short beard and moustache were gone, but his dark curly hair was still there. Hunter couldn't mistake the aquiline nose, deep-set brown eyes and short chin. He'd seen them only hours ago, back when the man was repeating platitudes about Allah's greatness on the floor of the insurgents' safe house.

Ashland was the tango Stella had captured, the one Hunter had recognized as Taliban in Afghanistan, and now the guy was posing as a Rubicon executive. The spook sure got around.

Ashland sailed a photo across the cheap wooden desk.

"You know this man?"

Hunter picked it up and glanced at it a little longer than he needed to in order to buy some time to strategize his answer. Hunter held Ashland's gaze and he was sure he knew Hunter had recognized him, so he assumed whatever game he was playing was for Kyle's benefit. He decided to play along—for now. "The dude looks kinda familiar, but I'm not sure I can place him. Close cropped hair, 5.11s and everyone here starts to look alike."

Ashland tossed him another picture. It was grainy and very dark, but showed Hunter at a loading dock, removing a crate from the back of a Ford Expedition.

"The good-looking guy is me. The other one is the dude from the first picture." Hunter smiled, but Ashland didn't respond.

"What are you doing in the photo?"

"My job. I'm transferring an arms cache we seized from insurgents to the EOD guys at ZapataEngineering. We do it every time we find weapons during a snatch and grab or a take down. We've been finding a lot of those lately—the intel seems to be getting better."

"What happens next?"

"I come back inside the wire, go to my hootch and jack off."

Ashland glared at Hunter, but without the intensity Hunter expected from someone really trying to learn about the photos. Hunter had been through brutal interrogations both in SERE training and in the field where he had been captured and held by the North Koreans and by Saddam.

This was no interrogation. Ashland's thoughts were elsewhere. Whatever was going on right now was a formality. Hunter shoved the photos toward Ashland.

"What happens to the explosives once you hand them over to Zapata?" Ashland said.

"I'm guessing the EOD guys blow them up—they live for that. That's been the SOP with seized weapons since day one." Hunter knew this wasn't true. His investigation had found that Rubicon was keeping the caches and shipping the weapons out of the country, but he hadn't yet learned the destination.

"Do you know of any cases in which seized weapons weren't destroyed?"

"Not any big stuff."

"So you are aware of some arms caches being diverted away from the disposal units?"

"Not on my watch."

"But you do know of some seized arms that were not destroyed?"

"Come on, every guy who's ever served here in Babylon has some kind of a trophy."

"Do you have a trophy?"

"This is all the trophy I need from this hellhole—a scar I'll never heal from." Hunter rolled up his left sleeve. A heart tattoo on his bulging bicep was ripped in two by pink scar tissue. The letter J was mostly intact, but the remaining tattooed letters had been stretched, cut away or were so poorly seamed that they were illegible. "Tattered heart says it all."

"Who did you turn the arms caches over to?"

"I told you. ZapataEngineering." Hunter pointed to the top picture. "You even have a picture of me doing it. So what's the problem?"

"Zapata has no record of receipt."

"That's bullshit. The guy signed for them every time, plus he always gave us a Zapata bill of lading."

"You mean these." Kyle pulled a stack of documents from his attaché case and waved them at Hunter.

Hunter reached out for the papers and quickly glanced through them. "Yeah, these are the ones. And that's my signature on the bottom of each of them. Proof they got them."

"Zapata confirmed that these aren't their documents and the man in the photo has never worked for them."

"Then who the hell was I handing the arms caches over to?"

"You tell us."

"Zapata."

"Do you have any idea how much those arms are worth?"

"I'm a shooter, not a businessman."

"Can you explain this?"

Ashland's aide handed Hunter a statement from a savings account at Bank of America.

"Let me see that. I don't bank there." Hunter studied the statements. The cover name, fake social security number and the faux Mrs. were the ones that Force Zulu had created for him as part of the cover identity used to infiltrate Rubicon, but they had not gone this far.

"This is your account—Greg Bolton and Julia Lewis-Bolton with your social security number—and it has some big deposits every month. Twenty-six thousand, thirty-two thousand. There's even one for over forty-k. They start a few weeks after you became deputy project manager at Rubicon and got command of your own team."

"Where's the money coming from?" Hunter said, still holding the statements.

"All of the deposits are from a business registered in the Bahamas that's tied to an Islamic charity. And guess who that charity happens to be charitable to—al-Zahrani and his al Qaeda faction."

"This is total bullshit. Someone's trying to set me up and you know it." Hunter took a deep breath and wondered if his cover had been blown, if they knew the Pentagon had infiltrated their operation and if the accusation of theft and arms trafficking were Rubicon's attempt at getting him out of the picture without tipping their hand, but that still didn't explain what Ashland was doing in the insurgent safe house or what he was doing working for Rubicon, for that matter. Hunter suddenly considered that maybe Ashland was doing both Rubicon and the Agency. Ever since Rumsfeld created Force Zulu, a cold war had been raging between the two clandestine services. It wouldn't be the first time that the CIA had sent someone to spy on a Zulu operator to make sure that the Pentagon didn't beat them to any significant intel prize. "Sir, I need to talk to you privately about something."

"Anything you have to say you can say in front of my aide, Mr. Kyle."

"Not this."

"I said anything."

"Suit yourself." It was time to go on the offensive. "What were you doing dressed up as a *muj* in the insurgent's compound tonight?"

"I don't know what you're talking about," Ashland said with a smile. "You must have mistaken me for someone else."

"Right. Add a scruffy beard, ratty moustache and some smelly rags and everyone here starts to look alike. And the same goes for Afghanistan where I saw you last. You were dressed up like one of the Taliban goat fuckers."

"You're in serious trouble."

"Why is a Rubicon exec hanging out with tangos? And not with just any tangos, but some with a lot of serious toys." Hunter glanced at Kyle's face. He displayed no signs of astonishment, so whatever his boss had been up to in the safe house, he was also involved.

"Ridiculous accusations will get you nowhere."

"So did you really go private with Rubicon or are you still spying for the Agency?" Hunter said as he stood to leave, inching his hand toward his SIG Sauer.

"I think this conversation is over." Ashland stood as well. "Mr. Kyle will escort you to our detention facility and see that you're on the next transfer shuttle to our Abu Ghraib facility."

Hunter drew his pistol just as Ashland and Kyle reached for theirs. Kyle blocked the door.

"I have another matter I need to attend to," Ashland said as he moved toward the door. "Mr. Kyle will see you to the facility. I'm sure we can clear this misunderstanding up in the morning." Ashland forced a crooked smile and made brief eye contact with Hunter as he left the room.

Hunter recognized the icy gaze of a man who had just ordered an execution.

Kyle pointed an HK .45 at Hunter. It looked ridiculously oversized in Kyle's petite hand.

"I'm not going to cause you any trouble," Hunter said, pretending to slowly lower his weapon. His training as a spook told him it was best to let Rubicon play things out— at least until they were outside of the building in the darkness—but, more than anything, Hunter was a warrior and this part of him wanted to fight his way out.

Suddenly, the door burst open. Kyle shifted his aim toward the intruder.

Stella stomped into the room, glaring at Kyle. She had removed her Kevlar vest and the bulky ceramic plates. Her sidearm was still holstered to her leg, her knife strapped to her ankle. Her brunette hair was pulled back into a ponytail and her Under Armour T-shirt clung to her, accentuating her curves. She glanced at Hunter without acknowledging him.

She kept moving toward Kyle, who still pointed the gun at her. "What the hell does Rubicon think it's doing stealing my jobs? And put that gun away now," Stella said in a commanding voice a drill sergeant would envy.

"I don't think I've had the pleasure, madame." Kyle lowered his aim, but kept the weapon pointed at her hip.

"Lower your weapon."

Stella still ignored Hunter as she focused on Kyle. Hunter took it as a hopeful sign that she didn't feel the need to protect her flank from him, then he realized how desperate his thoughts were.

As she held Kyle's gaze, she took a deliberate step toward him and he inched closer to the plywood wall. Hunter knew better than to interfere. He would much rather be facing Kyle's pistol than Stella's temper. For a moment, he pitied Kyle. He knew the fool believed he had the advantage because she hadn't drawn a weapon. The poor bastard didn't understand that he was facing the force majeure that was Stella.

"Rubicon is not going to fuck with me anymore. Put it down now," Stella said, pushing into his personal space. Kyle stared at Stella's perky breasts as she backed him against the wall. Now Hunter was having second thoughts about trading places with Kyle.

"Don't come any closer."

"You afraid of an unarmed girl? Oh, I get it. You don't like girls." Stella turned her upper body as if moving away, then without warning she pivoted, clearing herself from the line of fire. In a single flow of movement, she put her hand on the gun, twisted his wrist backwards, then used her other hand to shove his wrist into further pain until he let go. She snatched the weapon and sprang backwards like a cat.

Hunter fought back a grin. Watching Stella in action was like watching a prima ballerina; no matter how highly choreographed, her movements flowed so naturally. Although she appeared delicate, she was steel.

Stella was a weapon.

Stella was hot.

He only wished he were watching her in a girl fight.

"I take it that you're Camille Black," Kyle said, rubbing his wrist.

"And I take it that you're the Rubicon exec around here." She inspected the impounded HK .45, pulling out the magazine to check if it was loaded, then shoved it back into the gun. "I know that Rubicon is racing me to job sites to seize huge weapons caches. And I suspect you're selling them right back to the insurgents."

"You can't prove anything."

"I'm not a cop—I don't give a damn about proving anything. I'm a businesswoman—all I care about is making money and eliminating the enemy, preferably both at the same time. And as I see it right now, Rubicon is the enemy."

She tossed Hunter the .45 and slammed the door behind her as she left.

Stella, you tease. Hunter laughed to himself as he caught the gun with his left hand. He stuck it away and kept his own weapon aimed at Kyle's chest.

"Face down, on the floor, asshole. Make any sound and I'll pop and run." He reached into his own cargo pockets. He still had zip-ties from earlier in the evening. He fastened Kyle's arms and legs together, then patted him down, but found no other weapons. "Why are you trying to frame me?"

"You know you don't have time to get me to talk. Ashland will be back here any moment."

"You're lying," Hunter said.

"Does it matter? You can't afford that risk."

Hunter opened a drawer, found duct tape and slapped a piece over Kyle's mouth. To make absolutely sure he wouldn't be yelling for help, he wound several layers of tape around Kyle's head.

He turned out the lights and paused for a victory moment in the doorway. "Oh, I almost forgot. Tell the boss I quit."

THREE

Before the 1990s privatization push, private firms had periodically been used in lieu of US forces to run covert military policies outside the view of Congress and the public. Examples range from Air America, the CIA's secret air arm in Vietnam, to the use of Southern Air Transport to run guns to Nicaragua in the Iran/contra scandal. What we are seeing now in Iraq is the overt use of private companies side by side with US forces.

—THE NATION, May 20, 2004, as reported by
William D. Hartung

Camp Tornado Point, Anbar Province

Hunter left the building and stepped into the darkness. Dashing from one shadow to another, he crept along any structure that could conceal his profile. A ditch bag prepared with survival essentials was in his hootch where he had also concealed identity documents behind a picture of a woman who was supposed to be Greg Bolton's mother. He would grab them, then wake his men with the news of an escaped prisoner roaming the compound so that the ensuing chaos would give him the opportunity he needed to slip away. Standing at the side of a building, he waited for a security guard to turn his head before moving to the next structure.

He wanted to sprint directly to his trailer, but instead forced himself to take a darker, more circuitous path. He skirted the edges of a wide swath of light and squatted down behind a Humvee to look around and see if anyone had noticed him. Out of the corner of his eye, he thought he saw movement. His hand on the sidearm, he froze, staring into the darkness. After a few minutes, he decided he was imagining things and crawled through the Black Management motor pool, behind a half dozen Humvees and Lincoln Navigators. He stopped and jerked around to listen. An alley cat scurried between the cars. His caution was making him lose too much time. Just then he heard something hit against a Humvee behind him. Reaching for his knife, he turned his head just as a hand slammed into his jaw. Pain shot through his mouth like a lightning bolt branching out across the sky and he tasted metal.

He grasped his knife and turned to strike at his opponent, but the figure jumped backwards out of his reach.

"You son of a bitch," Stella said. Her voice was forceful—and loud.

"Stella?" He felt blood pooling in his mouth and spat.

"So Rubicon is resorting to slashing my tires now. And guess who volunteered for the duty. I should've known."

"Shhh. Not now. It's not what it seems. And you knocked out my tooth." Hunter put away his knife as he ran his tongue along his teeth. He stopped when he found a hole.

"I've heard that one too many times. I even believed you once."

"I'm telling the truth. Want to feel the hole?"

"I believe the tooth part. I'm sorry. I really am. Is the tooth still in your mouth?"

"You have to believe all of it. I love you." He pressed his tongue hard into the tooth socket to try to stop the bleeding. It distorted his speech. "I spat it out. I'd never do anything to hurt you. Rubicon is trying to kill me." He bent over to search the ground for his tooth before he lost track of the general area where it must have fallen. As he patted the ground, a burst of bullets ricocheted off the armored Lincoln Navigator behind his head.

Camille dropped to the ground. Her left hand hit something moist and hard. She fingered it and recognized the shape. "Oh, gross. Found your tooth." She pressed it into his hand, then drew her USP Tactical pistol, searched for the shooters and then fired at the same time as Hunter. They crawled behind another vehicle. Her NVGs were back in the Black Management office along with her Kevlar vest. "Rubicon's out of control."

"They're not after you. They want me."

"You? You're one of their grunts."

"I work for the Pentagon."

"Then I was right the first time. Now I'd say your cover's blown, secret agent man." Camille laughed as she reached up to the door handle of a Navigator. It was locked. Another burst of gunfire pinged against the trucks. She returned fire.

"I've got to get out of here."

"I have a platoon of Special Forces types itching to go head-to-head with Rubicon. We need to get to them."

"Rubicon's got people on the inside—"

Rounds hit the ground between them, sparking as they skipped on the asphalt. Camille said, "To be clear, I'm only helping you because I feel bad about ruining your beautiful smile. I'm not sure I believe you and I still want to kill you."

"Will you take a rain check?"

Camille pulled herself along the ground until the SUV was between them and the gunmen's last position. She scraped her forearm on the rough asphalt and it stung. "It's too damn dark." She tried another door. It was also locked. She whispered to Hunter. "I've got it. Go to the next Navigator and when I signal, bounce it as much as you can and set off the car alarm. Rubicon uses the old PVS-7 NVGs, doesn't it?"

"Yeah. Why?"

"They take forever to resample the image and refocus. The flashing headlights will flare them out. They'll be blind. Plus, my men might sleep right through gunfire, but not car alarms coming from our own motor pool."

Hunter scooted on his belly to the next Lincoln, clutching his tooth in his left fist. If there were any chance of saving it, he knew he had to keep it moist. As he fired toward the shooters, he kept his mouth closed and sucked as if he were getting ready to swallow a pill without water. Once a small pool of saliva collected, he popped the tooth into his mouth and tasted blood and dirt. He spat, but he could still feel the grit. His tongue moved the tooth to the side of his mouth and he tried to ignore it.

He emptied Kyle's .45 and tossed it away because he knew he would never find any more ammo that caliber. Ready to rock the vehicle to set off the alarm at Stella's signal, he grasped the SUV's door handle and tried pushing up on it, just in case it wasn't locked. It opened. Relieved that the automatic cabin lights had been disabled, he crawled into the backseat and then climbed to the front. He felt under the dashboard, but it was enclosed. He ran his hands over it until he found the release and pulled it off.

"Now!" Stella yelled and a few seconds later one of the Navigators started honking and flashing its lights.

Hunter couldn't set off the alarm from the driver's seat, so he did what he could to mimic one. He flipped on the lights, switched them to bright and punched the horn, then he returned his focus to the tangle of exposed wires. When the other vehicle's headlights flashed on, he could see the wires, but by the time he focused, it was dark again. After the next cycle, he closed his eyes and tried to recall the snapshot he had just seen. He reached for the two wires he thought were red and touched them together. They arced and the engine turned over.

Placing his knife behind the steering wheel between it and the column, he jammed the blade down and tried to turn the wheel. It didn't move. Careful to keep his body out of the way of the air bag in case it deployed from the force, he shoved the knife down harder until he felt it knock the locking pin away from the wheel. He turned the switch to put the truck into four-wheel drive, jerked down the gear shift and stomped the gas, then drove directly toward the white muzzle bursts.

"Damn him," Camille whispered to herself as she watched Hunter plow her Navigator through trash barrels, spare tires and anything else in his path as he tried to run down the shooters. She could never rely on him to cooperate with her. He was a team player with everyone else, but not with her.

Five of her men ran toward her from two different directions, their assault rifles pointing at her while two others remained with their backs to the nearest building, ready to eliminate any threats to their comrades. Stella threw her arms up and stood motionless, waiting until they were close enough to positively identify her.

Brakes screeched and she watched Hunter backing up into gunfire, redirecting the shooters away from her. The son of a bitch was on her side, at least. He just wasn't on her team.

Hunter saw motion in the rearview mirror. Stomping the brakes and turning the wheel at high speed, he threw the SUV into a U-turn worthy of the Batmobile and backed the armored vehicle into the gunfire. He couldn't see much, but kept steering the vehicle toward the muzzle flashes.

Several armed men ran toward Stella. He made a hard right and gunned it, barreling toward them. They didn't fire on him, so he flashed on the lights for quick identification. At the last second, he recognized them as Stella's troops and veered sharply left, then swerved right, weaving in between them at fifty miles an hour.

Hunter really wanted to take Stella up on the offer to help him, but he knew from his time at Rubicon that they had a man on the inside at Black Management, feeding them information about upcoming jobs. The mole was probably no threat to Stella, but he couldn't trust her outfit to keep him safe. Her men were protecting her and she didn't need him, not that she ever needed him. And with her holding off Rubicon's men, he was now free to head for the main gate. Any moment they would put the compound in lockdown and he would be trapped.

Camille heard the Navigator's engine roar as Hunter peeled off toward the compound's main gate, running away from her as fast as he could. Her chest tightened with each breath, but she was too angry to notice the hurt. He had used her for the last time.

GENGHIS jogged up to her. "Orders, ma'am?"

"Two Rubicon gunners were firing at me. Get them—alive, if you can."

"What about the SUV?"

Camille shook her head. As much as she wanted to, it wasn't right to send her troops to carry out her personal business. Hunter was her problem, one that she had to resolve herself. "Everyone knows Navigators are Black Management. He'll dump it as fast as he can. Give him two hours, then go search Ramadi for the vehicle. I want it back before the Iraqis find it and decide to detail it."

FOUR

The Pentagon, expanding into the CIA's historic bailiwick, has created a new espionage arm and is reinterpreting U.S. law to give Defense Secretary Donald H. Rumsfeld broad authority over clandestine operations abroad.

The previously undisclosed organization, called the Strategic Support Branch, arose from Rumsfeld's written order to end his "near total dependence on [the] CIA" for what is known as human intelligence.

—THE WAHINGTON POST, January 23, 2005, as reported by Barton Gellman

Camp Tornado Point, Anbar Province

The stench of smoldering garbage and medical waste kept all but the rats and strays away from the burn pit. The dump was the best site for a private nighttime rendezvous on a base where there was very little privacy. Larry Ashland closed his cell phone and lurked in the shadows, wondering whatever had happened to the glamour of his profession. The collapse of the Berlin Wall had not been kind to spies.

Ashland clutched a thick brown flip chart his assistant Kyle had prepared months ago at his request when he had first suspected Force Zulu had a man on the inside at Rubicon. Greg Bolton, whoever he really was, was a risk that Ashland had anticipated. A single spy was not going to be allowed to destroy his progress, even if by accident. For two years Ashland had been working his way into a highly secretive project code-named SHANGRI-LA and thus far knew only peripheral details, none of which added up. CIA funds were being dumped into Rubicon to run it, but he still couldn't tell if the money was because it was a covert Agency project or because another rogue CIA case officer was setting up lucrative retirement plans with corporate America.

As Ashland worked his way deeper into SHANGRI-LA, he had studied Rubicon personnel files of its top operators in Iraq, searching for anyone who could blow his cover. He recognized the photo of a man whom he had first encountered in Afghanistan, an operator who had then been working with Force Zulu, the Pentagon's new espionage and counterterrorism unit, the vanguard of the Pentagon's push into the CIA's realm. The man's Rubicon personnel file had told a very different story, one that Ashland had no doubt had been professionally crafted by Force Zulu to cover for one of its spies.

A BMW SUV drove toward him with its lights off. It stopped and Ashland jumped inside.

"Jesus, that stinks. Shut the door fast," Joe Chronister said as he held his hand over the dome light.

"Sorry to get you up at this hour, but we've got a situation."

"It better be worth it. Security firm supervisors and oil company execs don't generally meet in the middle of the night even if they do have the same parent company. Covers are wearing thin, even for around here."

"Rubicon busted a small-time crook tonight. One of our team leaders got greedy and went into business for himself."

"With the tangos?"

"Yeah and worse. With al-Zahrani's faction." Ashland handed Chronister a dossier.

"Crap. All it takes is one little guy to fuck up and someone thinks they've got something and they start pulling at threads. I assume you've taken care of him."

Ashland took a deep breath and slowly exhaled before speaking. He was counting on the pause to add drama. He had to burn the Force Zulu operator so badly that not even his own guys would believe him, let alone help him. Even if Rubicon managed to eliminate the man tonight, Ashland had to make sure that Force Zulu would not come around to investigate the death of their man. They had to believe their own man had gone bad. Joe Chronister had the connections, credibility and creativity to make sure that happened. He'd see to it that every government and private operator on the planet believed the Force Zulu spy was radioactive.

Ashland cleared his throat. "We could use some help. He took out Kyle, my best man. We're after him right now, but he's good."

"The way I see it, it's a Rubicon personnel problem. Jesus, this smell is too much. The hospital must've tossed a bunch of body parts in there tonight." Chronister turned up the air conditioner. Gunfire popped in the distance, but they ignored the typical sound of Iraqi nightlife.

"You've got to help us make sure he's neutralized," Ashland said. "Pull the right thread and you can unravel a whole sweater."

"The Agency can't be part of a manhunt. Too public. Eliminate him yourself. Jesus, you've got more hunters on the payroll here than we do. Tell the guy's family he died killing terrorists and let them collect the death benefits. No one will think twice about it, let alone call for an investigation. The family will probably be happy not to have to deal with Rambo coming home and fighting the war at the local 7-Eleven. The guys who succeed over here make lousy civilians and families know that."

Chronister wasn't cooperating and Ashland had worked with him long enough to know that he was losing patience and any moment would cut off the conversation. He didn't like giving away any more secrets than he had to, but he realized it would take the CIA's fear of the Pentagon to get Chronister on board with his plan. He still hadn't figured out the guy. Ashland knew that Chronister was CIA, but the deeper he got into the SHANGRI-LA project, the more he suspected that the Agency knew nothing about SHANGRI-LA, that Chronister had gone rogue and was using CIA resources to help the secret Rubicon project. The more he thought about it, the more Chronister disgusted him. But at the moment he needed Chronister and his contacts. Ashland took a deep breath and said, "There's a little more to it. Bolton—or whoever he is—works for Force Zulu. They've infiltrated Rubicon."

"Fuck. We take out their spook, we're painting a bull's-eye on ourselves." Chronister folded a Kleenex, held it up to his nose and breathed through it. "You know I actually typed up a resignation letter the day I heard the president authorized Cambone and that born-again whack-job Boykin to round up a bunch of soldiers and start playing *I Spy*. I predicted this was going to happen—us tripping all over each other. You know the Pentagon's real goal is to shut us down and corner the market on intel. Those fuckers spying on us is just another goddamn brick in the wall."

"If they learn that one of their Bushmen has started playing ball with the tangos, they might take care of him for us."

"Not without asking a lot of questions. And I have a lot I'd like answered—like how deep has Zulu penetrated Rubicon." Chronister shined a penlight on the file and thumbed through it.

"You have to burn him with Zulu. Make them doubt everything he says."

"Let me keep this." Chronister tapped his fingers on the file. "I can fuck him up with Zulu." A picture fell out of the file and fluttered to the car floor. Chronister picked it up. "Hey, I know this motherfucker. He was engaged to someone I used to work with. You know, I might be able to help you out with a silent solution after all. You ever meet Camille Black? She's a real ballbuster, in the best kind of way."

FIVE

"Anbar is controlled by terrorist groups," said Sheik Yaseen Gaood, [Iraqi] deputy minister of the Interior overseeing the western provinces. "The Anbar government has no authority. The ministries of Interior and Defense have no influence there."

—THE LOS ANGELES TIMES, June 11, 2006, as reported by
  Megan K. Stack and Louise Roug

Anbar Province

As Hunter drove out of the gates of the camp and into Anbar province, he gritted his teeth and immediately felt pain. His tongue checked on the tooth, still tucked into the side of his mouth. He had to get it back in the socket soon.

Like he had earlier in the night on the way to the raid, he turned right toward Ramadi. His unit had worked out an emergency exit plan for him—the only problem was he had to get to the insurgent stronghold, Ramadi. The escape plan had been set up before the insurgents had returned there yet again and no one in the Pentagon had ever gotten around to modifying it. He knew an American armed only with a SIG Sauer and a little over thirty rounds wouldn't make it far on the dusty roads of Anbar province. A goat in an Afghan mujahedin camp had a better chance of dying a virgin.

He had to go local.

The guys at Rubicon were constantly leaving things in their trucks but a quick scan of the back of the Navigator confirmed what he already knew—Camille Black ran a tight ship. A break-down kit was in the back along with ammo cans he'd check out when he got a chance, even though he was sure it would be 5.56 rounds for assault rifles, not 9mm for his sidearm. What he wouldn't have given for a stray rifle or even a different vehicle, one outfitted for a trunk monkey—a machine gunner with a mounted weapon designed to punch out the back window with the first round and surprise the road hazard with the following ones.

With one hand on the wheel, he reached under the driver's seat, hoping something useful had escaped inspection, but he found nothing. Leaning over to the passenger seat, he patted the floorboard and his hand bumped up against something, but it rolled away. A water bottle. Hopefully it had a few swallows left in it. The tooth was driving him crazy and he had to do something about it. Already on the edge of Ramadi, he pulled over to the side of the road, unbuckled his seat belt and reached for the water bottle. It was half full.

He turned the overhead light on and opened the door. He poured some water into his hand, he spat his tooth into the palm, then swirled it in the water. Although he had stitched up comrades more than once and had even carved a bullet from his own thigh, teeth were different. He'd rather face a horde of tangos than a dentist. It was all he could do to force himself to look at it. At least it seemed to be free from dirt.

Careful not to touch the roots, he picked it up and turned it around as he tried to figure out which way it went in. The water rolled out of his hand onto the ground. He leaned back into the truck to look into the rearview mirror to find the hole. Checking one more time to make sure the tooth was turned the right way, he took a deep breath and shoved it into the socket. Pain zinged his mouth. After another measured breath, he bit down firmly, pushing the tooth farther down. He jumped from the jolt.

He swirled warm water in his mouth. As he leaned out the door to spit, a knife thrust toward him. He jerked out of the way and yanked the door shut to the sound of bone being crushed. A man screamed and the knife fell to the ground.

Unsure if the carjacker had buddies with him, Hunter threw the SUV into gear, grabbed the arm and held onto it. This was the break he needed and he wasn't about to let go.

The man howled as he was dragged alongside the Navigator. Hunter glanced into the mirror and even though he saw no accomplices, he still wanted to get a little distance from the carjacking site, just in case. The man was going for a short ride. Hunter sank his fingers into the guy's hairy forearm, digging his fingernails into the skin, but he couldn't get a good grip. The arm slipped away. He hit the brakes, came to a stop, then sprang from the vehicle.

The young man lay unconscious in the dirt, his arm twisted into an unnatural position. Hunter yanked off the assailant's headband, headscarf and beanie and dropped them onto the hood of the SUV. He wrestled with the body for its clothing, a dishdashah, the traditional white mandress worn throughout the Arabian Peninsula. He worked the skirt above the man's hips, exposing his genitals. Keeping with local customs, the carjacker wore no underwear. Hunter averted his eyes.

"This is why guys in Detroit never go out carjacking free-balling under a dress. It's not only the cold," Hunter said as pulled the dishdashah over the man's head. He wadded it up and grabbed the headdress. He smiled when he found a small wad of cash. It wasn't much, but would be enough to get him by for a while before he could sell the gold chain necklace that he always wore for such emergencies. He jumped into the Navigator to drive back to where the guy had lost his slippers.

The dirt streaked across the front of the white cotton garment would draw some attention, but even so, the mandress would help him blend in a lot better than his 5.11 pants and Under Armour T-shirt. Back on the tango turnpike to Ramadi, he yanked off his shirt and undershirt, then pulled the dress over his head and down to his waist. The Velcro crackled as he pulled the sheath off his leg and lay his knife on the seat beside him. Steering with his knee, he unzipped his pants and pulled them down to his ankles where they got stuck around his combat boots. Peeking up over the dashboard just enough to see the road ahead, he untied his boots and took off his pants. For a few moments he debated with himself whether he really needed to lose his jockeys, but knew he had to do everything he could to blend in. His knife could have been a spoil of war, he told himself as he strapped it back onto his bare leg, but as much as it pained him, he would have to leave the firearm in the SUV. He had no way of concealing it and passing as an Iraqi was a far more powerful defense than a single bullet.

Deciding to forego the beanie, Hunter folded the black and white checkered cloth in two and draped it over his head. The black cord of the headband smelled like a goat. He doubled it around the top of his head to hold the headdress in place, then pulled down the sun visor to check himself out in the vanity mirror. The cruel Iraqi sun had given him a deep tan that was darker than many of the locals. His beard could have been a little longer and rattier, but he could pass. Score one for the loose Rubicon dress code that had no restrictions on hair length or facial hair.

The first rays of sunlight streaked orange across the sky and soon calls to prayer would echo in the streets. He could already smell smoke from firewood and diesel fumes from generators. The Iraqis didn't let much of the day get away from them, he'd give them credit for that. He spotted a dark alley with an assortment of cars where he could change and trade in Stella's SUV for something less conspicuous. He looked in the rearview mirror as he started to turn.

Two Ford Expeditions sped toward him.

Rubicon.

SIX

At the Pentagon, which has encouraged the outsourcing of security work, there are widespread misgivings about the use of hired guns. A Pentagon official says the outsourcing of security work means the government no longer has any real control over the training and capabilities of thousands of U.S. and foreign contractors who are packing weapons every bit as powerful as those belonging to the average G.I. ". . . they are not on the U.S. payroll. And so they are not our responsibility."

—TIME MAGAZINE, April 12, 2004, as reported by
Michael Duffy

Camp Tornado Point, Anbar Province

The first rays of the morning sun were turning the sky orange and a distant wail of a muezzin called the faithful to prayer as Camille marched into Saddam's former palace. It had been a day since she'd slept and nearly as long since she'd eaten. Her body was achy and her emotions were whitewater, churning with eddies and undertows with no clear main channel. She and Hunter played rough together and delighted in pushing one another to the edge in their own war games, but the heat of their battles usually resolved in wild passion. During their last vacation they had spent days tracking one another throughout Panama and it ended in a sugar cane field where she surprised him and overpowered him, though she was sure he would claim that he was the one who had prevailed. They had made love there for hours, the sharp blades of the cane slicing their skin. This morning had the appearance of another game, but his mood had not been playful. Their sparring suddenly felt strangely real. She grabbed a handful of

M&Ms from her pocket and popped them into her mouth. The M&Ms had saved her life more than once, keeping her blood sugar hyped when her body was ready to tank. She chewed fast and swallowed before entering the head-quarters of the base commander, USMC Colonel Michael Lukson. Camp Tornado Point was still officially a Marine base and the contractors were guests even though they out-numbered the Marines twenty to one. An aide showed her inside the colonel's makeshift office, one of Saddam's for-mer bedrooms.

Camille tried to play cool, but the cavernous room screamed for attention. It was a bold play of volume and void that had all the class and splendor of an Atlantic City casino. The original furnishings had long ago been stripped away, but gold-plated gargoyles perched atop green malachite pillars protected the granite walls and marble floors. A recessed archway and blue lapis columns framed a life-sized mural of Scud missiles with flames shooting behind them. At least the Iraqi flags on the mis-siles had been chipped away. Saddam's military murals competed with fantasy scenes of iridescent dragons men-acing chesty blondes that would have been better suited to black velvet than a palace wall. A beam of light shined onto the floor. She looked up, following it to its source. A mortar had knocked a hole in a ceiling dome and it had missed a stylized Saddam leading troops into Jerusalem by only a few inches. She shuddered when she realized she was standing in the middle of Saddam's wet dream.

The base commander had set up his office in a corner of the grand room. File cabinets and scavenged office fix-tures surrounded a simple wooden desk half covered by an old computer monitor. A wall map of the al-Anbar Area of Operation was tacked over the groin of one of Saddam's nymphs. The colonel sat at his desk, across from a man Camille hadn't seen or spoken to since the outbreak of the second Gulf War when she had quit the CIA. Joe Chronister was the reason she had joined the Agency and he was also the reason that she left it to start Black Management.

Colonel Lukson stared at her, his thick arms crossed. As was custom when in combat, his short sleeves were down, not rolled up in a cuff. One forearm was tattooed with the Marine Corps' globe and anchor with the words Semper Fidelis above it; the other arm had the image of an alligator on tracs.

Camille stood perfectly erect beside an empty chair. "Colonel Lukson, sir, I'm Camille Black, president and CEO of Black Management."

"I know who you are."

The large empty room behind her made her uneasy, but she continued to stand in silence, waiting for the colonel. She averted her eyes. The military controlled the bases in Iraq and the private military companies were guests on their turf. Camille's troops at Tornado Point did covert work for the CIA and some secret military units—almost all of it outside the purview of the base commander. It was no secret that Colonel Lukson and other field officers did not like their new roles as landlords for higher paid civilian mercenaries and would relish the eviction of one of them.

After a long minute, Lukson spoke. "Anything you want to tell me, Black?"

"Sir, I was fired on tonight by Rubicon troops."

"And that's why you decided to play cowboys and indians on my ranch? You might not take orders from me, but I sure as hell can kick your sweet ass off my base."

"Sir, I had to defend myself, sir," Camille said like an enlisted Marine. She flashed back to her childhood when she had to stand before her father and answer for her mistakes in the same way. At the time it had felt severe, but now, it seemed more like good training. She had a lucrative contract to protect and couldn't risk any missteps with her Marine host. It was time to use the word "sir" more than she had in the past year.

"And you had to defend yourself from Mr. Kyle as well?"

"Who's Mr. Kyle, sir?"

The CIA case officer Chronister interrupted. "I believe you encountered the gentleman tonight in the Rubicon offices."

Camille continued to stand erect in front of the colonel and ignored Chronister. "Sir, Mr. Kyle threatened me at gunpoint. I had to disarm him, sir."

"By tying him up and breaking his fucking neck?" Chronister said with a laugh. "Camille, I always loved that matter-of-factness about you. You really should've been a Marine."

Fuck you, Joe. She continued to stare straight ahead at the colonel. She wasn't going to fall for his bait—not this time. She wondered why Hunter had done it. He was one of the most deadly men she knew, but also one of the most moral. He wouldn't kill without reason.

"Black, answer the question. Did you tie Kyle up and break his neck?" Lukson said.

"No, sir. He was alive, sir, when I left, sir."

"Did you threaten Mr. Kyle?" Lukson leaned back in his chair causing a caster to fall out. He grabbed the desk to catch his balance.

Chronister laughed. Camille remained stoic, silently thanking her father, who would've beaten her senseless if that had happened to him when dressing her down and she had so much as cracked a smile. She was exhausted and trying hard not to tremble before the Marine. "May I help you, sir?"

"Goddamn piece of Iraqi shit." Lukson got down on the floor and shoved the caster back into the base of the wooden chair. "I'm still waiting on your answer, Black. Did you threaten Kyle?"

"Sir, no, sir."

"Come on, Camille. Did you not tell him . . ." Chronister pulled a pair of reading glasses from his pocket and put them on. He unfolded a piece of paper and read from it. " 'All I care about is eliminating the enemy . . . and as I see it right now, Rubicon is the enemy?' "

Camille stared straight ahead.

"Answer him, Black."

"Sir, those are my words, sir. Sir, the only way he could know that is if the Agency is bugging Rubicon offices."

"What's it to ya if we listen in on your competitors? What were you doing there?" Chronister gnawed on the end of his reading glasses.

"Black!"

"Sir, Rubicon has been muscling in on Black Management assignments. I suspect, sir, that they're trying to beat us to big arms caches. I also suspect, sir, that's why the Agency is keeping an eye on them," she said stiffly, as if she were at a legal deposition.

"Cut the cloak-and-dagger bull-crap. I don't have much use for spies and I don't like mercenaries, but one thing I really hate is a traitor. Fuckers should be shot on sight," Colonel Lukson said to her as he leaned forward. "The OGA has evidence that a few individuals in Rubicon have been in contact with al-Zahrani's people. Kyle got too close and they popped him. We're missing the big guy in this picture and I want to know who he is. We might not see eye-to-eye about spies and mercs, but I think we're all working from the same field manual when it comes to traitors. You seem like a nice, well-mannered girl. Now do the right thing, sweetheart, and tell us the truth about last night."

"Sir, I am telling the truth, sir. The only thing I have to add, sir, is that after I left Kyle's office, some Rubicon troops fired on me and tried to kill me. Maybe they got to Kyle first."

"Was Mr. Kyle alone when you left the office?" Chronister said.

Camille hesitated.

"Was he alone?" The colonel said, his voice rising with irritation.

Even to cover for Hunter, for some reason she couldn't bring herself to lie to the Marine's face. Camille turned toward Chronister as she spoke. "Yes. Kyle was alone."

SEVEN

A sprawling agricultural and smuggling hub on the banks of the Euphrates, Ramadi has long been one of the U.S. military's stickiest problems. The largest city in Sunni-dominated Al Anbar province, Ramadi has degenerated into a haven for insurgents. Even now, when U.S. forces are working to scale back their presence throughout Iraq, daily combat continues to roil the city.

—THE LOS ANGELES TIMES, June 11, 2006, as reported by Megan K. Stack and Louise Roug

Ramadi, Anbar Province

Every time Hunter entered Ramadi, he felt like a black man in the Deep South during Jim Crow; there were no friendly faces, only hateful stares and the lynch mob was never far away. The people of Ramadi carried their disdain for the Americans as civic pride. Hunter had been shot at on at least three occasions by the American-trained municipal police force and he couldn't begin to count the number of times civilians had lit him up. He had personally helped rid the city of scores of insurgents, one bullet at a time, but even after years of campaigns, the main roads were more hazardous than ever for Americans.

Hunter was counting on it.

He took a left into a neighborhood where he had once gone door-to-door trick-or-treating and found enough candy to keep the bomb disposal guys happy for a week. It had taken his Marine unit four days to clear a particularly nasty five square block area and about the same amount of time for the insurgents to return once the Marines had pulled back from the area. The neighborhood had been a real fixer-upper even by Iraqi standards and that was before the Marines had trashed the place searching for insurgent nests. While some parts of Ramadi had pallets of bricks on the sidewalks and residents busy repairing the crumbling walls, mortar holes and twisted metal gates, in this part of town the new occupants hadn't bothered to cover broken windows. Whoever was living here now was not putting down roots.

The two Rubicon SUVs followed him down the narrow street. His own men were now chasing him. It was time to see if they had learned anything from him. He doubted it.

Time to party in haji-land.

He honked the horn, rolled down his bullet-resistant window and stuck his head outside. The black checkered cloth of his headdress flapped in the wind as he yelled in Arabic, "Help! Americans!"

The language he had once delighted in learning back when he was part of the Marine security detachment at the Cairo embassy now made him cringe. He hated the sound of his voice speaking Arabic; the language of poets and scholars had been reduced to his language of combat. He honked again and repeated himself as he drove circling the block.

Halfway into the second circle, he heard the rapid pop of an AK, then several long bursts of gunfire. He hit the brakes and the Navigator skidded to a halt sideways in the middle of the street, blocking traffic. Hunter jumped from the Navigator shouting, *"Allahu akbar."*

The flip-flops were at least two sizes too big, but his toes gripped them as tightly as they could as he ran through the back alleys in search of Khalid the tailor.

He could hear the bullets pelting his pursuers' armored vehicles and hoped for their sake they had been smart enough to immediately call for reinforcements—it would be their only chance.

EIGHT

Private military firms are business providers of professional services intricately linked to warfare. That is, they are corporate bodies that specialise in the sale of military skills. They do everything, from leasing out commando teams and offering the strategic advice of ex-generals to running the outsourced supply chains for the US and now British armies. Such firms represent the evolution, globalisation, and corporatisation of the age-old mercenary trade.

—LONDON NEWS REVIEW, March 19, 2004, as contributed by
Peter W. Singer

Camp Tornado Point, Anbar Province

Camille stood in Saddam's former bedroom before the Marine base commander, ignoring CIA case officer Chronister and staring at a point just behind the colonel at one of Saddam's murals depicting a serpent constricting around a pin-up girl. Camille was thinking about how much she hated herself for once again protecting Hunter. Using the sidearm she had left him with would've been loud and Hunter was the quiet type. She had little doubt he had broken Kyle's neck shortly before he surprised her in her motor pool. She wasn't about to take the rap for him, but then again she also had no desire to help Chronister nail him. She may have wanted to hurt Hunter for how he had repeatedly betrayed her, but she was loyal in the face of an outside threat and Chronister had long ago proven himself to be just that.

"Colonel Lukson, may I borrow your office for a few moments?" Chronister said as he shooed away a fly. "I need to discuss some things with Ms. Black in private. I might be able to clear this up so you don't have to hand the investigation over to the Army's Criminal Investigation Division."

"After how they screwed us at Haditha, I'm happy to keep those CID turds from nosing around my base." Lukson nodded once, stood and walked away.

Camille and the CIA case officer listened to the squeak of his footsteps across the marble floor. As soon as Lukson had left the room, Camille sat down.

"Really, Camille. I didn't expect you to protect Hunter Stone."

"You're a piece of shit, Joe."

"You just made yourself a murder suspect. We now have reason to detain you. And detention in Iraq can last a very long time."

"Fuck you. You're desperate. You can kill anyone you want in this Allah-forsaken country and, unless you're a grunt fragging an officer, no one gives a damn." She reached into a cargo pocket of her 5.11s, pulled out a half-pound bag of peanut M&Ms and threw a handful into her mouth.

"But you handed me a little more leverage to persuade you to come back to work for me," Chronister said as a pigeon flew near them. Both turned their heads and watched as it landed on a headless statue covered in bird droppings. Chronister continued, "And yeah, I'm getting desperate. As soon as I get some loose ends of a project squared away, I finally get to retire."

"Work for you again? Go to hell."

"You've done well for yourself since leaving the Agency. You're a rich lady now. Looks to me like you should be thanking me."

"I got out because I saw an opportunity to do what I've always wanted—something I never had at the CIA—despite your promises." She held the M&Ms in her sweaty hand so long the color was rubbing off them.

"You're a damn good operator, but you never would've survived in the Special Activities Division—no woman ever has. Come on, Camille, you know those operators. They're all Delta and SEALs. They don't play with girls. They're the Agency's military—they never would've let you go out on a mission with them no matter how desperate they got. If I hadn't stepped in, you'd still be at the Agency making coffee for the boys."

"Right. And if I were still working for you, I'd be servicing dead drops, sticking messages under things and marking the spots with chalk—takes real skill. You know, I found out that Iggy had actually approved my transfer over to them. I certified in all the Black Book standards—the exact same standards all the Delta operators train to."

"Camille, honey, no one doubts you're every bit as good as they are." He held his hand out and pointed at the M&M bag. "Gimme."

She hesitated, then poured him a handful, took more for herself and dropped the bag onto the desk. Joe was the one who had gotten her hooked on them back when he had taken her to Algiers on her first undercover mission for the Agency.

"I trained all my life for that kind of action." Camille wiped her green- and red-stained palm on her pants. "You lied to me that I'd get it in the Agency."

"I told the truth. I thought it would be different."

"It would've been if you hadn't sabotaged me."

"You're like a daughter to me. I was protecting you," Joe said. "They would've fucked you good, left you alone, hanging in the cold on some mission, expecting an extraction that would never come. I've seen them do it to others."

He picked up the bag of M&Ms and held it out to her. Camille stared at him, studying him as she took the candy. He was an expert at deception and manipulation, but he actually seemed sincere. She wanted him to be sincere. "Quit shitting me."

"You were the best student I ever had. I got a real kick out of mentoring you. I didn't want to lose you. You know what they say, 'all's fair in love, war and the Agency.'"

She held up her index finger and bowed her head slightly while she finished chewing, then she swallowed. "What do you want?"

"A job done right."

"I have contracts for anything the Agency wants. Have someone else contact one of my ops officers, give him a target and my boys will take care of it."

"I want you to do it personally." Chronister paused, looked her in the eyes and appeared for a second as if he was going to crack a smile. Then he said, "I want you to kill Hunter Stone."

NINE

Troops and civilians at a U.S. military base in Iraq were exposed to contaminated water last year and employees for the responsible contractor, Halliburton, couldn't get their company to inform camp residents, according to interviews and internal company documents.

—ASSOCIATED PRESS, January 22, 2006, as reported by
Larry Margasak

Ramadi, Anbar Province

Ramadi was an unending stretch of bombed-out houses, neglected alleyways and decaying two-story concrete tenements. Garbage heaps and twisted car frames cluttered even the best neighborhoods. Roosters crowed from behind walled courtyards and dirty, skinny children were everywhere, playing in the streets and on rooftops. Hunter walked along an open ditch that smelled of sewage as he headed toward his contact's tailor shop in the downtown *souk*. With his white dress and checkered headscarf, he looked like an Iraqi, but he walked like an American and he knew it. He continually forced himself to slow down and amble along, reminding himself he was in no rush. Rubicon didn't have a chance at finding him. At that moment his biggest threats were the blister on his left foot and his growing thirst. He could live with that.

After a few hours of walking, he entered the market district. Sticky bodies, hawkers' cries, stale urine, diesel fumes, grilled lamb, smoke—the *souk* was a sensory explosion and lack of sleep and high levels of adrenaline made the assault worse. And everyone but him seemed to be carrying an assault rifle.

The tiny shops spilled out onto the streets, blocking already crowded sidewalks. Vendors carrying their entire inventory in small crates clogged the throng of people, thrusting watches, chewing gum and CDs into the faces of anyone careless enough to glance their way. He even spotted two vendors selling automatic weapons and grenades. Car horns competed for attention with the latest pop divas from Egypt. Hunter shoved his way through the sweaty masses, searching for Khalid's tailor shop among the many small stores selling satellite dishes, pirated DVDs and small appliances.

In the middle of a busy street corner, an old woman was hunched over a metal tub filled with large chunks of ice and plastic bottles of desalinated water imported from Kuwait. She wore head-to-toe black. Her hair was gray, her teeth rotten—Hunter guessed she was in her forties. Poor women did not age well in this part of the world.

Hunter fished a water bottle from the tub and checked to make sure the seal was intact. *Saddam's revenge* because of some unscrupulous vendor selling rebottled Euphrates water was the last thing he needed. He pulled the carjacker's money from his pocket. The crisp bills were pressed together in tight folds. He peeled off a pink 25,000 dinar note, the biggest they had printed and the smallest the guy had. On the black market, it was worth about twenty-five bucks in real money. The woman wrinkled her nose and said something he couldn't hear and he shrugged his shoulders. She stood, told him to wait, then disappeared into the crowd. He gulped down a bottle, then a second one. Even though he was thirsty, the desalinated seawater tasted flat. A few minutes later, the woman reappeared and handed him a wad of purple, brown and blue bills and some coins. He shoved them into his pocket without counting and walked on.

Merchant stalls sold baskets of pomegranates, mounds of spices and stacks of melons. A seller held out a handful of pistachios and Hunter took a sample. He broke it open and ate it, but the first nut was bad and the aftertaste bitter. He had once loved exploring exotic Third World markets, but his three combat tours in Iraq had drained away the joy. Now every car concealed explosives, every merchant harbored an AK, each sleeve cloaked a knife and a crowd was only one incitement away from a mob. He loathed this place for what it had taken away from him.

He strolled past a bakery with a display window stuffed with honey-drenched sweets. His mouth watered. Promising himself that someday after the war he would return with Stella to enjoy it, he kept walking, but he couldn't get over the pleasures the place had taken away from him. He stopped. Iraq was not going to defeat Hunter Stone. Hell, it wasn't even going to get to him today. He returned to the shop and bought a bag full of treats. Standing on the street corner taking in the bustle of the market, he shooed away the flies as he downed a half-dozen gooey, nut-filled pastries. The day had definitely taken a turn for the better.

TEN

Although the U.S. government says the hunt is still on, the CIA recently closed its Bin Laden unit.

—MORNING EDITION, *National Public Radio*, July 3, 2006, as reported by Mary Louise Kelly

Camp Tornado Point, Anbar Province

"Kill Hunter Stone?" Camille laughed. "I don't know who you're talking about. Who's Hunter Stone?" Camille wasn't sure how deep the Agency had nosed around into her relationship with Hunter. Out of fear for each other's safety, they each had gone to extreme efforts to protect their privacy, but they apparently hadn't gone far enough.

"Come on, Stella."

"Camille Black, please."

"We've known each other too long to fuck around with games like this. And quit hogging those M&Ms."

"Help yourself, but you've got to be kidding if you think I'm going to eliminate Hunter for you." She held out the bag while he fished out a handful. "What the hell did he do?"

"He's put this Agency in a very difficult position, but I think the same can be said about what he's done to you."

"I try to stay out of CIA politics, especially since 9/11 when the Pentagon started trying to short-sheet you guys at Langley."

"Short-sheet us, hell. They've been out for blood and they're not going to be happy until they're standing over the Agency's lifeless corpse. But this isn't about Washington politics. Stone's gone over to the other side."

"Bullshit." Camille leaned back in the chair and left the bag of candy on the Marine colonel's desk.

Chronister reached into a worn leather attaché on the floor and removed a stack of papers. He passed Camille a photo of Hunter handing over a crate to someone on a loading dock. She glanced at it and immediately handed it back to Chronister.

"This shows nothing."

Chronister passed Camille a stack of photos depicting Hunter at the same warehouse with the same man. He also included other shots of Hunter with a dark beard and in Iraqi dress meeting with the same figure in a crowded bazaar. Chronister continued speaking. "The man he's turning the weapons over to is a lieutenant of al-Zahrani. It doesn't get much more serious than supplying weapons to one of the two men scrambling to become bin Laden's successor."

"OBL's successor. I've been hearing a lot about that lately. So did some al Qaeda lieutenants finally catch on you've been holding the fucker for years and seize the opportunity to take over the network? Did they figure out that you've been running him, stringing them along, releasing just enough messages to make them think he's in charge from some rathole in Pakistan?"

"I don't have a clue what you're talking about." Chronister grinned.

Camille knew Hunter was part of the team that, less than a year after 9/11, had caught bin Laden, barely alive, hiding in a cave in a northern Pakistan. Of course, Hunter would never come right out and tell her, but instead had spun a wild yarn about a successful hunting trip for the world's rarest animal, his excitement betraying the thinly disguised metaphor. "Don't patronize me. You've had bin Laden on ice in Afghanistan for years. I've heard so many specifics from so many different units, I could take you to the cell block where you're holding him. Hell, I even know the names of the kidney specialists you've got keeping him alive—if he's still alive."

"Al Qaeda sure has been an organizational disaster for years, hasn't it?" Chronister laughed.

"Looks to me that might be changing with al-Zahrani and Abdullah fighting to pick up the pieces."

"It's not going to happen, unless, of course, they enlist a lot of traitors like Hunter Stone to help them out."

"Hunter is not a traitor. No way."

"Not knowingly. My guess is that he believes he's selling stuff to run-of-the-mill insurgents. I'm willing to give him the benefit of the doubt when it comes to betraying his country. You, my dear, are a different matter. Do you know how Stone got those arms caches—by staying one step ahead of Black Management. You really have to hand it to the guy. He's got balls—crossing not only us, but Rubicon and you. He didn't go after Triple Canopy, Blackwater or any of the others. Think about it. He chose to mess with Camille Black's very own Black Management. Think anything personal went into that decision to fuck Black Management? I think he wanted to screw you, Stella—screw the great Camille Black."

"Anything personal between myself and Mr. Stone is none of your goddamn business." Camille struggled to keep her voice steady, not wanting to show Chronister how furious she felt. Part of her couldn't believe that Hunter would do anything to intentionally hurt her, but she had suffered so much over his fictional death, it was getting easier and easier to believe. She grabbed the bag of M&Ms and chomped down as many as she could shove into her mouth. Her anger grew with each bite as she studied the photographs. Chronister sat back and waited.

"Am I supposed to believe that he was working for you at the Agency when he infiltrated Rubicon?"

"He *was* ours."

"Word on the street is that he was hooked up with Task Force Zulu." Camille tossed the photos onto the desk.

"He did try to go to the Pentagon black units first, but

they all turned him down. You know how strict certain units are about the operators having their lives in order so they're not vulnerable to blackmail. His was a fucking mess. I assume you might know something about this."

"You're talking about financial hangovers from his ex-wife?"

"Ex-wives. According to his file, he's still paying on two separate boob jobs for those gals. Didn't he knock up that last one—the crazy one—when you and I were undercover after those suitcase nukes in Turkmenistan?"

"We were both seeing other people—sort of."

"Sort of."

"As a good Southern boy, he felt he had to do right by her and marry her." Camille wiped her hands on her pants.

"I'm from Brooklyn. The South doesn't make a fucking bit of sense to me. But seems like he screwed you big time."

Camille stood. "Look, I've got to go."

"Stone approached the Agency a couple of years ago when things got a little too confusing for him. We helped him simplify his life by faking his death."

"A couple of years ago. When exactly?"

"A little over two years ago—it was early March."

"You mean a month before he was supposed to marry me?"

"I mean a month before he was supposed to marry you *and* Julia Lewis."

ELEVEN

Ramadi, Anbar Province

After another hour of exploration, Hunter found Khalid's shop in a quiet corner on the edge of the *souk*, near a busy mosque. Bolts of colored fabric were stuffed into the small salesroom and color pictures of the latest Middle Eastern fashions snipped from magazines were plastered over every square inch of the walls. The floor was littered with swatches of fabric, pin cushions and even a pair of scissors.

A man yelled a greeting from behind a red cloth curtain, "*Salaam alaikum.*"

"*Alaikum salaam,*" Hunter said and continued in Arabic. "I might have left my wallet here last week. It had a special picture of my daughter, Barika."

"Was she wearing the wedding dress I sewed for her?" A portly man stepped from behind the curtain. He carried scissors and wore a tape measure around his neck.

"No. The dress was from her aunt in Amman." Hunter said the final identification phrase as he studied the man's eyes.

He saw fear.

"Come. I've been expecting you." The man held the curtain open and motioned with his hand.

No one at Force Zulu had yet been alerted that he was coming in. "You've been expecting me?"

The man hesitated for a second longer than Hunter would have liked. "I meant when people leave their wallets in your shop, you expect them to return." He smiled. Several teeth were missing. "Come and I will locate your wallet for you. My wife will bring you tea and sweets."

Hunter waited in a sandy courtyard while the midday call to prayer blared from loudspeakers mounted throughout the district. Hunter ignored it as he sat in a plastic chair beside an orange tree, not sure if he should believe Khalid's assurances that his unit would be there any moment to escort him to safety. The agent had been vetted long ago, Hunter reassured himself, but something didn't feel quite right. Sipping tea, he twirled a fallen orange blossom between his fingers until it disintegrated, then he sniffed his fingers and smiled. His tongue checked on his tooth. It moved too easily and he knew it had to be stabilized soon if it was going to be saved. He hoped to be sitting in an American dentist's chair at a base in Baghdad by late afternoon. He wished the Zulu Bushmen would hurry up.

Just as the drone of the muezzin's call to prayer was ending, three Force Zulu operators burst into the courtyard, their guns sweeping the area. He had expected them to come posing as civilians, not wearing full combat gear. Hunter held his hands in the air, aware they would instantly judge him to be an Iraqi and a potential danger because of his man-dress. He'd worked with all of them and was surprised they didn't seem to recognize him.

"SABER TOOTH. Coming in from the cold. And it's damn chilly out there." Hunter laughed.

One operator approached Hunter, two others stayed by the door, their guns trained on him. They were all from his squadron and they should've seen past the Iraqi clothes and his new beard and recognized him by now.

"On the ground, you douche bag." Stutler kicked Hunter's left foot, knocking him slightly off balance. "Face down."

"What the hell are you doing? It's me—SABER TOOTH." Hunter dropped to the ground. He knew better than to fight overwhelming force. "I've been deep undercover and my cover was blown. Check with General Smillie at SSB."

"Smillie is the one who sent us." Stutler zip-tied Hunter's hands behind his back, then patted him down and found the knife. He ripped the sheath from his leg.

"I'm not offering any resistance. At least leave my feet free so I can walk without falling all over myself. Come on, Scott."

"No way, man. You could take out Bruce Lee with those legs. I've been on too many missions and in too many bar fights with you."

"Yeah, I've saved your sorry ass from the bad guys and from your wife more times than you can count."

"That's why I'm saving yours right now. Everyone else in Zulu wants the honor of killing the only fucker ever to betray the unit to the *muj*." He shoved the plastic tie under Hunter's ankle, then pulled it tight.

"I would never betray Zulu. Never. Rubicon's framing me. You've got to believe me."

"Dude, you're the last guy I ever thought would work for al-Zahrani." Stutler pulled Hunter to his feet.

Hunter shuffled into the tailor shop. A fourth team member waited inside.

"Move, you dumb-fuck," Stutler shoved him.

"Hey, it's hard enough walking in a dress and these zip-ties don't make it any easier." Hunter stumbled as if he had tripped on his dishdashah and intentionally fell to the ground on top of Khalid's sewing clutter. He rolled over on his back. "You're going to have to help me get up." He patted the floor until he found the pair of scissors he'd seen on the way in. Cupping them in his hands, he hoped Stutler didn't notice in the exposed moment before the wide sleeves of the dishdashah covered his hands. He had no idea what he was going to do with them, but he had to start expanding his options.

Hunter waddled from the tailor shop and looked around for the team's Humvees. He spotted them halfway down the block, on the other side of the street. Logistical nightmares like this were why the soldier in him hated markets, but the spy in him had fallen in love with them all over again. The crowd parted for Stutler's team. Friday prayers had ended and men streamed from the corner mosque. Hunter made eye contact with a young man. He was accustomed to the acidic glares of the Iraqis, but he felt sympathy coming from the guy. Then Hunter understood. They didn't see American soldiers taking away another American; they saw the American occupiers dragging away another Iraqi resistance fighter.

"Keep moving. Don't stop." Stutler pushed him.

Hunter slowed down and didn't say a word. He knew the team was bound by rules of engagement that were tighter than the plastic ties around his legs. Killing him in an escape attempt was undoubtedly permitted, but they all had been in the sandbox long enough to know better than to shoot a bound Iraqi in the middle of a crowded market. As far as the masses were concerned, Hunter was one of them, another innocent victim of the evil Americans. The old Arab proverb kept running through his mind: *never give advice in a crowd.* Hunter worked the scissors around in his hands to the right angle, then he stopped.

"Move, I said. Now!"

Hunter dropped to his knees, lowered his hands and cut at the plastic tie at his ankles.

"Get up, you asshole." Stutler grabbed Hunter under the arm and pulled him to his feet.

Hunter shuffled forward as if his legs were still bound. He instinctively turned the scissors so that they pointed to- ward Stutler, but he knew he couldn't bring himself to stab a fellow Bushman, so he stopped, threw back his head and shouted at the top of his lungs, "*Allahu akbar*! *Allahu akbar*! Allah is great!"

Hunter saw a piece of a brick fly toward Stutler, then a hail of rocks pelted the operators and angry shouts closed in from all directions.

The last thing Hunter saw was a chunk of concrete fly- ing toward his head. It was painted green, the color of the Prophet.

TWELVE

"They're pretty freewheeling," the former CIA official said of the military teams. He said that it was not uncommon for CIA station chiefs to learn of military intelligence operations only after they were underway, and that many conflicted with existing operations being carried out by the CIA or the foreign country's intelligence service.

—THE LOS ANGELES TIMES, December 18, 2006, as reported by Greg Miller

Camp Tornado Point, Anbar Province

Camille opened her mouth, then closed it slowly. Resting her chin on her hands, she stared some more. The betrayal sliced so deep, she didn't know what to believe. Hunter's story had never felt quite right and she had always sensed he was hiding something. She took a deep breath and pursed her lips. "You're telling me Hunter was engaged to someone else when he was engaged to me? I don't know what to say."

"Say you'll do the job," Joe Chronister said.

"How do I know this is true?"

"Because of how it resonates. You *know* it's true, Camille. Deep down inside, you know it."

Chronister gave her another stack of photos. On top was one of Hunter with a woman who looked like she had stepped out of the pages of a Neiman Marcus catalog. The bitch was obviously edgy, high-maintenance and totally out of Hunter's league. She was probably insane, which would make her within his reach, but not his grasp—his favorite type of gal, totally Hunter. "He could never afford a woman like that—not even if his official death had absolved him of alimony and child support."

"But you know he'd have the hots for a broad like that, don't you?"

Camille tossed the photos onto the desk. "Pictures can be doctored. Give a trained monkey Photoshop and you could be showing me shots of Marilyn Monroe giving him head."

"Stella—Camille—he faked his death so he could get away from you to be with her. It wasn't cold feet, it was a hot—"

"Stop. Don't say it." Camille held up her hand and looked away from Chronister so he couldn't see her fighting back tears as she remembered his lame excuses. Hunter had played her for a fool and she let him do it—over and over again.

"But in case you want more evidence, here are some intercepted e-mails between—"

"E-mail is the easiest thing in the world to fake. Untrained monkeys can do that."

Chronister reached back into his attaché and pulled out a thick dossier. He handed it to Camille. "You'll also find copies of several handwritten cards, love notes and letters with his signature."

Camille flipped through the pages, shaking her head. The handwriting was his. The adoring sticky notes were familiar—too familiar. She slapped it closed and pressed her hands against each side of it.

"I've seen enough."

"No, you haven't. I still have copies of statements from his joint bank account with her. Three months ago when Rubicon started raiding Black Management job sites, it went from chronically overdrawn to a six-figure surplus."

Camille threw the folders onto the desk and looked at Chronister. "As I said, I've seen enough. You have my attention. So why isn't the Agency handling this job in-house?"

Chronister took a deep breath. He recognized the look on Camille's face and he liked what he saw. Things were progressing better than he had hoped, thanks in no small part to the Marine father-figure who had unknowingly softened Camille up for him. In thirty-two years with the Agency, he had recruited hundreds, maybe even thousands of spies, convincing them to betray their countries for one reason or another. Money. More often than not money made them do it, but sometimes it was for love, other times for revenge. Every once in a while some poor sap gave his country the Judas kiss out of a belief in peace, democracy or the American way. The real art in turning someone into an agent was getting under their skin and figuring out what they needed deep down inside. And he knew exactly what Camille needed. There was something she yearned for from both her father and from him—an apology. They had both pushed her relentlessly and made her promises that she could become something that she would never be allowed to be because of her gender: a Special Forces operator.

The only difference between Chronister and her father was that her father had really believed it could happen for her one day. In the late eighties, after her father had taken her along on a covert mission to Soviet Uzbekistan to clean up some Agency business and he had debriefed them both, Chronister knew he had to have her working for him. He had never seen raw talent like hers. When she was old enough, he had dangled the opportunity to enter the CIA's paramilitary force in front of her to convince her to join the CIA over the Marines, even though he knew a woman didn't have a chance with the Agency's Special Activities Division either.

He glanced at Camille to see if his dramatic pause had gone on long enough. She was starting to look concerned.

"Is something wrong?" Camille said. "I asked you why the Agency isn't handling the hit in-house."

Chronister took another handful of M&Ms and talked while he chewed them. He took a deep breath and looked directly at her with the most remorseful expression he could muster. "Because I owe you."

He caught a glint of hope in Camille's eyes. *She wants it.*

"What do you mean, you owe me?"

"I'm facing retirement. Things look different when you get older and that lifelong dream of a fishing cabin in Michigan is only a few months away."

"What are you saying?" Her face softened, but her arms were still crossed.

"I'm saying you start to regret mistakes when you get older. Maybe even want to make things right."

"It's too late for that."

"Maybe. Like I said, you were like a daughter, but I shouldn't have protected you. I should've sent you over to Iggy and the Special Activities Division with my blessings. You would've made a damn fine operator for them." He sighed and shook his head, pretending not to notice the tears he saw welling up in her eyes. "Camille—Stella, forgive me. I'm sorry."

She turned away for a second and wiped her eyes. It almost felt genuine to him as he got up and hugged her. He cared for her.

He really did.

As he hugged her, he thought about how perfectly his plan was falling into place. He had worked too long and hard on SHANGRI-LA to allow one of Force Zulu's wannabe spooks to come in and fuck it up. The last thing he wanted was the Pentagon muscling in on the project. Convincing Camille Black to take out Stone was the cleanest way to get Zulu off his ass. The Pentagon would write it off as a crime of passion, a lover's spat. No one would suspect the CIA's hand in the murder of a US military spy. It was too bad he could never explain it all to her, because Camille was one person who would really appreciate the genius in his design.

He touched her face and wiped away a tear.

Camille pulled away and sat down. "Sorry." She averted her eyes in shame from the tears. "What's your time frame?"

"Soon as possible. But it's not a straightforward wet job. We need information from Stone. He's had SERE training from us and the Marines. He's not only been a guest of Saddam without breaking, he was held by the North Koreans for weeks before we bought him out. You've seen his fingernails. The man is not a talker."

"He'll talk to me. What do you need?"

"Stone is a bit player trafficking arms to al-Zahrani because his wife has high maintenance costs. But he knows who al-Zahrani's main man is inside Rubicon. I need you to extract this information for me, then kill him. You can make it as slow and painful as you want." Chronister knew the Force Zulu types—they were the über-patriots who teared up when they heard the "Star Spangled Banner." One of them would never work with al-Zahrani's organization, unless he was doing so under orders, orders that were bringing him too close to SHANGRI-LA. He wanted to know Stone's mission, but doubted even Camille could get it out of him.

"You sure you don't want him back alive?"

"Come on. You know how the world works. If an Agency analyst betrays us, US courts try him for treason. If a case officer betrays us, we eliminate him. Stone betrayed us." Chronister took another handful of candy and ate a green one. "Stone's made a fool of you—more than once. What say you, my dear?"

THIRTEEN

A former US army colonel, Alex Sands, declared: "The whole point of using special operations is to fight terror with terror. Our guys are trained to do the things that traditionally the other guys have done: kidnap, hijack, infiltrate."

—NEW STATESMAN [London], May 17, 2004, as reported by
  Stephen Grey

Anbar Province

Hunter lay with his eyes closed, half awake, half asleep. He was aware that he was dreaming in Arabic and that made him happy. The unconscious didn't bother messing around with a language it hadn't mastered. As he floated toward greater consciousness, he realized he wasn't dreaming in Arabic, but was listening to it. His forehead throbbed and he remembered the concrete fragment coming at him. He couldn't sense anyone's presence nearby, but he didn't want to take any chances, so he kept his eyes closed and tried to make out what was being said, but the voices were too distant and muted. Then he heard a loud thump and a voice shouting in English.

"Help me! I'm Jackie Nelson. If anyone can hear me, I'll reward you. American dollars. Help me." The voice was hoarse and it seemed to be coming from the next room.

Muj. The tangos had somehow snatched him and he knew far too well what they did to their American prey— Internet beheadings, bodies dragged through the streets, and severed heads delivered to American bases. He had long ago vowed he would take his own life and as many of theirs as he could before they did anything like that to him.

Lying motionless so he didn't alert any mujahedin guards that he had come to, Hunter peeped, but saw no one, so he opened his eyes and sat up on the stained sleeping mat on a filthy floor. He was still wearing the clothes he had stolen from the Iraqi carjacker. The room was empty and the door was shut, but the window had no bars and no glass. A warm breeze blew through it.

"If you can hear me, help me! Get the Americans. Reward. Dollars. Dinar." The voice weakened as she repeated herself.

When Hunter stood, the blood rushed from his head and he saw swirls of flashing light and blackness. He sat down again, took a deep breath and waited for his blood pressure to rise. His lips were chapped, his mouth dry and he was hungry, but he was no longer zip-tied. Why had the tangos cut him free? At once he understood: the *muj* weren't his captors—they were his liberators.

Hunter opened the door and stepped into the main room. Most of the outside wall was missing and the gnarled wreckage of a bombed-out car was visible through the hole. A sliver of a mirror clung desperately to the opposite wall, which was pitted with craters from the blast. A small perimeter had been cleared of debris around a makeshift table constructed from a door and saw horses. Scattered about one end of the table were a brick of plastic explosive, wires, detonators, pliers and a Colt long gun. Three men sat around it, each with an AK-47 at his feet, and a teenager leaned against a wall, an AK slung over his shoulder.

Hunter forced his thoughts into Arabic. "*Marhaba.*" He nodded his head in greeting as he waded through the rubble.

"*Marhaba,*" they said, echoing one another as they looked up. Two were twins, probably in their late teens, no older than twenty, and the oldest of the three couldn't have been more than twenty-two.

"Thanks be to Allah that you saved me from the Americans." Hunter placed his closed fist over his heart and bowed his head. Cries from the trapped American woman drifted through the walls. He ignored the hostage's desperate pleas and wished she would stop before she got them both killed. Any English he heard could break his concentration and cause a deadly slip of the tongue. "I am in your debt."

"The enemy of my enemy is my friend," the twenty-something one said. He avoided eye contact with Hunter. "Do you have a name? I am Fazul."

"I go by Mu'tasim," Hunter said. He had practiced this moment over and over, expecting to someday go deep undercover with the tangos. His Egyptian-accented Arabic was fluent, but he knew there were too many subtleties, too many opportunities to use an awkward word or the improper inflection. "But my given name is Sergei."

The men laughed. "Sergei. You're Russian?"

"I kill Russians. I am Chechen."

"Chechen? So that's why the Americans want you. I've trained with Chechens. They know no fear. I've seen a single Chechen with an AK-47 kill an entire platoon of Marines. They shot him, but he kept at them." Fazul picked up the AK and pointed it at each of his friends, pretending to shoot them one by one. "He killed them all—even the Marines who ran."

Hunter forced a laugh. "*Allahu akbar*. What else is there to say?" *Other than "You fucking lying muj. Marines do not cut and run."*

"Who are you with, Sergei?"

"I'm on my way home, *insh'allah*—Allah willing. I'm no longer with a cell and if I were, you know I cannot say."

"No. I mean, which leader do you follow? Abdullah or al-Zahrani?"

Hunter hated politics, but he knew enough about them to understand that he hadn't been captured by ordinary insurgents, but by the much rarer al Qaeda cell—or at least al Qaeda wannabes. The last thing he wanted was to get trapped in the middle of the growing schism inside al Qaeda over bin Laden's successor. He wasn't even certain what that was all about. He had heard rumors that bin Laden had finally died, but those had been floating around for years and he was pretty sure bin Laden was still alive in the secret prison in Afghanistan where he had been held since Hunter's team of operators had captured him in early 2002 in the mountains of Waziristan. The US government had wanted to avoid creating a martyr or rallying al Qaeda supporters into seeking his freedom by increasing attacks on American targets, so it instead made the al Qaeda leader fade away. Hunter wasn't officially read into the project, but he knew that the CIA and Pentagon immediately took joint control of al Qaeda, feeding its lieutenants with useless orders which rendered the organization ineffective. It cost the Administration plenty in terms of political capital because the public believed it still hadn't nabbed bin Laden, but the fiction was a small price to pay to keep the world and America safe.

Hunter didn't know what had happened, but something with the plan had clearly gone wrong over the past year. The best he could figure out was that a couple of bin Laden's more ambitious lieutenants either had figured out the American scheme or simply had sensed a weakened leader and staged a silent coup. Both Abdullah and al-Zahrani had declared bin Laden dead and were now fighting each other for control of al Qaeda. The internal violence in the organization had escalated so much in the past year that the two main factions were inflicting more casualties on each other than on the West, mirroring the Iraqi civil war between Sunni and Shi'a Muslims. Hunter took a deep breath as he looked around the terrorist safe house for clues as to which sect the tangos were with. He found none and said, "I follow the only true heir to bin Laden."

"Of course." Fazul smiled. "And his name is? . . ."

The teenager pushed himself away from the wall, stood straight and pointed his AK at Hunter.

"Long ago in Chechnya I pledged my life to bin Laden, may blessing be upon him. Now my loyalty is with . . ." Hunter studied them for signs that it was time to go on the offense. If he caught the right moment, he could use Fazul's body to absorb the boy's bullets while he reached for a weapon. He continued, ". . . al-Zahrani."

Fazul put his hand on Hunter's shoulder and held it there for a few moments. "You are a wise man, Sergei."

And a lucky one.

Fazul's cell phone started vibrating and a synthetic muezzin beckoned to midday prayers, "*Allahu akbar. Allahu akbar. Ashhadu an la ilaha illahhah . . .*"

Hunter knit his eyebrows, then smiled as he stared at the phone. Fazul picked it up, allowing it to finish playing the call to prayer. "It has a timer to play the *adhan* five times a day and it adjusts to the new time each day or if you move into a different location. It even has a direction finder for Mecca."

"Amazing," Hunter said. He couldn't bring himself to choke out a few more words to praise their god, even though he knew he should have added them.

Several small rugs were rolled up in a pile along the wall. One of the twins passed them out.

"Give our guest Amir's prayer rug. He no longer needs it. May Allah bless his soul," Fazul said, his countenance suddenly dropping.

Each tango carried his AK along with his prayer rug to the barren courtyard behind the house and Hunter followed them. A goat gnawed at the sparse scrub and heat rose from the sun-scorched sand. He squinted, waiting for his eyes to adjust to the blinding light. As he had feared, they were in the middle of the desert with no other structures in sight. He could forget about slipping away quietly in the night.

Hunter walked over to a well and picked up the bucket to fetch water for the pre-prayer purification ritual. Fazul grabbed his arm. "No, my friend. It's nearly dry. We have little water. We must use sand."

To confirm his suspicions that they were Sunni like most of al Qaeda, Hunter paused for a second to see if they washed their hands rather than their faces first in the cleansing. He did the same, first rubbing his hands with sand, then his face, ears, arms and feet. During the first Gulf War when he was in the desert for days with Task Force Ripper, he had used the coarser Saudi sand for a dirt bath, but the powdery Iraqi sand left a dusty coating where the Saudi sand had come away clean. Next he only pretended to rub it on his teeth.

The four mujahedin turned toward Mecca, put their arms in the air and declared Allah's greatness. Hunter listened for other insurgents as he said the prayers along with them, but he heard no other voices. The four to one ratio wasn't great, but he could work with it. All he needed was one opportunity.

His teammates at Force Zulu had thought he was insane, practicing the Muslim prayers over and over until they became second nature. Those drills in both Sunni and Shi'a prayer customs were all that was preventing him from looking like the new guy at a dance class, struggling to mimic the others while tripping over his own feet. He folded his hands over his chest and recited the first verse of the Koran in Arabic.

He bowed.

He stood.

He prostrated himself.

He recited the prayers all the while watching for any

opening to take them out. Fazul's rifle was within reach, but the others were slightly off in their timing so that at every moment during the ritual one of them was on a prayer mat within reach of his AK. He could probably take out one or two, but not all of them and not before they got him. He stood, turned to the twin on his right, then Fazul on his left and exchanged the last prayer with each of them. "Peace be unto you and Allah's blessings."

Yeah, right.

FOURTEEN

"But DIA [the Defense Intelligence Agency] is now engaged in doing far grander things with regard to trying to penetrate foreign organizations," said [Col. W. Patrick] Lang, the former DIA official. "They're trying to penetrate jihadi organizations. . . . It's happening all over the Islamic world."
    —THE LOS ANGELES TIMES, March 24, 2005, as reported by
    Mark Mazzetti and Greg Miller

Anbar Province

Fazul ordered the teenage boy to fetch food and drink for Hunter. He returned after a few minutes carrying a plate mounded over with white cheese, olives and flatbread. He handed it to Hunter who stood near the table, eyeing the AK underneath near Fazul's feet. Fazul was becoming more and more focused upon the bomb he was cobbling together.

"Rubbish." Fazul studied the markings on a blasting cap, then tossed it onto the floor. "This is useless rubbish. Amir, my bomb-maker, killed himself in an accident a few days ago. We're supposed to be ready for a wedding this afternoon, *insh'allah*—Allah willing."

"Thoughtful wedding present." Hunter balanced the plate with his left hand and ate. The cheese was mild and very salty. So were the olives.

"Here. Sit with us." Fazul pushed aside some tools, clearing a space for Hunter's plate. He picked up the sidearm from the table and set it on his lap.

Hunter sat at the head of the table where Fazul had indicated. He would've preferred a spot beside the ringleader since it would've made an assault easier. "Why strike a wedding and not the American infidels?"

"The families are prominent and they both came out in support of Abdullah. You know the teachings of al-Zahrani, may the Prophet bless him. We first have to clean our own house. Those who follow Abdullah are a pox on us all. Tell me, Sergei, do you know anything about bombs?"

"Enough not to wear one." He chewed on an olive, taking care not to chomp down on the pit and hurt another tooth.

One of the cell phones was in pieces and Fazul attached blasting cap wires to a circuit board. Then he crimped a wire to the end of a cap and taped the wire to a small battery. Fazul looked up at Hunter. "Where were you trained?"

"I was in camps in Afghanistan." *Where I killed fuckers like you.*

"Those days must have been glorious. Had I only been born earlier, *insh'allah*."

"Where did you train?" Hunter said.

"Uzbekistan."

Hunter had never heard of al Qaeda bases in the former Soviet Republic. During the early Afghan campaign, the Uzbeks allowed the US to take over former Soviet bases, but the arrangement dissolved after their government massacred a few hundred protesters and the US objected. Radical Islam scared the crap out of the Uzbek leaders, but it wouldn't be the first time a dictatorship played both sides. Pakistan had it down to a fine art.

"Uzbekistan? The Uzbek government sleeps with the Americans and prohibits teaching of true Islam," Hunter said.

"Not anymore. Al-Zahrani has an arrangement. As long as we keep to ourselves, we are most welcome—for a price, I'm sure."

"Keep your friends close and your enemies closer," Hunter said and grinned. "Where is the Uzbek camp?"

Fazul laughed. "If you showed me a map, I could not find Uzbekistan. The camp was a hole in the desert. I saw nothing but sand and voles." Fazul took the slab of plastic explosive and sunk the cap into the Semtex.

Hunter hoped Fazul really did know what he was doing, but his trembling hands hinted otherwise. He set the bomb down and looked into Hunter's eyes. "You ask many questions, my friend."

Hunter felt his body tense up and forced a deep breath to relax himself. "I was in Uzbekistan as a child, when it was part of the Soviet Union. I remember standing with my Young Pioneer group in Samarqand. The turquoise domes of the mosques, they were like nothing I had ever seen. At that moment, I realized that Islam had a glorious past and the communists were lying to us. I wanted to go in and pray, but I was told it was forbidden. The mosques were museums."

"Patience. The Russians will pay one day, along with the Americans." Fazul looked intensely at Hunter for a little too long.

A few minutes later the boy returned with a tray carrying glasses of tea and a bowl of sugar. The sugar had ants crawling in it, but the *muj* didn't seem to mind. Fazul stopped playing with the explosives to scoop up a teaspoon of sugar and drop it into Hunter's tea glass.

Hunter could never figure out why Iraqis didn't use cups with handles for hot beverages. The tea glass burned his fingers, but he knew better than to show weakness and set it down—or to fish out the ants now swimming in the brew. The first sip was hot enough to scorch the hide off a camel and it singed his taste buds. He smiled and complimented them on the excellent tea.

The twins picked up their weapons and stepped into the room with the American hostage, leaving Hunter alone with Fazul and the teenager, who still carried an AK slung over his shoulder.

"No! Stop! No!" The American woman screeched. "No!"

Without thinking, Hunter grit his teeth and pain from the tooth immediately electrified his mouth. He searched for options, fighting to conceal his emotions while white-hot anger seared his gut. At Fort Bragg, Hunter had spent long hours with his team day after day running through live-fire hostage rescue exercises in the Force Zulu shooting house. Suddenly their worst-case scenarios seemed so naïve.

The boy looked toward the door and laughed. Then he turned to Fazul. "May I go, too? I never get my turn."

Ignoring the boy's whines, Fazul fiddled with the wires of a blasting cap fastened to an AAA battery. He sat in the line of fire between Hunter and the boy's AK. Hunter eyed a screwdriver laying on the table and he inched his hand toward it while he watched Fazul sink the blasting cap into the Semtex. Hunter would need the full force of his right arm to shove the screwdriver into Fazul's temple, so he would have to use his left one to grab the gun from the terrorist's lap to take out the boy before he could fire the AK. He figured that the twin waiting his turn at the woman would come running out of the bedroom with his AK before Hunter would have time to switch hands. He was glad that he had trained so hard shooting lefty.

The woman's screeches grew fainter, more haunting.

Hunter snatched up a screwdriver and lunged across the table. His chair fell to the floor. At the last moment, he saw Fazul with a wire in each hand, moving them toward one another, about to close the circuit and accidentally detonate the bomb.

Hunter let the screwdriver fall to the floor as he seized Fazul's hairy wrists and held them apart.

"*Allahu akbar*. Praise be to Allah. You almost detonated it," Hunter said before the boy could react. He then pulled the yellow wire from Fazul's hand, gave it a tug and the cap pulled out of the Semtex. He reached over to the battery and ripped the tape off, separating the wires from it.

Alerted by the commotion, one of the twins ran out of the bedroom and pointed his assault rifle at Hunter.

Hunter and Fazul stared one another in the eyes without moving. Then Fazul glanced down at the screwdriver and Hunter recognized the flash of doubt.

"I kept you from blowing yourself up," Hunter said.

Fazul was shaking. "You saved my life. Thanks be to Allah, the merciful and compassionate."

Grunts and screams came from the bedroom. The one twin was still going at her. Hunter hated himself as he tried to block out her screams and said, "Yes, thanks be to Allah, the merciful and compassionate."

"Come." Hunter followed, aware that the teenager was behind him, carrying his weapon. Fazul walked over to the doorway to the room where the woman was being held. Her blouse was ripped and she was naked from the waist down. Her legs and arms were covered with fresh red bruises and older ones that had turned shades of yellow and brown. "Now I reward you."

"But I'm supposed to be after Gamal! Not him!" The boy said.

"Gamal! Off her! Now!" Fazul pounded Gamal on his back as if he were beating a stubborn donkey. "Off! I said off her!"

Gamal ignored him and continued to hump her. Fazul picked up his AK and whacked him with it in the kidneys. Gamal rolled off her, reaching for his back.

"Why did you do that?"

"Obey me." Fazul kicked him.

The woman's shoulder-length brown hair was matted from dirt and tears. Her lips were parched and cracked and her eyes sunken. The woman needed fluids badly. She turned on her side with her back to them and moaned. If she had been an animal, Hunter would've shot her to put her out of her misery.

"My friend, here is your reward. You may have her." Fazul stretched his arm toward the woman as if presenting a gift.

"No. It is *haram,* forbidden to know a woman who is not your wife."

"The Prophet, peace be upon him, blessed temporary marriages, particularly for those away from their wives when on *jihad.* It is *halal.* Declare your *mut'a* and take her. Then it is pure." Fazul looked into Hunter's eyes and grimaced. "My friend, you are not thinking of dishonoring me and refusing my gift?"

The room where they were holding the American woman had to be well over a hundred degrees and it reeked of stale urine and feces. Sweat dripped down Hunter's face and he wiped it away with the sleeve of his dishdashah.

The twins and the teenage *muj* blocked the doorway. They carried their weapons and so did Fazul. Hunter was helpless to try and help the woman without getting both of them killed. Insulting Fazul by refusing to rape her could have the same effect. He understood the scenario well. When his unit had been cross-trained at the Farm, his CIA instructors had spent the better part of an afternoon making them role-play the dilemma. He had gone along with the playacting, but he had always believed that if this happened to him, he would be clever enough to figure out an innovative solution.

Now it was for real and Hunter Stone saw no way out.

FIFTEEN

Anbar Province

"My gift awaits." Fazul swept his arm toward the American woman lying on a ripped mattress in a fetal position, sobbing.

Hunter despised the *muj*, but at that moment he hated himself more as he pulled up his dishdashah and climbed on top of the woman, upon Jackie Nelson. She let out a low groan, a sound that penetrated Hunter's bones.

Forgive me.

SIXTEEN

The days when journalists could move around Iraq just by keeping a low profile—traveling in beat-up old cars, growing an Iraqi-style mustache, and dyeing their hair black, or when women reporters could safely shroud themselves in a black abbaya and veil—are gone. When Jill Carroll of The Christian Science Monitor tried such tactics this January, she was kidnapped while trying to get to an interview with a Sunni politician . . .

—THE NEW YORK REVIEW OF BOOKS, April 6, 2006, as reported by Orville Schell

Ramadi, Anbar Province

Camille took off her Oakley sunglasses and rubbed her eyes. The bustling market was a security nightmare. Everyone and everything seemed to be in constant motion and the honking of car horns was deafening. Worst of all, they all were armed. She had long ago given up on trying to keep track of the flow of people for someone who might be watching them. Some of her best operators were close by dressed as locals, in case someone decided she was a target of opportunity and tried to snatch her like they had the American geologist a few weeks ago. Whatever the *muj* were doing to that poor woman, they were not going to have the chance with Camille Black—even if that meant premature death.

A hawker jumped in front of her with a display case of Iraqi bracelets and necklaces. She brushed him aside, remembering how she and Hunter were once enjoying a night market in Istanbul when two men had tried to rob them at gunpoint. They neutralized the threat and, rather

than deal with the hassle of the police, Camille had wanted
to flee the country. Hunter had surprised her with a better
idea: kick up their vacation a notch and tour ancient ruins,
staying one step ahead of the Turkish police, putting their
skills to the test. Hunter knew how to treat a woman to a
good time. She'd give anything to live like that again, she
thought, as she and her Lebanese interpreter walked into
yet another store selling satellite dishes and cell phones,
Iraq's two postwar obsessions. It was the fourth Omar's
Electronics they had visited in the past two hours. Since
nowhere in the town seemed to have electricity unless it
was from a generator, she couldn't imagine that business
was exactly booming.

"*Marhaba*," Camille and her interpreter said.

A voice returned the greeting from the back room.
Camille nosed around. The shop was hardly bigger than
a dog kennel and it was crammed with every imaginable
cell phone accessory and pizza-box-sized satellite dishes
were mounted along the top of the walls all the way
around the room. Camille stretched and peeked behind
the counter. A prayer rug and a sleeping mat were rolled
up and stuck in a corner. A picture of a man with the
cuddly look of an Islamic extremist was tacked to the
shelf. She pointed to it and whispered to her interpreter.
"Any idea which one that is? I've seen his picture all
over today and I can never remember which is which.
Long mangy beards, serenely rabid eyes—they both
look alike to me."

"It's al-Zahrani. He claims he is bin Laden's chosen
one. He says al Qaeda has become weak because of heresy
from within. He says its membership must be purged of all
of Abdullah's heretics."

"I know, Abdullah, the other Crown Prince of Evil. Succession problems will get you every time." Camille picked
up a Hello Kitty cell phone skin. "Isn't that how the whole

Sunni/Shi'a thing started? Not that I'm comparing Mohammad's ascent to heaven with Bin Laden's descent to
hell."

The shopkeeper ducked down as he squeezed through the
low doorway. He spoke in Arabic, revealing a mouth full
of gold fillings. Camille assumed that he was apologizing
for the delay.

"I'm Sally Winston, a correspondent for *Newsweek*. I'm
doing a story on yesterday's skirmish here in the *souk*."
She paused for the interpreter, hoping Omar hadn't caught
on that American journalists hadn't dared to venture out
on their own in Iraq in years, but rather relied on their Iraqi
staff to do the real reporting.

The man pursed his lips, shook his head and waved his
hand. She didn't need a translation. She had received this
same message all day.

"Look, all I want to know is how this guy got away from
the soldiers. Was anyone helping him?" Camille showed
the man an old picture of Hunter. He was clean shaven and
his hair was shaved in a Marine flattop, a look she much
preferred to his current beard, civilian-length hair and
moustache. She pulled out a hundred-dollar bill and waved
it in front of him. "I'm really getting sick of everyone
playing dumb." Camille turned to the interpreter and said,
"Don't translate that last part."

Omar spoke, then the interpreter said, "Perhaps I know
someone who saw him leave the *souk*. Perhaps he had
friends."

The shopkeeper snatched the banknote between two
fingers. Camille held on.

"I need more, Omar," she said.

"You made an offer. I answered your question." He tugged
on the bill.

"You're right. You did." Camille released the bill and he
jerked it away.

"Come back in one hour and bring more of these. Many more." The shopkeeper shoved it into the pocket of his dishdashah.

As soon as they left the shop, Omar flipped open his cell phone and hit speed dial.

SEVENTEEN

Anbar Province

The hokey-pokey started blaring from a cell phone in the other room while the tangos stood around, watching Hunter as he gyrated on top of his temporary wife, the American hostage named Jackie Nelson. Every thrust was like a knife stabbing into his gut. He despised what he was doing, what he had to do. Hunter tried to get the hokey-pokey out of his head, but it wouldn't leave.

He heard footsteps as someone ran to the phone, then the music stopped and Fazul's voice answered it. Fazul listened for several moments without speaking, then he shouted at the caller. Hunter closed his eyes and focused on the jerking motion of his hips as he tried to listen in, but he couldn't make out the words above Jackie Nelson's cries.

A few moments later, Fazul jogged back into the bedroom and kicked Hunter.

Hunter rolled away from Jackie and Fazul pointed his AK at him.

"My cousin tells me that a woman came into his shop today in Ramadi. She's looking for her friend—the one the Americans were taking away at the *souk* yesterday. Her friend is an American, she says."

Stella. Oh god, what have I done? Hunter's gut clenched so tightly that he felt like vomiting. *Stay in character. It's the only way out.*

"It's a CIA trick," Hunter shouted, channeling his rage through *Sergei the Chechen*. He felt the heat rising up his neck. "They lie. They lie that I'm American so that no one will help me. I am the enemy of your enemy. You saw them taking me away." His voice raised in a crescendo. He threw up his arms and took a measured breath. "I am helping you prepare for the wedding, *insh'allah*. Would an American do that? Do you want a car bomb or a martyr vest? I recommend a car bomb because I can wire it for remote detonation with one of these cell phones, but you could send the boy in a vest, *insh'allah*." He pointed at the teenage boy.

The boy snorted. "I am not a martyr. I am an executioner."

One of the twins waved his finger at the teenager. "You, an executioner? You only hold their feet down while I am the one who chops off the heads."

"Someday, I'll be the one who whacks off the heads. You wait and see." The boy pointed to himself.

"Enough!" Fazul held one hand in the air; the other kept the gun pointed at Hunter. "You will build a car bomb, then we will decide if you live."

Hunter sifted through the nest of wires, tape, blasting caps, rusty tools, torn brown paper sacks of nails, screws and other unrelated hardware. The half brick of Semtex was not much for a serious car bomb and would be better suited for suicide vests, not that he was going to volunteer any advice. At first he hadn't liked the idea of building a bomb for tangos, but then he'd realized that helping one al Qaeda splinter group take out another was probably a good thing. If he could get at least two of them to leave for the wedding, he was confident he could take the ones that remained and rescue Jackie. He piled the blasting caps together and started to untangle the wires.

"What are you doing?" Fazul said. "We don't have time for this. We need to leave within an hour. You have more to work with than you know. Come." Fazul motioned with his hand and stepped toward the doorway.

An old Passat station wagon was parked beside a beaten-up seventies-vintage Nissan pickup missing its passenger door. Several blue plastic gas cans were crammed into the small truck bed along with a rotting wooden pallet. Fazul lifted the pallet. Underneath it were two faded green artillery shells with Russian markings. *Duds*. Hunter had been on enough training missions to Twenty-nine Palms to know that even a good percentage of American artillery shells didn't go off—fuses malfunctioned; propellants were faulty; shit happened—and these puppies were unstable and dangerous.

"Use these," Fazul said as he knocked on the weathered shell.

"Stop! Don't do that!" Hunter waved his arms in the air. All it took to set off a shell with a piezoelectric fuse buried in the ground was for a shadow to fall across it on a hot day, and movement would generally do the trick for most other detonator types. Shells were designed for rough handling and the brutal launch from howitzers and their cousins, but the firing sequence began a process that successively withdrew the safeties. For some reason that Hunter would rather not find out, at least one of the safety mechanisms in each of the shells had failed to withdraw.

That could change at any moment.

He took a deep breath. The hot air carried away the last drops of moisture from his sweating body. "You found this in the desert somewhere?"

"How do you know?"

"It's armed. Don't touch it again." Hunter pointed to the slanted grooves cut into the copper rotating band around the base of the shell.

"But it will work. I know it will. Amir, may Allah's blessings be upon him, used to make them work for us until—"

"Until he did something stupid like you just did and blew himself up? I can make it work for you, but only if you promise me you won't touch any of the explosives. I want to be in one piece when I meet Allah."

One of the twins helped Hunter place the tools he needed in a flimsy cardboard box while the other twin stood guard a good ten feet away. Jackie's hoarse cries from when he was on top of her haunted him and he knew he would have to figure out a way to take out the tangos and save her. The bastards were going to pay, *insh'allah*.

At Hunter's insistence, the twins off-loaded the blue plastic gas cans and the wooden skid. He wanted as large a working space as possible and his body odor had grown so strong, he didn't want to hassle his nose anymore by adding gasoline fumes to the mix. Sweat poured down his face as he squatted in the back of the truck bed, hunched over the unexploded ordnance. He said a quick prayer to the real god, then checked to make sure a weapon was still pointed at him. It was. Then he said a second prayer. His explosives courses had been long ago and making truck bombs from old Russian shells was not on the standard curriculum. He knew some Russian and could make out the Cyrillic lettering—OF412—but didn't have a clue whether it meant it was a fragmentation high explosive or even an armor-piercing round. This is why EOD guys had manuals. For all he could tell, the shells could contain propaganda leaflets.

The most explosive parts were at the tip and the least explosive at the base—that much he did remember as he tapped the metal at the bottom with his finger to determine its temperature. Bacon would fry on it. Nice, crispy, *haram* bacon. He could almost taste it.

"I am watching you." Fazul waved his finger at Hunter. "I have seen Amir build many bombs and I know what it should look like. If you try to deceive me, I will know and I will kill you."

"Don't worry, my friend. I'll make it right, *insh'allah*." Hunter waved his hand, while in his mind, he had only his middle finger sticking up.

He considered smashing the Semtex between the 122 rounds, but was afraid such a crude detonator might not do the trick. He would have to build a proper bomb. He picked up a monkey wrench and adjusted it. Trembling, he reached for the fuse. It contained the highest velocity explosive in the round and the most unstable. He stopped himself short of touching it.

Breathe, man. Steady.

He stared at his arm and tensed his muscles. All he could think about was his friend Demo Dave, may Allah bless his soul, who accidentally threw a wrench down on a fuse. Without letting himself think about it anymore, he took the wrench, placed it around the fuse and adjusted it to fit. He turned his hand in the air as if unscrewing a lightbulb to make sure he would turn in the right direction, then he pushed down on the wrench. It didn't move, so he pushed a little harder.

No movement.

If the thing went off, the blast would be so large he figured it really didn't matter which body part was closest to it, so he shifted his position and straddled the 122 millimeter round. He ratcheted up the force, but it was stuck. The damn thing had come out of the gun spinning like crazy in the opposite direction, tightening the fuse even more as it had soared through the air. He didn't think he would ever get it to budge.

The sun burned the back of his neck. He took a deep breath and let out a curse in Arabic which was not nearly as satisfying as an English one. The blood vessels in his neck felt like they were going to burst. When he thought he had it, the wrench slipped. He picked it up and banged on the shell, cursing it in Russian. That felt better. The Russians knew how to curse.

He pushed harder than he thought he could, harder than he would've dared a few moments earlier, then he pounded the damn thing with the wrench and tried again. It turned. He removed it and set it aside in the truck bed, but felt no relief. If the second shell went off, it would detonate the first one, too—not that it mattered. One was more than enough to take out him, the tangos and a good chunk of their safe house. Apparently, one already had.

He sat down beside the shell and wiped the sweat from his forehead and waited for his breath to steady.

The second one was no less of a struggle, only a shorter one because he started at it with more force. He unscrewed the second fuse and pulled it from the shell. The bottom of it cleared the round, but something was attached. A six-inch cylinder was stuck to the bottom of the fuse. Hunter didn't have a clue what it was.

"You broke it!" Fazul pounded his fist on the side of the truck.

"Stop! A jolt can set these things off." Hunter wrapped them in his headscarf to keep them from knocking against one another as he climbed from the truck, then he placed them in the sand at the base of a date palm.

"Where are you going? You must finish." Fazul pointed a pistol at him.

Hunter ignored him, stayed in the spotty shade of the palm and began drawing a wiring diagram in the sand. Two footprints represented the Russian rounds and a handprint the cell phone. Hunter rested his chin on his hand as he stared at the desert floor. The sand burned as he raked his finger through it, connecting the two footprints and the handprint in a single big loop. Linking the ordnance in a series like that meant that the entire circuit had to be good or nothing would go off. Hunter wanted it to go off. The tangos were going to pay for what they had done to Jackie Nelson—and for what they made him do to her.

The faded, kinked wires of the old blasting caps did not inspire trust. A break in one of them could prevent the entire circuit from closing and the IED would be a dud. He kicked the sand and made two new footprints and a new handprint. They had to be wired parallel so that only one circuit needed to be completed to initiate a detonation. He pursed his chapped lips as he tried to remember how to do it. As he traced a line with his finger, he thought of Stella and wished things were different. Something about explosions brought her to mind. If only things between them were less volatile.

Careful not to shake the truck too much, Hunter sat on the tailgate and swung his feet up into the back. He took two blasting caps and twisted their yellow leads together, then repeated the procedure with their red ones. He checked the time on the cell phone. It was running out—only thirty minutes until the phone's timer would call the *muj* to prayer and complete the circuit, well before they arrived at the wedding.

With a few twists of a screwdriver, the back of the phone came off. Working as quickly as he could, he fastened blue and green wires to each side of the chip that controlled the ringer. He then completed the loop, connecting the blue wire to the two yellow leads and he saved the green wire—the color of the Prophet—to connect with the red wires. He wrapped the phone in tape to hold everything in place.

Returning to the centerpiece of his creation, he studied the fuse well at the top of the 122s, then pinched off a tennis-ball-sized chunk of Semtex. The pink substance had the consistency of bread dough and some of it rubbed off on his hand. He made a mental note not to eat anything or touch his hand to his mouth until he got a chance to clean off the residue. If the Czech-made plastic explosive was anything like its American counterpart, ingestion of it could cause a different kind of explosion.

He stuffed Semtex into the cavities in the top of each 122 and shoved a blasting cap into each mass of the plastic explosive, praying that his plan would work. His improvised explosive device was now armed. The blast would be enough to rip the truck apart. Hunter climbed from the truck and waved his arm, presenting his work to Fazul. He knew he shouldn't be, but he was proud of his very first truck bomb. He was even prouder of his choice of victims. But the real beauty was that the bomb would detonate when the cell phone played the call to afternoon prayers.

Allahu akbar—Boom.

Man, he deserved a cold beer—Allah willing or not.

Fazul approached the side of the truck and looked inside. Moving his finger in circles in the air, he traced the wiring through several loops. Nodding his head in approval, he clutched Hunter's shoulder and shook it lightly. "All appears as it should. You have saved your life for now, *in-sh'allah.*"

"When you're ready to detonate it, all you have to do is call the cell number—935-7949." Hunter read out the number of one of the phones that was not hooked up to the IED, just in case he got some wires crossed. He wanted either his timer to work or the whole thing to be a dud. The more he thought about it, being an accessory to blowing up a wedding was not something he wanted on his conscience.

"How far away should we be?" Fazul said.

The answer Hunter wanted to give was sitting on top of the goddamn thing, but he shaved off several hundred meters from how far he would personally distance himself and said, "One hundred meters."

Hunter gathered the tools into a cardboard box and carried it into the house. One of the twins followed him, his gun always pointed at him. Then he went back outside where Fazul was barking orders at the teenager. The twins piled into the truck and the teenage boy jumped into the back with the IED.

"Mufid, out!" Fazul said. "I told you, you're guarding our friend and the American whore. Get me a piece of rope, now! We're going to be late."

The boy shuffled into the house and returned a couple of minutes later with a half meter long piece of rope. If it were his operation, he would've used the extra wire to hog-tie the prisoner, but who was he to dispense advice? He held out his wrists and Mufid bound them tightly in front of him. *Big mistake, muj-man.*

The Passat's door was jammed. Fazul pulled on the handle, then gave up and climbed in through its missing window. Hunter guessed it was more macho than circling to the passenger side of the getaway car.

Fazul leaned out and gave final orders to the boy. "Keep your gun on him at all times. If he tries to get away, kill him. If the bomb works, when I return we'll send him on his way with our blessings. If it does not, it's not our blessings that he will need." He started to drive off, then stopped and shouted, "And stay away from the American whore."

EIGHTEEN

Ramadi, Anbar Province

Camille and her interpreter returned to Omar's Electronics exactly one hour later. This time she noticed the thick layer of dust on the satellite dishes and assumed the inventory was not turning over very fast. If business was slow, then he'd be even more receptive to selling information. With the way the day had gone, it probably only meant what she already knew—that Iraq was a very dusty country.

She greeted him.

"I am sorry. The man you are looking for is similar to another customer who was in here yesterday. I was mistaken." The shopkeeper waved his hands.

Camille pulled out a one-hundred-dollar bill, but Omar averted his eyes. She took out another, then another. When he didn't even glance at them, Camille knew it was hopeless.

"I cannot help you." Omar held up his hand, turned and wedged himself through the doorway, disappearing into the back room.

NINETEEN

Anbar Province

The boy kept his AK trained on Hunter as they watched the cloud of dust and sand kicked up by the Passat and the truck bomb disappear into the distance. Hunter flexed and twisted his wrists, trying to get as much play as he could from the ropes, but he only caused rope burn. They were tied too tightly. He'd have to work around it. The boy led Hunter back into the house. Either by instinct or training, the boy kept himself just far enough away from Hunter so he couldn't disarm him. He ordered Hunter to sit on the floor up against a wall. Like a good Arab, Hunter squatted instead.

"Help me!" Jackie Nelson started pleading again.

The boy stared at the door to the bedroom where she was being held. Hunter was relieved they hadn't broken her spirit—yet. They had sure fucked with his.

"Why will they not allow you to have her?" Hunter kept his eyes on the hostage's doorway. "You must not be man enough and they know it. They are your friends. They save you the humiliation."

"I am a man." The boy jumped to his feet.

"Of course you are. That's why you're the one holding the infidel's feet when the others cut off the head." Hunter grinned as he calculated how much farther he needed to push the little bastard. "Tell me, Mufid, do they take you when there's no woman around? Maybe you like that too much and that's why they don't permit you to know her."

"I am man enough! I can have a woman whenever I want." He pointed the barrel of his AK at Hunter, then toward the bedroom door. "Get in there. I have to keep an eye on you."

The boy ordered Hunter to stand beside the wall where he could watch him. Mufid pulled up his man-dress and climbed on top of Jackie Nelson, the AK in his right hand. She screamed and he slapped her.

With Mufid distracted, Hunter inched himself along the wall, moving out of the boy's main line of sight into his peripheral vision. The boy wiggled, trying to position himself. Jackie struggled and he smacked her harder.

Hunter couldn't restrain himself waiting for the optimal moment any longer. She had suffered too much. He jumped onto the boy's back, slipped his bound wrists around his head and jerked upwards. The neck snapped with a loud crack. His hands still around the neck, he lifted the body off Jackie and dropped it onto the floor.

She screamed even louder than before.

"Jackie, you're safe," Hunter said as he checked out the AK. He dropped the mag, pushed on the rounds and felt some give. It was a few short.

Jackie continued screeching, her eyes tightly closed.

He raised his voice. "I'm rescuing you. You're safe. I'm American."

She opened her eyes. "You're one of them." She started crying, then sobbing. He wasn't sure if she knew where she was and what was happening or if she had totally broken with reality in order to survive.

"No. Calm down and listen to me. I'm with the US government. I'm getting you out of here."

His arms were still bound, so he couldn't stroke her or put his hand on her to reassure her. He sat beside her on the smelly bed waiting for his words to sink in. After a couple of minutes, her sobs faded into a whimper. *Progress*.

"You're going to be okay, Jackie, but I need you to get a

grip on yourself. We have to go." He couldn't believe he was taking time to get in touch with his softer side, but he felt like he had to after what he'd done to her. Besides, he wouldn't be able to get far with her unless she pulled herself together.

Hunter heard a vehicle approaching the house.

"Oh, fuck. Stay here and keep low." Hunter sat up and grabbed the AK. He rushed into the main room, tripping on his man-dress. Reaching inside the cardboard toolbox, he groped around, but couldn't find the knife to cut himself free. When he heard the engine turn off, he gave up and dashed out the back door with his hands still tied up.

Hunter circled the building, constantly trying to get a better grip on the AK. The red Nissan with his bomb in the back was parked directly in front of the house, close enough that it would take out the entire structure if it detonated. He should've told Jackie to run out the back and take her chances with any gunfire.

"*Marhaba*," the twins called out and didn't wait for a response from the boy. "Guess who ran out of gas in the Passat?"

Hunter wanted to spray the truck with bullets, but feared that a stray might set off a detonation. But he also didn't dare wait long, because it would be prayer time at any moment. He was sure as hell praying already.

As one of the twins slid from the cab, Hunter fired a burst into his chest. The recoil from the AK jarred Hunter and his bound hands struggled to target the second tango. The *muj* ducked behind the truck, then popped up to hurl rounds in Hunter's direction. Hunter shot another volley, then ran as fast as he could, circling around the back of the house. When he got to the other side, the tango had his back turned toward him, trying to figure out what had happened to his assailant.

"Hey, you fucking *muj*!" Hunter couldn't stand to shoot a man in the back—even one of them.

The twin spun around and Hunter squeezed the trigger. The man's face burst into chunks of pink flesh and dark blood, then he collapsed beside the truck.

The bomb.

Hunter ran as fast as he could to the truck and vaulted over the tailgate into the bed. He grabbed one red wire and yanked on it. It pulled free. Then he tugged on a yellow wire.

It came loose, disconnecting one of the two circuits.

He exhaled and let his head drop while he waited to catch his breath, but only for a few seconds. The shells could be unloaded later when he and Jackie were ready to use the truck to make their escape from this hellhole. Shaking his head, he couldn't believe how close it had come to detonating.

He went back inside and found a knife to cut his hands free. When he walked into the bedroom, Jackie sat up on the ripped mattress, trying to pull her torn blouse shut. He took this as a good sign. The room where she had been held contained no furniture other than the filthy mattress and a slop bucket in a corner. There was nowhere even to search for her pants. Hunter pulled the dishdashah from the boy with some difficulty. His limbs were already starting to get a little stiff. Rigor happened fast in the hundred and twenty degree heat. He rolled the corpse so it was facedown, more out of respect for Jackie than the dead tango. He shook the man-dress out, opened the hole for the head and handed it to Jackie.

"I'm sorry, but this is the best we've got right now." He helped her get it over her head and put her arms into the sleeves like he was dressing a child.

"What happened?" she said, barely moving her lips.

"Don't worry about it. The twins are dead and so is the boy. We're the only ones here." He took her arm and gently pinched her skin. It tented and very slowly settled back to normal, indicating severe dehydration, but he already knew that. "We've got to get you some fluids."

"There was one more."

"He's at large. Out of gas somewhere between here and town—wherever the hell that is." Hunter extended his hand to her and she took it and pulled herself to her feet.

"I want him dead." She stared at the corpse of the teenage *muj,* then kicked it twice. She bent over, removed his sandals and put them on.

"You'll get no arguments from me."

"I mean I want you to track him down and kill him." She wobbled from the room.

Fazul was baking in the Passat at the side of the small desert road. The twin morons couldn't be trusted to do anything right. All they had to do was throw a can of gas into the back of the truck without hitting the IED and come back for him. They were probably indulging themselves in the pleasures of temporary married life with that American harlot. He regretted ever taking a hostage. They were too much distraction and he still hadn't found anyone to pay enough ransom for her to make it worth his trouble. The husband had seemed uninterested.

He flipped open his cell and called his cousin who agreed to pick him up. Praise be to Allah that Omar had closed his electronics store early and was nearby, so it would only take a few minutes to swing over. He hung up the cell. If the twins were not back by the time Omar got there, he'd have him drive to the house and he'd kill both of them along with the American whore. He snatched a prayer mat from the backseat, got out of the car and used his cell phone to check the direction toward Mecca.

Any moment, it would be time for afternoon prayers.

Jackie walked through the main room and out the back door. Soldiers lived with their guns in combat and Hunter was still on the battlefield. He was not going to make the mistake of letting his guard down a second time, so he picked up the AK and ran after her. One of its sharp edges cut his hand.

"I've got to get out of here," Jackie said. Her eyes were glazed and she didn't seem to be looking at anything in particular.

"Sit down." He pressed lightly on her shoulder as she tried to walk away.

"No, I have to go."

"You're severely dehydrated. You're not thinking straight." He took her by the shoulders and guided her toward the shade of some date palms about fifty meters from the house. "Sit here in the shade."

She ignored him and walked out of the compound's back gate and into the desert. Hunter reminded himself that he needed to be patient, when he really wanted to shake her to her senses and if that didn't work, knock her out and carry her to safety. He followed the crazy chick into the desert.

Hunter thought he heard something and turned back to the compound in time to see a brilliant white flash, then an orange fireball rising into the sky. He shoved Jackie to the ground and threw his body over hers just as he heard the loud clap. The earth shook as the blast wave passed. A piece of tangled red metal fell near Hunter's head, missing him by inches. A hailstorm of concrete cratered the desert around them, then smaller debris pelleted his back. As if someone were sifting the particles by size, sand followed. Then suddenly everything was quiet and a dust cloud enveloped them, making the air hard to breathe.

He rolled off her the moment he thought it was safe and he hoped to god he didn't re-traumatize her by throwing his body on top of hers so suddenly. The last thing he wanted was to go back to ground zero with her. He coughed, then pulled the sleeve of his dishdashah up to his face. "Breathe through your clothes," he instructed as Jackie pulled herself up off the ground. "Everything's going to be fine now."

"What happened?" She pulled the dishdashah over her nose and mouth.

"Their truck bomb detonated somehow." Except Hunter knew how. He'd pulled out only one set of yellow and red wires. He couldn't believe he had disabled one of the parallel circuits but had forgotten the second set of wires. Too many things had been going on at once, but still he couldn't imagine that he'd been that careless. It didn't take long for him to convince himself that one of the tangos must have survived longer than he had thought and caused movement that had set it off. That would be what he'd tell the guys in the unit, anyway. Then he remembered he no longer had a unit.

"I have to find some water for you. Come on. Let's hope those palms are still intact so you can have some shade to sit in." He took her hand and helped her to her feet. Sweat evaporated so fast he didn't notice it anymore. As soon as the dust cleared, the midafternoon sun would be relentless. They needed water fast.

Most of the mud wall circling the compound somehow had held together, testament to the years of baking in the desert heat. The house had not fared as well. It was gone. Disappeared. Poof. Rubble littered the ground, but not nearly as much as Hunter had expected. Some of the dust he was breathing had probably once been the house. A twisted section of truck chassis no bigger than a bicycle was all that remained of his escape vehicle. Hundreds of flies swarmed in several places. He had been in combat enough to know to avoid those spots marking fresh flesh and blood.

The house had shielded the well from the worst of the blast. Hunter dropped the bucket into it and waited for a splash. It clanked as it hit the dry bottom.

He pulled the rope, hoisting the bucket back to the surface. The well was shallow, not more than twenty feet deep.

Since mud coated one side of the bucket, water couldn't be too much deeper. The rope was long and it didn't seem too badly frayed. Peering into the dark pit, he knew what he had to do if he didn't want them both to die from lack of water.

Hunter tied the rope to one of the date palms. Jackie sat watching him, her arms crossed, rocking herself. No way was he going to leave his AK with the unstable lady. It was going down the hole with him.

He kicked off his sandals and threw his leg over the side. His man-dress caught on a broken brick. He couldn't stand maneuvering in the awkward thing any longer. He had no doubt why the man-dress had never gone over in the West. They totally sucked. Man-purses like some Europeans carried at least had some practical advantages he could understand, but not the man-dress. He vowed never to give a woman a dress as a gift again. It wasn't right.

Hunter turned to Jackie and shouted. "Look the other way, okay?"

She shook her head and didn't turn away as he propped the AK-47 up against the side of the wall and peeled off the dishdashah. He reached for the gun again, then talked himself out of taking it with him. It would be an extra hassle and it was very unlikely that a target would lean over the top and into the very narrow range of fire he'd be afforded from the bottom of the well.

He lowered himself unarmed and naked into the well. He liked fast-roping, but not without protective gloves, so he kept his descent slow.

The bottom of the well was cooler and slightly damp, a virtual spa. The mud felt somehow comforting as it squished between his toes. For a moment, he was a kid again, skinny-dipping and running up a muddy riverbank in the Ozarks. He smiled to himself as he got down on his knees and started using the bucket to dig. At least there was enough sunlight for him to see what he was doing.

He dumped pail after pail of mud alongside the wall. Each successive load was wetter than the previous one. He paused to take a break, straighten up and look at the sky and remembered his grandmother telling him stories of well diggers being in such darkness that they could see stars. When he glanced back down at his hole, water was seeping into it.

Back on his knees, he cupped his hands and drank. The water was sweet—silty, but sweet. He laughed as he splashed it all over himself.

Several buckets of mud later, the well was running with enough clear water to fill the pail. He drank all he could, and then poured a bucket of it over his head. He refilled it and started to climb up the rope, using the wall for footing. Then he thought he heard a car. The higher he climbed, the louder the engine sound became.

Fazul.

Fazul stared at the rubble of his former safe house, his mouth agape. It had vanished, as if Allah had scooped it up and left only a few handfuls of dirt and stone behind. A swarm of flies buzzed near the ground and hundreds more covered something in the sand. He shooed them away from a strip of pink flesh.

"May Allah bless them and grant them peace," Fazul said.

Omar made eye contact with him and Fazul nodded. Omar understood it was the twins.

The American whore perched under a tree, rocking herself, watching him. She was no threat. He would deal with her later—like he should have long ago. He scooped up a handful of sand and spilled it out, covering what was left of the twins.

After the last grain of sand had left his hand, he turned toward Mecca and raised his arms. "*Allahu akbar.*" Omar did the same. They folded their hands over their breasts, the right one on top of the left. Both men stood as they recited as much as they could remember of the *Janazah*.

Hunter paused, hanging on the rope about six feet below the top of the well as a car door slammed shut. It was followed by the sound of a second one, which made no sense to him. Maybe it wasn't Fazul. His toes dug into the earth on the side of the well as he grappled for something firm enough to help him support his weight. His muscles burned as he hung there, listening to sounds that didn't make sense. Fazul's voice was distinct and he seemed to be praying, even though prayer time had passed.

Hunter climbed hand over hand further up the rope. Straining to hold on, he pulled himself high enough to peek over the edge. Fazul and a tall man had their backs to him as they recited a funeral prayer. He hoisted himself over the side, teetering on his belly while he reached down to where he had stashed his gun.

It was gone.

Hunter looked around and saw Jackie Nelson slowly wading through the debris. She held the AK at her side, aiming it at Fazul. Their loud prayers masked the sound of her approach. They appeared unarmed. Hunter shifted his weight to pull himself over the rim of the well.

"Jackie, no!" Hunter shouted and waved his arms, not bothering to cover his nudity. "Don't do it. Keep it pointed at them and bring the gun back to me."

The Iraqis spun around, but neither drew a weapon. Fazul knit his bushy black eyebrows and glared at Hunter. Hunter snatched up his dishdashah and slipped it over his head.

"You can't shoot them in cold blood." Hunter approached her slowly. At least when the tangos held an AK, he knew what they were going to do with it. She was so out of it, she could spin around and shoot him without warning.

"Stop. Stay right where you are or I'm taking them both out." She looked over her shoulder at Hunter, then back at Fazul. "You, get undressed."

"I don't think he speaks English. And he's not going to do that," Hunter said.

"Before he dies, he's going to get a taste of how he humiliated me. Tell him to strip."

Hunter translated.

Fazul laughed and spoke in heavily accented English. "No woman commands me."

"Take it off, you fucker." Jackie fired a burst at his feet, kicking up a cloud of dust.

Fazul tore his clothes off, then put his hands over his genitals as fast as he could.

"Don't do this," Hunter said. "You're not thinking straight because of the dehydration. It's not right to execute an unarmed man. You don't want that on your conscience all your life." Hunter walked around her, careful to stay within her line of sight so he didn't startle her.

"I don't want to spend my whole life regretting I didn't kill the fucker who kidnapped and raped me. We all know there's no justice in this fucking country." She continued toward Fazul. When she was fifteen feet away, she fired a burst into his groin and the hands covering it. Blood gushed from what remained of his genitals as he collapsed to the ground, moaning loudly.

The lanky Iraqi screamed, then threw his hands into the air. "I have eleven children. I have four wives to care for. Please."

Flies lit on the meat as Fazul pawed at himself with the stubs which were all that remained of his hands. He let out an eerie howl that sounded more animal than a human.

"For god's sake, finish him off. No man deserves to die like this," Hunter said as he edged closer to her. The other Arab didn't move, even though she kept the gun trained on Fazul.

"No. You know he made me watch while they executed a German oil worker? The little fucker held Wolfgang's feet while he begged to be the one to chop off his head. What kind of people are they? You know what they did to me!" Tears streamed down her face.

Hundreds of flies crawled over Fazul as he writhed on the ground, moaning. The sand turned dark from the blood. Hunter looked away. A buddy in Afghanistan once bled out from a groin wound and Hunter knew death took a hell of a lot longer in reality than it did in the movies. The guy had the worst twenty minutes of his life ahead of him.

"I have much children. Please," the Iraqi said in English.

"It's over. They can't hurt you anymore." Hunter slowly walked up beside Jackie, put his hand on her shoulder, then grabbed the barrel of the gun with his right hand, spoiling her aim while his left hand came off her shoulder, took hold of the stock and pulled it to him.

He jacked a round, aimed the AK into the tango's kill zone and squeezed the trigger.

The wailing stopped.

Hunter lowered his head and turned away. Earlier in the day he had actually looked forward to the moment when he would kill Fazul for what he had done to Jackie Nelson and for what he had made Hunter do to her. Now there was neither revenge nor justice in what he did, only mercy and mercy made him feel a little more human in a place where he didn't want to feel anything at all.

TWENTY

"You won't find MI6 agents in any country where you can't buy a cappuccino."

—FOREIGN CORRESPONDENT, Australian Broadcasting Corporation-TV [Australia], March 29, 2005, interview with Craig Murray, former ambassador for the British Crown

Anbar Province

The sun was finally lower in the sky and the temperature was only moderately miserable when Hunter and Jackie climbed into the old VW Beetle that Fazul had returned in. The lanky Arab was slumped against the date palms, fingering Muslim prayer beads and muttering something to himself. Hunter had taken his cell phone, but had assured him that he would call one of the numbers on speed dial and tell them where to find him after they made their escape. He turned the key, but the car didn't make a sound. The only thing that seemed to be going his way was that Jackie was snapping out of it and she didn't seem to have any association between him and the repeated rapes. Unfortunately he did.

He got out of the car and slung the AK over his shoulder. "You know how to start it by popping the clutch?"

"Yeah, I had one of these when I was in grad school." After slurping down most of the bucket of water, her voice was stronger. She crawled into the driver's seat, stomped the clutch and shifted into gear.

Hunter hiked up his man-dress and dug his feet into the sand and braced his hands on the car. The metal was almost too hot to touch, but he would've picked up burning coals to get out of there. Hunter pushed, but felt resistance. "Steer it away from the loose sand."

The car gained traction and started rolling faster.

"Pop the clutch! Now!"

The engine started.

Hunter glanced back at Omar. He was still fiddling with the beads, probably praying. He opened the driver's door and threw the AK into the backseat.

"Move over," he said. "You still need a lot more fluids. Dehydration affects judgment."

"That didn't really happen, did it? Oh my god. You're not going to tell anyone?"

"I have nothing to tell and no one to tell it to," Hunter said. If only this were the first time he had had this conversation. Iraq had a way of testing morals and sooner or later, everyone failed. Revenge was too easy, the opportunities too many. Multiple combat tours had taught him that it only took a moment of righteous rage to guarantee a thirst for justice that would never be quenched and a faint taste of blood that would never leave his lips.

Hunter stuck his head out the window and spat, even though his mouth was dry.

The insurgent's safe house was in the middle of the desert with no real road leading to it, only a trail that had been packed firm from years of constant use. In spots the desert rippled across it, hiding it from view. So much of Iraq was covered with hard, baked sand, but in this area it was as loose as it was in Saudi. The late afternoon sunlight cast shadows that made the path even trickier to follow. He couldn't believe that anyone was foolish enough to bring a vehicle with such low clearance through the desert. The road forked and he chose what appeared to be the firmer path. He navigated between ruts and drove as fast as he dared—which was only a little faster than he could've walked it.

A nearly full water bottle rolled out from under Jackie's seat. "Hey, the gods are finally smiling on us."

She opened it and drank, then passed it to Hunter. He

drank less than he wanted to and handed back the bottle without looking over at her.

"You haven't told me your name," Jackie said.

"Ray."

"Is that your real name?"

"Real as it gets."

"So you're CIA?"

"Don't overestimate the Agency. Most of them are cocktail party pimps. It's their local whores who screw the *muj,* not them." His voice was clipped.

"Somehow I didn't think my husband Brian sent you."

"He might have sent someone, but it wasn't me."

"Then what were you doing there, posing as one of them?"

"It's complicated."

She sighed and turned away from him. "I liked you a lot better when you first rescued me."

"I liked me a lot better then, too."

After a half hour of silence, Hunter spotted a line of palms, then he saw trucks and cars moving by, but the closer they got to the highway, the more loose sand covered the road. He stopped and got out to make sure that he was still on it. He was. A hundred meters later, the wheels spun in the sand, digging deeper and deeper.

"Don't you have that guy's cell phone still in your pocket?" Jackie said.

"You want to call AAA?"

"I could call my husband."

"You really want to give the *muj* your home number when their cell phone bill arrives?"

Hunter walked around the car, then ahead where he thought the road was, but his feet sunk into the soft sand. He returned to the car.

"We're going to have to walk to the road," Hunter said. "Even if we get it out, we can't get through this. We'll get stuck again. I don't know how the hell he got it here, unless maybe we should've taken a left back when the road branched."

"I don't know if I can make it," Jackie said.

"I'll get you there."

He dug through the junk in the Arab's backseat, then through the trunk searching for food or water. The guy had stashed away a bottle of whiskey, assorted porn magazines, but no more water. "You did the right thing letting the other Iraqi live. The guy's not al Qaeda. At least I don't think this is one of their training manuals." Hunter held up a dog-eared copy of *Playboy*.

With Hunter carrying the AK, they set out for the highway. Lingering alongside a highway in twilight was not his idea of a good time. With their night vision equipment, the Americans ruled the night, but twilight was happy hour for the insurgents—time to lob off a few mortar rounds or ambush a convoy rushing back to the safety of a green zone. The weak, shifting light of dusk played tricks on night vision goggles and Black Hawk pilots and others patrolling the main convoy routes could easily be confused. Friendly fire was the last way Hunter wanted to go.

"So what are you doing here in Babylon?" Hunter said.

"I came with my husband. He's an oil exec."

"I thought this was one of those posts where they didn't allow spouses."

"He's got some kind of pull. I'm a soil scientist and there was going to be all kinds of work for geologists because of the oil. Petroleum is not really my thing, but I've got the degrees."

A herd of camels grazed in the distance. Hunter couldn't tell if there was anyone with them or not. "The work didn't come through or what?"

"Oil here is a disaster. They're not back to prewar levels and if anyone tries to tell you they are, they're lying. The no need for geologists here. No one's looking for new fields. They need engineers to get things running again and to keep patching them up after they're sabotaged. They could also use about a billion guards to protect the pipelines and the facilities." Jackie stumbled and Hunter caught her by the arm before she hit the ground.

"You okay?"

"More or less—how far away do you think the road is?"

"Couple miles. Not too bad. I can carry you, if you don't think you can make it."

"I'm okay. But one question, what do we do when we get to the highway?"

"Hitchhike." Hunter gave her a thumb's up. "Except we won't use our thumbs—that gesture can get you in trouble in these parts. It's the local version of giving someone the bird. And I'll have to ditch the AK first."

"And how do you think we can get Americans to stop for us when we're wearing these things?" She tugged on her dishdashah.

"They won't, unless you do something crazy like pull off your dress. They'd probably stop for a naked lady. We're going to have to hitch a ride with the locals and take our chances."

"Then I'm stripping."

TWENTY-ONE

In the documents, which cover nine months of the three-year-old war, contractors reported shooting into 61 vehicles they believed were threatening them. In just seven cases were Iraqis clearly attacking—showing guns, shooting at contractors or detonating explosives.

There was no way to tell how many civilians were hurt, or how many were innocent: In most cases, the contractors drove away. No contractors have been prosecuted for a mistaken shooting in Iraq.

—THE NEWS & OBSERVER [Raleigh/Durham, NC], March 23, 2006,
   as reported by Jay Price

Anbar Province

Purples and oranges lingered in the sky when Hunter and Jackie spotted a Chevy Suburban leading a convoy of SUVs, American contractors zooming back to a green zone before nightfall. From the several different makes of vehicles, he guessed several companies had banded together for safety. White signs in English and Arabic on each vehicle warned: DANGER. KEEP BACK. AUTHORIZED TO USE LETHAL FORCE.

"Here's our big chance," Jackie said as she started to pull up her dishdashah.

"Don't." Hunter grabbed her arm. She shook him off, surprising him that she suddenly found so much strength.

"I'll do whatever it takes." She pulled the garment over her head and waved it at the approaching vehicles. "Help us! We're American! Help!"

The headlights of the first vehicle shined on her naked body. It slowed down, then stopped with the doors cracked open and barrels of assault rifles sticking out. H whispered to her. "This could be a problem for me. Follow my lead."

"What the hell are you talking about? We're saved."

"Hands in the air." Two contract soldiers wearing body armor and carrying AKs hopped out of the Suburban, their weapons trained on Hunter. The doors to the others were partially open and even though he couldn't see the gun barrels, he knew every one of them had an automatic weapon pointed at him. Whistles and shouts came from the convoy.

"Shake it, baby," someone shouted.

"Put your clothes on, Jackie." Hunter drew out his words, feigning a Southern drawl.

"I said hands in the air," the soldier said. "You, too, honey."

"Get dressed now. Slowly." Hunter turned his head toward the soldier and shouted. "Roadside strip show's over. She's had enough humiliation."

She slipped the dishdashah over her head, but the catcalls continued.

"Look, we need a lift. You can tell we're no threat to you. Feel free to frisk me or I can strip off my man-dress and give everyone another cheap thrill."

"I'll pass on that one." One of the soldiers patted down Hunter. "I don't suppose you have any ID on you. What are you doing here like this?"

"A mission went south. We're lucky to be alive." Hunter looked over the vehicles. There were three Ford Expeditions, a Lincoln Navigator and a RhinoRunner. He knew Stella had several Navigators and some RhinoRunners for VIP transport. But the Ford Expeditions concerned him. They were Rubicon's signature vehicle.

The soldier radioed his supervisor, then lowered his weapon. "There's room in the second vehicle. Welcome to civilization."

d on an Expedition's reinforced steel door, but ed. Hunter reached around her.

"I got it. These armored things are a workout."

Hunter boosted Jackie into the backseat and two men scooted over to make room for her. Two others sat in the third row of seats. All were dressed in khakis and ruby red T-shirts, Kevlar body armor and photographer's vests stuffed with ammunition. The real hunters usually didn't go out until late at night, so he guessed most of these guys were probably bomb disposal experts at the end of their workday. Elvis was blaring from the CD player. Hunter kept his head low, trying to shield his face as much as possible, hoping that whatever he had discovered about Rubicon, they wanted to keep extremely quiet and had not issued a general alert to all their troops. He only wished he knew what the hell the big Rubicon secret was that he supposedly knew. He kept racking his brains for clues and he didn't even have many of those except Ashland, the spy he recognized in the tango safe house.

Hunter pretended to check on Jackie, pulling down her lower eyelid, even though it really was too dark to tell if the whites of her eyes were as jaundiced as he assumed they were. She needed more fluids and he could use this to keep the attention on her and reinforce that they were together because Rubicon was searching for a lone runner. "You fellas got a medic kit on you? I need a saline bag to get her hydrated."

"Sure thing. We've got a medic in the other truck if you need one," one of the guys behind them said as he reached for a medic kit and passed it to Hunter.

"Thanks, but I can handle it right now." Hunter unzipped the soft case and set an IV bag, a needle packet and an antiseptic wipe on his lap. He handed the kit back.

One of the men in the backseat said, "Jimmy, you got any of that Gatorade left?"

"Yeah." Jimmy sat twisted to the side, looking out window, his gun ready for action. He stuck his hand seat without turning away. "Here. It's pretty warm

"Thanks," Jackie said. "Any of you guys have a cell phone," Hunter elbowed her, but she ignored him and continued, "that I could use to call—"

He put his foot on top of hers and tapped it, then pressed with increasing force.

"You bet," the guy next to her said and flipped open his Iraqna phone.

"I'm only going to tell him we got out alive," she said in a low voice as she punched in a number. Hunter reached over and hit cancel.

Two of the men glanced at each other, noting his odd behavior.

"Sorry," he mouthed to Jackie. She flashed him a disapproving look, but seemed to be playing along. Hunter rubbed the alcohol wipe on Jackie's arm, then attached the needle to the IV bag and inserted the catheter.

"What the hell happened to you two out there?" The team leader said from the front passenger seat as he turned down the music.

"Just another day at the office."

"Not at liberty to say, huh?"

"Sorry. It would make things a lot safer for us if you'd forget we were ever here." Hunter squeezed the IV bag to force the saline to flow faster as he monitored the traffic ahead. It was heavy and classic Third World style: every man for himself. Signs, regulations and even lanes were treated as suggestions to be ignored. It was a giant game of chicken at seventy miles an hour on roads broken up by bombings, tank treads and neglect.

"I don't know how you spooky types do it. I'll take working with bombs any day. Hell of a lot safer."

Hunter wanted to get the conversation off them fast and the best way to distract an EOD guy was to get him started talking about bombs. "So do you guys run with ECM?" Hunter knew the vehicles of the best contractors were all uipped with electronic countermeasures which would send out signals that detonate any radio-controlled roadside bombs ahead of them.

"They don't do much good anymore. The tangos have imported a passive infrared trick from Hezbollah—thank you Iran."

"ECMs really don't work?"

"Nope. Not with a totally passive infrared system. You enter the IR footprint of one of those and you're Swiss cheese—even in one of these armored babies."

"Anything you can do about them?" Hunter said as he watched a pickup overloaded with refrigerators and stoves slow down to give them room.

"The recommendation is to use thermal vision to spot a temp differential from the surrounding objects, but I think your best bet is never to ride in the front vehicle."

"Head's up. White van tracking us. Over there on the service road," one of the shooters said as he pointed his AK at the driver.

The Ford Expedition weaved in and out of traffic, speeding up. One hundred ten. One hundred fifteen. One hundred twenty miles an hour and the speed was increasing. Heavy bulletproof windows couldn't always be trusted to roll back up when it counted the most, so the men sitting by the doors cracked them open and stuck the barrels of their weapons outside. Without exchanging a word, the guy sandwiched in the middle passed Hunter his weapon. Hunter shoved the IV bag into Jackie's lap and opened the door just enough.

The white van sped up.

"What do you think?"

"Not good."

The Rubicon SUV ahead of them swerved toward the ditch, kicking up dust. Suddenly Hunter saw why. A compact car stuffed with a family was in front of them, creeping along the road and they were hurtling toward it. In a fraction of a second, they were on its bumper. The Rubicon driver swung into the shoulder, passing the car on the right, driving into the dust cloud. The Ford Expedition bounced so hard Hunter's head hit the doorframe and he started to fall out the door. He grabbed for anything he could find and held on to the seatbelt as he hung outside the door. Even though visibility was only inches, he was staring straight down at a blur of garbage, churned-up earth and discarded plastic bags.

He snagged his foot under the passenger seat and pulled himself upright into the cab. Seconds later they emerged from the dust cloud, four feet from the white van. The van's driver pointed something at him.

Hunter leaned out and started to squeeze the trigger, then he realized it wasn't a gun, but a finger.

"Hold fire!" Hunter shouted, but not in time. The van's window exploded into fragments. The driver slumped over the wheel and the van veered toward them.

"Look out!" Hunter said.

Their Ford Expedition took a sharp left, throwing Hunter back toward the door. He held onto the seat as the door swung open, then back a little. Hunter waited until the ride smoothed out, then held onto the frame, leaned back outside and pulled the heavy armored door shut.

They were back on the main road, again zipping between cars, trying to catch up to the lead vehicles in the convoy. He looked back and saw the white van hit one of the countless decapitated palm trees that line Iraqi highways. Then he glanced at Jackie. She was staring straight ahead, her eyes wide.

The Rubicon team leader turned up the music and Elvis was rocking over his new blue suede shoes.

Jackie whispered to Hunter. "That was a finger. He was pretending to shoot with his finger. He even mouthed 'Bang.' I saw it right before—"

"Yeah, he was acting stupid and it got him killed. But it's big boy rules out here." Hunter whispered, trying to keep his voice below the music. Now back in his seat, Hunter squeezed the saline bag as he returned it to his lap. "The Iraqis are fed up with the occupation and it's hard to blame them. Could you imagine carloads of heavily armed Iraqi contractors speeding down the Beltway in DC during rush hour and shooting at any vehicle that spooked them? But as long as we're here, it's got to be this way. A vehicle speeding up to approach a convoy is either a suicide bomber or someone committing suicide. You don't come close to an American vehicle and everyone knows it. That's why we have those little signs warning everyone to stay back. We're authorized to use lethal force. Like I said, big boy rules."

"It was a finger, for god's sake."

"There was a dust cloud and it was nautical twilight. It's a split-second decision."

The shooter in the backseat made eye contact with Hunter and grinned. "Road rage, man. Commuting is a real bitch."

"BK, you saying you're ready to get shipped home to avoid the commute?" the team leader said.

"No way. I'll take this over a civilian job any day. You know when I worked at Burger King I actually had to smile at people? You didn't hear me asking those tangos, 'You want fries with that?' Those days are over, man. I make in a day what I used to take home in a month. Hey, maybe I ought to start shouting that every time I shoot a tango. It could be my tagline." BK held his AK, pointed it at a truck and pretended to shoot. It veered off the road and into the ditch. "You want fries with that, tango-man?"

The men laughed.

Hunter didn't. He closed his eyes and saw the van driver pointing his finger at him. *Bang*.

TWENTY-TWO

Triple Canopy grew to over 800 employees and earned annual
revenues exceeding $100 million within its first year of operation.

—TRIPLE CANOPY, *INC.*

Blackwater was originally slated to be paid $229.5 million for five
years, according to a State Department contract list. Yet as of
June 30, just two years into the program, it had been paid a total
of $321,715,794.

—THE NATION, 28 Aug, 2006, as reported by
Jeremy Scahill

Camp Raven, Black Management Iraqi Headquarters
The Green Zone, Baghdad

The car lights glistened off the shiny silver retro-style trailer
in the former parking lots across from the presidential
palace. During Operation Iraqi Freedom I, when Hunter
was fighting his way into Baghdad alongside the legendary
Colonel Dunford, Camille quit the CIA and was in Hollywood mortgaging everything she owned and negotiating
with a movie studio to buy a luxury trailer that had become
too rundown for their starlets. Within six weeks, the trailer
was in Baghdad and Camille was courting military brass for
contracts in the Green Zone's first speakeasy. The war had
been good for business and the current drawdown of troops
was a bonanza. Each soldier pulled out meant a vacuum that
had to be filled. The Iraqis weren't up to the task and America was too deeply involved to roll over and allow room for
al Qaeda to move in.

Enter Black Management.

Enter Triple Canopy.

Enter Rubicon Solutions.

Enter Blackwater.

Only families cared about dead contractors—Pentagon body counts didn't. Relying even more heavily upon the private military corporations, the US was able to quietly maintain a constant level of influence while the American public celebrated the homecoming of the troops.

Alcohol now flowed more or less freely in the Green Zone and Black Management's reputation for the best operators in the Iraq and Afghan theaters pulled in the contracts, so the speakeasy had long ago given way to formal offices. Black Management headquarters had expanded into three low concrete buildings with four-foot-thick ceilings engineered with layers of cutting-edge materials designed to absorb mortar blasts. Two clamshell maintenance hangers housed helicopters undergoing repairs and their Baghdad fleet of Black Hawks, Little Birds and Super-Cobra attack helicopters were parked on the ramp. But upon Camille's insistence, the original Hollywood trailer had been preserved.

Camille stepped inside it, fondling those early dreams.

Sue "Pete" Peterson swiveled in her Aeron chair and jumped to attention as soon as she saw it was Camille. Her hair was even more closely cropped than Camille remembered, but she still wore enough Old Spice to make Camille nearly gag. Pete worked as the Black Management deputy project manager for logistics for the Baghdad area of operations, but whenever Camille was in town, she reassumed her old role of personal aide to the boss.

"At ease. I thought you were going to salute for a minute there," Camille said.

"Sorry, ma'am. Old habits die hard."

"We crapped out in Ramadi. The trail's cold," Camille said as she pulled apart the Velcro shoulder straps of her Kevlar vest. Pete helped her out of it and hung it on a coatrack. Camille was very aware of how the sweat made her

T-shirt cling to her breasts. So was Pete. Camille would never admit it, but she liked the attention and Pete was more of a gentleman than most of the guys she worked with. It wasn't that often that Camille let someone make her feel like a lady.

Camille continued speaking. "We must have talked to two hundred shop owners and vendors. Hundreds of people were there yesterday during the riot and they all say they saw nothing. I even believed one or two of them. Iggy back from Afghanistan yet?"

"Tonight. Don't worry. Virgil's holding down the fort, but he hasn't been too happy about it. It's his shot at being the alpha dog and there's no one to play with. It's been quiet lately—real quiet."

"Quiet makes me nervous. You don't know where the tangos are. They're moving around, regrouping for something big."

"You want some ice water? A soda?"

"I got it. I miss the old speakeasy days. I could use a cold one right now." Camille opened an apartment-sized refrigerator and pulled out a can of Coke with white Arabic script. She took a sip, then set it on the coffee table and sunk herself into the black leather sofa, closed her eyes and took a long breath as she savored the air conditioning. The unit for her trailer was twice the recommended BTUs for the space and seemed to be one of the few that could stand up to the desert heat.

"I can send one of the boys for whatever you want and I could rustle up some whiskey a little faster than that." Pete set a glass of ice on the coffee table in front of Camille and poured the soda into it.

"No need. I'm good."

"Can I be frank with you?" Pete was the kind of woman who, even if you didn't ask, would tell. It got her into trouble. It got her out of the Army. It got her a job with Camille.

"You always are."

"We're not a mom and pop shop anymore. You don't need to do this yourself. I heard from Virgil that you went out on a run and led a takedown last night. That's too dangerous for the president of a billion-dollar company."

"We're not there yet. Though the accountants are projecting we'll hit it in November if current trends hold." Camille sipped her Coke. "Things have gotten hot with Rubicon and I needed to see for myself."

"Is that all?"

"I like to keep my skills sharp."

"I hear you on that one. I sneak out every once in a while with the boys just to pop a few fly balls. But that wasn't what I was talking about." Pete stood and walked over to a cabinet beside the stainless steel sink. "You've been at the Kandahar base so much lately, I've gotten out of the habit of stocking up for you. Looks like all I've got to offer you to eat right now are some corn nuts, pretzels or a stale Ding Dong."

"Pass on the Ding Dong."

"Yeah, I wouldn't touch it either." Pete ripped open a vending-machine-sized bag of pretzels and dumped them into a blue ceramic bowl hand painted with a geometric pattern and stylized Arabic writing. She offered some to Camille, then set the bowl on the coffee table.

Camille bit into a pretzel. "Business is too good in Afghanistan—actually most of our work at the moment is unofficially over the border in Waziristan, tracking down Abdullah. The Taliban and al Qaeda run that part of Pakistan, but no one wants to admit it any more than they want to admit the US is active there. Even though Pakistan is our good friend in the fight on terror, as far as I'm concerned Pakistani intelligence is the most functional part of al Qaeda."

"The tangos have sure been going after each other without OBL to hold them together." Pete plopped down in the armchair across from her. Camille sensed there was something bothering her. Pete's expression suddenly became more serious and she continued, "I'll tell it to you straight. You have no business running after this guy."

"Abdullah? You've got to be kidding. He and al-Zahrani are the world's two most wanted terrorists now that it finally leaked that bin Laden's long dead."

"Come on. You know who I mean—Stone. I've never seen you put out an alert to all supervisors like this morning. Asking them to grab Stone, sure, but the part about you reserving deadly force for yourself—that was out there."

"I want him brought in alive. He has some information I need."

"Right. Come on, Camille. You and I go back to the days when this trailer was sitting at Shuwaikh, impounded by the Kuwait Ports Authority because we didn't have some trumped-up permits. The amazing part is I hauled it up to Baghdad in one piece, more or less. Sure couldn't do that now, too damn dangerous."

"Amazing you wrestled it away from them. I thought Black Management was sunk then and there along with everything I owned. Of course, I thought that several times—like when we couldn't get any operators to join us because they didn't want to work for a woman. Thank god Iggy joined me. He really turned things around. Without him, we wouldn't have hit critical mass."

"Iggy was sure a magnet for the best operators. But you're selling yourself short. There are a lot of boys who wanted to work with you. You've got star power, too."

"More like sex appeal. I know these guys. All they think about is pussy and that's all a woman's good for." She ran her fingers through her hair, pushing it back behind her ears. "You recognized him from the picture?"

"Oh, yeah. And I'm sure I'm not the only one." Pete grabbed another soda and drank a swig from the can before filling half a glass. She opened a file cabinet and pulled out a bottle of Wild Turkey. She added a shot, then set the bottle in front of Camille.

Camille dumped some whiskey into her Coke too, even though she was more of a vodka kind of gal.

"When did you find out he wasn't KIA?" Pete said.

"Two months ago. What I just now found out was that the Agency helped him fake his death so he could marry someone else—a hell of a way to break off an engagement."

"Ouch. You gonna take him out?"

"You do know me, don't you?"

"We've been around together and I've seen more than I should." Pete shook her glass and the ice cubes clinked against the side.

"What you don't know is that I've been hired personally for the job. Temp Agency stuff. He was working for them inside Rubicon and apparently the new hussy is high maintenance. He got greedy and stupid. Sold seized weapons caches to the tangos."

"You believe it?"

"I believe enough." Camille took a deep breath. "It's a knife straight into my heart. And the more I find out, the more it gets twisted."

"What if it's been twisted? You know the Agency. They're not exactly in the truth business."

"Even if only half of it is true, choosing death over me is enough to make me want to help him get his wish."

Pete chuckled. "I hope I don't ever cross you, but I gotta say, there's no one I'd rather have watching my back than you. Don't get me wrong. The boys working for us are the best, but they all do it for adrenaline or money. You're old-school like your daddy. It's all about loyalty—loyalty to country, family, friends."

Camille smiled at the thought that she was like her father when it came to loyalty, but she knew it wasn't true. Her father was a true Marine—Semper Fi—always faithful. As much as she had dreamed of becoming the same, the Corps wouldn't allow her to follow his path. Combat operations were off-limits to women. Her father had seen to it that her long-range marksmanship skills could compete with the best scout snipers and her surveillance, weapons and survival skills could match any recon Marine. But as a woman, she would have been relegated to combat support. On the day she graduated from college, she went to the Marine recruiter's office with her father, but left without signing the enlistment papers and instead called Joe Chronister and accepted the CIA's offer.

She still resented that she was denied the camaraderie that forged a Marine. But Camille was a girl and girls were supposed to leave their families and their names behind when they married. They changed sides to go with the highest bidder; they were the original mercenaries.

Like it or not, Camille was one, too.

Camille set down her drink. "You know, I used to think Hunter was the only man I'd ever know who had an even stronger sense of loyalty and honor than my father. He'd agonize over doing the right thing when all I cared about was being the best."

"The floozy might have really gotten under his skin. People will do all kinds of strange things for a woman. I could tell you stories."

Camille laughed. "You know, the funny thing is he keeps trying to tell me he's doing it to protect me." Camille downed the Coke and whiskey, then poured herself a straight shot and raised the glass. "Like Daddy always said, Semper Fi."

TWENTY-THREE

The Green Zone, Baghdad

Entering into the highly fortified Green Zone in the Iraqi capital reminded Hunter of crossing from drab communist East Germany into the glitzy, affluent enclave of West Berlin. West Berlin was a subsidized showcase of just how good things could be if only the commies discovered the wonders of the American way of life. Fast food, relatively safe streets and the absence of poverty in the Green Zone made similar promises to the select Iraqis allowed inside its razor wire and blast walls. Nearly two decades after the fall of the Berlin Wall, things still weren't going very well for the East Germans and Hunter suspected the Iraqis would face similar disappointments—*if* the situation were ever stable enough to remove the blast-proof concrete T-walls, checkpoints and tanks that kept the Americans and the Iraqi government safe from Iraq.

The Green Zone was the safest place in Iraq for all Westerners—all Westerners except him. All he could think about was getting out of there. The zone had a high concentration of security forces which would be searching for him and it also had paranoid Westerners who would turn in anyone accused of supporting the insurgency. It wouldn't give him much room to maneuver to figure out why Force Zulu had cut him loose. But the red zone—the rest of the country—was too hostile to give him the breathing room he needed to sort things out and formulate a game plan for clearing himself. He needed to fall back to neutral territory—somewhere that wasn't color-coded. He needed to get the hell out of Babylon.

* * *

Once inside the zone, the convoy vehicles dispersed toward their various corporate military camps. They let
Hunter and Jackie out near the al-Rashid hotel. He ducked
into the shadows and Jackie followed. The Arab man-dress
that had saved him in Ramadi made him stick out in the
Green Zone, particularly at night without most of the Iraqi
support staff around.

"Are you sure you don't want me to take you to the hospital?" Hunter said.

"There's not much they can do for me. I want my own
bed and I don't want the press around. I live around the
corner." She took his hand. "There's no way I can thank
you enough."

"We're good. I need to get moving." He pulled his hand
away.

"What's this all about? What's so dangerous?"

"Good-bye, Jackie. Take care of yourself and get out of
this place as soon as you can." He pecked her on the cheek
and walked away without looking back.

"Ray! Wait!"

Hunter kept moving even though he heard her light
footsteps jogging after him. He thought about trying
to find Stella. She did have a large facility in the bubble,
but he couldn't take the risk of getting nailed by her
security if she wasn't there. The one thing he was sure of
from his time at Rubicon was that it had infiltrated
Black Management. He couldn't trust anyone there
other than Stella and he wasn't even so sure about her.
She had a temper and he could sort of see how she might
really be pissed at him, particularly over him stealing her
SUV and not apologizing for standing her up in Dubai.
The best thing he could do was to get out of the country,
maybe even head to Saudi—no one would expect an
American to flee there. But first he needed food, rest and
money.

Jackie kept trying to catch up with him. She yelled after him. "You don't have anywhere . . ." Jackie gasped for breath, then continued, ". . . to go . . . do you?"

Hunter stopped.

TWENTY-FOUR

The logistics task order contract awarded to Halliburton subsidiary KBR for food and living services in Iraq in 2003 has cost more than $15.4 billion so far, according to the GAO.
—UNITED PRESS INTERNATIONAL, December 29, 2006

At the lowest level, Blackwater security guards were paid $600 a day. Blackwater added a 36 percent markup, plus overhead costs, and sent the bill to a Kuwaiti company that ordinarily runs hotels, according to the contract.

That company, Regency Hotel, tacked on its own costs, and a profit, and sent an invoice to ESS. The food company added its costs and profit and sent its bill to Kellogg Brown & Root, which also added overhead and a profit, and presented the final bill to the Pentagon.
—THE NEWS OBSERVER [Raleigh/Durham, NC], September 29, 2006, as reported by Joseph Neff

Camp Raven, The Green Zone, Baghdad

As soon as she got word of a possible sighting of Hunter, Camille jogged back to her trailer from the Black Management Ops Center to meet with the informant, one of her employees who had just returned in a convoy to the Green Zone from a job site near Ramadi. She went inside and it reeked of sweat and Pete's Old Spice, a putrid cocktail. Sitting on one of her leather armchairs was a man in his late forties. His skin-tight tan T-shirt was streaked with dirt and had his blood type written on it with a Magic Marker. Like many of her frontline personnel, he had the Black Management black panther logo tattooed on his forearm. His belly hung over his khaki slacks. He would never pass a military physical and she was surprised he had passed hers, except she knew the shortage of skilled technicians had caused them to loosen up standards in some occupations, particularly for Explosive Ordnance Disposal guys.

Camille extended her hand to the man. "Hi, I'm Camille."

"Mark Fields, pleased to meet you." He leaned forward, using his weight to help him stand to greet her, then he wiped his hands on his pants, renewing their dirt coating. "Ma'am, I'm sorry. I would've taken time to shower if I knew I was meeting the big boss. We hit a hundred and twenty-three today at the site. Hot enough to make a camel sweat like a pig."

"Don't worry about it," Camille said, even though he reeked of body odor. She stifled a gag as she sat down. "Pete, can you get Mr. Fields a bottle of water?"

"You got it." Pete walked over to the fridge. "Fields here is an EOD supervisor for a team working on a site near Ramadi. They're Baghdad-based and they convoy with some guys from Rubicon and Zapata."

"Whoa. I know this isn't why you're telling me this, but why are we going through the risk and expense of the commute when we have personnel at Camp Tornado Point in Ramadi? That road is nasty." Camille started to raise a hand for emphasis, then stopped herself. She wasn't there to micromanage.

"There's a big job in Ramadi and everyone's EOD units are stretched thin." Pete tossed Fields a bottle of water.

"Thanks, Pete," he said.

"So I hear you've got some information for me?" Camille said.

"I think I saw your man."

"You think?"

"It was getting kinda dark and he was dressed like a towel head, uh, I mean like a local. And he was with a girl."

"An Iraqi?"

"Dressed that way, but I'm sure she wasn't one of them. She stripped to get the convoy to stop. She was as thin as a twig."

"Where is he now?"

"Somewhere here in the Emerald City."

"In the Green Zone?"

"Yeah. We were packed to the gills, so they had to ride with Rubicon. I knew you'd want to know more, so I called one of my buddies who works for them. I've been trying to get him to switch over to Black." Fields picked up the water bottle and gulped down half of it, then let out a sigh. "Anyways, my buddy was in the SUV with him. Jimmy said the guy was some kind of a spook. Apparently he and the girl infiltrated the insurgents and things got too hot for them. Jimmy said she was so dehydrated, they pushed in two bags of saline between where we picked them up outside of Ramadi and here. She was skin and bones. She was definitely American from what Jimmy said. Oh, and he couldn't stop talking about how bad they smelled. Said it was all the guys could do to keep from puking. Now I could identify her for sure. I got a real eyeful when she flagged us down." Fields flashed a conspiratorial smile at Pete. "You shoulda been there."

"So does Rubicon have him? Did they take her to the hospital?" Camille tried to get her mind off Fields' intense body odor. It was starting to make her queasy and she worried she might not be able to get the place aired out well enough by bedtime.

"Nope. Said they'd be fine and they got out over by the al-Rashid. Jimmy said they were real cagey."

"Pete, what was the name of that geologist kidnapped in Anbar a couple of weeks ago?" Camille ran her hand through her hair and leaned back while she tried to come up with an explanation for Hunter hooking up with a woman in that condition. Her best guess was that he had come across a woman being held hostage and she knew him well enough to know that he would either free her or die trying.

"I remember that. The woman was freelancing for an oil company when they grabbed her. One of the al Qaeda splinter groups backing al-Zahrani sent out a ransom demand, then I didn't hear any more. I don't think they have her back yet."

"Get on the Internet and pull up a picture."

Pete handed Camille a color printout of a studio shot of the abducted geologist. She had shoulder-length brown hair and the complexion of a movie star. She passed the photo to Fields, stretching herself to get it as close to him as possible, so he didn't have to raise his arm to take it from her.

"Bingo! That's her." Fields tapped the picture with his index finger.

"Who is she?" Camille said.

"The article is printing out. Just a sec," Pete said. She took a sheet from the laser printer and glanced at it before handing it to Camille. "Her name's Jackie Nelson—I know who she is now—she's the wife of a Rubicon exec who tried to lure me over to them once."

"What's his name?"

"Brian Nelson, a VP for Rubicon Petroleum."

Camille glanced at the photo again. If she didn't know the Rubicon exec's spouse was a geologist, she would've guessed trophy wife.

"Rubicon does oil, too?" Fields said.

"Their fingers are in everything," Camille said. "Don't you know the Rubicon story? When Dick Cheney left Halliburton to run for VP, some of the execs split off and formed Rubicon Group. The government throws nonbid contracts at them all the time. Rubicon Solutions is the security subsidiary they started after 9/11 and they've also got a consulting firm that does studies for the Pentagon, recommending the mother ship's services. Then, of course, there's their PR firm that constantly reminds the world that everything they do is really for Third World widows and orphans. Think of them as Halliburton's evil twin. Frankly, both of them scare the shit out of me."

Fields grunted. "Didn't know that. I always thought they were small potatoes because that's where the guys go when they get fired from us or TC. They're known for being a little loosey-goosey. I know one Rubicon shooter who claims he's wanted in—"

"Thank you so much for bringing this to my attention." Camille stood and extended her hand to Fields. She couldn't stand to look at how his sweaty T-shirt clung to the rolls of his beer belly any longer and she needed to track down her lead before Hunter slipped away. She pulled three one-hundred-dollar bills from a pocket where she had stashed them in Ramadi and held them out for Fields without looking down at them.

"I can't take that from you, ma'am. I'm happy to help out." Fields waved his hand.

"Then do me a favor. Take it and go treat your crew to a few rounds of drinks on me." Camille smiled as she walked him to the door. As soon as he left, she opened the windows and said to Pete, "Find out where Jackie Nelson lives. And check the hospitals, just in case. I want to have a chat with her—tonight."

TWENTY-FIVE

The Green Zone, Baghdad

Jackie Nelson's apartment might not have been up to middle class American standards, but it was the most luxurious place Hunter had been since he last left the States. He'd slept inside plywood walls in the Rubicon barracks and he worked in cinder block houses or mud-brick homes clearing them of weapons and insurgents. The walls of Jackie's apartment were Sheetrock and they were covered not with oriental carpets, mirrors or pictures of some bearded mullah, but with dozens of charcoal portraits and pencil drawings of American troops and Iraqi civilians. The furniture was a jumble of Iraqi antique chests and Ikea basics, but the TV was flat panel; the stereo was Bose and he was sure the beer was cold. It felt almost American. It felt almost safe.

Hunter knew he had to be careful.

"Walk me through it. I want to know how you know your husband won't be coming home tonight."

"You're as paranoid as Brian is. Like I said, we have a system. See these two drawings?" Jackie pointed at a pen and ink drawing of an Army medic bandaging the arm of an Iraqi girl and at a sketch of a bearded spice merchant in an Iraqi market. "When the one with the medic is on the right, he's in the country. When it's on the left, he's abroad. He's out of the country. Don't worry. Brian never gets home at night."

"And why do you think he'd still be doing this weeks after you were kidnapped?"

"He's a creature of habit. I could be dead for a year and he'd still be doing it."

"He travel a lot?"

"Constantly. There's always some big secret project. So secret, he won't even tell me what continent he's going to." Jackie took a glass pitcher from the fridge and poured two glasses of water. She handed one to Hunter, then held hers up in a toast. "To my hero—Secret Agent Man Ray."

Hunter flashed her a smile and wished he could forget what the tangos had made him do to her. He couldn't believe she didn't seem to have any memory of it, but then he knew all too well the tricks the mind had to play in order to survive torture. He gulped down the entire glass without pausing. She refilled it.

"Don't you want to call your husband and at least tell him you're alive? You couldn't wait to call him earlier."

"I don't know whether he gives a damn anymore, but it doesn't matter. He's in Uzbekistan and he doesn't have his cell with him. God forbid that he leave a trail of anything." Jackie grabbed a box of Ritz crackers and ripped it open. She popped a whole one into her mouth and held the box out for Hunter. "I have to shower. I can't stand being like this a second longer. Afterwards, I'll call my sister."

"Wait a minute. Uzbekistan? I thought you said he wouldn't tell you where he went."

"I have my ways."

"Gonna tell me?" Hunter followed Jackie into the hallway and stood outside the bedroom door, nibbling on a handful of Ritz.

"Why not? You're going to disappear from my life forever after tonight, aren't you?"

"Afraid so."

"I told you I'm a soil scientist. I do forensics. When I was stateside I did a lot of expert witness gigs—tying soil samples to remote crime sites, that kind of thing." She opened a wardrobe and pulled out a polo shirt and pair of Dockers and threw them on the bed. "If these don't work for you, help yourself to something else."

"So you scraped soil off his shoes?"

"I almost forgot shoes. Hope you wear a size eleven, otherwise you're out of luck." She handed him a pair of deck shoes. "I think he's been cheating on me. I wanted to know where he kept disappearing to, so I analyzed the soil. He's up to something in Uzbekistan, somewhere around Zarafshan."

"You can be that accurate from little chunks of rock?"

"Actually, it's the microfauna and microflora that are the dead giveaways. Well, it wasn't that easy. In grad school I worked summers for Neuberg Mining Corp. We did some extensive studies of the Muruntau deposits—they were trying to figure out the most environmentally friendly way to get the gold out of low-grade ore. As soon as the bastards realized they could buy off the Uzbek government and get away with heat-leaching, my trip there got cancelled along with my job." Jackie took out a bathrobe for herself. "Anyway, all I have here is an old microscope, but I thought I recognized some plant fragments in the soil unique to that region of the Kyzyl Kum desert. I couldn't imagine what the hell Brian was doing there. Uzbekistan has oil in the south, but nowhere near where the truffles are found. So I sent a sample to a friend in Ann Arbor for an elemental analysis. And guess what she found when she ran an ICP-MS?"

"Not a clue."

"Gold—along with extremely high levels of methyl mercury concentration in the truffles."

"You're way over my head now."

"I was dead-on—Uzbekistan, Muruntau mines, somewhere near Zarafshan. The Soviets were shameless in using mercury in the mining process—that sample could only have been from a gold mine. And one of my old professors confirmed it was the Kyzl Kum truffle." Jackie walked into the bathroom and grabbed a towel. "I still think Brian's been cheating on me—even if he's doing it in an old gold mine."

He followed her to the bathroom doorway. "Uzbekistan, huh? You're damn good."

"I'm damn bored." Jackie turned on the shower with Hunter watching. "You keep standing there. You planning on joining me or something?" she said in a way that made him think she was flirting with him.

She was one messed up lady and Hunter realized he needed to move on before she latched onto him even more.

"I'm sorry. I didn't mean to be following you. I was curious about what you were saying and I wasn't thinking." He started to shut the door, then paused. "So your husband works for some kind of an oil company?"

"Yup. Rubicon Petroleum."

TWENTY-SIX

The Green Zone, Baghdad
One hour later

Camille was surprised when Jackie Nelson cracked open the door, but she guessed a lone Western woman at the doorstep didn't appear too threatening, particularly since they were so rare in the Green Zone. Jackie stood, blocking the doorway, wearing a fluffy white bathrobe and a towel wrapped around her hair. Civilians were such a trusting bunch.

"Jackie Nelson?" Camille held up her corporate identification card—her real one. She knew Rubicon would find out that she had paid a visit to the wife of one of their VPs and she preferred to do it brazenly. She loved to pull Rubicon's chain—then run like hell. "I'm Camille Black, president and CEO of Black Management. I need to talk to you about this man. He's in danger." She showed her a photo of Hunter.

Jackie glanced at it and looked away. Her face was gaunt. "I've never him seen before."

"I've heard he rescued you. You owe him your life."

"I don't know what you're talking about."

"Don't give me that. I know." Camille made eye contact and held her gaze. Jackie's eyes were bloodshot and slightly jaundiced. "You rode here with a Rubicon crew, but you didn't tell them who you were. Why not? Your husband's one of their VPs. I'd think they would have been even more helpful if they'd known."

"Ray said it was too dangerous."

"Was Rubicon the one holding you captive?" Camille had no idea who had held her hostage, but she couldn't figure out how Hunter got hooked up with her if Rubicon weren't involved. Last she knew, Rubicon was trying to kill him. Even if there were no Rubicon link, it couldn't hurt to wedge some doubt between Jackie and Rubicon. Like Joe Chronister had taught her many years ago, this was how informants were born and she could use one with inside connections to Rubicon. Camille stepped closer, into the cracked door and Jackie moved back a few steps into the apartment.

"Why would Rubicon ever want to hold me hostage?" Jackie said.

"Maybe as an executive perk. Word around here is that your marriage isn't going too well." Camille bluffed, but she knew the odds were in her favor. Hardship posts and relationships didn't mix well.

"I think you better come in and shut the door."

"Is he here?"

"I stretched out for a few minutes while he showered and nodded off. I woke up and he was gone."

"He couldn't stick around in a Rubicon apartment. They'll be here soon. They tried to kill him a couple of times yesterday. I know because I helped him get away." Camille listened for any noise hinting that Hunter was in the apartment. It was quiet, except for the hum of the refrigerator and the air conditioner.

"Why would Rubicon want to kill Ray?"

"Do me a favor and play this for me. Background noise." Camille gave Jackie a CD. A former NSA scientist in Black Management's expanding intelligence division had mixed special privacy "music" composed of sounds that could not be easily identified and filtered out. It was grating, but effective.

Jackie took it and sighed. "I know the routine." She turned on the player.

"To answer your question, I honestly don't know why Rubicon's targeting him. Maybe he saw something they don't want him to know about."

"Rubicon is a paranoid bunch, but it looks like you're that way, too." Jackie sat on the sofa and pulled her legs up onto the cushions. She stared blankly down the hall.

"Rubicon is dangerous. Paranoia can mean survival."

"Why do you want to help Ray?"

"We have to keep it quiet." Camille hesitated. She didn't want to have to go there, but it was the best way to get the woman to help her. "Ray and I are engaged," Camille said, fighting a tempest of emotions. She knew she had to play the part and force herself to be happy about it. The random sounds of the music were irritating and only made her more agitated.

"That's wonderful. Have you set a date yet?"

We did. "No, not yet. We're waiting until we can have a big wedding back home." Camille smiled and it made her feel more hollow inside.

"He's in trouble and on the run. I do know that much," Jackie said and then relayed the story of her rescue from the terrorists. She paused frequently, stared down the hallway and shook her head as if another dialogue were going on internally.

"You keep looking down the hallway. Is he here?"

"No." Jackie avoided eye contact with Camille.

"Was he here?"

"Yes."

"I can help him, but I've got to find him first. When was he here?"

"He left over an hour ago. I don't know where he went."

Camille wasn't sure if she believed her, but the woman had no reason to lie, except to protect Hunter. She was already pushing it, coming into the apartment of a Rubicon executive and interrogating his wife. Searching down the hallway would have consequences she didn't want. To be on the safe side, she would post observers outside the building just in case he really was hiding down the hall. If he really had left an hour ago, he could be anywhere, inside or outside the Green Zone by now.

Once it became clear that Jackie didn't have any useful information, Camille stood to leave. The woman needed to debrief, but Camille didn't have time or inclination to be her confidant. And she couldn't stand another moment of pretending everything was like it had once been between she and Hunter. She had forgotten how happy she had been just to be with him and watch him move about in the world, interacting with people and animals. He had such strength and compassion. He was a warrior and a lover. There was such a balance of opposites about him. And his mind—he made her think so hard and laugh so hard. *God, I miss him.*

She gave Jackie a glossy black business card as she tried to stuff her emotions back where they belonged. "I've got to get moving if I'm going to find Ray. If you think of anything that might help me, call me. If you get scared and want out of here or you need an escort to the airport or need protection from Rubicon, call my assistant Pete. My men will be here in a flash. We're not far away— just across from the old presidential palace." She stopped the music and retrieved the disk from the CD player.

"I know the place. I hope you can help him. Ray—or whatever his name is—is an incredible guy. You've got to be one of the luckiest women on the planet."

"He is amazing." For a moment, Camille really did feel lucky. She always did get into her cover stories a little too much, she scolded herself. But he was amazing.

TWENTY-SEVEN

At least 13 DynCorp employees have been sent home from Bosnia—and at least seven of them fired—for purchasing women or participating in other prostitution-related activities. But despite large amounts of evidence in some cases, none of the DynCorp employees sent home have faced criminal prosecution.

—SALON.COM, August 6, 2002, as reported by Robert Capps

The Tribune's series, which documented the deaths of 12 workers who had been trafficked from Nepal to Iraq, raised a specific alarm because it detailed alleged abuses involving contractors and subcontractors "employed directly or indirectly by the U.S. government" at American facilities in Iraq under a multibillion-dollar privatization contract. That contract, which has cost taxpayers more than $12 billion, is held by Halliburton subsidiary KBR.

—THE CHICAGO TRIBUNE, January 19, 2006, as reported by Cam Simpson

The Green Zone, Baghdad

The rushed shower, shave, self-inflicted haircut and clean clothes made Hunter feel like a new man. He only wished they also made him look like one. As long as it was dark and no one looked too closely, he could probably pass as one of the thousands of contractors in the Green Zone. It had been risky enough to take the time to clean up and the danger of any extra minutes to alter his appearance in a Rubicon-leased apartment was too great. He stole a Leatherman utility knife and a swatch of duct tape, an operator's best friend, from Jackie's husband. He felt bad sneaking out while Jackie was asleep, but he felt a lot worse about other things he had done. He tucked a pebble in his right shoe to alter his walk, but the rock poked him so much as he walked down a flight of concrete steps in an alley, he stopped and emptied his shoe. *Tradecraft be damned.*

The streets were empty of foot traffic. At night the Green Zone was an American enclave and Americans drove everywhere. He needed wheels and money. He didn't find any in the predictable spots at Jackie's and he didn't want to ransack the entire apartment. Dozens of new American-made pickup trucks were parked along both sides of a street that seemed to otherwise be abandoned. He had only been there once, but he knew he had found the place he was looking for.

He walked down an alley toward the sound of loud music coming from a basement. As he got closer, he could see an Iraqi bouncer standing at the door.

The Western-dressed Iraqi had a cigarette dangling from his mouth and an AK slung over his arm. He looked Hunter over, then nodded and opened a blue painted door to a bar tucked away in a basement. Hunter stepped inside and the thick cloud of smoke immediately made his eyes burn as the beat of the blaring hip-hop music pulsed through his body. The place was packed with American contractors and a few privileged Iraqis. Strings of Italian Christmas lights hung over the bar, the brightest spot in the otherwise dark establishment. No one knew whether the few nightclubs and bars in the Green Zone were illegal or not, but everyone knew they had to be treated as such if they were to avoid offending local Muslim sensibilities. It was the best stocked bar in the Middle East outside of Dubai. Thanks to Western contractors importing cheap foreign workers to staff their service contracts, young Filipino and Thai bar girls kept the men entertained. Southeast Asian women always looked young to Hunter, but no one could have convinced him that any of these girls were over fifteen. Hunter watched a constant stream of them escorting American men and rich Iraqis into a back room.

Assault rifles were placed on tables and empty chairs—always within easy reach of their owners. Hunter had been counting on the fact that the real operators worked at night and the guys in the bar at this hour were mainly construction workers, bomb disposal guys and run-of-the-mill security guards. But for some reason tonight there were too many familiar faces and that made him nervous. He knew a lot of the guys there by their call signs, or names that didn't really belong to them. The Special Operations world was a small one and Hunter had been a part of it for over a decade.

Hunter picked up an empty beer bottle and carried it as camouflage as he worked the crowd, searching for an easy mark. Contractors always carried too much cash to places like this and he needed money and credit cards. The cash would get him out of Iraq and the credit cards would buy airline tickets as part of a fake trail to destinations only his pursuers would visit—he definitely wouldn't.

Someone put his hand on Hunter's back. "Well if it isn't Jack Russell. How you doing, flyboy?"

Hunter swung around. The man was in his midforties and wore a brightly colored Hawaiian shirt. He looked part Chinese with a lot of something else thrown in. Hunter vaguely remembered him as an instructor in a gentleman's course where Force Zulu had sent him to learn the basics of handling a helicopter so he could pick up enough to land one safely in case a pilot became incapacitated. It was one of the most humbling experiences of his life. The first time he took the controls, he couldn't keep the helo inside an area the size of a football field. It spun. It whirled. The beast had a mind of its own and he doubted it could ever really be tamed, only forced into temporary submission. Two courses and many simulator hours later, he could almost keep it in the air without making himself quesy.

Hunter pretended to sip from the empty bottle as he kept

an eye on the door. "Keeping myself in the crosshairs. So what are you up to nowadays?"

"Still flying them whirlybirds. You ever get that ticket?"

"Never. I like my wings either fixed or honey barbequed. Helos flip too easily." Hunter sat down the bottle down. "You're going to have to help me out with your name."

"No, problem, Jack. It's Wayne Akana. But everybody calls me Beach Dog."

"So what outfit are you with here, Beach Dog?"

"I retired from the Night Stalkers. I keep planning on moving back to the North Shore, but right now I'm flying for Black Management. As a matter of fact, this afternoon I flew Camille Black herself from Ramadi into the bubble."

"Camille's here in the Zone?"

"Sure is. See that big guy over there?" Beach Dog pointed to a man whose belly hung over his Bermuda shorts. Several men crowded around a table with him. "He's buying drinks for everyone on his crew, says the rounds are on Ms. Black's tab."

"Any idea where she is right now?"

"What do you want to know for?"

"We used to have a thing."

"Sure you did. I've heard that from a lot of guys." Beach Dog smiled and gulped his Heineken.

A Rubicon security team walked into the bar, dressed for work, not a night on the town. They wore photographer's vests with bulging pockets over Kevlar body armor and they carried AKs. Hunter hunched down a little and moved so that Beach Dog was between him and the door. "Can you get me to Camille?"

"Now?"

"She's got some big problems and I have something she needs." Even if Stella were really furious at him, Hunter was sure he could talk her down. All he needed to do was get her to understand the truth. And besides, he had to find a way to make things right with her. He ached inside as he thought about how much he wanted her. Suddenly it didn't make any sense to flee Iraq to save his ass if it meant leaving his heart behind.

"Yeah, right," Beach Dog said. "I don't think she needs anything in your pants." He waved to a waitress, then pointed at his empty beer bottle. "I've heard talk from the guys that she might even have something going on with Pete. You know, the woman with the short hair and comfy shoes who works in her Baghdad ops."

"I'm not joking." Hunter grabbed him by the arm. The Rubicon operators scanned the crowd. Hunter slouched lower and looked around for options.

"Dude, you are one intense guy." He stared at Hunter's hand grasping his forearm.

"See those two men working their way to the bar? They're Rubicon operators and they're here to kill me. Keep yourself between them and me."

"Hey, I'm here for a good time, not to play combat-flashback with you." The helo pilot put his hands in the air as if surrendering.

"If you were with Camille Black today you had to have heard her talking about problems with Rubicon. I'm not crazy and I have critical intel for her about Rubicon. There's going to be money in this for you. You know she's generous with those who go out of their way to help her."

"How serious of a problem is it?"

"You saw the look on her face today, didn't you?" Hunter gambled. He could almost see how the two vertical lines formed between her eyebrows when something was bothering her. That look used to scare him because it usually foreshadowed trouble between them, but now he would have welcomed it just to see her again.

"I've never quite seen her this way," Beach Dog said as a waitress handed him another beer.

"I'm telling you, big bucks."

Beach Dog sighed. "Follow me." He approached three

men talking to two girls who had barely reached puberty. He put his arm around the waist of a petite Filipina and looked at the men standing around the tall table with her.

"Hey, what are you doing, Dog? Hand's off. I just bought her," a man twice the girth of Beach Dog said as he pushed Beach Dog's arm away. He pointed to a passport from the Philippines lying on the table.

"Rob, remember how we ducked the Aussies at the bar in Patpong? I'll have her back to you in two shakes."

"She better still have that new car smell." Rob shrugged his shoulders and reached for his drink.

"Take the other one," Beach Dog said to Hunter as he led the bar girl to the back of the bar. "You need one of these to get into the brothel in the back. It's got plenty of exits."

Hunter took one of the Filipino girls by the hand. He expected to follow Beach Dog, but instead, the girl immediately started leading him to the whorehouse. Beach Dog and another girl were right behind him.

A small Asian man sat on a stool in front of a glass door with newspapers stuck to the panes to obscure the view. He nodded to the girl and let the group pass.

It took a few seconds for Hunter's eyes to adjust to the darkness, but his ears were immediately oriented to the sounds of sex: heavy breathing, moaning, grunting and assorted fucking sounds which sounded like a giant orgy coming from all around him, but there was no laughter, no signs of lingering. When he could see, he understood. It was a place where you wanted to do your business and then get the hell out. He was walking through the most sorry-ass brothel he'd ever seen, and as a Marine he'd seen some pretty bad ones. Sheets hung from wires crisscrossing the ceiling, creating small cubicles. They stopped short of the concrete floor, well above the thin mattresses. Clothespins attempted to hold the corners shut, but not much was hidden and from what he saw, he wished it were. The Iraq War had gone on long enough for proper whorehouses to be established, so the only way he could explain the place was that the proprietors had designed it for quick disassembly in case of a police raid. Either that, or they were cheap fuckers.

The girl tugged at his hand to lead him into a cubicle. He planted his feet and shook his head.

She formed a circle with her index finger and thumb and thrust two fingers from her other hand in and out of it: "Ten dollar." Then she puckered her lips and blew. "Five dollar."

Hunter shook his head. "No thanks." He looked behind him to Beach Dog. "Where the hell's the door?"

"Straight ahead, past tent city."

The girl grabbed Hunter's arm and tried to pull him back. "Why you no like?"

He shook her off and kept going.

Ten minutes later they were in Beach Dog's extended cab Ford F-150 truck approaching the Black Management compound.

"I think I'm better off if I get under a blanket in the backseat for the security point," Hunter said as he ducked low in the seat.

"Dude, chill. I'm telling you, It's just like going onto a base back home. Right stickers, right look and nobody says boo."

Beach Dog rolled to a stop at the security shack and held out his thumb and little finger, flashing the guard the Hawaiian shaka sign. "Hey, Kimo, been catchin' any waves lately? I hear we had some big sets come in yesterday."

"You too funny." A heavy Hawaiian man let out a deep belly laugh.

"Too much beach and not enough water in this place." Beach Dog held up his plastic security identification badge.

"Your friend, he have ID?"

The guard pointed at Hunter who looked at Beach Dog and shrugged his shoulders. He needed a backup plan fast, but at the moment he was stumped. He would not take out an innocent security guard. *Come on, Beach Dog.*

"I can give him one visitor pass, but I need an ID," Kimo said.

Beach Dog grimaced. "He can't leave a trail. No one can know he was here with me."

"He some kind of spy or something?"

"Promise me you won't tell anyone what this is about." Beach Dog leaned out the window and lowered his voice. "Steamy, hunky man-love."

"For real?" Kimo cocked his head and inspected Hunter as if he had just arrived on the planet.

Hunter let his wrist fall limp in his most effeminate wave while he told himself Beach Dog couldn't possibly be serious.

"Go, go, go. But next time, his place." The guard raised the barrier.

"Now you keep that long board waxed. I feel a big swell coming on." Beach Dog winked at Kimo.

"You too much. Go!" Kimo closed his eyes and shook his head.

As soon as they cleared the guard shack, Hunter turned toward Beach Dog. "Dog, you don't really—"

"I like surfing the big waves, if that's what you're getting at." Beach Dog smiled in a way that gave Hunter the feeling the guy really was coming on to him. "That trailer over there. That's the boss-lady's." He pointed to a retro-style trailer, but drove past it.

Hunter had nothing against gays and even had intervened several times to keep some poor guy from getting the shit kicked out of him just because he had lost the chromosomal luck of the draw. But he still felt a wave of nausea when he thought about two guys. Two chicks were a big turn-on, but two guys were just gross, particularly when one of them was him.

As they drove past several helicopters, Hunter said, "Why don't you pull over there out of the streetlight?" He wished he didn't have to deceive the guy. He would be careful not to injure him permanently.

"My trailer's just over there by the helicopters."

"I can't wait, dude—if you know what I mean."

TWENTY-EIGHT

Brown & Root's open-ended logistics contracts from the Army and Navy indeed much of the military privatization campaign are grounded in a 1992 study the company did for the Defense Department that several analysts said formed the template for privatization of logistics for a downsized U.S. military. Soon after the company delivered the classified study, which reportedly concluded that the Pentagon could save hundreds of billions of dollars by outsourcing, Brown & Root won its first competitively bid logistics contract. Vice President Dick Cheney was defense secretary when the first Brown & Root study was done, and he became chief executive of its parent company, Halliburton, when he retired . . .

— THE LOS ANGELES TIMES, January 24, 2003, as reported by Mark Fineman

Camp Raven, the Green Zone, Baghdad

"Are you sure you wouldn't rather stay at the al-Rashid?" Pete said as she unfurled a sheet and guided it as it fluttered down onto the leather sofa in the Black Management trailer. Pete had insisted on helping Camille make the bed and Camille got the feeling she was hanging around, wanting something.

"No way. It's run by Halliburton. I trust them about like I trust Rubicon." Camille held a down pillow under her chin and worked it into a pillowcase. "Here I get 600-count cotton sheets and I don't have to worry about suicide bombers or cockroaches. Roaches creep me out almost as much as Halliburton does and I'd be hard-pressed to say which one of them is more likely to thrive after a nuclear war."

Pete laughed. "Any guesses where Hunter is?"

"He won't stick around in the Green Zone. Too many

people can recognize him here. If I had to guess, I'd say he's already out of the bubble. He can pass for an Arab and he's got the balls, so I wouldn't be surprised if he heads to Saudi. It would sure throw anyone off his trail. No Westerner in his right mind would rush into the flames of hell." Camille shook her head. "I can't think about it anymore. I'm driving myself crazy mulling over the possibilities."

"I laid out some fresh towels for you in the bathroom. It's a little cramped in there, but it works. I'll bet a shower will feel real good right now."

"A lot of things would feel good right now."

"I can arrange for anything you want. Massage. Anything." Pete smiled, her eyes undressing her.

Camille unzipped her carry-on-sized Swiss Army suitcase and took out a USP Tactical pistol, a cosmetic case, then a lacy, black nightgown. She held up the negligee just to play with Pete. She had bought it only a few weeks ago before Hunter stood her up in Dubai. It had been two long months since she'd had sex and for a guilty second, she actually entertained Pete's offer. Camille was one of the few females among thousands of men in the Green Zone and she could have had any one of them she wanted. The top operators kept their bodies hard and well-sculpted and she liked that, but she had hardly paid attention in the last two months since she had learned that Hunter was still alive. It was time to get over him, do the job for Chronister and go on the prowl again.

The more she thought about it, the more she wanted sex. She even considered Pete again, but decided she liked her women femmier. "Thanks for the offer. But I don't think you have what I want tonight."

Shortly after Pete left for the night, Camille closed her eyes and stuck her head under the shower stream. For a few choice moments she could forget about Hunter and quit worrying about what she was going to do when she found him. It scared her how much she wanted to kill him and that she knew deep down that she really could. As long as he was alive, he would keep hurting her and the pain got worse each time. Chronister had given her an easy way out. She wouldn't be killing him for personal reasons that she might someday feel guilty about; it was for god and country. She didn't have to decide what she was going to do now. Instead she focused on the sensation of the warm water caressing her skin and savored each steamy breath. It was good to breathe humid air again. She was so sick of the desert, she was ready to move into a terrarium.

She poured shampoo into her hands, rubbed them together, then ran her fingers through her hair. It felt bristly from all the dust and dirt.

A sudden cool draft brushed her body. She looked up, but the glass shower stall door was fogged over and a towel she had slung over it obscured everything else.

"Pete?"

No answer.

"Pete, is that you?" She felt a wave of fear as she quickly assessed how vulnerable she was, naked and without anything to use to defend herself. Water rolled down her face and shampoo burned her eyes. She splashed water on them and looked around the stall to see if there were anything that she could use as a weapon. A plastic Bic razor was her best bet and it wasn't a very good one. She listened, but couldn't hear anyone over the sound of the shower, even though she sensed a presence.

She smacked the safety razor against the stall and broke off the head. With enough force and at the right angle, the jagged plastic handle could puncture a neck. She took a deep breath and kicked open the shower door.

Hunter sat on the closed toilet seat. He didn't move, but looked her over with elevator eyes and smiled.

"You're looking damn good, Stella. Damn good."

TWENTY-NINE

Camp Raven, the Green Zone, Baghdad

Shampoo suds slid from Stella's hair onto her shoulders, then flowed down to her breasts where the stream forked. Hunter traced each shifting tributary with his eyes, starting with the ones that curved around the sides, the foamy bubbles making each breast seem even softer than he had remembered. He watched the suds drip from her nipples toward the floor, but his gaze stopped halfway at the swirls of her pubic hair. Her curly brown hair danced with the flowing bubbles, a shimmering veil teasing with fleeting glimpses of pink.

He reached for her just as she lunged at him with a plastic razor handle. Dodging, he grabbed her arm and stood up, throwing her off balance so that she slipped on the sudsy linoleum. He bent her hand backwards, forcing her to drop the plastic weapon. His foot crushed it. Just as her head was about to smack against the sink, Hunter jerked her up by the arm, pulling her close. She tried to get away from him, but his strength overpowered her.

As Hunter seized her wrist, Camille raised her foot to strike him, then felt her other foot slide across the slick floor. Suddenly the edge of the sink was right in front of her. She raised her free arm to catch herself and pain shot through her other wrist as Hunter twisted. She struggled to regain her balance, but everything she touched was wet and slippery and then she found her body pressing against Hunter. For an instant, she liked it. She squirmed, but he held her locked in a bear hug.

"Let go of me."

"Not until you quit fighting me. Why do you attack me every time you see me?"

"And why do you stab me in the back every time you see me?"

"It's not what it seems."

"You keep saying that—right before you screw me again."

Hunter captured her gaze for a moment before he spoke. "Whatever you think I've done, forgive me. I love you—more than anything. I've never intentionally done anything to harm you."

She drew back her leg, preparing to ram her knee into his groin, then she looked into his eyes and wasn't all so sure. Something about his eyes made her feel that he really did love her. She lowered her leg.

His eyes pled with her as he spoke. "And right now I need you. A lot of people are trying to kill me."

"And I'm one of them. You know, I was ready to forgive you and help you—that's when you stole my truck."

"I was trying to tell you when you wouldn't let me get a word in edgewise. Rubicon has someone on the inside at Black Management. That's how they got the information about your job sites. I couldn't take the risk."

"But you can now?"

"I'm desperate."

"You know I want to believe you." She tried not to notice how natural it felt for her body to scrape against his, then she realized he probably had the same feelings about her. She tilted her head and looked up at him, inviting a kiss. He lowered his head toward her and gently touched his lips against hers. She kissed him hard and lost herself briefly. But she wanted to lead him to the edge and make her move there. Whether or not she went ahead with Chronister's contract, she had to escape from Hunter's grip. It was a matter of pride. The only problem was that it felt good, too good. Her tongue played with his, luring it into her mouth, but he would only dart inside for a few seconds, so she sucked his bottom lip into her mouth, then she bit down hard.

Hunter was experiencing a joy he'd almost forgotten over the past few days, even years. His mind raced to restore everything that had been between them, then a sharp pain jolted him. "What the—" He jerked his head away and accidentally bit down on the loose tooth, ramming it deeper into the tender socket.

The second he realized he'd let up a little, he tightened his hold but the soap made his hands slide. Her naked body rammed against him and he bumped back. He gyrated with each thrust, twisting, turning together, a dance of warriors. Her fingernails dug into his wrist. God, he wanted her. "You're the only woman I've ever loved."

"That's not what I've heard." Her elbow smacked him in the ribs. He was starting to think that maybe she really didn't want him.

"Whatever they're telling you about me isn't true. I couldn't get the evidence, but I know Rubicon is working with the tangos. They think I know something and I wish I knew what the hell it was."

"Why don't you run to your CIA friends for help?"

"I've been burned, even with my unit. And I'm not OGA. I'm with Force Zulu."

"My contact told me you were with the Agency—that the Bushmen wouldn't have you. The Agency helped you fake your death so you could get away from me and marry that Julia bitch." Stella jabbed her thumb into the tender spot under his arm. It brought tears to his eyes as her thumbnail cut his skin and dug into the tender flesh, but he breathed deeply and resisted the pain. She knew how to do it right.

"What the hell are you talking about? You can't be serious. The Julia thing is part of the legend Zulu created for me to use when I infiltrated Rubicon." He hooked his foot around hers as he pivoted away, then swung back suddenly, slamming himself against her. She tripped. He guided her head away from the sink as he forced her down. The floor space in the trailer's bathroom was barely large enough for her. He straddled her, pinning her on her back. Her breasts looked a little smaller, but rounder and her nipples were now perked out. Maybe she did want him, but then the air conditioning was blasting. "There is no real Julia Lewis from Tacoma. You've been in this business long enough to know how things work. She's part of my cover—that's all. Whatever Rubicon is telling you is a lie."

"It didn't come from Rubicon. It was CIA. I find it hard to believe that my Agency contact is lying."

"Really? With all the people leaving the profession to go work for Rubicon and outfits like yours, don't you think it's possible that someone's positioning himself for retirement? Or that the Agency's finally getting it that Force Zulu is a bigger threat to them than the KGB ever was? We're better at human intel and direct action than they've ever been and someday the president is going to realize that and force the Agency to step aside." She wiggled underneath him, but didn't try hard to resist. He knew Stella. She was only making it look real while she waited for the right opportunity, so he had to make sure she didn't find it. Holding her wrists, he stretched out on top of her. Her velvety skin was right there pressing against him, but his clothes were sandpaper, irritating him with each movement. He wanted to rip them off and feel skin. "I want you."

"Yeah, I can feel that." She bumped her thighs against his pelvis. "I'd give anything to step back in time and stop you from faking your death and trying to shield me from whatever baggage came along with being a Bushman."

Stella moved her hips back and forth underneath him, back and forth. Hunter wasn't sure if it was for real or if she was working on a distraction so she could attack. She knew he couldn't resist danger, the warrior's aphrodisiac. His groin moved in rhythm with hers. "I wanted to protect you."

"More like you chose your career over me."

"I said I was wrong. I can't change what I did. Please forgive me. I love you."

Stella cracked a smile. Hunter could see hints of a deeper emotion radiating from her green eyes. As a soldier, he knew he had to exploit any weakness he found in an enemy. Stella wasn't exactly an enemy in the traditional sense, but he had learned long ago the difference between war and love made the battlefield the safer endeavor—or at least the less painful one. He had suffered the loss of friends in combat and moved on, but he knew he could never recover from losing Stella. The battle with her was one he had to fight to win.

"I'm the old-fashioned kind of guy who believes there's only one woman in the world out there for me. Stella, honey, you're that woman. Look me in the eyes. If you can tell me you don't have that feeling way down inside that we belong together, I'll walk away and I'll never bother you again. Look me in the eyes and tell me you don't love me. Can you do that?"

Stella opened her mouth, then closed it. She blinked several times, but Hunter saw the tears anyway.

"I was hired to kill you," she said.

"So you're saying you think we belong together?"

"I'm saying I agreed to kill you."

"You gonna do it?" He sensed such anger underneath the surface and such a sense of betrayal in her that he really didn't know the answer and he wasn't entirely convinced that she'd give him an honest one.

"They didn't say how they wanted it done." She raised her head toward his, her mouth open just enough so he could see her sharp little teeth.

THIRTY

Camp Raven, the Green Zone, Baghdad

The leather sofa in the Black Management trailer really wasn't wide enough for Camille and Hunter, but it was bigger and more comfortable than the bathroom floor, so they made it work. Camille woke up with Hunter spooning her, his muscular arms wrapped around her, keeping her from tumbling off the edge. Her skin was clammy, her hair matted with shampoo and she smelled of sex, but she was happy. She caressed his arm and felt a scar on his left bicep that she didn't remember. She traced its outline with her finger. Hunter muttered something and shifted his legs.

"You awake?" Camille said.

"Yeah, my body's been so constantly blasted with adrenaline for the last few days, I can't come down."

"I don't remember this scar. What's it from?"

"A tactical mistake I'm not going to make a second time."

Camille reached for a penlight on the coffee table. Hunter pretended to let go of her and she put her arms out to break a fall that never happened. She turned on the penlight and shined the thin beam onto his arm. "Ouch. That looks like it hurt. A knife, huh? I was expecting a bullet wound. You get in a bar fight?"

"Something a little rougher than that." He reached for her hand, deflecting the beam. "Give me that. I'm going to use it to inspect you over from head to toe."

"That's a tattoo there underneath the scar, isn't it? I thought you hated tattoos?"

Hunter immediately pulled the sheet up over his arm.

"What are you hiding from me?"

"Nothing. Get back here and let me show you why they call us Bushmen." He laughed.

Camille flung the sheet back and shined the penlight on his arm. A scar ripped through a tattoo of a heart. Much of the black lettering had been cut away with the damaged tissue, but she saw all she needed. As in a Rorschach test, she tried to see an "S" in the first mangled letters; then she looked for a "C" even though he never called her Camille, but she had known even before she pulled down the sheet that it was once a "J."

"J" for Julia Lewis.

Hunter had once had a tattoo for his ex-wife and after having it removed, he swore he would never do it again—and he wouldn't for Camille. But apparently he felt differently about Julia Lewis.

"I should kill you." All she could think about was getting away from him before he hurt her even more. She sprang from the sofa to grab her clothes and turn on a light.

When Stella jumped off the sofa, Hunter was sure she was going for a weapon. Earlier he had made note of a USP Tactical lying on the coffee table and he caught another glimpse of it as she moved the penlight away from him. He lunged for it and beat her to it. He flipped off the safety just as she flipped on the light.

"Hand's up. Don't move." Hunter pointed the gun at the center of her chest.

"You son of a bitch. You're screwing me again." She held her hands out, but seemed to be shifting her body weight to her left leg.

"Listen to me, dammit!"

"Fuck you!"

Camille could feel the heat rise from her chest, up her neck and into her face. What the hell was he doing, pulling a weapon on her—her own gun—when she was trying to turn on a light? The fucker was lying and he had plenty to hide.

Hunter said, "It's not what it—"

"—seems. Go to hell." Camille lowered her hands and took a step toward him, glancing to where she always kept her Ka-Bar knife on the right side of her desk. She wanted to slice. She wanted blood. She wanted pain, ripping, cutting pain. "I'd rather be dead than hear you say that one more time. Shoot me, you motherfucker. Do it!"

"Stop!" Hunter said.

Stella was calling his bluff, closing the gap between them. She moved smoothly, a panther, sensing weakness, moving in on her prey. He could never shoot her and she knew it. Her eyes were wild with rage. As she looked around the room, she averted them from the Ka-Bar knife on the edge of her desk. She wanted that knife. He took a step closer to where his clothes were piled on the floor to make it a little easier for her to get to it. At the moment she lunged for the knife, he tripped her and knocked her to the floor, snatching the weapon for himself.

As fast as he could, he scooped up his clothes and ran from the trailer.

THIRTY-ONE

Camp Raven, the Green Zone, Baghdad

Hunter didn't understand why she was reacting so strongly, but he had scars that reminded him not to stick around and try to find out. He sprinted naked across the Black Management compound, circling behind her trailer so she wouldn't have a clean line of fire when she ran out the door. Knowing her, though, she might blow out a window to get to him. The sun was just coming up and no one was outside. A few hundred yards away, a dozen Black Hawk helicopters and several Little Birds were parked unattended. He knew that like all military helicopters, they would be serviced and ready for flight. With a natural sense for roll, pitch and yaw, he could fly anything—anything which was meant to fly. As far as he was concerned, god intended flight only for things with wings and anything else was begging for trouble, particularly helicopters. But he didn't see much other choice if he wanted to make it out of the Green Zone alive. Stella would be after him any second.

He ran toward the helicopters, trying to figure out which one to try for. The Little Bird observation and assault helo was favored by black-ops types for its heavy weapons and maneuverability, but the Black Hawks had greater range and his limited piloting skills meant that he wouldn't be able to take advantage of the Little Bird's greater maneuverability anyway. He ran to the nearest Black Hawk and jumped inside. He slung his leg around the stick and reached for the ignition, but the key was missing. He used the knife as a screwdriver and worked as quickly as he could to remove a metal plate below the ignition like he'd seen pilots in his unit do whenever they had lost a key. The first rays of the morning gave him barely enough light to see what he was doing. His big fingers fumbled with screws and he pried off the panel, sliced through the wires leading to the ignition, then twisted them together.

Keyless entry, Zulu-style.

There was still no sign of Stella, but he knew the only indication of her could be a small red laser dot ranging the distance between her rifle and his chest. He reached to the overhead console and flipped on the APU, then the generators and the start button for each engine.

Silence.

The engines didn't even let out a whimper.

The trailer was spinning and Camille touched her forehead to see if there was any blood where Hunter had made her smack her head on the desk. As soon as she could stand, she grabbed for a desert tan T-shirt and khaki shorts, not bothering with a bra or panties. An M-4 assault rifle in hand, she dashed from her trailer, still sticky from sex and burning from anger. Pete stepped from her trailer.

"Which way did he go?" Camille said.

"Who? What's going on?" Pete said.

"Stone. I want all personnel on the alert for him. Deadly force is authorized. I want that lying son of a bitch dead."

Hunter's mind raced through the start-up sequence. If a helo were on the tarmac, it had to be airworthy. These things were kept in top shape and it wasn't like a car which might have run its battery down from leaving the lights on all night. He leaned back and glanced at the battery behind the copilot's seat. It was unplugged—standard operating procedure for military helicopters. He turned everything back off, then wedged his body between the seats, leaned back, but couldn't get to it. Counting the seconds, he jumped from the cockpit and shoved the plug into the battery.

He sprung back into the pilot's seat without bothering to strap himself in and flipped the overhead switches.

"Come on, baby."

He pressed the starters and breathed again when he heard a welcome hum. At first the huge blades lumbered past the window and in moments turned into a dark distortion in the otherwise clear early morning air. He shoved the throttles all the way forward. With his left hand, he pulled up on the collective and the bird lifted into the air.

Textbook.

Camille heard the whoosh of the Black Hawk starting up and dashed around the trailer in time to see it lift into the air. She wouldn't even take Chronister's money. This one was on her. She dropped to one knee, aimed the M-4 at the vulnerable tail rotor and she squeezed off a burst.

Hunter heard bullets pinging against the hull. Only a dozen feet off the ground, the helicopter immediately yawed to the right, turning clockwise along with the rotors. None of the warning lights on the dashboard had gone off and he knew the bullets weren't his problem—he was. He stomped the left pedal and the helicopter spun the other direction and didn't seem to want to stop. His heart pounded as he hit the right pedal and it whirled again the other way. Saddam's Presidential Palace blurred past him, then Stella's trailer. A hundred feet off the ground, he danced on the pedals as he struggled to compensate for the gyrations while the helicopter spun around out of control.

Camille stopped firing, stood and watched as the helicopter twirled around like a Tilt-A-Whirl, all the while gaining altitude.

"That was a damn good shot." Pete stood beside her and watched it spiral upwards.

"I don't think so," Camille said. "If I hit it, it would be-
have that way, but he wouldn't be climbing. Without the
tail rotor he should enter auto-rotation and take her down
immediately. I think he's just a really lousy helicopter pilot. That asshole better not crash my bird."

Hunter was dizzy and his stomach felt like it had been left
behind several rotations ago. He realized he was overload-
ing the machine with inputs before it could even respond.
His eyes closed and focused on finding balance. With each
spin he forced himself to go easier on the pedals, overcompensating a little less as he slowly gained command.

As soon as Camille realized Hunter was getting the hang
of it, she ran toward the helicopters on the ramp. "Get me
a pilot, now!"

Hunter clutched the cyclic control so hard, his fingers
were growing numb. The bend in the Tigris was in sight
behind him, its deep green waters still a dark strip in the
early morning light. He could see the famous cross sabers
on Saddam's old parade ground in front of him. More or
less in control of the helicopter over Baghdad, Hunter had
now executed his plan in full and didn't know what the
hell he was going to do next, other than get dressed. Flying
in the nude was not what it was cracked up to be. His ass
was sweaty and sticking to the NOMEX seat, but the rest
of him was freezing to death. The troop doors in the back
had been removed for combat and the cool air was whipping around. He pulled the shirt on, then managed to
slither into the Dockers without sending the helo into a
spin.

He checked the fuel indicator. There was enough to fly a
little over four hours, depending on the winds, so he was in
range of Iran, Saudi, Jordan, Syria, Kuwait and probably
even Turkey, although the altitude would zap his fuel. All

of the choices sucked. He couldn't find any charts and the last thing he wanted was to run out of fuel in the desert, so he was limited to following the Tigris or the Euphrates. The port of Kuwait offered ships to anywhere in the world, but travel by sea took too much time and the place had too many Americans and too many bad memories. He pressed on the left pedal, shoved the cyclic forward and headed away from the rising sun into the desert. He would hit the Euphrates, hang a right and follow it north to Syria. With any luck, his old contacts in Damascus would still be alive.

THIRTY-TWO

The Green Zone, Baghdad

The Rubicon security executive Larry Ashland had just dozed off when a phone call from the CIA case officer Joe Chronister woke him up with good news: Hunter Stone had been spotted in Baghdad. It wasn't good news to Ashland, because it meant that he was still in danger of exposure. As long as the Force Zulu operator was alive, Ashland's cover with Rubicon was at risk. Stone had recognized him from Afghanistan and also from the Iraqi insurgents' safe house and the Zulu operator knew he was a spy. Judging from their middle-of-the-night encounter in the Rubicon offices at Camp Tornado Point, Stone didn't seem to understand who Ashland was working for or what he was doing spying on Rubicon. But it didn't matter. If the Zulu operator passed along the information about him, some analyst along the way might put the pieces together and blow his cover. He couldn't allow that to happen. Stone had to die.

Seven hours later word came in that Stone had stolen a Black Management helicopter. Ashland immediately dialed the Rubicon Baghdad chief of operations, stepping into his pants while he waited for him to pick up.

"It's Larry." Ashland said into the secure phone as he zipped his fly. He gave the Rubicon ops chief a situation report. "I don't care how much of a head start he's got on you. Find some helicopters in the direction he's headed, scramble them and neutralize him. I'm on my way." He slammed down the phone, cursing his own stupidity. Ashland sensed that the blowback was just getting started. All he'd wanted to do was keep Stone from tying him to that earlier operation in Afghanistan and blowing his cover. He should've taken Stone out himself instead of relying on his former assistant Kyle to do the cleanup work. At least his own tidying up with Kyle was a little more thorough.

THIRTY-THREE

Camp Raven, the Green Zone, Baghdad

Camille didn't care why Beach Dog was peeling duct tape off his wrists as he hurried over to the Little Bird. All that mattered was that Pete found a pilot and he seemed to be sober. Beach Dog hopped into the aircraft, reached into his pocket and pulled out a small white figurine of a cat with its paw in the air. He stuck it to a piece of Velcro that was already on the dashboard. Camille guessed it was some kind of talisman. In less than a minute, the blades were turning. Camille jumped into the copilot seat. Pete finished her phone call and started to climb in, but Camille stopped her. "I want you to find out everything you can about this Julia Lewis he was supposedly married to."

Pete glared at Camille, irritated at having to stay behind.

"That's an order," Camille said, then turned to the pilot as she pulled out a Bose headset. "You understand the mission? I want my Black Hawk back in one piece and I want the pilot in as many pieces as possible."

"Gotcha, ma'am," Beach Dog said as the Little Bird rose into the air. "What do you want me to tell the big military?"

"He was heading toward the airport, so I'm guessing he's flying until he hits the Euphrates, then he'll use it to navigate visually to Syria. Tell the air traffic controllers we're sightseeing today, heading to Camp Tornado Point via the Euphrates."

The nose pitched up as they climbed out over Saddam's old parade grounds, passing above the oversized crossed-swords monument.

"Ma'am," Beach Dog said. "The Hawk's maximum speed is about ten knots above ours. We're not going to catch up with him."

"Then let's cut him off at the pass. He's following the river and it's not the most direct route. Take us direct to Fallujah. Contact the ground radar and see if they're carrying his track."

"You bet."

"And turn off our transponder. I want to sneak up on him."

Camille stared down at the Baghdad slums, remembering Hunter's touch, his eyes, his smell—and her joy. The cityscape beneath them turned into desert and Camille could feel its harsh emptiness.

THIRTY-FOUR

Anbar Province

About thirty-five minutes into the flight, Hunter decided that helicopters were pretty cool machines after all. His hand had finally released its death grip on the cyclic and he was playing around a little, zigzagging along with the river, cautiously improving his skills. Sunglasses, tunes and a mug of strong coffee would've made the ride a lot more fun. He started humming to himself, "Born in the USA."

Daybreak at five thousand feet was beautiful, even near Fallujah, but since Anbar was a very active area of operation, he decided he'd better go low and fly below radar. He pushed the cyclic forward to tilt his nose and pushed down on the collective to decrease power. The bird did exactly what he wanted, descending to two hundred feet. Toys like this were reason alone to make up with Stella.

The Rubicon Mi-8 helicopter crew was barely five minutes out of Camp Tornado Point when they made visual contact with the Black Management helo. The Bulgarian pilot, Boyko Koritarov, had been briefed that the Black Management pilot was a novice and probably was flying visually. He knew exactly what he was going to do and he took his time to give the target a wide berth, then Koritarov brought his Russian-built aircraft in behind him, careful to hug his blind spot. When he calculated that he was ten rotor disks away, he ordered his gunner to open fire.

Camille watched through binoculars as an old Soviet-made helicopter approached Hunter's bird from his right rear. As if the cheap Russian equipment hadn't been enough of a giveaway, she also recognized the fuselage's distinctive diagonal ruby stripe bordered in white. Rubicon. "What the hell's Rubicon doing?"

"Sneaking up on him, using a blind spot. If I didn't know better, I'd say he was getting ready to—"

"He's firing." Camille could see sparks as the bullets hit the airframe.

Hunter was singing to himself when he thought he heard something over the roar of the turbine engines. He stopped for a minute, didn't hear anything and resumed his jam session.

Boyko Koritarov couldn't figure out why in the world Rubicon got its gunners from the tropical paradise of Fiji. Fijian mercs were cheap, but there was a reason. The idiot was shooting up a self-sealing fuel tank and a crew cabin that had no crew inside. The Black Management pilot was safely on the left side of the craft, apparently oblivious to the assault.

"Retarget tail rotor gearbox," Koritarov said in heavily accented English.

Hunter had enough of Springsteen and moved on to the Stones—he loved classical music. A few seconds later the Black Hawk yawed to the right and kept spinning. Hunter stomped the left pedal, but didn't get anything. It kept going around and around, faster and faster. He rammed both size elevens into a space barely large enough for one foot and pushed the pedal with everything he had while he jammed the cyclic forward. Then he saw the warning lights go off at the same time he caught a flash of another helicopter.

Stella.

Stella had finally nailed him.

Camille keyed her microphone. "Unidentified Rubicon Hip, this is Black Management Six, hold fire or we will engage. Repeat, Rubicon stand down." She turned to Beach Dog. "Please tell me this is one of the Little Birds we out-fitted with the 20 millimeter Gatling guns."

"Yeah, but we're not in range—too high and too far."

"Get in range."

"Hang on."

The Little Bird dived so fast Camille felt like she was in a freefall—inside and out. She had been too angry in the trailer to grill Hunter and find out the truth she needed to know about that Julia chick—and he had pulled a gun on her. Now she realized she was in danger of losing that chance permanently. And how dare Rubicon shoot one of her Hawks out of the air? She took the targeting controls of the Gatling gun.

She watched Hunter's helo gyrate out of control as her Little Bird dropped down behind the Rubicon Mi-8. She estimated the range to target now at two thousand meters and closing fast. A few seconds later she opened fire on the tail boom. Metal flew and the tail rotor slowed. She kept fir-ing and now prayed that Hunter survived. The tail boom began to sag as the Rubicon Mi-8 whirled around.

Beach Dog turned toward Camille, his eyebrows raised. "Don't you think that's enough? The dude's going down."

The Rubicon helicopter spiraled toward the ground.

The gyrations were getting faster and faster. Hunter reached up and brought back both throttles, then struggled against the G-force to bottom out the collective so the damn thing would auto-rotate and quit spinning the cabin along with the rotors. It was like putting a car in neutral and now all he had to do was coast down a hill—straight down. The rotors would spin with the air and, if all went well, lower him to a rough landing. Fighting vertigo, he scanned the ground for a landing site. A village lay di-rectly below him. He had to get clear of it or at least aim for a street, but he was plummeting fast. Pulling back on the cyclic to flare the craft, he pitched the nose up and used the momentum of the main rotor to brake the descent. The spinning slowed, but he was coming up on a rooftop. He wrestled with the two functioning controls and squeezed out a little altitude and a few more meters of distance. Barely clearing the house, he smacked down hard between two buildings. The specially designed pilot's seat collapsed onto the floor, cushioning most of the blow, and he swallowed something.

He shoved down the collective, pulled on the brakes and blasted out of the door with Stella's gun. The main rotor was still moving, kicking up dust and sand. He had to find cover before Stella flew overhead and gunned him down.

On the run again in Anbar, this time with no pants on—man, he'd have given anything to have that damn mandress back.

THIRTY-FIVE

Anbar Province

The Black Management Little Bird hovered low over the village while Camille scanned the area, trying to get a peek through the dust cloud. *Please be alive.* She keyed the mike to call to her Baghdad ops center. "LIGHTNING SIX to RAVEN. We have a Black Hawk down. Repeat, Black Hawk down." She relayed the GPS coordinates. "Beach Dog, take us in low and hover. I want to see if he made it."

"Not a good idea in this neighborhood. The bad guys we've chased out of Fallujah and Ramadi like to hole up in these parts. This is the Wild West."

"Things get too hot, we'll pull out." Camille studied the area. Children looked up from the streets and adults were running outside to see what was going on. So far, she didn't see any weapons.

The cloud began to dissipate around the Black Hawk. It had hit level, sandwiched between two buildings on a vacant lot. Its back landing gear had broken off, but it otherwise seemed intact. If she could get a salvage crew to it before the locals trashed it, it could fly again.

"Circle to the other side and dip down. I want to see if he's inside and injured."

"You got it." Beach Dog maneuvered the Little Bird in low and pitched it slightly forward. The Hawk's door was open on the pilot's side and Camille could see through the front windows. No Hunter.

"He must've split when the dust was kicking up," Beach Dog said.

"He's got to be in one of these houses. Set it down. I'm going in."

"With all due respect, Lady Rambo, you're fucking nuts."

Beach Dog had a point and she knew it. She didn't take time to grab body armor or even extra rounds for the M-4. No way was Hunter going to come to her after she had shot at his helicopter this morning. She wouldn't be surprised if he even thought she was the one who knocked him out of the air. He had no more reason to trust her now than she'd had to trust him, maybe even a little less. "Fall back to a safe distance. I'm bringing in the cavalry for a door-to-door search."

THIRTY-SIX

Jabal ad Dhibban, Anbar Province

Hunter heard the thud of the second helo hitting the ground as he hauled ass down the alleyway. A tango's RPG must have hit Stella's bird. He hoped to god she survived the crash with only enough injuries to keep her from coming after him. His tongue probed the inside of his mouth and confirmed what he had feared: he'd swallowed the damn tooth during the hard landing.

He ducked into the first open doorway he found. An old lady was rubbing raw wool between her palms, making yarn while she watched a game show on TV. A horde of kids was playing with a half-inflated yellow balloon. She screamed and the children joined in as they scrambled to get behind the woman.

"It's okay. It's okay. I'm not going to hurt you," he said in Arabic, as he pulled on his pants. He raised his voice and repeated himself so she could hear him over their high-pitched shrieks, then he heard a helicopter moving above the building. It wasn't as loud as a Black Hawk; it sounded smaller, more like a Little Bird. What was a second helo doing there so fast?

The woman started to settle down and was now breathing hard, trying to catch her breath.

"Don't hurt us."

"Give me the biggest jilbab you've got and a headscarf and I'll go. You're going to be all right. Get me the clothes. Now!" He grabbed her arm and pulled her to her feet as gently as he could without losing any speed. Manhandling an old lady got to him, but he had to get a sense of urgency across to her. Women aged so fast here. He told himself she was probably not more than ten years older than he was. But even if they were the same age, it still didn't make it right.

THIRTY-SEVEN

Jabal ad Dhibban, Anbar Province

The belly of the Little Bird deflected some light gunfire from the locals as it hovered low over the village while Camille and Beach Dog searched for any sign of Hunter. Wherever he was, he was staying put. When she realized the sound of their helicopter was probably making him feel pinned down, she ordered Beach Dog to climb to a safe altitude. Camp Tornado Point was less than fifty kilometers away and it would take the Black Hawks under ten minutes once they were airborne. Beach Dog flew in a high holding pattern while they waited for the Black Management troops to arrive. With any luck, Hunter would chance a dash between buildings and they'd get a bead on his position.

The airframe of the Rubicon helicopter had rolled on its side on impact a few hundred meters outside the village. There was no movement around it, but Camille knew that didn't mean much. The cabin was a defensible position, offering shelter from the sun, which was already starting to bake. The crew could be sitting inside, waiting for rescue. The downed crew was Rubicon's problem, not hers. She would help with a little close air support only if the tangos moved in around them in serious numbers.

Using binoculars, Camille watched two helos flying toward them from the direction of Camp Tornado Point. From their last reported position, she didn't expect to have a visual on them yet, but she guessed that she could see farther than anticipated in the clear desert air.

"Whatcha gonna do about Rubicon shooting down our bird?" Beach Dog worked the cyclic as they circled above the village. "You're not going to let them get away with it, are you?"

"No way. I'd say they've crossed the Rubicon."

"Huh?"

"The die's cast." The two helicopters were now close enough for Camille to get a good look—Russian-made, with diagonal ruby stripes bordered in white: Rubicon. "When Julius Caesar marched his army across the Rubicon River, he knew he was starting a civil war in Rome. Rubicon crossed the line today. I'd say we're looking at the same thing—civil war."

PART TWO
Civil Wars

Through most of the Bush administration, the CIA high command has been engaged in a bitter struggle with the Pentagon.
  —CNN, September 27, 2004, as reported by Robert Novak

"This is a turf battle," said retired Army Col. W. Patrick Lang, former head of Middle Eastern affairs for the Defense Intelligence Agency. "All of this represents that clandestine human intelligence in the Department of Defense is a growth industry and that it is no longer regarding itself as under the control of the CIA."
  —THE LOS ANGELES TIMES, March 24, 2005, as reported by Mark Mazzetti and Greg Miller

THIRTY-EIGHT

Jabal ad Dhibban, Anbar Province

Camille and Beach Dog hovered over the village in the Little Bird and watched the Rubicon Russian-built Mi-8 helos come in low over the field near their downed aircraft, but they didn't stop. One landed at the side of the village and the other continued on. Camille shook her head. "Unfucking believable. Rubicon's going after Hunter before helping their own guys. It really is a war. What do you think? Have you ever taken on two birds at once?"

"You have to waste them now while they're on the ground and vulnerable. Our guns have a longer range, but Hawks can take a beating Little Birds can't," Beach Dog said as he scanned the skies.

Camille radioed her base at Camp Tornado Point and her ops center at Camp Raven in Baghdad to see what was taking them so long and learned that something big had happened a half hour ago near the Syrian border and the Marines were asking for everything Black Management had. Her operations officers were scrambling to redeploy equipment from Mosul and Tikrit so they wouldn't be left shorthanded. She couldn't believe that she owned a small army, but when she actually needed it, it was stretched too thin to give her the resources she requested. It was little comfort to know that Rubicon was probably in the same position and couldn't afford to send many additional helicopters to their private skirmish.

Rubicon troops piled out of the first helicopter while the second one moved into position on the far side of the village. Camille leaned over and read the altimeter—3200 feet. "Let's show them we're serious. You up for a high angle strafing run?" Camille wanted to swoop down fast with the machine guns blazing and blast her own line in the sand, daring Rubicon to cross it.

"The Beach Dog's always game." He checked the gun switches, then looked down to study the terrain.

"Then let's add some pep to their step. I don't want to hurt anyone right now. You see any Iraqis in the way, abort."

"Unless you've done a lot of these, I'd feel more comfortable working the gun, ma'am."

"All yours, Dog."

"Got your leash on nice and tight?" Beach Dog tugged on Camille's restraints. "Initiating firing pass. Hang on, we're surfing air!" The words had hardly left Beach Dog's mouth when the nose of the Little Bird suddenly dipped.

Camille gasped as the helo dropped. The angle of attack was so steep, the four-point safety harness was all that held her back from crashing through the windshield and the bubble window of the Little Bird didn't help steady her nerves—it gave her an unobstructed panorama of the approaching red earth. They were a good thousand feet away from the second Mi-8 helo, still gaining speed when Beach Dog fired a burst and started leveling off. A line of dust and sand puffed into the air, fifty feet away from the Rubicon helo. Beach Dog kept firing, drawing a line almost up to the wheels of the Rubicon Hawk.

"Yeah, baby!" Beach Dog shouted as he broke away

from the target with evasive turns that tossed Camille back and forth in her seat.

"Now get us the hell away from here. I want out of range of their guns. As far as I know, Rubicon's helos are outfitted with old M60s, but we're starting to go back to Mod Deuces on ours, so keep over two clicks between us at all times just in case they've also switched over to the older, longer range runs." She turned away from Beach Dog, gazed down at the village and whispered to herself, "Hang in there, Hunter. We'll get you as soon as we can."

THIRTY-NINE

Jabal ad Dhibban, Anbar Province

The old lady was tiny even for a withered Arab grand-mother and she barely came up to Hunter's chest. Black covered her from head to toe. Hunter helped her yank an oriental carpet off an antique brass chest with intricate geometric forms engraved into it, a treasure chest from *A Thousand and One Nights*. Under other circumstances he would've enjoyed taking a good look at it.

Praying out loud for mercy, her frail upper body rocked back and forth as she lifted stacks of clothes from the chest. It was taking her forever, but Hunter didn't have the heart to push the petrified woman any harder.

Then he heard the familiar whoosh of large transport helicopters. Stella was bringing in reinforcements. He couldn't believe it. She had to be bringing in troops for a block by block search and he knew he had to get out of the area before they sealed it off.

"Come on! Hurry it up!"

The woman prayed louder and her arms began to shake. She lifted up a light gray Muslim woman's overcoat. He took it and shook it out. It was several sizes too large for the old lady, but many times too small for him. Originally, he had just been looking to make his head and shoulders blend in while they searched from the air, but if they were doing a ground search, he doubted he could pass, not with his facial fuzz.

Without warning, the rapid pop of machine-gun spray came from the street. The woman and children fell to the floor in a cacophony of screams while a helicopter shrieked low overhead, a Fury swooping down from the heavens in relentless pursuit. At the moment it was easy to picture Stella with wreathes of snakes on her head.

Hell hath no fury like a Stella scorned.

FORTY

The Green Zone, Baghdad

With all of its plasma flat panel monitors, satellite uplinks and people running around with wireless headsets and microphones, the Baghdad Rubicon Solutions command center reminded Joe Chronister more of a high-tech television studio than the ops centers he'd known back at Langley. Private companies sure had the money for all the latest toys and he could definitely understand why so many operators went over to places like Rubicon.

The CIA veteran's cover as a Rubicon oil exec made it plausible that he would be seen in the headquarters of the company's military branch, but he still didn't like being there. Rubicon's upper management was aware that he worked for the Agency and they had arranged for his cover. And Ashland, as his liaison to the local component of SHANGRI-LA, also knew, but he didn't want anyone else getting suspicious.

Chronister had to straighten out Larry Ashland before the eager beaver created a mess he wasn't sure they could mop up. He didn't slow down as he passed the desk of Ashland's new assistant. Ashland was on the phone, talking on one of those fancy wireless headsets. Chronister shut the door and motioned for him to hang up. He had the kind of boyish face and self-righteous smirk that made Chronister want to take a swing at him. He'd give him three more seconds and if he didn't stop the conversation, he'd personally rip the silly headpiece off his head.

"What the hell were you thinking, ordering your men to knock off Hunter Stone?" Chronister leaned on Ashland's smoked glass desktop, intentionally smearing it with handprints. "I had it all set up so that Camille Black would take care of him for us. If Rubicon does it, she'll be on our ass forever. Trust me. I've known this woman for years. She's powerful, connected and she doesn't forget."

"We can't let him get back to Zulu."

"And that's why you ordered Rubicon to shoot down his Black Hawk a few seconds before he got into Camille's crosshairs? You dumb ass." Chronister could hear his Brooklyn accent get stronger as he raised his voice. "The whole goddamn mess would've been over with right then and there. Zulu would've chalked the whole thing up to a lover's spat and Camille would've blamed Stone for Rubicon poaching her job sites. Now we've got a bona fide goat fuck on our hands. Zulu's going to find out Rubicon's either killed or is trying to kill one of their boys and eventually, they're going to trace it back to me. And linking it to me is as good as fingering the Agency. And if that happens, we are really fucked. The Pentagon's been looking for an excuse to put us out of business and they'll be all over SHANGRI-LA, you dumb-fuck."

Chronister could feel his chest tightening as he continued, "And Camille Black, she's a fucking barracuda. You can't just send her flowers and say 'whoops, I'm sorry.' You started a war with the lady and she owns one of the best militaries around." Chronister pointed to the door. "And why isn't your ass out there monitoring the action in real-time?"

"I will be as soon as we end this pleasant conversation." Ashland smiled wide enough to show off his perfect set of teeth, just begging for some emergency dentistry at

Chronister's hand. "Stone could've talked to Black. We had to make sure he didn't."

"Hello? She was about to shoot him out of the air, you dickhead. And I hear she spent all last night fucking his brains out." God, he loved Camille. That woman had balls. Big hairy balls.

"Is she insane?" Ashland squinted and shook his head in his pretty boy version of does-not-compute.

"You're going to find out if you don't get your ass in there right now and stop a war. First you better make sure word goes down the pipeline not to hurt Stone. I want to have a heart-to-heart with the guy, find out exactly how much Zulu knows about the project and if he told anything to Black. I'm sick of relying on you fuck-ups and it's time I find out for myself."

"It may be too late."

"What the hell are you talking about?"

"We have troops on the ground searching for him. They have orders to neutralize on sight."

"Let's get this straight," Chronister said as he thrust his finger at Ashland as if it were firing off a missile. He hated his guts so much, Chronister was starting to think his feelings were making him cut the asshole too much slack and chalk up everything to incompetence. He had assumed Ashland's aggressive actions to try to take out Stone were because the guy was a prick, but maybe there was something else to him. He would have to keep an eye on him more closely to make sure he didn't have another agenda. Chronister continued, "I want to know exactly what Stone and the Pentagon know about my involvement with SHANGRI-LA. You better bring him to me alive. Whatever happens to Stone—for whatever reason—is going to happen to you, but much slower. That's a promise you can take to the bank."

FORTY-ONE

Jabal ad Dhibban, Anbar Province

Hunter shoved his arms in the women's overcoat, ripping the seams along the way. The old woman glared at him. After a deep breath, he sucked in his chest, pulled the light gray jilbab closed and managed to button the top. His pant legs were rolled up as high as he could get them, but they still showed under what should have been a floor-length garment. He didn't need a mirror to know his disguise looked like crap.

Rummaging through the brass chest, he found a couple swaths of cloth. He stuffed scraps of cloth into a bundle while the kids watched in fear from the bedroom doorway. Even though it made him feel sick to take away one of their few toys, he picked the partially deflated balloon up off the floor and worked it into his bundle, rounding out the front. He tied it up, then using the longer piece of material he fastened it low around his midsection in a sort of cummerbund. Soldiers didn't tend to stare at pregnant ladies; they usually looked away pretty quickly. He was counting on it.

He slipped back into the overcoat and tied the scarf over his head, wishing he had shaved off the moustache and beard when he'd had the chance. Arab women did often seem to have a bit of a five o'clock shadow, but his was really pushing it. He hunched down, bowed his head and waved at the terrified family as he stepped out the doorway.

FORTY-TWO

Anbar Province

Camille's Little Bird intercepted the Black Management Hawks a few kilometers before Ramadi. Camille ordered the lead Black Hawk to set down in a field there, so she could swap places and equipment with her Chief Operations Officer, Manuel "Iggy" Ignatius. Camille knew her proper place was in the Little Bird, directing both air and ground battles, but this was too personal and her passions too dangerous. She was putting Iggy in charge of the skirmish and herself in the middle of it. Iggy was an alum of Delta Force, Gray Fox and CIA Special Activities Division and she could think of no better hands to place herself in, even though one of those hands was made from carbon composites, a prosthetic hand, courtesy of the Taliban.

The Little Bird landed in a field with patches of green, thanks to irrigation waters from the nearby Euphrates. The crop had been harvested and she guessed from the withered vines that it had been some kind of melons. The lead Black Hawk touched down twenty meters away while the other continued on to the village. She squinted her eyes and breathed through her T-shirt, trying in vain to protect herself from the swirling dust and sand as she jumped down from the Little Bird and ran over to the Hawk.

A little less than halfway there, she passed Iggy. He was the only operator she had ever known who wore shorts into battle. He claimed long pants restricted movement in his prosthetic leg, but she suspected he also did it to remind the troops in case they hadn't noticed his prosthetic arm. She grabbed his new arm as they passed and wished him luck.

The rear crew door of the Black Hawk had been removed

for combat. Camille climbed inside. Metallica was blaring "Enter Sandman" over the intercom, thanks to a jury-rigged iPod. She caught the pilot's gaze, glanced at a speaker and slid her finger across her throat, then pointed her index finger straight up and moved it in circles. He nodded, cut the music and the bird lifted into the air. Someone reached out to help steady her while she held on to whatever her hand could find.

Ten operators and their full combat gear were crunched into the troop space. Several of them were the same ones she had ridden with a couple nights ago in the Cougar, including GENGHIS. She recognized the distant, hardened looks on their faces, warriors headed into battle. This time no one was smiling and joking around like they did when they went after insurgents. Tangos were a ragtag bunch, poorly trained, barely equipped, but Rubicon had equipment which more or less equaled theirs and its soldiers were schooled by the very same American units. And they were Americans.

Camille plugged her headset into the intercom. "You all heard the sitrep, so you know what's going on." The ride smoothed out and she squatted on the floor in the middle of her troops. "Rubicon shot down one of our Hawks with our man inside. The guy we've been searching for, Hunter Stone, is one of us. He infiltrated Rubicon to find out why they were beating us to job sites and whatever he found out, they want to kill him for it." Camille pleased herself with her ability to lie on the fly. The CIA had taught her well. She really didn't like deceiving her troops, but the truth was far more complicated and far less motivational. "I know it has something to do with Rubicon selling arms caches to the *muj*. Stone survived the crash and he's on the ground running for his life. Rubicon brought two Mi-8s filled with operators ordered to hunt him down and they have a good ten-minute head start. They shot our bird down and they lit me up. You're authorized to use lethal force against Rubicon. We're at war, gentlemen. Hunter Stone is counting on us. Let's go get him."

"You really going in with us?" GENGHIS said. A pinch of tobacco bulged in his cheek.

"Hunter Stone is one of us and I leave no man behind. Now where's my gear and the clothes you're supposed to have for me? I can't go into combat in a T-shirt and shorts. And someone tell the pilot to turn Metallica back on."

Suddenly she was very aware that she wasn't wearing underwear. From the way the guys were looking at her breasts, they had noticed, too. Someone handed her a pair of desert camouflage pants. She unbuckled her belt and shouted above the music. "Everyone close your eyes— that's an order."

Everyone complied, except Genghis. He sat there leering at her.

No man was going to intimidate Camille Black. Struggling to keep her balance as the helicopter maneuvered, she pulled off her shorts and paused for a moment. She stood naked from the waist down, glaring at him.

GENGHIS spoke. "I thought you'd be sitting pretty in the Little Bird, ordering us around like your own toy soldiers." He squinted his eyes and nodded his head, pausing a few seconds before he spoke. "Your daddy would be proud. His little princess has balls."

FORTY-THREE

Jabal Ad Dhibban, Anbar Province

The ground hadn't heated up yet, but Hunter had already stepped in enough goat turds to be on the lookout for the nearest mosque so he could help himself to some sandals left outside the entryway. One of the nasty little pellets had wedged between his toes and others were smashed onto the bottom of his feet. He heard some occasional AK and M4 fire, but nothing serious. Two more Black Hawks had flown in operators and a Little Bird was hovering overhead. Kids were playing in the streets, running and pointing at the circling helicopters. Locals went about their routine business, apparently numb to helicopter swarms. Hoping to slowly work his way outside of their search grid, he kept his head tucked and did his best to waddle down the dirt road like a very expectant Muslim lady. He laughed to himself. His buddies were right—Stella really was a ball breaker. She had reduced a warrior to the kind of guy his buddies had always insisted that she wanted—barefoot and pregnant.

Gunfire echoed from a few streets away. In seconds, the casual shots turned into a heated exchange. The locals melted into the buildings as one of the Black Hawks dipped down and the Little Bird seemed to maneuver low to get a better view of the action. Suddenly, several AKs fired and the place sounded like New Year's Eve in Chinatown. The celebration was moving toward him.

FORTY-FOUR

> But if one is sitting at home as an Iraqi, and all one can see are civilian contractors bristling with weapons, it begs the question who are these people? Who ultimately do I turn to if, God forbid, they shoot my son or my husband, who do I turn to? From our own point of view we would find it pretty extraordinary to have armed civilians from a plethora of nations walking our streets, and in certain cases, as has happened in Iraq, setting up vehicle check-points and getting involved in controlling the population with no clear legal authority to do so.
>
> —FILE ON FOUR, THE BBC, May 25, 2004, interview with Duncan Bullivant, owner of Henderson Risks, a private military company active in Iraq

Jabal Ad Dhibban, Anbar Province
A Few Minutes Earlier

In '04 Camille had personally joined one of her advance teams, quietly paying house calls to some special residents on the eve of the Battle of Fallujah before the Marines moved in. Together with her operators, she had raided apartment buildings with sarin and VX chemical weapons labs. She had liberated torture chambers and walked through execution rooms right after tangos had finished live Internet broadcasts. All of that was preferable to bursting through the doors of innocent civilians, violating every inch of their lives, and having to make split-second decisions as to whether they were grabbing for a gun. Anyone raising a weapon against them was an insurgent, they all told themselves as they squeezed the trigger.

The village was quiet except for stray gunshots and the whoosh of the helicopters. As Camille and her team left a building, she noticed the streets had suddenly cleared of children and locals. Her team leapfrogged across an intersection to the next block. When GENGHIS was halfway across, an AK began popping nonstop and his right leg collapsed under him.

Rubicon.

GENGHIS tumbled in a roll, stopping behind a rusted-out truck and returning fire. Camille had a clear shot at a Rubicon soldier. Whether she liked GENGHIS or not didn't matter. He was part of her team and if a teammate was hurt, so was she. Without a thought to the larger political consequences, she squeezed off, but not for Black Management. Those shots were for GENGHIS.

The Rubicon pilots were fucking crazy, even by Beach Dog's admittedly low standards. Everywhere he tried to move his Little Bird, one of the Rubicon Mi-8s blocked him. Twice they'd come within two rotors' distance. He could feel their breath, pushing hard against his helo.

"I say we take them out before those dickheads accidentally get us all killed," Beach Dog said as he hung nose to nose with a Rubicon bird.

"Maintain position," Iggy said as he watched the movement on the ground.

Beach Dog flipped them off. They returned the salute.

"Feel better now?" Iggy said.

"Not yet, sir."

Camille keyed her mike and contacted Iggy. "TIN MAN this is LIGHTNING SIX. We're taking fire. Request some heat."

"I'm having trouble keeping an eye on you and don't want to risk friendly fire. Rubicon's birds are playing chicken with Beach Dog," Iggy said.

"Understood. Do what you can."

Camille instructed her team to lay down suppressive fire

and work their way one by one across the intersection to join GENGHIS. Just as she started across, movement from a rooftop caught her eye. An arm holding an AK dropped over the side and blindly pelted the road. Camille ran ahead anyway and slid onto the ground beside GENGHIS. "You okay?"

"Nothing like a little fresh lead in the morning to kickstart the day." GENGHIS ignored the wound, fired, and a tango collapsed. Without missing a beat, he retargeted and shot another one.

Weapons fire erupted from the rooftops. Iraqis with assault rifles jumped outside of doorways, fired, then sprang back inside.

"Fucking Jack-in-the-box *muj*," GENGHIS said. A spot was growing on his 5.11s as if he had sat down in blood. The unit's medic ran over to him and started cutting away the seat of his pants.

Camille leaned around the old truck and fired at a Rubicon soldier. The sound of AKs got louder by the second as word of the action spread from one Iraqna cell phone to another and more and more insurgents joined in.

The ants had discovered the picnic.

Beach Dog maneuvered the Little Bird toward the highway that bordered the village. It was the main road linking Fallujah and Ramadi—the tango turnpike. They swooped down low enough to get a good view of a parking lot that was filling with mopeds and old trucks that looked like they wouldn't move even on a downhill slope. Over one hundred men stood around, each of them carrying an AK. All of them wore the green headbands of the Mahdi's Army and several carried green flags.

Iggy keyed his radio. "CHALK ONE this is TIN MAN. We're monitoring hostile traffic coming into town. I'm moving you to join up with CHALK TWO. Head back west, two blocks, then take a right and stand by."

"LIGHTNING SIX here. Situation deteriorating. Taking

it from all sides—Rubicon and tangos—pinned down. You're authorized to use necessary force."

Iggy studied the crowd through a pair of binoculars. Beach Dog was amazed at Iggy's use of the prosthetic hand. The digits didn't seem to move all that well, but the guy sure knew how to get everything he could out of them. Another truckload of tangos arrived.

"I'm telling you, man," Beach Dog said. "They're not here for a church picnic. Those dudes are looking to pick up chicks—as in seventy-two virgins."

"I don't like turkey shoots if there's a chance civilians are mixed in."

"There's going to be a turkey shoot, but our guys are going to be the turkeys," Beach Dog said.

Beach Dog thought he saw a *muj* carrying a long tube. Something flashed and a smoke trail streaked toward them.

"RPG!"

Beach Dog slammed the controls and the Little Bird went sideways up into the air, leapfrogging over a Rubicon Mi-8. Before he could take a breath, a fireball engulfed the Rubicon helo. Like a cartoon character who had run off a cliff, the helicopter spun around once in place in the air, then plummeted straight down to earth. A main rotor hit a house, then the others snapped off one by one. Beach Dog pushed the Little Bird into a steep climb and looked away. Witnessing a bird's death throe was too painful.

Camille saw a flash of flames in the sky. She and GENGHIS made eye contact. She was thinking it, but GENGHIS said it. "Mog." Mogadishu. The Somalian capital was the site of the battle that every operator had on his mind as soon as things started going to hell.

"I'm telling you, man, we're looking at Mogadishu—Black Hawk down. I know what I'm saying. I flew strafing runs nonstop thirteen hours straight," Beach Dog said, shaking his head as he remembered the afternoon mission in 1993 that was supposed to be a thirty-minute cakewalk, but instead had dragged into a long, bloody night of urban warfare that left eighteen dead and every one of the one hundred sixty warriors wounded—one way or another. Beach Dog stared at the downed helicopter and could remember the thick black smoke from the two downed Black Hawks curling into the dark blue African sky that day. What he was staring at didn't look so different. He could feel his frustration from trying to direct lost Delta Force and Rangers through Mogadishu's windings streets and his helplessness as he had watched thousands of militia crawl all over them. He took a deep breath and felt his stomach muscles clench as he watched more tangos arrive in the parking lot below. "I'm telling you, we've got to take them out now."

"I know," Iggy said as he watched more packed trucks pull up. "We're not going to have a repeat on my watch. Waste the motherfuckers before they scatter. I don't want a single *muj* to walk out of that parking lot."

"You got it. I'll work the gun unless you have a real hankering for it."

"Do it."

The comm was jammed with everyone talking at once. Iggy raised his voice to shut them up, then gave instructions to the two Black Management Hawks which were flying under the call signs PANTHER ONE and TWO. "PANTHER ONE, TIN MAN. Your sector of fire is the northwest side of town. Engage tangos turning off the highway. Do not engage Rubicon vehicles at this time. PANTHER TWO maintain your overwatch position in the center of town and engage rooftop targets at your discretion."

Beach Dog calculated his approach and egress options with a single glance. The Little Bird would come in steep and fast from the southwest side of the village, hit the target and cease fire right before the highway. He would throw the helo into evasive turns as he climbed out over the gravel piles of a crude cement factory on the other side.

He headed the Little Bird to the southwest side of the village. When he had the distance he wanted, he swung it completely around, aligned it with the main road coming off the highway and checked the Gatling gun switches. "Initiating first pass." He threw her into a steep dive and yelled, "Banzai!"

A few seconds later, Beach Dog pressed the trigger and scores of bodies tumbled to the ground as if someone had jerked a giant carpet out from under them.

"Nice shooting," Iggy said with a smile. "And Beach Dog, those of us on the ground that night in Mog appreciated you working overtime."

"Is that where you picked up the spare parts?" Beach Dog threw the helicopter into a steep climb.

"Afghanistan. Operation Anaconda."

"Now I heard Anaconda was a real turkey shoot."

"A cluster fuck's more like it. Turkey shoot's the military's official version." Iggy looked down to assess the damage. "Take us in for a second pass."

Hunter recognized the sounds and did his best to make a mental picture of the battlefield, but he couldn't figure out what the hell was going on, except that Stella had her hands full with insurgents flocking to the action. There was a reason the good guys worked at night and she knew better than to stick around anywhere for more than a few minutes in the daylight. Her passions always did threaten her judgment, not that she would ever believe it. She would claim it only happened with him and, on second thought, she might be right. They had a way of stirring passion in one another.

He watched the RPG slam into the Rubicon Mi-8, then

felt the thunder of the crash. Black Management's Little Bird swooping in behind it with its machine guns blazing blew his mind. He had never imagined that Stella would ally with Rubicon to neutralize him, though he wasn't going to completely rule out that they were both after him, getting in each other's way. At least the woman was making more sense to him as he felt his own anger. The more he thought about Stella in the trailer reaching for a weapon to kill him right after they'd made love, the more the anger grew. A little jealousy over the tattoo with another woman's name on it, he could understand, but she had been out for blood. Before, he had not been able to understand her ferocity, but now he, too, had something burning inside, the flames leaping higher as he thought about the audacity of Stella sending her own private army after him.

He was on fire.

No way in hell was she going to get him.

Gunfire came from all directions. He hunched behind an old wooden cart, closed his eyes for a moment and listened for the distinctive crackle of M4s. The constant AK fire made it nearly impossible to localize any sounds, but he made his best guess and headed away from the Americans, toward the tangos.

Camille knew they would take more casualties if they couldn't stop the rooftop action. Had it been Rubicon instead of the insurgents, she was sure that she and her troops would all be dead, but the tangos were sloppy. She was deciding who she would take with her if they had to fight their way to the rooftops when the call came in from Iggy that the machine guns of a Black Hawk were on their way.

"Inform PANTHER TWO that as soon as their gunners engage, CHALK ONE is moving," Camille said.

"That's affirmative," Iggy said. "Stay with a compass heading of 220 for one-half click for the nearest possible

LZ. We're too tied up here to direct you to CHALK TWO. You'll rendezvous there."

Camille listened for the whoosh of the Black Hawks and realized she heard only AK fire and the wailing call to prayer coming from the distance.

Rubicon had pulled back.

She hoped the downed helicopter was enough of a black eye to get them to focus on the insurgents and quit messing with her. She had to get her troops out of there before more tangos arrived and pinned them down.

PANTHER TWO roared overhead and its staccato machine-gun fire was deafening. Camille flashed hand signals to her men to move out. She extended her hand to GENGHIS and he surprised her by taking it. He pulled himself to his feet, then pushed her away.

Their guns fanning the streets ahead, they worked their way toward the pick-up zone. The situation had gone to hell faster than she'd anticipated and she couldn't risk her troops any further.

Hunter was on his own.

God help him.

None of the Iraqis seemed to look twice at Hunter. No one cared about a big, ugly pregnant woman, not with so much action around them. Since he could pass as one of them at a distance, he stuck to the tight back alleys, somewhere usually far too dangerous for an American. The narrow alleyways made the streets seem all that much wider and more vulnerable. He stood ready to cross what seemed to be a main artery.

He first looked left, then right at Stella.

The Black Hawk gunners were working their magic, making the tangos disappear and Camille and her unit were jogging toward their extraction point when something made Camille take a second look at an expectant mother.

"Hunter?"

The idiot turned and ran.

Hunter's gait was so wide, he popped the buttons on the overcoat as he sprinted. He emerged from between the buildings and ran onto a wide street, directly into a group of soldiers, Rubicon troops.

"Hey! That's the guy! Grab him!"

A dozen Rubicon troops were a few yards in front of him and Stella was right behind him. He had a fraction of a second to decide his fate. The bitch would probably down him as soon as she got a clear shot, but Rubicon would want to talk to him before killing him. Rubicon and Black might be working together to capture him, but as soon as one side caught him, the cooperation would end. He knew which side would give him the better chance of survival.

Hunter ran to the Rubicon soldiers with his hands in the air.

"I surrender."

FORTY-FIVE

More than 1,500 South Africans are believed to be in Iraq under contract to various private military companies.
—The Cape Times, February 4, 2004, as reported by Beauregard Tromp

Jabal ad Dhibban, Anbar Province

As soon as Camille spotted the Rubicon troops, she stopped and held her fist up in the air, signaling her men to hold their positions. She was stunned as she watched Hunter raise his hands and give himself up to Rubicon.

Hunter, you stupid, stupid man.

She got on the radio. "Tin Man, I need your eyes now!"

"Lightning Six, stand by. Panther Two, can you assist?"

"Lightning Six, this is Panther Two. We got ya. I see about a dozen of you standing in a street that's at least one house wide."

"Negative Panther Two, not us. You're looking at Rubicon troops." AK fire came from across the street from Rubicon's position, but she figured that was their problem. She ignored it and described her position and what she needed from him. The Black Hawk pilot directed three teams through the maze of streets and alleyways so they could take position, flanking Rubicon. One stayed behind to close the trap.

So far so good, Hunter thought. The Rubicon troops seemed to accept his surrender. They took his knife and gun and he stood with his arms in the air while a young kid, probably a former Ranger, stripped him of his costume and shoved him down onto his knees. The kid glared at him the same way he had glared at hundreds of tangos. AK fire ricocheted on the ground. A Rubicon soldier held his weapon in one hand and popped off a burst.

The kid zip-tied Hunter's hands behind his back, then shoved him in front of an older South African merc who had clashed with Hunter before on previous Rubicon missions. Hunter had seen him kill several noncombatants in cold blood, but reports of that to his Rubicon superiors had only been enough to get the merc kicked off his team, but not enough to get him fired.

"My original orders were to kill you on sight." The South African grinned, exposing yellow teeth. "But now I understand that we're going to let your girlfriend do it for us."

It was already in the nineties and Camille was breathing hard as she took position between two walled courtyards. Rubicon troops rushed down the street only seconds later. She signaled her chalk of ten men to step out of hiding and surround the two dozen Rubicon soldiers. The Black Hawk hanging above them added to the illusion of superior force, but she knew it was only for show because the numbers were not on their side. They could pick off a guy or two, but once things started mixing up, they'd have to pull out. The Black Management troops emerged from the alleys and circled the Rubicon unit. Camille pointed her M4 at the face of the operator nearest Hunter. Her men selected their own targets.

"Hand him over," Camille said. "And give me back my gun. The fucker stole it."

"Is this your gun?" In a split second, the operator drew Stella's USP Tactical and held it against Hunter's head. "I'll hand it back to you after I'm done with it, doll," he said with a peculiar accent that Camille suspected was South African.

"No!"

"I suggest you inform your men to stand down and permit us go about our business."

"He'll do it. Go!" Hunter said, standing perfectly still. "I thought your orders were to let her kill me?"

"They were. But I neglected to mention I got new orders." The South African cocked the pistol. "What'll it be, love?"

Camille slowly lowered her weapon and keyed her mike. "All chalks, LIGHTNING SIX. Fall back." Camille looked Hunter in the eyes and said, "I was trying to save you, not kill you."

"Touching, but I don't have the whole bloody day. Lover boy is the only thing holding me up. If he's dead, I can get out of here. So, love, if you don't leave in three seconds . . ."

Just as a Rubicon soldier shoved a hood over Hunter's head, Camille mouthed, "I love you."

Camille's team made it to the pick-up zone in less than five minutes. As they piled into the Black Hawk, she could feel their heaviness: mission not accomplished. And she felt like a personal and professional failure. She wanted to hit something, but knew better than to let her men see her frustration. She had no idea if she could save Hunter now. They apparently wanted information from him, so that meant he probably had a few days, if not weeks, to live, but that was only a guess. Rubicon had the means to make anyone disappear—hell, they did it under government contract all the time. She would never know if the Julia Lewis thing was real, like Joe had said, or if, as Hunter kept trying to tell her, things weren't what they seemed. She fought back tears as they lifted into the air.

The one surviving Rubicon Mi-8 helicopter was sitting on the ground only a few hundred meters away. They seemed to be having problems trying to jam everyone into the single helo. Rubicon might have Hunter, but they were going to pay the price—starting now. She leaned over to her pilot.

"Order your gunner to target the Rubicon helo's tail. I don't want him getting off the ground."

"With pleasure, ma'am."

The Black Management helicopter rotated in the air, her guns pointing at the Rubicon Mi-8. They fired a deafening burst and the Rubicon tail rotor splintered as the blades turned into the path of the bullets.

Camille and her men cheered.

FORTY-SIX

The Green Zone, Baghdad

Jackie Nelson pressed the charcoal pencil to the paper and made a sweeping line that she could already see as the flowing traditional Iraqi male dress. In a few minutes she tried to capture the mysterious eyes of a man moving about in another man's clothes, engulfed in a lie. She still couldn't get the depth of pain and isolation she had seen. She tore the page from her drawing pad and set it beside the other sketches of her liberator, her hero, the guy she knew only as Ray—her secret agent man. Her small kitchen table was covered with charcoal drawings of Ray.

Her husband, Brian Nelson, stuck the large brown envelope he was carrying under his arm and picked up a drawing. Shaking his head, he dropped it back onto the table. "Do you think you should get some counseling or something? For christssake, you can't draw pictures of this guy for the rest of your life. The embassy flies in a shrink from Amman once a week. How about I have Rubicon pull some strings and get you in to see him?"

"I want to know who Ray is." She ignored him and started another drawing. "You could learn a lot from him."

"I'm sure hoping to."

She raised her pencil from the paper and looked him in the eyes for several seconds without speaking. "You know something, don't you?"

"I've got to go for a short walk." He broke eye contact and kissed the top of her head.

"Maybe you're right. I could use a break right now. I could use a walk, too. I guess it would be safe enough to go out if I'm with you."

"Are you sure you don't want to stay home? Give it some

more time?" He pointed to a drawing of Ray in combat garb, clutching an M16. "Maybe we can set up an exhibit at a gallery when we get home. These really are damn good."

"You really think so?" Jackie smiled. It was one of the softest things she'd heard from him in ages.

"The swoop of the line says movement to me. I want to see how you develop that." He motioned to the one she had begun a few moments ago.

"I'm trying to catch the action. I see him running, firing his weapon while he's using his body to shield the little girl." Jackie roughed out the figure of the child in seconds. "I can really feel this one. Go on without me. Enjoy your walk."

Joe Chronister kept the large brown envelope with the file tucked under his shirt as he walked to the site of the dead drop. Camille Black was asking questions about Julia Lewis and he wanted to make sure she got the right answers. He wished he could have done better, but with such short notice the best he could do was to recycle the Julia-Lewis-Fucks-Hunter-Stone file which she had already seen. Camille was a sharp cookie, but she had flipped through the file for less than a minute and he was banking on it that she had missed some things that would feel fresh to her.

A couple of guys were tossing garbage bags into a big blue Dumpster. He ignored them and walked past. A few seconds after he heard the lid slam shut, he looked back to make sure they had gone. He doubled back, slid the envelope with the file in it out from his shirt and peeled off an adhesive strip. Bending over, he slapped the envelope onto the bottom of the Dumpster. With a stroke of the wrist, he marked it with a streak of chalk, trying to imitate the swoop of Jackie's line, stylizing the Z. He thought to himself that someday he'd have to use the code name Zorro for himself. It was a hell of a lot more fitting for him than "Brian Nelson."

FORTY-SEVEN

Civilian employees at the prison were not bound by the Uniform Code of Military Justice . . . One of the employees involved in the interrogations at Abu Ghraib, according to the Taguba report, was . . . a civilian working for CACI International, a Virginia-based company. Private companies like CACI and Titan Corp. . . . were permitted, as never before in U.S. military history, to handle sensitive jobs.

—THE NEW YORKER, May 17, 2004, as reported by Seymour Hersh

Camp Tsunami, Abu Ghraib Prison

The scratchy cloth hood blocked Hunter's sight and he breathed the hot, stale air which he had just exhaled. The heavy material was wet from sweat. His hands and feet were now cuffed with plastic ties. He no longer heard the voices of the operators who had captured him and escorted him along several transfers. A couple of hours had been spent in a SUV, but a lot of the time was spent sitting and waiting. They shoved him through a doorway and he could sense the presence of two, maybe three guards.

"Greg Bolton, Staff Sergeant, 491 . . ." Hunter rattled off the name, rank and social security number for his cover identity with Rubicon, then repeated himself again and again. Regardless of what his colleagues at Force Zulu thought of him, he would not betray them to Rubicon. He had to keep up his cover story so Rubicon didn't learn that Zulu was investigating them. They might suspect it, but he wasn't about to confirm anything.

"Like I give a rat's ass who you are, you fucking trai-tor," his Rubicon jailor carefully enunciated each word.

Hunter guessed Minnesota or Wisconsin, a refugee from a blue state.

The other man shoved him to the ground. He twisted his body to break the fall, but it didn't do much good against the hard concrete. The guard kicked him and rolled him over, facedown. A knife blade scraped against his back, then the man slit his shirt and ripped it from him. He did the same with his pants and underwear. Then Hunter heard the click of a camera.

"I will now be conducting a body cavity search."

A latex glove slapped against the man's wrist and Hunter knew it was for the sound effect. It worked.

"I hear you're a *muj* lover." The man grabbed Hunter's testicles and squeezed. "You know, I could do this all day."

His hands were a vice. Hunter gasped and nausea washed over him like a tsunami, but didn't recede. The jailor twisted and grasped even harder. Hunter thought he was going to pass out; he wished to god he would.

The guard let go and stood there. Hunter drew himself into a fetal position and rubbed his thumb against his missing fingernails, a reminder, courtesy of the North Koreans, that he could survive anything. He tried to focus on controlling his breathing, but it smarted too damn much. His eyes teared up and he was sure his balls were badly bruised and swelling up like a bull's.

Hunter had gone through far worse in North Korea and he knew this was only the introduction to the Baghdad Hilton—a tour of the hotel grounds and a welcome cocktail. Thanks to those commie bastards, he knew himself better than any man should. Love for America, pride in the Corps and his belief that he was a warrior on the side of democracy and all things right had kept him going in the catacombs of hell somewhere north of the 40th parallel. The North Koreans were pros, but they couldn't get inside him where it really mattered. What the North Koreans couldn't do in six weeks with their bamboo sticks and

electrodes, Rubicon had accomp...
got inside Hunter and twisted and squ...
his very soul.

None of his training had prepared him for torture ...
hands of another American.

Underneath the hood, a Marine cried.

...e trade in military services
...veiled. There are no possibili-
...or dissolution, as no international
...e existence of the firms. There is
...ing with clients who hire the firms . . .
...al sanction available applies not to the
...employees, and only in very limited
circu... ...individuals working for the firms are captured,
they mig... ...their rights provided in the general laws of war.

—COLUMBIA JOURNAL OF TRANSNATIONAL LAW, Spring 2004, as
contributed by Peter W. Singer

Camp Raven, The Green Zone, Baghdad

At the Black Management Baghdad headquarters, Camille looked at Pete over the top rims of her sunglasses, shook her head and walked past her into the trailer, favoring her right foot. She couldn't get Hunter off her mind and she wanted desperately to stop thinking about him, even for a few moments. She knew all too well what Rubicon would be doing to him to motivate him to give up whatever information he possessed and Hunter was not the kind of guy who would let go of anything. His will could scratch diamonds.

Pete followed her inside. Someone had straightened up the trailer. The blanket and fresh sheets were stacked on a chair in the corner. Camille tossed her sunglasses onto the coffee table and they slid across it and fell to the floor where they stayed. She then opened a metal file cabinet and rooted around. When she didn't find what she was looking for, she slammed it shut and went on to the next.

"Whiskey's third drawer down. But you might not want

it, though. I managed to rustle up a bottle of Beefeater," Pete said as she walked over to the cabinet in the kitchenette. She took out a bottle of gin and held it up with both hands as if it were made of expensive crystal. "I couldn't bring myself to go with the vodka, because it was all cheap stuff you wouldn't like."

"Best news I've heard all day. So you ran down to the local package store to please the boss-lady?" Camille knew it was a little more complicated than that. Café Babylon sold bottles out of the backroom, but their overpriced stock was hit and miss.

"Anything for her." Pete flashed a smile as she got ice and a bottle of tonic water from the fridge. "I traded a favor with the boys over at the Bechtel party trailer." Pete mixed a gin and tonic, then poured herself a straight whiskey. "So do you want to hear the latest Julia Lewis installment now?"

"Let me drink in peace for a few minutes. It's going to take a few stiff ones until I can handle any more today." Camille sat down on the sofa and unlaced her Merrell hikers. The boys in the Black Hawk had brought her one size too big and it had rubbed blisters. She had only really noticed them burning in the past couple of hours after adrenaline levels in her body had started to settle. Pete tossed her a bag of pistachios. She caught it and set it aside.

"I almost had him. I was within ten meters of Hunter, then that stupid, stupid man took off running and the next thing I knew he had his paws in the air, giving himself up to Rubicon." Camille rubbed her foot while she inspected the blisters. The biggest had already burst. Gritting her teeth, she ripped the dead skin off.

"You were shooting up his helicopter this morning—"

"My helicopter."

"I stand corrected—your helo. My point is, this morning you were trying to kill him. What does it matter if Rubicon does the deed instead of you? Dead is dead."

"It matters." Camille rubbed the dead skin between her fingers, then flicked it away toward a wastebasket. She leaned back and sighed. "It matters. Rubicon is not going to get away with shooting down one of my birds."

"You want him only because they want him?"

"Works for me."

"Not for me. It was because you let him get to you last night."

"Fuck you." Camille gulped down the gin and tonic too fast and felt the gas building up inside. She put her hand over her mouth and stifled a belch. "You talk to our lawyers?"

"Yeah, Sarah Wang was out of town—Minneapolis again—she must really love it there. But I spoke to Patrick Jones. When I told him you wanted to know if you could sue Rubicon for taking out the Hawk, he couldn't stop laughing. Said you'd be better off visiting Rubicon's HQ in Herndon and staging a slip and fall than trying to nail them for shooting down your helicopter here in Iraq. Ain't gonna happen."

"We paid Marr Hipp Jones and Wang for that?"

"You always say they're the best. To be fair, he covered all the bases. You want the detailed analysis?"

"Cut to the punch line." Camille untied the bag of pistachios and pried open a nut. Her mind kept going back to how she had failed Hunter. Rubicon was probably torturing him right now.

"He said your best option is write the whole thing off and watch your back. The bottom line is we're all operating outside of Iraqi law and the Uniform Code of Military Justice doesn't apply to private security companies like us." Pete poured herself another glass of whiskey. "That's why we can do whatever the fuck we want."

"It's the only way we can do the job the government wants us to do." Camille shook her drink and the ice cubes clinked against the glass. She struggled to keep herself focused on the conversation. "The last thing we need is to pay for some creative legal work, set a precedent that somebody's law actually applies here in the Wild West and have it come back and bite us in the butt. Can you imagine the civil liability for property damage alone? Black Management has taken out over five thousand insurgents and we all know the definition of an insurgent is pretty damn loose around here. It's more or less anyone we take out. I don't even want to think about the wrongful death claims Iraqis could come after us with."

"Patrick did mention something like that."

"Sometimes I lie awake at night—you know Washington is a mercurial place. Sure, we're saving the president's ass in Iraq, but you ever stop to think about what could happen if the other guys sweep the next election?" Camille got up to pour herself another gin and tonic. "I shouldn't be talking like this. It's been a hell of a day. You want another round? Oh, forget it. I'll bring over the bottles." Camille braced the three bottles between her forearm and belly and balanced her own glass. She set them on the table, then plopped onto the sofa. "I'm going to hurt Rubicon. I just don't know how yet. Any more reports of them taking aggressive action toward us?"

Pete reached for the Wild Turkey. "Things were hopping today along the Syrian border. It started in Tal Afar, then spilled over into the Syrian side. The first rumor I heard was they thought they had al-Zahrani, then some of our guys came back with conflicting reports they'd nailed a French spy in Syria. We were all out in numbers. A few of our guys and some from Rubicon tripped over each other, but I'm pretty sure that's all it was."

"Rubicon has what they want, so maybe they're going to leave us alone and hope I leave them alone. What I can't figure out is why they wanted Hunter so badly. I'm starting to think some of what he was telling me is true. He told me Rubicon has a mole on the inside here."

"No way." Pete set down her drink, pursed her lips and shook her head. "Our boys are loyal."

"I don't care what we call them, they're mercenaries. They'll kill for a price, which is about eight hundred bucks a day."

Pete kept shaking her head. "A lot of the boys are very loyal to you—to the legend of Camille Black."

Camille cringed at Pete's words. She had proven today that she was no legend. She started thinking about touching Hunter's missing fingernails last night and she wanted to cry. She paused before speaking to compose herself. "The operators come to me because I buy them the top-of-the-line toys and they stay only because I pay top dollar. And they don't really stay. They all move around—some come back, though."

"We've got a lot of former recon Marines who thought the world of your father."

"I have no illusions. We're not the Marines. We don't get them while they're young and use borderline cult tactics to mold their loyalty." Camille waved her hand in the air. "Don't get me wrong. I think the world of the Corps. No organization has ever produced better warriors, better patriots or better human beings, but they have something we don't that goes beyond tradition, beyond patriotism. The Marines have got some kind of core truth that grabs people inside, bonds them with each other and gets them to push themselves to give their all in a way the Army could only dream of. They fight for each other, not money or flags. No military in the world has been able to replicate it and god knows they've tried."

"You really miss your dad, don't you?"

"Like you wouldn't believe." A couple of tears rolled down her face. She looked away and tried to wipe them off before Pete noticed.

"Hunter reminds you of him, doesn't he?"

"Don't go there." Camille picked up her drink. "Now how did I get started on that?"

"I think you were getting hungry and starting to ramble.

Which reminds me, I hear Halliburton is starting up a new lunch wagon right outside our front gate."

"You're getting me off track, though I am starting to think about real food." Camille grabbed a handful of pistachios. "I remember where I was going with all of that. A Rubicon spy is the only explanation for how they knew to intercept Hunter's helicopter this morning." Camille's fingernail broke as she pried open a nut. She twisted the splintered nail off and rubbed her finger against the jagged edge. She closed her eyes. "Who else knew about Hunter other than you?"

"The entire base. I issued a general alert right after you told me he was inside the wire. A couple of guys saw him run out of your trailer and streak across the compound. Anyone with a brain could've figured out it was him spinning around in the helicopter you were shooting at. It was quite a spectacle and word travels fast around here, especially when it involves a buck naked man running from the boss-lady's trailer and stealing a helo. I'm sure guys were laughing about it all over Afghanistan today."

"Great." Camille sighed. "Be very cautious. Keep as much as you can compartmentalized. From here on out, we're working on the assumption that Rubicon's got someone planted among us." Camille refilled her glass, but didn't dilute the gin with tonic water. "Okay, I'm ready now. So what did you find out about that Julia Lewis bitch?"

"You're not going to like it."

"I'm numb. Bring it on, baby." Camille leaned back and ran her hands through her hair. It was like straw, but she could wait to get back under the shower, given fresh, raw memories. She picked up her drink and gulped it down.

A few minutes later Camille closed the file and dropped it onto the coffee table. Except for the headers at the top of each page which made it appear to have been faxed from the Black Management Virginia offices, it looked like a duplicate of the CIA file Chronister had shown her a few days earlier. "That was a waste of time. I've already seen this. Get me something new. She's got a Maryland address. Send someone over to interview her—today."

"It's getting kind of late."

"It's still afternoon there." Camille threw a nut into her mouth. "Is there anywhere here you send someone out for pizza?"

"You really want to ask someone to make their way across town during D.C. rush hour?"

"Set it up so they go there first thing in the morning. And pepperoni would be great, though that lamb kebab and goat cheese one was pretty good the other day." Camille rubbed her eyes. She knew Pete didn't approve of her being with Hunter—or any man for that matter—but it was starting to annoy her. "I want to know everything about her relationship with Hunter. Get me dates, pictures—everything."

"That's not going to be easy. You really think you can knock on someone's door and get them to spill their whole life history for you?"

"Don't send a soldier. Send one of the spooks. Trust me. Any decent spy will know how to get what I want—including the pizza."

FORTY-NINE

Sixteen of the 44 incidents of abuse the Army's latest reports say happened at Abu Ghraib involved private contractors outside the domain of both the U.S. military and the U.S. government. Army investigators have reported that six employees of private contractors were involved in incidents of abuse . . . But so far nothing official has actually been done. Much as the civilian leadership at the Pentagon escaped unscathed, the corporate leadership at the firms has avoided investigation and possible punishment. So far, the only formal investigation has been one conducted by the firm involved; CACI's investigation of CACI cleared CACI.

—THE WASHINGTON POST, September 12, 2004, commentary by Peter W. Singer

Camp Tsunami, Abu Ghraib Prison

Hunter had grown accustomed to the high summer temperatures and even though it was probably in the upper seventies in the cell that night, he was chilled. His lips were burning, his stomach growling and his bruised balls throbbing. They had given him neither food, nor water, nor clothes, so he sat on the filthy cold concrete hungry, thirsty and naked. A lightbulb inside a small cage burned all night and loudspeakers blasted Chinese opera. The music selection made little sense, except that the voices were screechy and the nasal sounds damned annoying. He listened for hours, picking apart the sounds so he could filter them out, but couldn't hear any other prisoners. That worried him.

"Here's your Red Cross package, you mother fucking *haji*," a guard yelled through the slots on the solid metal door. The incessant music had masked their approach. The cell door opened and a book came flying toward his head. While he raised his arm to deflect it, they dropped something else by the door, then locked it without showing themselves.

Hunter walked over and picked up a small Muslim prayer rug and a copy of the Koran in Arabic. He was sure the bastards didn't realize he could actually read it, but he knew better than to ever let them see him doing it—not that he even wanted to crack it open. He sat on the tiny rug, drawing his legs up against his chest for warmth and when he couldn't fall asleep, he tried to meditate. All he could think about was Stella mouthing those three words that he'd waited so long to hear again. He only wished he could be sure she meant them and wasn't just caught up in the drama of the moment.

He nodded off, then woke himself up shivering. Lying with his face on the prayer rug to protect it from the grimy concrete floor, he tried to go back asleep, but the deafening Chinese music made his head pound. The cell reeked of stale urine and feces. He slept in fits, his body aching more and more each time he awakened.

The music blast suddenly stopped and Hunter jolted awake, jerking his head around, trying to figure out where he was. "*Allahu akbar,*" a canned muezzin blared from a tinny loudspeaker, calling to prayer.

He stretched and everything hurt. A hint of morning light came through the grate in the ceiling above him. He peed into the drain in the floor, sat down on the prayer rug and waited, but no breakfast arrived, not even thin gruel.

Hunter counted the cinder blocks in the cell: one hundred ninety-three.

* * *

Hunter counted the slits in the grate above his head: eight hundred and fifty-seven.

He flipped open the Koran, but the first words, "*Allahu akbar*" were such a turn-off, he slammed it shut. Allah didn't seem so *akbar* at the moment. Man, he was getting thirsty.

FIFTY

Camp Raven, The Green Zone, Baghdad
Two days later

The sweat on Camille's body evaporated almost instantly as she jogged around the perimeter of the Black Management compound. The temperature was bumping against a hundred ten and she was daring it to climb higher. Even though she knew she shouldn't be pushing herself to extremes, she couldn't stand another minute staring at the monitors and comm equipment in the operations center. Her entire intel staff was working on finding Hunter, but nothing had happened the entire day and his trail had dried up like moisture in the desert air. She was feeling light-headed, breathing hard and she knew she should stop and go work out in their air-conditioned gym, but she kept running. She waved as she passed some of her troops tending a garden. With a few seeds and some camouflage netting for protection from the unrelenting sun, they'd figured out a way to bring a taste of normalcy to their lives after a day of combat. She envied them. She needed a garden.

Near the shipping containers of fresh ammo, Pete pulled alongside her in a John Deere Gator and motioned for her to jump in. Camille waved her off and kept running, but Pete drove along behind her, yelling over the Gator's engine and waving a manila folder in the air. "We got her—Julia Lewis."

"Do I want to open it? What's your read? I know you looked at it," Camille said. She stopped, hopped into the moving utility vehicle and snatched away the file.

"Camille, honey, yesterday I talked to Pam Summerlin, the retired FBI agent we hired to interview her. I didn't want to say anything until I had something you could sink your teeth into. It's not good."

"Don't ever hold anything back from me again." Camille scanned the stack of papers, careful to keep them from blowing away as they drove along. It seemed like everything Greg Bolton and Julia Lewis-Bolton did, they put in both of their names—electric bills, phone bills, vet bills. They had even made a joint donation to the Marines' Toys for Tots charity. It seemed like a little too much togetherness for the man she knew, but the bitch could be the clingy type. "Are we absolutely sure 'Greg Bolton' is Hunter?"

"Keep going. There's a copy of a Maryland driver's license with his picture and signature. There are several other papers with joint signatures. I'm no expert, but they all looked genuine to me." Pete stopped the Gator in front of Camille's trailer, turned off the engine and pulled up the parking brake.

"Nothing I've seen here can't be faked." Camille fished a bottle of water out of the open glove compartment. It was warm, but she drank it anyway. "I want absolute proof."

"I thought you said he admitted to you he was using the Greg Bolton cover."

"He did. That's why I want absolute proof that Julia-baby isn't part of his legend."

"Do you want to see the pictures? I was really hoping you didn't want to go there."

"Dammit, Pete. Quit trying to protect me." Camille tossed the empty bottle into the bed of the Gator. Just then she heard the single boom of a mortar round going off. She moved her head as she followed its whistle through the air. "Sounds like the fucktards got the parking lot again. The damn thing has enough holes in it without them."

Pete reached for a clipboard that was shoved behind the seat and removed a second folder file. Camille snatched it away from her and opened it.

She sat down on the steps of the trailer and could feel the sun burning her skin as she thumbed through photo after photo of Hunter with the anorexic supermodel. She couldn't figure out what Hunter could ever see in such a woman. Camille was too big-boned and too muscular to ever look like that, no matter how well she cleaned up. It had been a long time since she'd primped herself. Makeup and pumps didn't exactly work well in a combat zone.

She kept looking through the photos. Each one had the date in red in the lower right hand corner, but those could have been easily faked. They seemed to have been taken in spurts, with long breaks in between which was what she would expect if he was on deployment, undercover as a shooter with Rubicon. All of the private military companies had three- or four-month rotations with thirty paid days off in their country of residence. "Did you see any dog or cat pictures in here?"

"No, but what does that have to do with anything?"

"I saw a couple of vet bills in the file with both their names on it. People with pets take their pictures with them all the time. We should be seeing at least one Fluffy shot."

"You're grasping at straws."

"I don't think so. I'm going to find that lost dog." Camille marched into the trailer, opened the first file and studied the vet bills. The Lewis-Bolton family had a puppy named Jordan, a yellow lab/Brittany spaniel mix. The dog had been fixed, received all of his vaccinations and had come in every six months for a checkup. Camille picked up the phone and dialed.

"Want to fill me in?" Pete hovered over her.

Camille shook her head and swiveled the chair away from Pete.

A woman's voice answered the phone. "Good morning, Chesapeake Vet."

"Hi, I'm hoping you can help me out. I've been calling around to all the vets in the area. My son found a big yellow dog. I think it's a lab. He's got a collar with tags, but they've hit against each other so much, I can't make anything out except the last name Lewis and the second name might be Bolton. You wouldn't happen to have any clients with the last name Lewis or Bolton would you? The dog is really sweet, but I can't take in another one."

"You know, I think we do. Hold on."

Camille rubbed her eyes and felt her chest tightening. She hadn't expected a vet's office to answer, let alone one that could identify the dog. Government spy agencies weren't that thorough with backstops for their agent's covers. Even in her days at the CIA, the best she ever got was a fake name, a recently-issued social security number, a PO box in Tysons Corner and a listing as a member of the board of a CIA propriety company. Force Zulu was military and no way were they even that thorough.

The woman came back on the line. "You're in luck. Julia and Greg Bolton have a yellow lab mix named Jordan."

The receptionist's words blurred as Camille stared at the file.

It's true.

Hunter had really wanted this Julia woman more than he had wanted her. Two years ago when she had cried so hard over his death, something inside her had died with him. Now she realized the happiness she wanted back so badly had never really been hers in the first place. It was all a monstrous lie.

Every man Camille knew was afraid of a true Amazon, but Hunter understood. She had always believed that they had challenged each other to develop further, train harder and think faster. Together the two warriors became a force.

She put her head down on the desk and tried to hide her tears. The Hunter Stone she had loved since high school was no more.

Camille Black was alone, an army of one.

FIFTY-ONE

Camp Tsunami, Abu Ghraib Prison

Hunter clung to the gift that Stella had given him as he was being taken prisoner, her full sweet lips mouthing "I love you." For two days, he had been pounded with over a hundred decibels of Chinese opera while waiting for his interrogation to begin. The bastards knew what they were doing. Time set the imagination loose and boredom numbed the will to resist. He pinched his forearm. The skin was taking longer and longer to spring back. He needed water soon and he would have to cut back on the exercise regime which he designed to do in the cell to keep himself in shape.

Without warning, the door swung open. Two men and a woman in gray prison uniforms with the Rubicon logo stood at the door; one man pointed an AK-102 at him.

"Time for your first therapy appointment, *haji*," a petite woman with a self-inflicted haircut said. "My friend here is kind of jumpy and the boss gets real pissed when he kills a prisoner, so do us a favor and cooperate. Put your hands behind your back and turn around."

Hopeful that he would eventually find his opening, Hunter complied as they tightened plastic cuffs on his wrists and shoved an olive-drab hood over his head. It reeked of vomit and instantly made him feel nauseous.

Fourteen stairs and two hallways later, the guards led Hunter into an air-conditioned room and shoved him down on what felt to his bare butt like a cold metal stool. The air conditioner was blasting on him and it had to be set as low as it would go. Then suddenly someone threw ice cold water on him and laughed. A door slammed and locked, but he wasn't alone. He could sense the presence of at least one guard.

He sat and waited, shivering.

After what he guessed was an hour, he tried to meditate, but couldn't. Screeching Chinese opera was still running through his head and every time he started to dry off, a guard doused him with ice water again. He rubbed his fingers over his missing fingernails and focused on an image of Stella, standing in the village, bulked up with body armor and telling him how she really felt.

She loves me.

The door opened and he felt a breeze and movement, then it closed. Silence. Papers rustled, then a voice spoke. "Remove the hood."

A guard walked over, unbuckled the hood and pulled it off him. Hunter squinted from the bright fluorescent lights. A middle-aged man sat behind an old metal desk. He seemed fit, but Hunter was confident he could take him out, even in his dehydrated state.

"If it isn't the one and only Master Sergeant Stone. I finally get to meet you," the man said with a heavy New York accent.

"Greg Bolton, Staff Sergeant, 491-83-1430."

"You can call me Mr. Zorro."

"Greg Bolton, Staff Sergeant, 491-83-1430."

"You think you're fucking cute, don't you? Sergeant Stone, your own Force Zulu has designated you an 'enemy combatant.' The Geneva Conventions don't apply here. You're free to talk to me and I'm free to do whatever the fuck I want."

Zorro reached into his attaché case and removed a bottle of water and placed it on the desk in front of Hunter.

Hunter looked away from it and repeated, "Greg Bolton, Staff Sergeant, 491-83-1430."

"You want the water, don't you?" Zorro twisted the top

open and took his time pouring it into a plastic glass. "I'm a reasonable man. I'm willing to give you all the water you want."

Hunter flashed back to the waterboard in North Korea and instinctively gasped for air and held his breath.

"Did that bother you, Master Sergeant? I thought you'd be happy with an offer of water. Did something bad happen with water? Maybe in Pyongyang?"

"Greg Bolton, Staff Sergeant, 491-83-1430."

"I've read your dossier, Sergeant Black-Stones. Those nuts look pretty bad, by the way. You really ought to see a doctor." Zorro drank some water. "I'm so sorry. I'm not some goddamn torturer. I'm a civilized man and I'm here to help you."

Hunter repeated his cover identity's name, rank and social security number, barking out the words like a drill instructor.

"You do need to know I'm a man with very little time. I'm not here to dick around with you. Here's the deal: You give me something; I give you something. It's that simple." Zorro shrugged his shoulders and smiled. His teeth were yellow, probably from too much nicotine.

"Greg Bolton, Staff Sergeant, 491-83-1430."

"I'll make you a deal." He shoved the glass of water toward Hunter. "All you have to do is tell me your real name and the water's yours. Hell, I'll throw in the whole goddamn bottle—a liter and a half of pure desalinated water."

Hunter took a deep breath. He tried to swallow, but his mouth was too dry and his throat burned. "Greg Bolton, Staff Sergeant, 491-83-1430."

"I know you're Hunter Stone. What's it going to hurt if you tell me what I already know? You're only spiting yourself."

Hunter ran his parched tongue across his cracked lips. He looked at the water and knew it wouldn't be more than a day or two until his organs started shutting down and dying. Rubicon already knew who he was. They knew. He wouldn't be betraying anyone. "Hunter Stone," Hunter said as he reached for the glass. "Master Sergeant Hunter—"

"No, no, no." Zorro grabbed the water glass and pulled it back, sloshing water onto the desk. "I only asked for your real name, not your real rank, too."

Hunter burned with hatred toward himself as he said, "My name is Hunter Stone."

"Help yourself to the water, Hunter Stone."

Hunter snatched up the water bottle and gulped it down before the guards could take it away.

"Maybe we can help each other again some time soon." Zorro walked toward the door, then paused and turned around. "Sergeant Stone, if you find there's something you want, let the guards know and give them something in return. They're authorized to make trades for me. Tell me everything Zulu knows about Rubicon and SHANGRI-LA and you can have the run of the house."

FIFTY-TWO

The sun went down and the trailer had grown dark except for the blue glow of a digital clock. Camille sat alone with her head on the desk. Her face was sticky from tears and snot. Her head throbbed and her nasal tissues were so swollen, she had to breathe through her mouth, and that only dried out the membranes more. She heard someone come into the trailer, but she didn't look up. A hand stroked her back.

"I told you to go," Camille said, her voice hoarse.

"You've been alone here for hours," Pete said as she turned on a lamp.

The bright light burned her eyes and Camille shielded them with her hands. "Get that off."

"You can't stay like this in the dark." Pete switched the lamp back off.

"Just go."

"Can I get you something? Water? Something to eat?" Pete moved beside her and ran her fingers through Camille's hair.

"Get me a bottle of vodka."

"That's the last thing you need right now."

"Get it."

"Whatever you want," Pete said, her voice now stiff and cold. "You're the boss."

Camille didn't know or care how much time had passed when Pete returned. She hadn't moved, though it felt like even more of her world had fallen away. Her tears had dried into a salty crust.

Pete placed something on the desk. "Honey, you shouldn't

drink on an empty stomach. Not when you're like this. I got you some kind of a lamb stew and rice. Best I could do at this hour."

"You get the vodka?"

"I shouldn't have."

Camille heard a glass bottle clink against the desk, but couldn't identify the sound of what else Pete set down. She heard the click of a lighter and immediately shut her eyes.

"You can't drink in the dark. I brought some candles." Candles presumably lit, Pete kneaded Camille's shoulders. "You want to talk?"

"Nothing to say."

"Can I get you anything else? Water maybe?"

"No water, two shot glasses."

Pete made some noise in the kitchenette, then put three glasses on the desk. "You're getting water anyway."

Camille heard Pete pour the vodka, then say, "What are we drinking to?"

"We're not. Go."

A few minutes after Pete left, Camille raised her head. Her neck was so stiff, she could barely move it. Everything ached, but she was too numb to care. She opened the desk drawer and reached inside. She pulled out another USP Tactical, a replacement courtesy of the Black Management armorer. She checked the magazine, then positioned it on the desk to her right.

The vodka was some Polish brand she didn't recognize. She screwed off the top and filled the two shot glasses. Using a candle, she lit the vodka in one of the glasses. The blue flame flickered.

"This is for you, Hunter—for us," she said out loud, holding up the second glass in a toast. As far as she was concerned, the Hunter Stone she had loved really was killed in action in Iraq two years ago. She downed the vodka in a single shot. "I loved you so much. We paid the ultimate price." Her voice cracked. Reaching for the vodka to pour herself another shot, she glanced at the gun and decided to drink from the bottle instead. She pressed it against her lips. The alcohol burned her raw throat.

She watched the blue flames dance and thought about what had been. She remembered tracking one another in the Mark Twain National Forest, armed with paintball guns, but she could no longer feel the delight as they'd blasted away at one another. She recalled the times their martial arts sessions had gotten out of hand, turning into serious violence, then dissolving into tender lovemaking, but the passion wasn't there anymore. She was but a voyeur. Pain had stripped away joy and the memories were now flavorless. Everything was a blue blur as tears welled in her eyes and dripped onto the manila file folder. She looked down at it, then grabbed for the vodka. The alcohol rush made her feel warm and calm.

Half of the shot had burned off. It was almost over. She reached over to the pistol and flicked the safety off, but kept her thumb on it, hesitating.

She was happiest when she was with him, but it wasn't like she couldn't be happy without him. Before he had resurfaced in May, she was moving on with her life, missing him, but moving on. She loved Hunter and it hurt like hell that he didn't feel the same way, but she was a warrior.

A Warrior.

Warriors don't quit.

She shoved the gun aside.

She sat there staring into the air for several minutes, then she opened the top folder and looked at a picture of Hunter. He really was Greek-god gorgeous. She turned the page and looked at the next one. Why wasn't she the woman lying in his arms after that picnic?

Camille took a deep breath. The flame was nearly gone. She stared at the photo, wedging herself into Hunter's arms in place of that bitch. The other woman kept butting in and she was left staring at a snapshot. Then she noticed the date in the print's lower right-hand corner and squinted to be sure—May 11th of this year.

"Oh my god," she whispered to herself. "May 11th—Granny's funeral—he was with me." Tears streamed down her face and her body shook as she wept. He loved her. He really did.

She leaned over and blew out the flame before it could extinguish itself.

Semper Fi, Hunter. Semper Fi.

FIFTY-THREE

Camp Raven, The Green Zone, Baghdad

Camille tripped down the stairs of her trailer, shouting for Pete. She stumbled, but caught herself before she hit the ground. She heard the loud *bam-boom* of a rocket fire in the distance. A few moments later, Pete came running from her trailer.

"He loves me, Pete. He loves me."

"Camille, sweet pea, you're drunk."

She put her arm around Camille and led her to a bench someone had constructed from shipping crates. The generators were so loud, she could barely hear the palm fronds rustling in the warm breeze. A crescent moon hung low in the sky.

"It's a forgery," Camille said, slurring her words and breathing through her mouth.

"Even the vet checked out. You've had too much to drink. You need to down some water and sleep for a while."

"No." Camille shook her head. "The dates are wrong. The pictures. They're wrong. May eleventh."

"Why don't you let me help you take a shower and put you to bed?" Pete brushed the hair from Camille's face. It was soaked from tears. "You poor thing. You've cried a lake."

"He couldn't have been with her. On May eleventh Granny Lusk was buried. No one knew he was there. No one but me." Camille stifled a yawn.

"I know how badly you want to believe him, but you're not making sense. You need to sleep. If it'll make you feel better, I'll take it and get some of our resident spooks to look over it and check it all out."

"No. It's a fake. Oh god, they've got him. We've got to get him away from Rubicon."

"We don't know where he is or even if he's alive."

"He's alive. I know he is. They want him to talk. They can't break him, but they won't know that yet. That gives us time." Camille stood, but Pete stayed on the bench. A mortar whistled in the distance. "What time is it?"

"Almost two."

"Bars still open?" Camille swayed.

"You don't need any more."

"Are they open?"

"Yeah."

"Get a dozen men down here immediately."

"With all due respect, you're drunk and heartbroken and you look like shit. And that's coming from someone who thinks you're one of the most stunning women she's ever seen." Pete stood and put her hand on Camille's back, nudging her toward her trailer.

"Get the boys. That's a fucking order."

Pete's square jaw was clenched. "Yes, ma'am. What do you want? Hunters? Pilots? Spies? Technicians?"

"I don't care. Whoever's up. Civilian dress is fine— no gear. I expect them in front of my trailer in ten minutes." Camille weaved more than she liked as she walked away. She had ten minutes to sober up, print some pictures and try to make herself look like a boss—one who, under the right circumstances, they would follow to their deaths.

* * *

As soon as Camille got back into the trailer, she flipped on the computer, grabbed a stack of twenties from petty cash and shoved them into the pocket of her running shorts. While waiting for the computer to boot up, she shoveled the rice and lamb stew into her mouth, barely chewing before swallowing. She would've preferred her favorite peanut M&Ms, but she didn't have time to search for a bag.

The laptop was finally displaying the Windows desktop and the wallpaper was still the picture from three years ago that Hunter had taken at arm's length of them laughing together, both splattered in Day-Glo fuchsia and orange paintball paint. She smiled this time as she remembered the high of that day. God, they had had so much fun.

She leaned over and clicked into a personal file and opened a more easily recognizable picture of Hunter. She set it to print two hundred copies, hoping to get as many as she could before time was up. On her way to the bathroom to clean up, she stopped to shovel in a few last mouthfuls of food and to guzzle as much water as she could stand. She had no doubt she really did look a wreck. A few splashes of cold water, a Black Management baseball cap and some sunglasses would have to do the trick. At least vodka didn't taint her breath.

Iggy entered her trailer without knocking just as Camille was putting her hair into a ponytail and threading it through the back of a baseball cap. Papers were falling out of the printer tray. Then he noticed the candles, the empty bottle and the .45. He picked up the gun and flicked the safety back on.

"What's going on, Cam? Pete told me you ordered her to muster my troops. She also told me you're sauced."

"I love you, Iggy, but no time."

She snatched up the pile of papers from the printer. They all had Stone's picture on it. She weaved toward the trailer door and Iggy grabbed her arm with his artificial hand.

"Cam, listen to me. You're drunk. I can't let you make a fool of yourself in front of your men."

"Let go of me." She twisted and pulled away.

Iggy followed Camille outside the trailer, embarrassed for her. A dozen off-duty men stood around in front of her quarters wearing Green Zone casual—skin-tight Under Armour T-shirts, Royal Robbins 5.11 pants and assault rifles. They were a mixture of operators, shooters, spooks and techies. Whatever stunt Camille was about to pull, no way could Iggy contain it. Word would spread like gunfire in Fallujah.

Camille climbed back onto the bottom step. A mortar thudded and whistled across the sky. No one even turned a head. She cleared her throat, then said, "You have a mission. Fan out to all the bars here in the bubble—"

The men laughed.

She continued. "I'm serious. Cover all the bars and the private trailer parties. Tell everyone I'm offering a bounty of one million dollars cash for this man."

She held up the stack of papers. It was too dark to see anything other than that she was holding the sheets backwards. *Jesus.* Iggy leaned over to Pete. "Get those from her."

Pete slipped up beside Camille and took the flyers.

Camille paused, waiting for the whistle of a mortar to stop. "Tangos are sure busy tonight. Must've cashed another Saudi check. They always seem to shoot their wad on payday—I'm sure none of you can relate to that." The men laughed again. "I want you to find Hunter Stone—the one Rubicon captured between Fallujah and Ramadi. Hit the bars, but avoid media hangs-outs. Keep it in the family."

"Any idea where he is?" one of the computer weenies said.

"No. Rubicon's got him. Focus on getting word to Rubicon employees. Some of them know where he is," Camille said.

"Ma'am, with all due respect," a cocky operator known as COPPERHEAD said. He'd been a SEAL for only four years, but thought he could kick the world's ass. "That's not enough money if he's being held in one of Rubicon's facilities where they keep the tangos. It would take serious gear, a team of six top-tier operators with support, bribes for information—everyone would need a cut. It's got to be worthwhile. One million might work if you want some Gurkhas or other Third World mercs taking a stab at it, but if you really want him—"

"I want to turn heads," Camille said. Like she hadn't already, shooting after a naked man running from her trailer and now talking to her troops drunk. She was a damn fine operator, but this personal crap was making her lose it. Much more of this and he would take out Stone himself.

"Try five million. That would get my attention," someone shouted.

"Five it is. I'll toss in an extra two mill if he's not harmed in the op. One million for information that leads to his rescue."

Iggy thought about how things had changed since the early penny-pinching days of Black Management when the Marines let them rummage through piles of seized AKs to arm their troops. Now they had so many government contracts, it wouldn't even be a challenge for the accountants to figure out a way to bill the government for the five mil—chump change.

Camille pointed to Iggy. "For anyone from Black Management who convinces Iggy they have solid intel and a good plan, I'll furnish the toys. Spread the word. By noon tomorrow I want every employee at Rubicon dreaming of retiring to Hawaii."

FIFTY-FOUR

For help on contracting, the Defense Department sometimes turns to other government agencies, who take on such work for the money, keeping a fraction of the total value of the contract in the form of a fee. . . . After an internal Army report accused a CACI employee [at Abu Ghraib] of encouraging soldiers to set conditions for interrogations and said he "clearly knew his instructions equated to physical abuse," it took more than a week for the government to track down and release details on the CACI contract, which was originally an Army contract but was turned over to the Interior Department.

—THE WASHINGTON POST, June 9, 2004, as reported by
    Robert O'Harrow, Jr. and Ellen McCarthy

Camp Raven, The Green Zone, Baghdad
The next day

Camille's stomach churned and she chomped down on more antacid tablets. The chalky things even tasted pink. She swirled chamomile tea in her mouth to kill the taste, but the combo was even worse. Last night was a blur. She was certain Pete had escorted her back into the trailer and that she had fallen asleep in her clothes, but she awoke in a nightgown—the negligee she had bought to meet Hunter in Dubai and had never worn. She didn't want to ask Pete. It was too strange and she didn't want to know.

She was now a refugee from the bright Iraqi sun, holed up in her trailer, waiting and recovering. Over and over she kept telling herself she had to rest up as much as she could so she'd be ready when the moment came. She popped more aspirin and pounded water, downing an entire bottle at a time. Across the compound in the operations bunker,

Iggy and his staff were studying whatever information they could find about Rubicon's detention centers and drawing up assault plans for each of them. In addition to small holding facilities at all of their installations, Rubicon ran several prisons throughout Iraq, including the new prison at Camp Cropper and the older facility at Abu Ghraib. Even though the Abu Ghraib complex had been turned over to Iraqi control, Rubicon continued to run one of the five prisons in the compound on the American taxpayer's dime.

Black Management was still in the process of building up its intelligence capabilities, so it outsourced part of the search for Hunter. Her spooks were coordinating with AegeanA, a British firm, to purchase signals intelligence on Rubicon's Iraq operations and they were also working with the American agencies, Diligence and Lyon Group, to see if they had any assets on the inside at Rubicon that could be purchased.

Camille opened one of the forged files and admired the quality workmanship. The more she thought about it, the more the call to the vet disturbed her. Last night she had been too drunk to have grasped the full picture, but it was starting to sink in and it scared her. It was the craftsmanship in the cover identity that was so upsetting. It took so many resources and such expertise to create and maintain a fictional paper trail like that. She only knew of a few instances in which the Agency had gone as far as issuing a *quasi-personal spouse* to backstop an alias in use overseas. And even then, they had done it only for particularly valuable aliases that they had used and developed over the years.

The Pentagon used aliases like disposable MRE wrappers, its operators longing for that *Mission: Impossible* moment when they could yank off the mask and reveal to the villain not only that he had been duped, but who had done it. Agency spooks were long-term players who were most satisfied when the bad guy died happy and ignorant, having been exploited by the same deception most of his life. The approach was the difference between checkers and chess, the Boy Scouts and the mafia. Deep down, Hunter was an Eagle Scout, but whoever had crafted his cover was at heart a criminal conspirator. She saw invisible fingerprints all over it, but not from the CIA. The Agency didn't create sophisticated aliases in-house anymore, but outsourced them to a boutique firm called Abraxas.

Someone had a strong desire to deceive her, one that was backed up with a serious budget. She knew only one person who would go to such lengths. And it was the same man who had tried to convince her to kill Hunter using all of the alias garbage—her old mentor at the CIA, Joe Chronister. Joe had taken the Pentagon's lame alias and handed it over to skilled hands at Abraxas so they could spin the yarn of Greg Bolton and Julia Lewis into a tale which could be used to incite her to kill Hunter. She had no idea as to why, but it was becoming clear to her that the CIA wanted Hunter Stone dead and they wanted it to look like a crime of passion.

Even though it was midafternoon, Camille felt so hungover from both alcohol and her tears, she decided to sleep it off. The day was so hot, the trailer's supersized air conditioner could barely keep up with the desert sun and it was warmer than usual inside. The lacy nightgown she'd woken up in was the coolest thing she had, so she slipped back into it, then grabbed her USP Tactical, checked the safety lever and stuck it between the sofa cushions.

As she squeezed the excess liquid from a pair of used chamomile tea bags, her mind was racing, but the pieces weren't coming together. The best she could figure was that Hunter must have stumbled across something going on between Rubicon and the Agency they didn't want her or Force Zulu finding out. They wanted Hunter dead, but the CIA couldn't murder one of the Pentagon's spies without all hell breaking loose and the Pentagon immediately investigating Rubicon and uncovering CIA secrets. So Joe Chronister, who knew her so well, thought he could manipulate her into hating Hunter so much that she would kill him out of rage, providing his death with the story they needed to satisfy Zulu investigators. Zulu would attribute it to a crime of passion and they would never realize that the CIA had killed one of theirs. She stretched out on the sofa, covering her swollen eyes with the tea bags.

Thoughts of the Agency kept coming back into her head. She sure didn't want to risk the several hundred millions of dollars of work they secretly funneled her way through contracts with the State Department, General Services Administration and even the Department of Interior, the guys who ran the National Parks—if they only knew. The CIA had friends in the military and all of her operators had worked closely with the Agency on one project or another. Providing employment to CIA non-official cover case officers as part of their aliases was a standard industry courtesy and at any time nearly a half-dozen Agency NOCs were attached to Black Management and many more Black Management employees were green badgers, former CIA staff leased back to the Agency at a nice profit. Even after the function of providing cover aliases to NOC case officers was outsourced to Abraxas, Black Management continued to participate in the program, cooperation which she would now be reevaluating and talking to Hollis about. When it came to the CIA, Black Management was completely compromised. She could only really trust the handful of people with strong personal loyalties toward her. Without removing the tea bags from her eyes, she felt around on the coffee table for the phone and punched in Pete's number.

"This is Camille. There's an operator named GENGHIS who works for us out of Camp Tornado Point. Locate him and tell him to bring his gear. I have a job for him."

"Will do."

She yawned as she set down the phone. The chamomile was starting to make her eyes feel better. She finally fell asleep, worrying about the CIA, thinking of Hunter and praying he was still alive.

FIFTY-FIVE

Camp Raven, the Green Zone, Baghdad

Camille was jolted awake by the sense that someone else was in the room. She pretended to be sleeping while her hand inched toward the sidearm stashed between the cushions. The damn tea bags were still on her eyes, so she couldn't even take a quick peek without tipping off the intruder that she was conscious. Listening intently, she thought she heard someone breathing, then the air conditioner kicked on and masked everything. Her hand felt for the pistol's plastic handle.

She drew the gun, aiming at the last location of the breathing sounds. The tea bags flew away from her face.

A man was sitting across from her, looking at her.

"I could've filled your bed with lead—or something else." GENGHIS shook his head as he turned on a lamp.

"And I could've shot you. I still can. What the hell are you doing in here?"

"I got word the boss-lady herself wanted me. So here I am, sweetie." He held his arms out and smiled, showing off his tobacco-stained teeth. "And you really should do something about the alarm system on your trailer. Piece of crap."

Camille sat up and glanced at the clock. She had napped for nearly six hours.

"You pick up that little number just for me?" GENGHIS said.

Camille remembered she was wearing the silly negligee. "You could be a gentleman and walk over there and grab me a sweatshirt and sweatpants."

"Could be, but I'm not. I like what I'm seeing. Like it a lot." He squinted as he smiled. Crow's feet etched deeper into his tanned face. He looked almost Mongolian, like his namesake, and Camille guessed he had a lot of Indian blood. "I hear the last man alone in this trailer with you ended up running for his life, buck naked."

"What are you doing working for me since you obviously don't have a very high opinion of women?"

"I love girls. Nothing sexier than a good looking chick who's packing."

"Enough bullshit. Why aren't you working for boys you respect over at Triple Canopy or Blackwater?"

"Seriously?" He stood and walked toward the built-in closet. "Is this where I'll find your sweats?"

"Yeah, second shelf down. How's your ass, by the way?"

"Sore, but nothing that'll slow me down. Want to see the stitches?" GENGHIS tossed her the clothes.

"Pass." She slipped on the black sweatshirt, pulled it down as low as she could, then put on the sweatpants with some modesty. "Thanks. So, seriously. Why are you working for me? We all pay about the same, though I like to think I have the best operators and best war gear."

"The top operators are split between you and Triple Canopy—Blackwater, too, to an extent, though you have a slight edge. Iggy pulls in a lot of them and the mystique of Camille Black lures the rest."

"Something tells me you haven't fallen for the je ne sais

quois of Camille Black since you probably remember her in diapers." GENGHIS and some of the older troops knew her real identity because of her father, but as true operators, they were silent professionals.

"Don't underestimate yourself. I've seen you in action. You're good. You still have a lot to learn, but you're young." He walked over to the door, opened it and spat tobacco juice. "Skoal's a nasty habit."

"You want something to drink?"

"I don't drink when I'm working and I think I'm working right now."

"I have sparkling water, some fruit juices, tonic water." Camille opened the fridge.

"Plain water."

Camille handed him a bottle and took one for herself. He didn't seem like the kind of guy who needed a glass and ice. "Answer my question. Why are you working for me?"

The expression on GENGHIS' face suddenly became serious and he sat there for a few moments looking at her before speaking. "Charlie Hawkins was the best warrior I ever met. He saved my ass in places I don't remember. No matter what I said a couple of days ago, I know he raised his little Stella to be one of us. The military won't let women do this kind of black work, but I figured I'd give you a shot. I owe it to Charlie."

"I vaguely remember you and dad arguing about his work for the Agency." The truth was that she barely remembered him, but she wanted to probe his attitude toward the Agency to convince herself one last time he wasn't the mole.

"We might've. I'm a soldier. There's no love lost between me and the OGA. What's it to you?"

"You ever consider working for them?"

"No."

"Come on, every man has his price. What would it take for you?"

"You trying to recruit me? If you are, pull off that sweatshirt because you'd have a lot better shot in that little clingy number. I don't want money. I have all I need. All I care about is staying in the game." He opened the water and drank the entire liter bottle without a pause, then crossed his arms and looked her in the eyes. "It's been fun playing around with you, but I'm getting bored. What's this interview all about? What do you want?"

"Someone to watch my back."

"Consider that pretty ass covered." He pinched a fresh wad of chewing tobacco and stuck it in his cheek. "You seem like a gal who likes to take care of herself, whether it's a good idea or not. Someone threatening you?"

"I don't know where this is all going, but I need someone I can count on at my side when it's time to play ball. The only ones I can really trust are Iggy and Pete. Iggy I need running the show and Pete's not an operator."

"Iggy's a good man. I'd trust him with the lives of my children."

Someone knocked on the trailer door. GENGHIS drew a SOCOM pistol and aimed at the entrance.

Pete stepped inside.

"You chicken shit, put that thing down," Pete said, then turned toward Camille before GENGHIS lowered his gun. "We know where he is. Abu Ghraib. The Rubicon compound."

"We have men in and out of there all the time," Camille said.

"Is the intel good?" GENGHIS said, chewing a pinch of tobacco.

"Iggy and Virgil actually agree on something. Both say it's actionable. The problem's going to be deciding which one of the Rubicon snitches gets the million bucks. We nearly had them lining up outside the front gate."

FIFTY-SIX

[Private military corporations] structure their organization very much like the military—giving employees "ranks" based on experience and training. They own military equipment such as Kiowa Warrior helicopters and train their pilots to fly them in Iraqi skies, Smith said. They deploy for months on end, train at military installations and work daily with U.S. commanders in any given war zone, he said.

—The Chicago Tribune, April 2, 2004, as reported by Kirsten Scharnberg and Mike Dorning

Camp Raven, The Green Zone, Baghdad

When Camille rushed into the Black Management war room, her senior operations officers were arguing around a conference table littered with laptops, blueprints and satellite images. As soon as they saw her, they stopped and stood. She was never sure if it was out of respect for rank, or old-fashioned chivalry, but either way it made her feel uncomfortable. She was the owner and president of the company, but she knew she wasn't in the same tactical league as her generals. That's why she kept her call sign as LIGHTNING SIX, the six denoting a field commander. She was comfortable calling the shots in a skirmish, but she left the war planning to those trained by the big military.

As usual, her Chief Operations Officer, Iggy, was wearing 5.11 tactical shorts, showing off his shiny new right leg. The Black Management dress code for employees in Iraq allowed khaki shorts, but senior staff usually wore full-length Royal Robbins 5.11s. Iggy was no bleeding heart liberal, but he was determined to convince the spec ops community that the loss of limbs didn't necessarily mean loss of combat readiness. At Walter Reed, before the wounds on his amputated arm had healed, Iggy had already broken his first prosthetic hand from too rigorous a set of push-ups. Over the next eighteen months he relearned how to field-strip an M4, parachute from planes, build improvised explosives and even insert an IV needle into a wounded man's arm. Despite the blisters, he ran for miles with full gear weighing down on his stump. Camille had seen him swap ammo magazines with one hand faster than most men could with two. He lived by the mantra: *mind over matter*—if he didn't mind, it didn't matter. Although he had exceeded all physical requirements for his old job, the CIA had offered him only a desk.

A few years earlier when they were both in the CIA, Iggy had certified Camille as meeting all standards for the Agency's Special Activities Division operators. He had been willing to make her the CIA's first female paramilitary operator until Joe Chronister had pulled some strings and blocked her transfer. In the late spring of 2003, when Camille had heard the Agency had written Iggy off as an operator, she recruited him. Camille wanted his strategic mind, but gave his body a chance, returning an old favor and sweetening it with a minority stake in Black Management.

Even though he didn't need to for his position, Iggy had passed the company's rigorous physical tests for tier-one operators and he again met all Delta Force black book certification standards. When things were quiet, he went on runs with the boys to maintain his combat skills. Despite his old Agency ties, she knew his loyalty to her was unwavering.

"Evening, gentlemen," Camille said, wanting to rush through formalities and get down to planning Hunter's rescue. "I believe you all know GENGHIS who's joining us tonight." Camille noticed how Virgil and Iggy shot each other glances. No one welcomed GENGHIS. Camille continued, "Where are Stout and Matsushita?"

"Running the Syrian engagement. It won't cool down," Iggy said.

"Pete gave me a sitrep on Abu Ghraib, so I know what's going on. All I need is the plan." Camille took a seat at the table and turned toward the screen with a satellite image of the five separate compounds which made up the sprawling Abu Ghraib prison complex.

Iggy cleared his throat, but didn't speak. She looked over at him. He stared into the air, as did the other senior ops officer.

"Is there a problem, gentlemen?" Camille said, tapping her fingers on the table. "You did make up the contingency plans I asked for? Come on, you have to have one for Abu Ghraib."

"Yes, ma'am," Virgil Searcy said in a Southern drawl. Searcy was Black Management's Deputy Operations Officer. "We have two plans and we're just trying to get our heads together on our approach."

"Let me guess. You want to stage a distraction, then fast-rope in from helos with overwhelming force and secure the whole goddamn prison. And Iggy wants to play *Mission: Impossible*."

GENGHIS laughed, but no one else did.

"In a nutshell, ma'am, you nailed it." Virgil smiled. The Vietnam vet and former SEAL commander's silver hair was almost civilian in length. Almost.

"We don't have much time. I want this to go down tonight while the intel is fresh." Camille studied the satellite image. Abu Ghraib had five main fortified structures spread out over several hundred acres, each one a separate prison. Clusters of tents were scattered throughout the fenced-in compound. "Virgil, unless you've got a unique twist to the overwhelming force scenario, I want to hear the one with the lighter footprint. Abu Ghraib's a legal black hole, but I don't want to hit so hard that we piss off the new Iraqi owners and start to wear out our welcome.

We have to go as black as possible with this one. What's your plan, Iggy?"

"Our hunter teams drop off captured tangos at the Rubicon Abu Ghraib facility almost every night—busy nights, we can make several deliveries." Iggy tapped something into his computer and the satellite image zoomed in on what must have been the Rubicon prison. He aimed a laser pointer at the entrance. "For the ingress, we send in a SUV with a prisoner delivery, but instead of tangos, we drop off a team of six armed tier-one operators posing as Iraqi prisoners. We use break-away flex cuffs on their hands and feet. Thanks to our colleagues at Lyon Group, we now have an arrangement with one of the Rubicon guards to make sure the metal detector is down and to provide a distraction that will allow them to bypass a body search so they can take in gear on their persons."

Camille shook her head. "I know Rubicon is sloppy, but I find it hard to believe that they ever take prisoners into their facility without searching them first."

"Their searches are secondary. They count on us to make sure the prisoners arrive clean. They conduct one at a holding area on the inside, but our contact will stage a diversion to prevent this."

"You ever see those Rubicon guards?" GENGHIS wrinkled his eyebrows. "They're not pick of the litter. They're the guys who can't get jobs in county jails stateside. I don't like counting on one of them not to fuck it up."

Iggy ignored him and continued, "The team takes in sidearms, night vision, C and all the fixings to blast the doors open. They grab our man and get out. The delivery team in the SUV usually has to wait three to five minutes for Rubicon guards to take the prisoners inside and come back out with the usual transfer paperwork, so they'll still be waiting outside for the egress."

"What transfer paperwork?" Camille said, looking up at Iggy.

Virgil looked up from his laptop. His comb-over slid and revealed the bald spot. Camille glanced away as if she had just seen the guy naked. "We've been pestering the shit out of Rubicon ever since we handed over three HVTs last month and they claimed they never received the bastards."

"Bullshit," GENGHIS said, shaking his head while avoiding eye contact with Iggy. "Rubicon did it the first couple of times, then they'd go inside and leave us hanging. We're the ones who fill those things out to keep you desk jockeys happy."

Iggy raised his voice. "It doesn't matter who fills out the goddamn paperwork, the point is everyone is used to the truck sitting there for a few minutes after the prisoners go inside. They can wait on the team and not arouse suspicion. As soon as the team is in the facility, our Rubicon insider takes them into a holding area here. Two and a half minutes after entering, our advance team cuts the lights using a remote triggering device for their charges." Iggy shined the red dot on fuzzy rectangular objects behind the main building. "These are the generators. The Iraqis supply the prison with power for four to six hours a day, always in the morning and late afternoon. The rest of the power is from the backup generators."

"As bad as here in Baghdad," Camille said, shaking her head.

Iggy reached for his coffee mug with his artificial hand and took a sip. "We send in a two-man advance team to rig a small charge on it for remote detonation."

"How?" Camille said.

"We rounded up some Iraqis for a routine prisoner drop earlier in the evening. We do it like always in a food delivery truck and use the tangos as cover to drop off a couple of extra men inside the wire. They set the charges, then hitch a ride out with the second chalk."

"I don't want innocent Iraqis swept up," Camille said with force.

"Don't worry." Iggy smiled. "Bad guys are easy to find. We're already baby-sitting a few of them over in the bunker that we grabbed in anticipation." He stood and pointed to one of the blueprints on the table. "The original British plans, courtesy of an SIS contact. He tells me that it hasn't changed and our collaterals confirm this. Sorry, we didn't have time to scan the prison drawings to add to the slide show."

"Good enough," Camille said.

Iggy traced the planned movement of his teams with his hi-tech hand, custom designed for combat. It was encased in carbon fiber and steel plates protected the motor and microprocessors in the palm. The pinky was made from an extra durable polymer since it was the more vulnerable digit. Iggy tapped a finger on the blueprint. "As soon as the power's cut, our team pops their plastic cuffs off, puts on NVGs and neutralizes the guards—like our friends say: swift, silent, deadly. After that a team of three heads down to the end of Broadway to isolation cells in B-Block. They blow the sliders to the block—"

Camille held up her hand to stop him. "Translate. You're talking to someone who can't stand to watch prison movies. The thought of being cooped up like that freaks me out."

"Sliders are the big barred doors that slide open. Block's a cell block and Broadway is what they call the main walkway between the rows of cells. So as I was saying, three operators blow the doors, and extract Stone. Meanwhile three from the team hang behind and eliminate any additional resistance, then plant charges on the doors to clear an escape route back outside."

Camille sighed. "You're taking out the Rubicon insider who's escorting us in?"

"Yes, ma'am. I recommend we eliminate all potential resistance," Iggy said.

"I don't like it. It doesn't seem right." Camille pursed her lips. "Alternatives?"

The three operators shook their heads and Iggy spoke. "It's a gamble what our insider will do when the lead starts flying and his buddies start dropping. I can't risk my men."

"I have no problem killing tangos, but I don't like taking out some poor working class slob trying to get ahead," Camille said as she absentmindedly tapped her pen on the table.

"Jesus. It's big boy rules around here." GENGHIS threw his arms into the air. "Play like a girl and you're going to get us all killed to save your boyfriend's ass."

Anger flashed in Camille and the kernel of truth in what he was saying made her more furious. "You're out of line, soldier." She jerked her head around and pointed at GENGHIS. Her finger was inches from his face. Snake eaters like GENGHIS knew only one type of ass chewing and she knew if she didn't throw in enough insults and profanities, he'd look at her, laugh and spit Skoal on her boots. She took a deep breath. "If you want to work for me, then shut your fucking cock holster long enough to realize who's in charge and then support me in my orders. Otherwise, you can just continue your little five-knuckle shuffle back in your hootch and go home."

She glared at him. He didn't blink. Neither did she.

Seconds passed.

"Are we clear, GENGHIS?"

"Yeah."

"Are we clear young man?"

"Yes, ma'am. I was out of line, ma'am." GENGHIS looked away and stared into the room, checking out like a grunt being dressed down by an officer. "It won't happen again, ma'am."

"If you want to work for me, you have to show respect. That goes for me and my senior staff."

"Yes, ma'am. Understood ma'am." His speech was clipped and military in cadence.

Camille glanced over to Iggy and Virgil. "I want to make sure this is clear to everyone. This mission is not about saving 'my boyfriend.' This mission is to extract an operator who infiltrated Rubicon and who possesses information that Rubicon wants to keep suppressed at all costs."

Iggy shined his laser pointer at the satellite photo projected on the overhead screen. "Back to business, everyone exits in the food truck. They have to peel off their disguises before they hit the gate. A third team will be providing overwatch from a building near the gate. We'll also have a little fireworks at their number two gate and Rubicon will be doing everything they can to rush their shooters outside the wire to quiet things down." Iggy turned off the projector. "That's the plan, unless you want the full SMEAC."

"No need. I'll be in on the mission briefing and the 'crawl, walk, run,'" Camille said as she studied the floor plans.

GENGHIS cleared his throat and said, "A couple of borrowed Ford Expeditions instead of food trucks would make it look like their own guys are going after the bounty. That way they might not tie the op to Black."

Iggy ignored him.

"Iggy?" Camille said. "We pose as Iraqi cops all the time, I don't know why we can't use Rubicon as cover. Is there a problem with that?"

"No ma'am. No problem. Rubicon's SUVs are parked outside the bars most of the night. I can send someone out for a joy ride."

"We have Rubicon uniforms and ID badges?" Camille said.

"The spooks stockpiled them as soon as we ran into the first trouble with them." Iggy powered down his laptop.

"Include me and GENGHIS among the fake prisoners," Camille said. "The mission's all yours, sir. Make it happen."

"You got it," Iggy walked toward the door to the main ops center. He had no sign of a limp and if he wore long pants, no one would suspect that he was missing his right leg below the knee.

"Ma'am. Any idea what that information is, ma'am?" GENGHIS said. "Is it related to Rubicon beating us to sites with large weapons stockpiles?"

"I'm guessing it is. I wouldn't be surprised if we find out they're selling seized arms back to the insurgents, but I'm only speculating."

Iggy stood in the doorway. "That would be enough to bring down the bastards. You ever think about how much business that would free up for us? Why the hell would they ever take a risk like that? They've got billions in contracts and that's not even counting Afghanistan and the drug work they're doing in South America."

"I know." Camille set down the pen. "Rubicon has raked in over fifteen billion in Iraq contracts. That's a hell of a lot at stake, but you know, if peace breaks out and things settle down here, all that goes away. Maybe they're doing us all a big favor and making sure it doesn't." Camille had seen the CIA flounder about for most of the 1990s, searching for a real purpose after the collapse of the Soviet Union and the end of the Cold War. She sure as hell didn't want to be in the same listless position if the War on Terror abruptly ended. Everything she had worked so hard to build up would be over and Black Management would be out of business. She didn't particularly like it, but she needed the War on Terror—a lot of people did.

"I wouldn't put it past them to bankroll the tangos to stay in business. They screw their own guys every chance they get." GENGHIS snorted.

"Can I see you in your office for a minute?" Camille said.

"Sure thing." Iggy motioned with his prosthetic arm for

her to walk ahead of him. They entered his office and he shut the door.

Blinds covered a window looking out into the operations center. They were lowered, but the slats were turned so that he could keep an eye on things. The office was just big enough for a desk, a few chairs and a vinyl couch. Stuck in the corner beside bookshelves were what Iggy called his dumb arms and legs. His running leg and swimming limbs were the latest of their kind, each costing fifteen to twenty thousand dollars, but they had no brains. The smart ones cost three to four times that.

Most of the time he wore his smart limbs, which had microprocessors that constantly compensated and adjusted to whatever activity he was doing—walking slowly, climbing stairs, driving, eating, typing. Servo-motors opened and closed hydraulic valves in his ankle and wrist, increasing or decreasing movement in response to the microprocessors that measured his movement fifty times a second. The limbs were Bluetooth-enabled so they could be adjusted remotely with a laptop. Out of concern that an enemy hacker could gain access to his body, he had refused to be outfitted with them until their programming was upgraded with 256-bit encryption. Only he, Camille and a handful of his doctors knew the alphanumeric password.

"What's the story with you and GENGHIS?" Camille said. She stood beside his desk and put her hand on a stack of papers.

"One I don't tell," Iggy said as he sat down.

"You're going to have to. I need to know whatever it is."

"You know I'm professional."

"But GENGHIS isn't. I want to know what you know about him and don't like."

"Did you know he's Carmen's godfather?" He pointed to a picture of one of his seven kids hanging on the wall next to a shot of him in jungle camouflage holding a sniper rifle.

Camille sat down. She had never considered that GENGHIS might have been his friend, let alone the godfather of his oldest daughter. Tonight was the first time she'd ever seen them together and they didn't exactly seem to get along.

"This stays between us."

"Of course."

"GENGHIS and I were both in Delta. He came up through Marine recon, then switched over to the Army. He's the kind of guy who didn't care about losing rank and that's pretty much all I cared about. They were looking at swapping my bird for a star and I got a chance for some field action that would help make the case for my promotion. I handpicked my team. GENGHIS, a guy named Pilkenton and I gave the Libyans a little technical assist in complying with international agreements on chemical weapon production."

"Meaning, you were on a black op to knock out a factory?"

"Flattened the goddamn complex. Woke up Qadaffi in his tent sixty miles away," Iggy grinned, pleased with himself. "Anyway we were on the egress to the rally point, outside of Rabta and ran into resistance. We neutralized it, but Pilkenton took a round in the face. We were running behind and racing to get the hell out of there. You take out a chem plant like that and you've got all kinds of fallout you don't want to be exposed to. The winds were light, but they were shifting and about to blow toward us. Pilkenton was slowing us down, bleeding all over the place and groaning. He couldn't help it, the poor bastard. Anyway, we heard another Libyan patrol coming, looking for their buddies. Pilkenton would've given away our position. There was hardly any mouth there to put your hand over to shut him up. GENGHIS snapped his neck, then carried the body to the LZ. Pilkenton never would've survived anyway." Iggy's gaze was distant, still somewhere in the Libyan desert. He took a deep breath. "It's hard to explain how someone with a gunshot wound to the face dies from a broken neck."

"That's a challenge."

"But I did it—under oath. Everyone knew I was covering for GENGHIS. And they all understood, too. They'd all been there. But I couldn't live with it, Camille. My word is everything. They made me a general and sent me to the Pentagon. That's when I left Delta for the Christians In Action. Lying is a lifestyle with those loveable bastards, so I thought that's where I belonged." Iggy picked up a pen and twirled it around his artificial fingers. "Haven't spoken to GENGHIS since."

"I understand," Camille said, even more convinced that she could trust Iggy. Especially considering what it had cost him, his loyalty to GENGHIS would've made a Marine proud. "But you're going to have to work with him and that's going to involve more than talking."

"I'm a soldier. You can count on me doing what it takes to accomplish the mission. And we have a mission to finalize right now. You'll meet your team at twenty-three thirty hours in the bunker to do some run-throughs first. Come as an Iraqi civilian—male, traditional dress." He looked her in the eyes. "I'm also going to have to ask you a question about a scenario involving our guy on the inside. If I don't like your answer, I'm pulling you, even if you are the boss."

"I'd expect no less." Camille left the room.

FIFTY-SEVEN

Camp Tsunami, Abu Ghraib Prison

Hunter's stomach growled as he sat naked on the prayer rug, heavy metal music now blaring over the loudspeakers. The one hundred ninety-three cinder blocks had been inventoried so many times that he was ready to name each one like he'd already done with the seven rats that regularly prowled his cell. He did another hundred pushups, but didn't want to work out too hard since he hadn't eaten in days and he was starting to feel it. All the water he could drink was a bitter reminder that he had let Zorro extract more information from him than he had ever given the North Koreans or Saddam's Mukaburat. Handing over his real name was harmless enough, he tried to convince himself, but he knew that was the way it always started. Each scrap was innocuous, you told yourself as you handed over more and more. He understood how denial worked—he had once dated a Catholic girl who called herself a virgin the next morning—time and time again.

He was man enough to admit to himself he had been screwed by Zorro and it wasn't going to happen anymore. Even though Zorro knew he worked for Force Zulu, he had refused to acknowledge it during today's interrogation session. It wouldn't take long for them to realize their only leverage over him was water. Then they'd start withholding it again. Soon enough a point would come when he would have to begin handing them the little details they already knew or die from cascading organ failure. Intense physical pain was less insidious, easier to resist. Old-fashioned electrodes-on-the-balls torture made things very black and white.

Zorro had kept coming back to something called SHANGRI-LA and he seemed to believe that Hunter knew something about it. Hunter assumed it was the code name for whatever Rubicon had going on with the tangos and it was probably related to the arms caches Ashland had accused him of stealing, something that Zorro didn't seem to care about. He wondered how the strange Uzbekistan connection fit in. Jackie's husband had worked for Rubicon Petroleum and she claimed he was up to something secretive in Uzbekistan—the same place the al-Zahrani terrorists had trained. It could be a weird coincidence, but he doubted it. No matter how much he thought about it, a clear picture wouldn't come together.

He opened the Koran and started reading it to kill time, but his mind kept wandering to Stella. She would be trying to find him, but he doubted she stood much of a chance.

The guards on this shift were still playing heavy metal at a deafening level. He wasn't sure if they had switched to heavy metal to annoy Arab inmates or for the guards themselves to relieve their own ears. Either way, he welcomed the change except that the sound level was about the same as a jet taking off. Constant exposure to the deafening sound left him with a splitting headache that wouldn't go away for days and he feared he was going to have a hearing loss. He flipped through the Koran, then unexpectedly heard some familiar notes on an electric guitar, but he told himself no way were the guards playing that song to get to the prisoners. It wasn't right. Not even they would stoop so low as to play the national anthem to torture inmates.

After another chord, Hunter got up. Jimmy Hendrix' electric guitar was screeching while machine guns, bombs and screams—the sounds of Vietnam, the sounds of Iraq— were going off in the background. He stood at attention in his Abu Ghraib cell, naked, singing "The Star Spangled Banner" while he chocked back tears.

Without warning, the door cracked open and a guard threw Day-Glo orange prison coveralls, an olive-drab hood and a pair of flip-flops at him. He carried an AK-102, the poor Russian cousin of an M4, but he didn't point it directly at him. Hunter could've taken him out, but he saw something in the guy's eyes; he wanted something from Hunter and he was afraid.

The guard yelled above the music. "Put these on. We're getting you out of here. Hurry!"

Hunter jumped into the overalls and zipped them as fast as he could.

The guard glanced at the door as he handed Hunter the heavy hood. "Pull this on, too. I'll stick the strap through, but I won't buckle it."

"Did Camille Black send you?"

"And get your hands behind your back so I can cuff them." The guard's body was shaking with tension.

"No cuffs."

"It's got to look like a prisoner transfer. Get your hands behind your back. We're running out of time. Do it!"

"I want my hands free. You don't know what you're doing, do you?"

"I'm making five million in five minutes. Hands behind your back." He pointed the Russian assault rifle at Hunter.

He hoped the guy's half-assed plan gave him an opening to escape before it got him killed. But he didn't hesitate to go along with him. He'd rather die from a bullet than organ failure. "Give me the tie and I'll hold it in place."

"Whatever." He handed Hunter the zip-tie.

The flip-flops were several sizes too big and Hunter struggled not to trip over them as the guard shoved him along. The hood obscured everything, but he heard the clank of heavy metal locks and guessed he was almost outside the cell block or had entered another one.

A woman's voice said, "What took so long? Nathan can't stay parked at the door much longer. They're starting to get suspicious." Her footsteps paced alongside them.

"Stop!" A man shouted. Hunter estimated he was ten meters from them at their six o'clock. He wanted so badly to rip off the mask so he could see, but he knew better.

One of his liberators grabbed him, spun him around, took his arm and started to run. He planted his feet firmly and refused to move, figuring it was his best and only chance. Hunter heard an automatic weapon pop and the guy holding onto him screamed, then let go. He wanted to yank off the hood, but knew any movement on his part would be interpreted as a threat, a threat to be neutralized. So he stood there as he listened to another burst of gunshots and he heard the female jailor scream. He forced his eyes closed and pictured Stella telling him she loved him—that was the last image he wanted to take with him to eternity. In a split second, he was being shoved to the floor. He didn't resist.

"Face down! Now!"

His heart was pounding so hard, it felt like it was shaking his body. Then he realized he was actually trembling. He really thought it was over. As he lay on the cold concrete floor, smelling blood and sensing death all around him, he understood his life was soon coming to a close.

And he also understood he had made a terrible mistake in staging his death, telling himself that it was to protect Stella. Now he realized it was more to protect him, to protect him from losing her. He had lost over two years with her·and now he'd never see her again.

A Rubicon operator kicked him in the kidneys. The sharp pain was almost a welcome distraction.

FIFTY-EIGHT

Camp Tsunami, Abu Ghraib Prison

The Rubicon prison guard Bobby Carmichael whistled to himself as he waddled into the guard's bathroom with a package of brown paper towels, dreaming of the mail order bride and the double-wide he was going to buy with his bounty money. With a million bucks, he could even buy a lot in that new gated trailer park just off I-44 in Joplin. He wiggled his butt when he realized that with that much dough he could really go uptown and get himself a white Russian girl instead of one of the Filipinos he'd been saving up for. Whoever Hunter Stone was, he wished he could plant a big one on his cheek. Having that guy on his cell block was the luckiest break he'd had in his entire life.

He glanced at his watch and wondered where Becky and Lew were. Come to think of it, he hadn't seen Nathan for quite a while either. They were probably having some fun with the inmates and had cut him out of the action again. If they only knew that for once, Bobby was going to be the center of the world. Only four guards were on the cell block instead of the usual seven, but what did he care? It would only make it easier for him to slip the team inside, bypassing the usual searches.

The guard's bathroom was not something he was going to miss. No wonder the Europeans called them water closets. It was tough enough to take a dump teetering over the stained porcelain squat toilet like a hen laying an egg, praying to god he didn't lose his balance and fall in, but it was nearly impossible when it felt like those shit-smeared walls were closing in. He wadded up a fist full of paper towels and tossed them into the hole as if he were shooting a basket. He crumpled most of the package into tight wads. Putting his foot there to pack them down the hole as tightly as he could made him want to saw his leg off, but he reminded himself it was for the big bucks.

It was time. He flushed the toilet and left the door ajar. The other guards were too spoiled. They depended upon their comforts and nothing caused a more serious crisis among them than their own toilet overflowing. In another five minutes, they would be screaming for Bobby to drop everything and come clean up the mess. But this time he wouldn't come.

In a few minutes, Bobby Carmichael would be a millionaire and everyone knew millionaires didn't clean crappers.

He hurried outside for a smoke, thinking of his very own slinky blonde Rooskie.

FIFTY-NINE

Army investigators were forced to close their inquiry in June 2005 after they said task force members used battlefield pseudonyms that made it impossible to identify and locate the soldiers involved.

—THE NEW YORK TIMES, March 19, 2006, as reported by Erick Schmitt and Carolyn Marshall

Camp Tsunami, Abu Ghraib Prison

The glue holding on Camille's moustache made her upper lip itch, but she couldn't scratch it because her hands were cuffed behind her back in special breakaway zip-ties. As they were getting outfitted for the job, she broke apart three of them to make absolutely sure she could get free. Even voluntary restraints made her antsy. She reassured herself that it only helped her play the part more realistically—any sane Iraqi being hauled into Abu Ghraib should be a basket case. The six fake prisoners were sitting on the floor, crammed into the back of the stolen Rubicon Ford Expedition. As they wound through the Jersey barriers in front of the outside perimeter gate of the Rubicon-managed Abu Ghraib prison, she fell against GENGHIS. He winked at her and pushed back. She wasn't sure if it was another come-on or if he was now being chummy.

The Iraqi guards at the main gate were taking forever, talking with their driver about something she couldn't hear. God, she hoped they got Hunter and didn't end up trapped inside with him. She imagined herself a wild animal, throwing herself against the sides of the cage until she collapsed in blood and exhaustion. Trailers for prison movies alone were enough to make her want to go outside for a run. She took a deep breath. The SUV lurched forward and she watched out the back window, staring at the razor wire as the giant gates slammed shut.

She kept thinking about Iggy's question before he cleared her to go on the mission. He had described a scenario in which she believed she had figured out who their insider was. Iggy had wanted to know if she was absolutely sure that if he was carrying a weapon, she could neutralize him without hesitation. She had said yes, but wasn't so sure she had told the truth.

"RUBY SLIPPER to all units," the driver's voice came through a small speaker hidden in Camille's ear. "We have entered the HAUNTED FOREST."

Camille thought *The Wizard of Oz* was an unusual choice of code names for a straight guy, but she understood Iggy's logic of choosing something all the men were familiar with since there was so little time to prepare the op. She also suspected it was related to his affinity for his own call sign, TIN MAN. The important thing was that even if the Agency and Rubicon had somehow broken into their encrypted radio traffic, the RUBY SLIPPER wouldn't fit until it was too late.

At the prison entrance three Rubicon employees leaned against the cinder block wall in their wrinkled gray prison guard uniforms, smoking cigarettes and waiting for a new delivery of prisoners to process. If they hadn't been carrying assault rifles, they could just as easily have been fast-food workers on break hanging in the parking lot. She wouldn't have been surprised if that's what they had done in the States before Halliburton started the working-class gold rush, offering white-collar salaries for blue-collar work in Iraq.

A man who had supersized far too many of his own

French fries threw his cigarette to the ground, crushed it with his shiny black shoe and grinned as he watched them drive up. Strange reaction, Camille noted. She hoped it wasn't some eager new employee's first day on the job. She took it as a good sign that the others kept puffing away. The SUV backed up to the building. It came to a stop and she tumbled over against another fake prisoner.

One of her men posing as a Rubicon operator walked around the SUV and opened the back hatch. "Get your ass out of my truck, *haji*," he said as he grabbed Camille's shoulder and yanked her from the truck. She twisted her body like a cat as she fell to the ground.

"I didn't say lie down. On your feet."

He jerked her up by her arm and she struggled to keep her hands and feet close enough together so she didn't pop off the plastic ties. She looked him in the eyes, then spat at his feet. The Rubicon jailors laughed, cigarettes dangling from their mouths. Her men unloaded the prisoners.

"You boys gonna stand there lollygagging all night or you gonna take these here peckerwoods off my hands," REBEL, their driver said, turning on his thick Cajun accent. He was one of the smartest and sexiest operators she had. "They're stinking my truck up to high heaven."

"Hold your horses, farm boy. Six prisoners tonight, huh?" a lanky blond man said, an AK-102 at his side. His moustache was so ratty that it made Camille feel pretty good about hers, at least until he lowered his head and started studying her face more closely.

REBEL tried to distract him away from Camille. "So you boys ever get to watch girls going after one another like in all of them prison movies? I bet it's nonstop lezzie action in there."

The young guy looked over at him and laughed. "Yeah, that's all we do all night in there, watch chicks getting it on with other chicks. It's a rough job, but somebody's got to do it." He pulled out a scuffed, off-the-shelf

Motorola walkie-talkie. "Open up, Milford. I want back in before the girls hit the showers."

The steel door buzzed open and the guards shoved Camille, GENGHIS and the other four operators inside. She was sweating from the plastic-wrapped C-4 taped to her belly to help conceal her breasts. A USP Tactical pistol was stashed in an ankle holster under her dishdashah. They all had weapons and night vision equipment stashed under their Arab dresses. The insider was supposed to ensure that the walk-through metal detector was broken. In case he didn't come through, she was ready to draw at the first sign of problems.

The lock clanked shut behind her and it echoed in her head. Then it was drowned out by radio chatter from their driver. "TIN MAN this is RUBY SLIPPER. SCARECROW has entered the WITCH'S TOWER."

"Copy that," Iggy's smooth voice said over the earpiece.

"TIN MAN, RUBY SLIPPER again. The MUNCHKINS have returned and report everything in place for POPPY FIELDS," the driver's voice said over the radio. The advance team was now safely back inside the SUV and the explosive charges were set.

The Rubicon jailers stopped the prisoners outside a set of bars through which Camille could see the main cell block. The cells were stacked two high and they were packed with Iraqi men. Two guards pointed AK-102s at them while the big jailor's walkie-talkie squealed. She didn't know which one was their insider. She didn't want to.

"Bobby," the voice said over the walkie-talkie. "The john's flooding us out again. Get up here now!"

"Do it yourself." The obese guard talked out of the side of his mouth as he spoke into the radio. "I've got some prisoners to strip search."

"No way. Get your fat ass up here. Someone else can do it or throw them in the intake for a few minutes and come on up. The water's almost to the fridge." The voice crackled. "Oh, gross. There's something floating. I'm climbing on the desk."

"Coming." The big guard turned to the other two. "You guys want to do me a favor and check their asses for me?"

"No way. You're the fudge packer," the lanky kid said. The other shook his head. "You heard Milford, we can lock them up in intake and hold them there until you're back."

"Man, I have to do everything around here. Hurry up. Rack the A-sliders." He knocked his fist against the sliding barred door and the young jailor shoved an oversized prism-shaped key into the lock and opened it.

Camille felt sorry for Bobby. She recognized his type from school—the fat kid who would do anything to be liked, but whom everyone picked on. She knew in her gut that Bobby was their insider. She hoped to god he managed to hustle to the prison office to fix the overflow before POPPY FIELDS went down. Even though she had complete faith that Iggy knew what he was doing, she still didn't want to kill their informant.

Since taking the prison over from Saddam, Rubicon had done nothing to renovate it—or clean it. Camille felt the grimy walls closing in on her as she shuffled through the bars. The place reeked from nearly fifty years of sweat, feces and urine. She looked for the nearest security cameras, but there were none. Rubicon was cheap and smart enough not to tape whatever their guards did there. The bars slammed shut with a metallic thud which she could barely hear over the thousands of prisoners catcalling to the new guys—to them. She stood at the end of Broadway, the main thoroughfare between the stacks of cells. It was the middle of the night, but the fluorescent lights glowed brightly and everyone seemed to be up. Scores of men pressed against the bars of each cell, watching and smoking. Over one hundred prisoners were squeezed into each cell. Saddam himself couldn't have packed them in much tighter.

Iggy's voice came over her earpiece. "TIN MAN to all units. Standby for POPPY FIELDS in ten seconds." The order POPPY FIELDS couldn't come fast enough for Camille. Her heart was racing and she was drenched with sweat. Captivity did not become her. She calmed herself with the knowledge that in a few seconds, she would be freeing herself from the plastic cuffs and getting down to work before the guards understood it wasn't an ordinary blackout. She only wished that Bobby would hurry it up and get the hell away from them before it was too late for him. But for some reason he seemed to be waiting until they were secured.

The young guard shoved a key in the holding cell lock, but couldn't get it to turn. Camille and the other five operators stood at the end of Broadway with their hands and feet in plastic ties, waiting on the young kid to find the right key to the temporary holding cell. Camille could see the floor inside. It was black from blood and grime.

"TIN MAN to all units." Camille knew what was coming and she took a deep breath to focus herself and shut out the roar of the prisoners. Iggy continued, "Standby for POPPY FIELDS in five, four . . ."

The guards' walkie-talkies squealed. "Bobby, haul ass, man. I'm in turd soup up here."

Iggy's voice continued, "Two, one—stand by. All units hold position and stand by."

What the hell?

The operators volleyed glances at one another as they tried to make sense of the disruption.

Radio silence.

Dammit, Bobby, get the fuck out of here.

The guard fumbled with the dozens of keys on his extendable key ring attached to his belt, but didn't seem to be able to find the right one. Bobby shoved him aside.

"You're going to have to learn how to do these things yourself. You know Big Bobby's not always going to be here."

Iggy was taking forever, then Camille heard someone key a mike and she steeled herself. "TIN MAN to all units. LIONS, TIGERS AND BEARS. Repeat to all units: LIONS, TIGERS AND BEARS."

Abort.

PART THREE

Secret Wars

The C.I.A. is awash in money as a result of post-9/11 budget increases. But because of the general uncertainty over the future, it faces a long delay before it can recruit, train and develop a new generation of spies and analysts. So for now it is building up its staff by turning to the "intelligence-industrial complex."

—THE NEW YORK TIMES, June 13, 2005,
op-ed contribution by James Bamford

[T]he contracting boom continuing unchecked . . . means, says [John] Pike of GlobalSecurity.org, that America's spy network could soon resemble NASA's mission control room in Houston. "Most people, when they see that room, think they're looking at a bunch of NASA people," Pike notes. "But it's 90 percent contractors."

—MOTHER JONES, January/February 2005,
as reported by Tim Shorrock

SIXTY

"LIONS, TIGERS AND BEARS." Iggy's abort command echoed inside Camille's head. She doubled over and let out a loud moan to distract the guards, hating herself for what she was about to do. All that mattered now was getting her team out alive. She twisted her wrists and spread her ankles apart. The zip cuffs broke away. She reached for her USP Tactical, slapped the trigger twice and fired two rounds into the middle of Bobby's forehead at the same moment GENGHIS did the same. Blood splattered onto the stained walls, the freshest strokes on the Abu Ghraib mural.

GENGHIS glanced at Camille, "Sorry. Didn't think you had it in you."

"I wish," she whispered.

The other guards died before they could discharge their weapons. The inmates erupted in cheers just as the power went out, courtesy of their advance team. Darkness was a relief. With their night vision equipment, they had the advantage.

GENGHIS yanked at Bobby's keychain, but couldn't get it off his belt. He unbuckled it and tugged, struggling to harvest keys from the corpse.

Camille turned away. She pulled the dishdashah over her head and tossed the man-dress aside. She was scared Iggy had ordered the abort because he had received intel that Hunter was dead. He would never say it over the comm for fear it would shake her up too much to operate. He was right.

It was pitch-dark and she smelled death. Every muscle in her body tensed up and the animal in her told her to run.

Breathing hard, she reached around and removed the night vision goggles from where they were taped at the small of her back. She put the NVGs on her head, turned them on and could see again—sort of. The place was so dark, there wasn't much light for them to magnify and everything seemed to be closing in on her. She knew she had to forget Hunter, pull herself together and concentrate on the egress, so she took a deep breath, forced herself to calm down and focus, but the surging adrenaline made her feel like a frantic beast.

An operator grabbed her arm and tugged. "Move."

She went with him. They met the team at the slider to the cell block and waited for too many seconds until GENGHIS and COPPERHEAD pushed through them with Bobby's keys. GENGHIS unlocked it and slid the bars aside. The roar of hopeful prisoners grew louder, wrestling sounds echoing in her head.

The team rushed to the steel door to the outside. COPPERHEAD shoved keys into the lock, but there were too many to try them all. Her breath was fast and shallow. She had to get out. Now. She wanted to body-slam the door and she realized she was losing it. She closed her eyes for a second and imagined she was with her father.

She knew what to do.

"Stand aside. We're blowing the door." Camille said as her training took over and she drew her knife from a thigh holster. She sliced off the block of C-4 duct-taped and contoured to her stomach along with a packet containing a set of four electronic blasting caps and a remote detonator, then cut the C-4 brick in two and gave the other half to GENGHIS. She pinched off a chunk of C-4 the size of a golf ball and ripped a strip of duct tape from her stomach. Pushing the C-4 against the lock, she shoved a cap inside, then slapped the tape on to hold it in place.

In less than ten seconds, she and GENGHIS finished setting charges on the lock and hinges.

"Get back and look away!" Camille said as she raced back through the slider onto Broadway and out of the blast range. "Fire in the hole." She pressed the remote. The explosion thundered through the cell block and inmates screamed.

She dashed through the open doorway, gasping for fresh air.

SIXTY-ONE

Today, anyone suspected of links to terrorism can be snatched anywhere in the world, put on a secret CIA jet and taken to a country, such as Egypt, for "out-sourced" torture. When [Michael] Scheuer developed his programme he stipulated strictly that only suspects who had been tried in absentia for terrorist offences or had an outstanding arrest warrant were to be targeted . . . . Today there only has to be the suggestion they are involved in terrorism—no convictions or warrants are needed, nor is the permission of another country.

—SUNDAY HERALD [Glasgow], Oct. 16, 2005, as reported by Neil McKay

Camp Raven, The Green Zone, Baghdad

In the past hour Camille had killed an innocent man, busted out of Abu Ghraib and torched a stolen Rubicon vehicle in the desert. Having to perch on GENGHIS' lap for most of the ride back to Camp Raven didn't put her in any better mood and she still had no information on why they had had to abort. Even though the radio was encrypted, Iggy didn't want to use it. It had to mean that Hunter was dead. Iggy just didn't want to tell her over the airwaves. She absolutely knew it was true when she saw Iggy, Pete and Virgil were waiting on them at the entrance to the ops center.

Camille climbed from the Black Management Navigator and made eye contact with Iggy, but couldn't read him.

"He's dead, isn't he?"

"I don't think so." Iggy shook his head. "Your bounty worked a little too well. Some Rubicon guards tried to spring him on their own a few minutes before you got there."

"They get him?" Camille stretched. The other operators stood around, listening. "Is he here?"

"They fucked it up. They're dead."

"Hunter?"

He put his prosthetic hand on Camille's back. "Let's go talk inside—in private."

GENGHIS and Pete followed Camille and Iggy into the operations center. Most of Black Management's business happened at night and the place was buzzing even more than usual. Oversized LCD monitors showed live feeds from unmanned aerial vehicles, helicopters and ground troops, all in the green tones of night vision. Like a television producer of a live event, supervisors with cordless headsets studied the screens, giving directions as they toggled between images.

"Just tell me. Is Hunter alive?"

"Best we can tell."

"Syria?" Camille watched fast moving terrain on one of the monitors, then saw the bright trail of a missile flying away from the Super Cobra helicopter. GENGHIS and Pete stood a few feet away, still within earshot, as they followed the live action on the screens.

"Over there," Iggy pointed across the room. "That's Iran you're looking at. It's really hopping tonight. Some recon Marines got into a little trouble. We're keeping the Revolutionary Guard busy while their comrades yank them out." He turned toward Camille. "I'm afraid we've lost our chance to grab Stone. They're moving him, probably out of the country."

Camille kept her eyes on the monitor, waiting for the flash as the Hellfire hit its target. It gave her a few moments to sort through a jumble of emotions. She was relieved that he was alive, but frustrated that they had lost their chance to rescue him by only minutes. "We need to find him before that happens. But I'll go wherever it takes—let's just hope it's Afghanistan where we have the infrastructure."

"Not much chance of that." Iggy laughed.

"What's your source?"

"The Brits at AegeanA came through with sigint. Some idiot in the prison made a frantic call to a Rubicon oil exec at home on an unsecured line."

"So Rubicon is giving its own operatives covers in their petroleum division. Pretty sloppy," Camille said.

"What makes you think he's one of Rubicon's?"

She shot Iggy a worried glance. "You're not thinking the Agency? But I don't care who's involved, I'm going after him as soon as we pick up a trail. Black Management can't get pulled in any deeper—we have too many Agency contracts. We can't risk it. This is going to take a very light footprint."

"Back up a minute," Iggy said. "You can't seriously be thinking of going after him on your own?"

"I'll take GENGHIS."

GENGHIS was watching the action in Iran. He swung his head around, opened his mouth, then shut it. He paused, then decided to speak. "You surprised me tonight. I didn't think you had it in you to do what you had to do."

Camille waited. "So? Are you in?"

GENGHIS nodded.

"Cam, can I talk to you alone?" Iggy said.

"Sure. Pete, set GENGHIS up with some quarters." Camille turned to GENGHIS. "Be ready to deploy on five minutes' notice."

"Yes, ma'am." GENGHIS saluted her and she knew he meant it.

Camille sat alone in the war room with Iggy, yawning and rubbing her eyes. "We don't even know at this point if we're going anywhere to rescue him, but I'll be honest with you. You'd be my first choice, but I need you here running things and planning the op to come bail me out if it goes south." She couldn't bring herself to tell him the other part of the truth—that she was afraid his prosthetic arm and leg made him too easy to spot. Artificial limbs were too noticeable if they had to slip through borders and maneuver undetected.

"Understood." Iggy sighed. "It's about my new gear, isn't it?"

"Don't make me go there."

"The truth."

"Iggy . . ."

"You don't want to rely on a guy who has to change his batteries every two days."

"I'd trust you with my life any day. You know that. We've been in the field together after you lost them. But . . ." Her voice trailed off as she grappled for the words.

"But what?"

"You're not one of the little gray men anymore. You can't slip around under the radar. You've got a signature." Camille felt her stomach knot. "I'm sorry."

Iggy looked at her for a few moments before speaking. His dark brown eyes were sad, his demeanor deflated. "Don't be. All I wanted was your truth. And you know, you're right. I don't like to think I have any limits, then I get some goddamn sores on one of these stumps that make me so mad, I'll run an extra mile just to spite them."

Camille put her elbows on the table and supported her head with her hands. "I hit some limits tonight, too, but I didn't run any extra miles. You know that scenario we ran through before you cleared me to the team?"

"Yeah."

"His name was Bobby." She stared into the ops center through the window that covered most of one wall of the war room. The image of her bullets blasting the holes in Bobby's head wouldn't leave her.

"You froze?"

"Perfect shot." She touched her index finger to the middle of Iggy's forehead. Fighting tears, she turned away. "Just like my Daddy taught me."

"Was he armed?"

"A shorty AK."

Iggy took a deep breath and held her gaze. "You had a responsibility to your men. You did what you had to do."

"Bobby wouldn't have hurt us. I know he wouldn't have." She closed her eyes.

"He could've. That's all that matters. The risk wasn't acceptable."

"It's not like I haven't killed before. I have no problem eliminating the enemy. I've done wet jobs, black jobs and I've been in combat, but tonight I killed some poor slob who probably didn't even know how to get the safety off his weapon."

"Look at me, Cam." Iggy reached over to her with his birth hand and took hers. "We've all been there. We've all made that call—the car coming up on us too fast, the kid waving what turns out to be a goddamn toy gun, the guy holding an AK trying to protect his family."

From the way Iggy looked her in the eyes she got the feeling he wanted to hold her. She would've liked that, but she'd shown too much vulnerability already.

Iggy continued, "I'll give you the same talk that I always give my boys in a debriefing after something like this. We all loathe ourselves afterwards because we all want to do the right thing and sometimes the right thing is wrong. But you know what I do then? I look at the guys I made it back alive with and remind myself that I did it for them, for their wives and kids back home because, sometimes, Bobby gets scared and squeezes the goddamn trigger."

"This isn't the first time," Camille said, her voice flat. "Or even the second."

"Not the last, either." He squeezed her hand. "You know

why? GENGHIS was right about something for once—you are one of us."

All of her life Camille had strived to be one of them, the elite shadow warriors. She had been part of operations with them dozens of times and together they had pulled off the impossible, but they'd never accepted her as their own. No matter how hard she trained, no matter how good she became, no matter that she was in charge of all of them, she was first a woman in their eyes. Now she finally had made it into the club, not because she had endured and achieved, but because she put a bullet through the forehead of a fat man named Bobby.

Camille and Iggy sat together in silence for several minutes, nodding to one another from time to time. Iggy understood and that helped take the edge off. She took a deep breath and exhaled loudly. She motioned with her head to the ops center. "It's getting late and they probably need you in there."

Iggy let go of her hand. "There was more in the intercept I need to talk to you about. I don't have all the pieces, but the way I see it, it could be one of two things. Either Stone's stumbled over an Agency black op that could compromise them so badly that they'll take out one of the Pentagon's men to protect it or someone in the Agency is planning on retiring to a cushy Rubicon position soon and is already doing his new employer some favors." Iggy turned on his laptop.

"That's the norm in government now, isn't it? Throw favors and contracts at a company before you retire, then go collect the fat paycheck. Any idea who it could be?"

"Sure do. That Rubicon exec whose phone call we intercepted. His name is Brian Nelson."

Camille looked up. "Jackie Nelson's husband? The geologist Hunter rescued?"

"The very one. Kind of makes you wonder if the whole

hostage thing was a way to get some insurance money and get rid of the need for a nasty, public divorce. Nothing spooks hate more than having their personal life dragged out of the shadows by a divorce court." Iggy waved his artificial hand. "But that's not where I'm going with this. AegeanA called me as soon as they picked it up; that's when I ordered the abort. A little later they e-mailed me the recording." Iggy launched the Windows media player on his laptop. "Listen and tell me if you hear what I do."

The voice came over the computer speakers. "Aw, fuck. I told you dickheads to start a guard rotation using your top operators. I wouldn't trust those jerk-off jailors to work night shift at a 7-Eleven. I want him transferred to BALI HAI. I want him where no one can interfere."

"Oh, my god," Camille said.

"You heard it, too, didn't you?" Iggy crossed his arms and leaned back in his chair.

The voice continued, but Camille quit listening. "You know, last time I saw him, he said something about retiring as soon as he wrapped up a big project, but he's such an old-school spook, I can't see him selling out to Rubicon. Not Joe Chronister."

"He sold you out, didn't he?"

"Yeah, but not the Agency. It's his life." She took a deep breath.

"Times change and people change."

"I should've told you earlier. The night everything blew up with Hunter at Tornado Point, Joe recruited me for a contract on Hunter. That's when the whole Julia Lewis story started. It was his. He tried to screw me one last time before retirement."

"You're going to have to put the personal stuff aside." Iggy scooted his chair a few more inches away from her. "Cam, with that info, I'd say it's getting pretty clear that the Agency wanted you to take out Stone so Zulu would believe it was a domestic dispute and not tie them to it."

"Maybe. But it could be Joe working on his own." She nodded without smiling.

"He could be, but if he didn't go feral, then Black Management's been sucked into the cold war between the Pentagon and the OGA. We don't want to get involved in a proxy war." Iggy lowered his voice out of old habit, even though the war room was swept for bugs several times a day. "There's no love lost between the Agency and the Pentagon's Force Zulu. If a Zulu operator like Stone was caught spying on the Agency—even if he's spying on a CIA project run through Rubicon—you bet they'd take him to their blackest hole for a nice little chat. The CIA got caught with their pants down on 9/11 and they've been fighting the Pentagon for their existence ever since. Right now with Zulu's recent successes, the future's not looking too good for our old friends at Langley."

"Yeah, but it still could be Joe freelancing for Rubicon and the Agency has nothing to do with this. He is getting ready to retire and it makes perfect sense if he's using Agency resources while he can to set himself up with Rubicon. Talk to your friend who used to be Baghdad's CIA station chief—the one who's working for that private spook agency—and see what he can tell you about the Agency's ties to Rubicon."

"You mean Whitley over at Diligent? Already have a call in to him." Iggy stood and reached across the table for his laptop. "Chronister mentioned taking Stone to BALI HAI. We got another intercept when he mentioned something called SHANGRI-LA. I couldn't tell from the context if they were the same place or not, but I'd bet money they're a couple of the OGA's black prison sites."

"What do you know about renditions and CIA prisons?" Camille craned her neck to read the e-mail that Iggy was responding to. It didn't seem too important.

"You do know I pretty much set up the operational side of that program? Compared to what we do now, it seems what we started with was kind of quaint—grabbing tangos off the streets as long as they're not in the US and dropping them off for questioning at whatever Third World country had outstanding charges against them."

"Your personal contribution to human rights."

"Ah, if the Agency's not violating someone's human rights, they're not doing their job."

"We're going to work from the assumption they're taking him to a black site. You ever been in one?"

"Pretty much all of them, first-tier and second-tier— Hotel California, Motel 6, Salt Pit, Bondsteel—even the party barge the Navy had floating out in the Indian Ocean for a while. A lot of the first-tier black sites are old KGB facilities—built like brick shithouses. But then there's Bondsteel. You know that Halliburton built it back when Cheney was running the outfit?"

Camille shook her head and Iggy continued, "You have to get to Stone before he goes into one of those because he'll never come out." Iggy shook his head. "But I've gotta say, I've never heard of SHANGRI-LA or BALI HAI. They could be new or they might have changed the designations since I left the Agency." Iggy chuckled. "SHANGRI-LA and BALI HAI make it sound like the Agency's got some PR guy advising them now."

"I don't like the idea of messing around with the CIA, but I'll do whatever it takes to intercept that rendition flight on whatever end we can get to it." Camille tapped her fingers on the conference table.

"The Agency hardly ever runs those flights itself— hasn't for years. Most of them are outsourced."

"Any idea who has the contract?"

Iggy smiled. "Our friends—Rubicon."

SIXTY-TWO

The Green Zone, Baghdad

Joe Chronister had run agents for thirty-two years and he still couldn't figure out why they thought he was like some overpaid doctor, on call 24/7. He had no problem getting out of bed to meet with them if it was a real emergency, but they were usually like welfare cases, clogging the ER with the goddamn sniffles. CRAWFISH was one of his senior agents, in the old days keeping him informed about what the military was really up to and now snitching on the private military. Never once had CRAWFISH called him in the middle of the night. He yawned as he parked his car and walked onto a construction site where he had arranged to meet his mole in Black Management.

CRAWFISH was in the darkest corner of the site, leaning against a backhoe.

"This better be good. I was sleeping like a baby," Chronister said.

"Passed out when you heard about the jailbreak, huh?" CRAWFISH said.

"I love Camille dearly, but she's becoming a real pain in the keister."

"She's going to get worse. I thought you needed to know that she's listening to you. I don't know all the details because she's starting to compartmentalize, working directly with Iggy, but somehow she found out about the Rubicon jailbreak immediately via sigint. I'm speculating, but I think it's safe to assume you were the one the Abu Ghraib guards called first."

"Listening in on my home phone, huh? That bitch."

"I don't know if she knows it or if she's guessing, but she thinks you're planning on moving Stone out of the country and she's gearing up to go wherever she has to."

"By herself?"

"With another operator."

"Make sure you're the one going with her. I think the world of Camille, but if she gets too close, she has to be eliminated. Under no circumstances can she come into contact with Stone again." Chronister wasn't quite sure which pieces Camille and Stone had, but his instincts told him that by now it was too many to risk them comparing notes. He wasn't about to have the capstone of his career come crashing down because Camille butted in where she shouldn't have. "Tell you what, I'll cut her a break and try to throw her off with a wild goose chase to some godforsaken place like Ukraine, but if she somehow manages to find Stone, you're going to have to take them both out."

"I don't want to kill Camille," CRAWFISH said.

"You will if you have to." Chronister wagged his finger and took a step closer. "Because I hear the JAG at Fort Bliss might reopen a cold case about a major stabbing her CO over thirty times."

"He raped me. He was going to kill me."

"Yeah, yeah, but you don't have any proof of that and the Agency's holding plenty of evidence, enough to send you to Leavenworth for life." Chronister smiled to himself. He absolutely loved it when groundwork he'd once done to recruit an agent kept spinning off interest for years.

"Camille's treated me well. Don't do this."

"That's not what I hear. I hear you treat her like a real lady and she teases you—quite the little coquette. Then she slaps you in the face and fucks Hunter Stone, regardless of how he jerks her around."

"No. That's not true. She has a hard time accepting her feelings."

"Bullshit. Give it up. Camille knows what she likes. She likes dick—Hunter Stone's dick, to be precise. Face it, Pete. You aren't even in the running."

SIXTY-THREE

> He [Bob Baer, former CIA case officer] says: "If you want a serious interrogation, you send a prisoner to Jordan. If you want them to be tortured, you send them to Syria. If you want someone to disappear—never to see them again—you send them to Egypt."
>
> —NEW STATESMAN [London], May 17, 2004, as reported by Stephen Grey

The Green Zone, Baghdad

The first calls to prayer were sounding when Joe Chronister drove away from his meeting with Pete. He hadn't yet given up on a few more hours of shut-eye, but he had something to take care of first. Camille was listening and he had to assume that even his cell was compromised. Rarely did he risk his cover by visiting the Baghdad CIA station, but he was worthless without a secure cell phone and he wouldn't mind shooting the shit with the guys over a cup of java. A few minutes later he was walking down the hall of the CIA station, peeking in every open door, looking for a familiar face.

Bill Copeland was sitting at a desk, studying a report. Copeland was one of the last of the old CIA bluebloods, with their Ivy League degrees and liberal leanings, who looked down at self-made types like Chronister. He knew his state school diploma and blue-collar habits had held back his career, but he wasn't about to kowtow to men who wouldn't get their manicured nails dirty.

"Hey, Joe, haven't seen you for a while." Bill Copeland looked up from a fax he was studying.

"That's because you pantywaists stay here in your bunker and only venture out as far as the OGA bar. Never see you outside the bubble where the real action is." Chronister grinned. "What's up with all the new faces around here?"

"The Agency has everyone on thirty-day rotations, sixty on rare occasions. As if this place weren't impossible enough for our kind of work. Try recruiting an agent when you can't go anywhere without half a platoon of security guards around you. Now if somehow you're lucky enough to snag one, you have to hand him off in a few weeks to some new guy fresh from Langley. And the agent's supposed to trust the stranger with his life. If I were an Iraqi, I'd never spy for us. Splendid system."

Chronister snorted. "Yeah, the big boys on the seventh floor keep setting up dumb-ass regs like that and I can't help but think the Agency's not going to be around much longer—between that and General Smillie's Force Zulu muscling in."

"That thought has crossed everyone's mind," Copeland said as he continued reading the fax.

"Anything interesting going on? I heard Black Management nabbed a French spook among the tangos in OPERATION RIVERBED a couple days ago. Fucking French."

"Take a look at this. Looks like Paris has another one messing around in our business." Copeland handed him the papers he was reading.

"You got a debriefing document from the interrogation already?"

"Low pain threshold. I hear he's being questioned at *Far'Falastin* in Damascus."

"Those Syrian bastards are tops," Chronister said as he skimmed the report.

"It gets more interesting. Skip ahead to the description of another agent here in Baghdad. Seems Paris is very interested in CIA ties with Rubicon." Copeland turned to his computer screen while Chronister read.

Chronister sat down and stared at the page, his mouth

agape. "Holy fuck. The spook's talking about SHANGRI-LA."

Copeland quit reading his e-mail and turned around. "Are you read into SHANGRI-LA? I've never heard of it."

"And you still haven't. Whoever didn't sanitize it out of the report is going to get reamed so hard he'll never sit down again." Chronister flipped the pages, moving his lips, talking to himself. He needed more information fast. Official channels would take forever and even worse, would demand a ream of paperwork. He needed Copeland to take a few shortcuts for him. "I need you to check on someone for me. He fits the description more or less of the agent we're looking for and he knows everything this guy said. He could be the spy. Get NSA intercepts—everything you can."

"I'm not counterespionage."

"Live a little. You nail this fucker and I promise you'll get an EPA for your personnel file." Chronister counted on the allure of an Exceptional Performance Award. He wanted to get to bed and he didn't want to get caught up all morning dogging the bureaucracy when he could use Copeland, the paper pit bull. "Sure ups your chances of retiring a GS-15."

"I am retired."

"You're shitting me?"

"Eight months ago. I went to work for a body shop—Lyon Group. They lease me back to the Agency to do my old job for thirty thousand more." He tapped a green ID badge clipped to his shirt.

"Whatever." Chronister handed Copeland back the report. "Nabbing that fucking mole will make you a legend when you get back to Langley. Legends get good parking spaces—even if they are contractors."

As Chronister walked into his apartment, the aroma of hot coffee greeted him but the coffeepot was empty and Jackie was perched at the table, churning out more sketches. The walls, refrigerator and every other goddamn surface were now covered with drawings of Hunter Stone. Everything had been going so well with SHANGRI-LA before that Force Zulu bastard had come along. He had gotten used to keeping regular office hours and he had even come up with a brilliant work-around for his marital problems, using Rubicon's connections with the tangos to arrange for death doing him and the missus part. The fucker Stone had not only rescued his wife, but he was keeping him up all night and now, when he finally got a few hours at home, the SOB haunted him, mocking him from his own kitchen cabinets.

Chronister picked up the empty coffeepot. "Hey, what's with the coffee? Couldn't you have saved me some?"

Jackie sat at the kitchen table in the same white bathrobe she hadn't taken off since she came back. She didn't look up from her latest tribute to the wonder boy—Stone holding a small lamb with an adoring Iraqi family surrounding him.

"This is really getting to be too much. You haven't even gotten dressed. And you're obsessed with this mother-fucker." He pointed at a picture of Stone.

"Ray saved my life. Did you find out anything about him for me?" Jackie stood and emptied the coffee grounds into the garbage.

"Now how would I ever do that? Oil execs don't have access to that kind of information."

"Do you think I'm stupid? I've had enough of your game. Oil execs don't sneak out in the middle of the night, except to visit a mistress. You don't come home smelling of women. You smell of blood."

"I do not."

"You drip with blood." Jackie filled the Mr. Coffee with water, then threw a half dozen scoops of Folgers into the white paper filter. "I'm not going to argue with you. I know you're a spy and I really don't understand why you go to all the trouble of hiding it from me. At first I thought it was to protect me, then I thought it was to protect your cover, and then I finally understood you get some kind of a sick thrill from toying with me, from tricking me into living a lie along with you. Well not anymore. It's over."

"You're not making sense. You can't leave me. I've explained to you about that." Chronister shoved a slice of white bread into the toaster. When he had first gone deep undercover as a Rubicon oil executive, he had quickly realized that he stood out without a spouse. At the time she had been fun, but it didn't take too long for the isolation of Iraq to change that and make him realize he had gone a little too far for the project. "Go see that embassy shrink and stop it with these goddamn drawings." He grabbed a handful of sketches lying on the cabinet, wadded them up, then tossed them into the garbage.

"No!" Jackie sprang toward the trash and scooped out the crumpled papers. He watched in disgust as she brushed coffee grinds from them, then sat down at the table crying as she tried to smooth out the coffee-stained pictures.

"Look at you. You're a fucking nutcase. No one's ever going to believe anything you tell them about me. And you know something else, you better give up on your fantasy boyfriend because he ain't coming back."

"You know where Ray is?" Jackie looked up, her eyes wide. "You've got to save him."

"Save him? You're fucking kidding, right?" Chronister laughed and tore down drawings taped to the kitchen cabinets. "I'm taking him to one of my favorite places tomorrow where I plan on taking the gloves off for a man-to-man chat."

"No!" Tears streamed down her cheeks.

"You gonna stop me? You can't even get dressed." He walked around the room, ripping sketches of Stone from the wall. Jackie trailed behind him, pleading. He reached for a drawing of Stone saving Jackie and she grabbed his arm, screeching something at him, but he didn't listen.

"Ain't gonna happen, baby. He's not going to save you now. No one can." He shredded the drawing, the pieces fluttering to the floor. Jackie got down on her hands and knees and crawled around collecting them.

He watched her, thinking about how he could snap her neck and end the drama in seconds, but he was a pro and professionals knew better than to act in rage. It was so soon after the kidnapping that it would be very tricky to eliminate her now without arousing suspicions. There had to be an option he wasn't seeing at the moment, something clever, something worthy of him.

She collapsed on the floor, sobbing, turning her shredded masterpieces into papier-mâché. The bitch wasn't going anywhere for now. To be on the safe side, he yanked the phone cord from the wall. He needed to make some calls, but he could use the bedroom phone and his new cell. A refreshing nap might open up the right possibility, something the Agency and the life insurance company would never question.

SIXTY-FOUR

Statements extracted under torture are totally unreliable, sometimes concocted by the interrogators themselves, the victim merely signing them. . . . Inevitably, the victim admits whatever he is asked to admit. A lie enters the stream of intelligence as the truth.

—SUNDAY HERALD [Glasgow], October 16, 2005, as reported by
Neil Mackay

In one video played to jurors last week [in the California terrorism trail], Umer Hayat admitted visiting several terrorist training camps. . . . But his account sometimes bordered on the fantastic, with tales of a thousand terrorists wearing masks "like Ninja Turtle" as they practiced twirling curved swords, firing automatic weapons and pole-vaulting rivers in an immense underground compound—a description that roughly tracks the Ninja Turtles television show.

—ASSOCIATED PRESS, March 11, 2006, as reported by Don Thompson

Camp Raven, The Green Zone, Baghdad

Stuffing her mouth with a granola bar, Camille stumbled from her trailer and toward the bunker that housed the ops center. The day shift had come on a few minutes ago and she could count on a steaming pot of fresh coffee. She needed it; she had slept for three hours and felt a wreck. Activity in the ops center had dropped to the usual daytime lull. Most of the monitors were dark and those that were on were rerunning footage from last night's action, the morning crew fighting vicariously. She grabbed her mug and yelled to anyone who was listening. "Who made the coffee today?"

"Curatalo—brace yourself."

"Great. I was afraid it was Iggy's troubled water." She dumped coffee into her cup, leaving room for more cream than usual. Without bothering to stir, she sipped some down, then headed to Iggy's office. He seemed to live there, typically working nights and well into the morning. She guessed he had to slip away to shower and sleep midday before things geared up for the evening's operations, but she suspected he often went for days without leaving the ops center.

Iggy looked up from a satellite image on his computer. "You get any shut-eye?"

"Not much, but I'm sure it was more than you did. It's hard not to worry about Hunter. Anything new?"

"Yeah, AegeanA picked up a short conversation between Joe Chronister and a guy named Larry Ashland, some kind of a supervisor in Rubicon. They discussed taking Stone to a black site in the Ukraine." Iggy smacked his lips as he shook his head.

"I take it there's something you don't like?"

"A lot. Joe initiated the call from his home phone on an unsecured line. Even though he openly referred to Stone, he used the current code name for the Ukrainian shithole—a program he knows I've been read into." Iggy made eye contract with Camille. "I've worked with Joe on at least a dozen projects and you can say a lot of things about the SOB, but his tradecraft is clean."

"He knows we're listening." Camille shoved some papers aside and set her coffee cup on Iggy's desk.

"Oh, yeah. He knows all right and that means we've got a leak a little closer to us than we thought. AegeanA has a wire to his cell. It's state of the art encryption, but you know what kind of code breakers the Brits are. Not a single call in or out. They did whatever magic they do and checked his records. He uses it constantly, except today." Iggy put his hands on the top of his head and chin and twisted. His neck popped. "I figure he wasn't sure if we were sophisticated enough to get through the cell's encryption, so he placed the call to Ashland on the open line, to make sure we were listening. He wanted to make damn sure we heard what he had to say."

"He wants me out of his hair," Camille said. "At least he didn't hire a sniper."

"You're too high profile. Everyone knows you're in a showdown with Rubicon. Anything happens to you right now, it calls more attention to Rubicon and whatever the hell SHANGRI-LA and BALI HAI are."

"We knew we had a mole problem." Camille sipped some coffee. "Any idea who it could be? Who around here knew about the jailbreak sigint?"

"Could be anyone on duty in the ops center last night. I made a reference to it in front of your team when you got back." Iggy sighed. "Doesn't narrow it much."

"Then let's play along. He wants to throw me off track and send me to Ukraine, then as far as everyone's concerned, I'm gearing up to intercept a plane there tomorrow. In the interim, do whatever it takes to find out where and what those code names could mean—talk to our green badgers inside the Agency if you have to. We've got spies on the inside at the CIA. Let's use them."

"Agreed. And I really think you should—"

Someone knocked at the door and both turned toward it. "Yeah. Come in."

"Sorry to interrupt you, sir, ma'am." An aide stood in the doorway. "I've got Kimo from the main gate on the line. He's got a barefoot woman in a bathrobe. She won't say who she is, but says her husband is going to kill her. She's insisting on talking to Ms. Black."

Camille reached toward the aide's radio. "Kimo's the big Hawaiian guy, right?" The aide nodded. Camille squeezed the button. "Howzit, Kimo? Can you let me talk to the lady?"

"For sure, Ms. Black."

"Hi, this is Camille Black. How can I help you?"

"I didn't know where else to go," the woman's voice said. "You said you'd help me. I'm Jackie Nelson."

Iggy and Camille looked at each other, then she turned to the aide and said, "Send GENGHIS to the gate immediately and have him escort her to my trailer. Tell him to stay with her until I arrive. He's to let no one else in except me."

Camille jogged up to her trailer with Iggy. An operator she knew only as BEAR stood on the steps, an M4 in hand.

"Where's GENGHIS?" Camille said.

"No one's seen him since last night, ma'am," BEAR said as he stepped aside to let them enter.

"Find him," Iggy said as he stepped into the trailer.

Jackie Nelson sat in the black leather armchair, staring into space. Her hair was stringy, uncombed and her eyes were red and puffy, but her face wasn't quite as sunken as when Camille had last seen the woman in her apartment. Still, sitting there barefoot with filthy feet and in a bathrobe, the woman looked deranged.

"Hi, Jackie. This is my good friend Iggy. He might be able to help us."

Iggy extended his artificial hand. She reached out, touched it lightly, then pulled her hand back.

Camille continued, "Looks like you left home in a hurry."

"He was going to kill me. He always said he would if I left him and I told him I was leaving." She rubbed her hands together as she sat down. "There's something about him. I know he could do it."

Iggy smiled. "You've got Joe's number all right."

Camille shot him a stern glance.

"Who's Joe?" Jackie said. Her arms were crossed and she slumped in the chair.

"Don't worry about it now," Camille said. "You're safe

here. I'll get you some clothes in a few minutes." Camille held herself back. Camille was afraid that, if she pushed too fast, she would never get anything useful from her.

"I'm so sorry I look like this, but I had to get away. He was in the bedroom. I couldn't get to my clothes."

"Smart move," Iggy said. "He would've popped you."

Jackie's bloodshot eyes grew wide. "You know Brian, don't you?"

"*Brian* and I go way back." Iggy nodded. "He can be quite a charmer when he wants to, but you don't fuck with him. He's a mean son of a bitch."

"His name isn't Brian, is it?" Tears ran down her face. Jackie looked up and took a deep breath. "This is going to sound crazy and I know I already look crazy, but I'm pretty sure Brian's a spy."

"We both know him as Joe Chronister," Camille said. "He's been a CIA case officer since Vietnam."

"I knew it. It was all a lie," Jackie said over and over, crying as she rocked herself. "I married some fake person." She cried harder.

Camille and Iggy volleyed glances. Iggy shrugged his shoulders and Camille rolled her eyes at him as she got up to retrieve a box of tissues. She handed it to Jackie and put her hand on her shoulder while they waited for her to calm down. As far as Camille was concerned, emotions were obstacles to be controlled and defeated, not something to be processed. Her own feelings made her uncomfortable and other people's were worse. She poured a glass of water, then handed it to Jackie, then she sat down on the couch beside Iggy.

The tears seemed to slow and Jackie grew quiet except for snorting sounds. She wiped her cheeks and nose with a tissue. "I'm sorry. I shouldn't bother you, but I know he was going to do it. Ray couldn't save me, he said. No one could."

"Who's Ray?" Iggy said.

"Ray—that's what he called himself. I don't know his real name. You were looking for him when you dropped by the apartment. Ray rescued me."

"His real name is Hunter Stone. Why did your husband say Hunter couldn't save you?"

"He told me Ray, uh, Hunter wasn't coming back." Jackie's voice cracked. She started to cry again.

"Everything's going to be okay. You don't need to cry. You're safe here and we're going to save Hunter. I promise," Camille said, keeping her words slow and steady as if she were trying to talk a jumper off a window ledge.

Jackie bowed her head, wiped away tears, then blew her nose. "Sorry."

"We need to know everything he said about Hunter. Everything, even if it doesn't seem very important to you."

Jackie nodded. "Brian, uh, Joe said he was taking Ray to his favorite place tomorrow. He said something about taking the gloves off for a man-to-man talk."

"Where the hell is that?" Iggy said.

"He's been working on some big project for the last couple of years. I know that's what he meant." She blew her nose into an already soaked tissue. "He wouldn't tell me a thing. He disappears for days, sometimes weeks at a time. That's how I knew he wasn't really an oil exec. He kept going to the same place, but there's no oil there."

Iggy held up his prosthetic hand. "Hold on a minute. I thought you said he wouldn't tell you where he was going."

"He wouldn't. I figured it out from the dirt on his shoes when he got home. I'm a forensic soil scientist." She sniffed loudly, sucking the phlegm back into her sinuses. It grossed Camille out even more than the constant nose blowing. "I don't know what his project is about, but whatever it is, I have absolutely no doubt it's somewhere near Zarafshan, Uzbekistan."

"You can be that specific?" Camille said.

"Only because I analyzed a zillion samples from the Muruntau gold deposits there for a summer job when I was in grad school. I was bored out of my mind and I used to study the microflora. I discovered a new member of the *Terfeziaceae* family—a desert truffle—on the roots of a . . . You don't want to hear all of this, do you?"

"I've heard enough to believe you know what you're talking about," Camille said, smiling to reassure her. "Did your husband ever mention SHANGRI-LA or BALI HAI?"

Jackie knit her eyebrows and stared into the room for a few moments. "You know, he did. One time when he came back from Uzbekistan and I asked him where he had been, he said he'd been to SHANGRI-LA. I thought he was just being his usual asshole self."

Camille and Iggy finished the interview and Camille gave Jackie a towel and some fresh clothes. She showed her into the trailer's bathroom so she could freshen up.

Iggy looked at Camille and sighed. "You were great with her. But please don't make me ever go through another interrogation like that again. I'd rather take a cattle prod to some guy's cajones. I don't know how therapists can stand it. Hell, a full day of that touchy-feely stuff and I'd fry my own nuts."

Camille laughed. "Use my computer and get some overheads of Zarafshan. There's an old KGB prison in the mountains north of there, near all the gold mines. You won't be able to see the prison—it's constructed inside an abandoned mineshaft." Camille walked to the sink and filled a coffee carafe with water, then poured it into her Braun coffeemaker. She wasn't about to go to Central Asia undercaffeinated.

"How the hell do you know all of that?"

"I was there on one of my first jobs with my dad—old Soviet days. The name was *gora*-something. You'll have to check with the spooks. I totally forgot about it. It was an

Agency contract to take out one of their own before the KGB softened him up to much." Camille shoveled coffee into the filter, spilling some on the stainless-steel counter.

"You don't have to make it strong just for me."

"You can water it down." She wiped up the grinds. "The KGB prison was built inside a mountain in an old gold mine that dated back to tsarist days before they started open pit mines in the region. It was an impossible job to get to anyone in there."

"Right. Your father didn't know the word impossible. How'd Charlie pull it off?"

"It wasn't his usual surgical work. We used the air vents. There was no other way. He felt horrible about it. I was thirteen, a kid on my first real mission behind the Iron Curtain. I just thought it was cool."

"You probably put a lot of poor bastards out of their misery." Iggy turned the computer on. "So the Agency's running an old KGB prison in Uzbekistan—one more hellhole under new management. I bet the Rubicon tie-in is that they've used those guys instead of Halliburton to renovate it for them. You know I don't have any qualms about doing whatever we have to do to keep our country safe, but why the hell do we have to use the same goddamn facilities the KGB did their dirty work in? I fought those monsters for years. We were the good guys, taking down the Evil Empire. It gets to me to know our guys are using the same electrodes, the same tubs . . ."

"You don't think we need to do it?" Camille turned on the coffeemaker, then retrieved cream from the fridge.

"I'm not saying that at all. The tangos aren't playing by any rules. You have to get rough with them if you want to find out anything."

"Seems to me like most of what you get that way is junk. The poor bastards say anything to make it stop."

"You know, Camille, interrogation is an art. The real masters can extract pure information. The problem is anybody can torture someone. Not everyone who can cut open a head is a brain surgeon. You get the jerk-offs who get off on it and the idiots who'll keep going cause they don't know how to evaluate the detainee's potential. Sometimes the torturers themselves make up shit. But then there are real masters. They're the ones who know when to quit."

"Not to change the subject, but I don't want to think any more than I have to about what they're doing to Hunter." Camille leaned against the counter while she waited on the coffeemaker. "GENGHIS and I need to get moving as soon as we nail down a plan. I'd like to bring in some serious hardware and some top operators from our Afghan shop."

"You know you can't do that. You have to have a light footprint. Find the nearest airstrip and take your best shots. The middle of the desert, they won't be running security quite as tight as elsewhere."

"Yeah, you're right." Camille pointed toward the bathroom. "Any suggestions on what to do with her?"

"That lady needs help—serious help. Joe's really fucked her. You know he's been widowed twice, don't you? I don't remember the details. Don't have to."

"He would've gotten away with it again. I'd like to nail his ass."

"Accidents happen." Iggy typed, using all the fingers on his left hand and hunting and pecking with his right. "We have to police our own. I hate it, but sometimes, it's the only justice. All I need is one more story I can't tell."

"You're saying we should take out Joe in some kind of vigilante justice?"

"It's been done before."

"I'm ready to grab him and see if we can extract specifics about where he's taking Hunter."

"He's not the type who'll break quickly."

"The voice of experience?" As soon as she got the words out, she wished she hadn't asked. Iggy was a good man and she liked to believe in good men.

"You don't want to know, do you?"

Camille pulled a box of corn flakes from the cupboard that Pete had recently stocked. "I guess we can fly her on a Hawk to Amman or Kuwait City and send her off to the States from there."

"Hell, Joe's got his hands so full, you could have a press conference send-off from the Baghdad airport and he wouldn't know it. Send some boys with her on Route Irish to Baghdad International or if you're feeling generous, a bird could drop her off there." Iggy entered something into the computer. "This is weird. I'm using our account to order Ikonos images and they're showing all satellite pictures for Uzbekistan are unavailable. I've tried several dates including one three years from now and nothing's working."

"Could be a Web site problem. They go over Uzbekistan several times a day when they're shooting Afghanistan. You think someone bought them all up?" The coffeemaker gurgled. Camille removed the pot before it was finished brewing and poured a cup into a mug with the Black Management black panther logo.

"Doesn't make sense. Why would you want to keep people from looking at some underground facility you couldn't see from the sky anyway?"

"Maybe SHANGRI-LA is aboveground, though I'll still put money on it that they're using the old KGB haunts."

"That's a given," Iggy said. "You always use whatever's already there. Look at what we do here. Not knocking down Abu Ghraib was obviously stupid, but we use all of Saddam's old facilities. I'll check in with the spooks and see what the KGB had going on in that neck of Kyzyl Kum. Looks like you're going to be tripping down memory lane there."

SIXTY-FIVE

Camp Tornado Point, Anbar Province

He should've snapped Jackie's goddamn neck when he had a chance, Joe Chronister told himself as he tried to find a chair with four legs in the former Iraqi Army brig. The place was such a dump that Rubicon hadn't bothered to take it over even though it was in their corner of the sprawling Camp Tornado Point compound. It smelled like an old slaughterhouse and it probably was. But the cells were intact and that was all that mattered since he had to hold Stone incognito somewhere away from the temptation of Camille's bounty. It sure beat an empty shipping container for ventilation. Three shooters, a black hood and an old key were all that he needed to hold Stone and a couple of his friends until he had the final piece he needed to start their transfer to Fuckistan.

He heard a car drive up and one of his men escorted Larry Ashland inside.

"My god, how do you stand this smell?" Ashland said, squinting his eyes.

"Hadn't noticed."

Chronister sat on the best chair he could find, then shoved one toward Ashland, who stared at the grimy wooden seat but didn't sit down. The pussy didn't have a clue they were on to him.

"It won't kill ya," Chronister said.

"Where's Stone?"

"You'll see him soon enough."

"I did not appreciate the rough handling on the way in. And I don't understand why they had to impound my weapons." Ashland flicked imaginary dirt from his starched white shirt.

"Can't be too careful around operators like Stone." Chronister pulled out a pack of cigarettes and held it out to Ashland. "Want one?"

"They'll kill you."

"Lot of things do that." Chronister lit his cigarette, looking over Ashland. "Working the Iraqi side of the op, you have to be curious what it's all about—how your little piece fits into the big picture. I was thinking it's time to take you to check out BALI HAI. You know, you can get a good look at SHANGRI-LA from there."

"BALI HAI. Not SHANGRI-LA?"

"You haven't figured it out yet, have you? BALI HAI's the prison; SHANGRI-LA's the project." Chronister took a long drag from the cigarette and felt an immediate rush. He had waited a couple of years for the opportunity to screw Ashland. He'd despised the fucker from the first time they had met. "Here's the deal. We're transferring Stone and a couple others overland to an out-of-the-way airstrip. No one's going to be watching for him. A Rubicon rendition flight will ferry them from there to Uzbekistan. You'll tag along."

"So SHANGRI-LA *is* in Uzbekistan?" Ashland nodded his head.

"Yeah and you can send a postcard to Paris from there. They have some nice ones with those turquoise blue domes—"

"What are you talking about?" His countenance fell and he was suddenly very serious.

"You tell me." Chronister drew his Glock and yelled for the guards. "My wife left me this morning. I'd love to kill someone right now, so don't push me, you fucking spy."

"I didn't touch your wife."

"Spoken like a true Frenchman."

A guard shoved Ashland down onto the gritty floor and plastic-cuffed his hands behind his back. "What the hell is this about?"

"We nailed a spy a few days ago on the Syrian border. And that man was a talker. Something he said about a spy and SHANGRI-LA started ringing bells. Next thing you know, I've got a file on my desk about some DGSE agent with your ugly mug in it." Chronister took a long drag from his cigarette, then blew smoke toward Ashland. "And what were you French thinking, calling your espionage agency the DGSE? Now KGB, CIA, SIS, those are cool, spy-cool. But DGSE sounds like some bankrupt trucking company." Chronister grinned and shook his head. "You know, you can either cop to it now in a civilized conversation or later when we start plucking off those manicured fingernails. Make it easy on yourself."

"Then Stone didn't tell you? You know about me from the other agent?" Ashland laughed. "He didn't understand, did he?"

"Stone didn't tell me a fucking thing. I tried some dumb-ass new interrogation method I learned at a seminar from an FBI guy. Didn't work worth a damn, but don't worry, we don't use that touchy-feely stuff at BALI HAI. It's strictly old school."

"What do you want from me?"

"I want to know what you French thought you were doing, nosing around a CIA operation. I thought we were all friends?"

"We used to be. Then you started kidnapping innocent civilians and torturing them in your secret prisons. You start wars under the pretext of preventing Saddam from getting nuclear devices, even though you know he doesn't have them—because you manufactured the evidence. Now America and its corporations are addicted to the War on Terror like a user to heroin. Your president flouts your laws and constitution. And what do the American people do? They supersize another order of French fries."

"When are you French ever going to get it through your

heads that you don't matter? *La Grand Nation* ain't a superpower. Hell, France isn't even a player. I'll never understand why you think you guys have to butt into other people's business."

"We have an obligation to defend freedom and democracy—something America *used* to understand."

"And I supersize my freedom fries." Chronister crushed his cigarette out against Ashland's cheek. "We're going to have some fun together. I can tell."

SIXTY-SIX

The CIA has been hiding and interrogating some of its most important al Qaeda captives at a Soviet-era compound in Eastern Europe,
according to U.S. and foreign officials familiar with the arrangement.

The secret facility is part of a covert prison system set up by
the CIA nearly four years ago that at various times has included
sites in eight countries
—THE WASHINGTON POST, November 2, 2005, as reported by
Dana Priest

The current transfers mean that there are now no terrorists in the
CIA [black site/prison] program. . . .

[T]he Supreme Court's recent decision has impaired our ability
to prosecute terrorists through military commissions, and has put
in question the future of the CIA [black site/prison] program.
—PRESIDENT GEORGE W. BUSH, Address to the nation,
September 6, 2006

Camp Raven, The Green Zone, Baghdad

Camille shoved a Leupold Mark 4 spotting scope into a
small suitcase stuffed with clothes she didn't like and
planned on dumping along with her other props as soon as
she passed Uzbek customs. She stuck an encrypted Irid-
ium satellite phone into a day pack. A few years ago she
would have been pushing it to take such an advanced communications device along, but with the proliferation of cell
phones, she doubted the border guards would take a second glance. "Hey, I thought you were picking up everything in-country like a good little assassin," Iggy said as he
stood in the middle of the small trailer and watched her
pack. "What's with the scope?"

"All you can count on getting there is old Russian equipment. I love Dragunovs, but their iron sights suck. The Russians have some great optics, but they can be hard to come by." Camille tossed a pair of Zeiss binoculars and a birding field guide to Central Asia into the small suitcase. "As long as I look like some nutty birder after a scissor-tailed whatever, Uzbek border guards won't think twice about a good spotting scope.

"Any sign of GENGHIS?" Camille said as she sorted through a stack of T-shirts, trying to lighten the load in the suitcase.

"None and I don't like it," Iggy said, shaking his head. "He told Pete he was off to a massage parlor last night after she showed him his rack. Our boys have quizzed every whore in the bubble. No luck."

"You think he's our mole?"

"He's a son of a bitch, but he's no traitor. I think someone didn't want him going with you."

"Not good." Camille stopped packing and looked up at Iggy. "Any word on the overheads?"

"That's why I dropped by." Iggy grinned. "I put the spooks to work on it. Best they could get from Ikonos was that two years ago some company called Tasopé bought up all their satellite images over Uzbekistan—for the next three years."

"Who owns Tasopé?"

"It's like opening one of those Russian nesting dolls—a bunch of shells. The mother company was an outfit called CRH Salvage. It's got a dozen names on its board of directors."

"Who are they?"

"Most of them are high-net-worth types—the kind you'd expect to be doing angel capital investments. The interesting thing is they only own forty-eight percent. Controlling interest is held by three mystery men. The spooks said they went through something like forty-six databases and nada. Can you imagine three people who've never had a credit card or a piece of junk mail to their name?"

"That has the Agency's fingerprints all over it."

"Get this, their birth dates were all in the forties, fifties and sixties, but the social security numbers were all issued in the past five years. Here's the kicker: they all have post office boxes in Arlington and Chevy Chase."

"So a CIA proprietary company is buying up every private satellite image of Uzbekistan for the next three years. The Agency is definitely up to something big there." Camille zipped up the carry-on suitcase.

"Hold on. We've got more. The boys at Lyon are good. When this is all over, we really ought to think about buying them up." Iggy picked up Camille's suitcase and carried it to the door of her trailer.

"You're not using our in-house spooks?"

"They're busy planning your trip. Had to outsource it to the friendly competition." Iggy carried her suitcase down the steps. Camille reached for the handle, but he pulled it away. "I got it. As I was saying, one of the guys recognized a name from the work we threw them a few weeks ago researching Rubicon's holdings."

"Overlapping directors?"

"Yup. One name—Garry Hoyes. Someone messed up and used him twice. Hoyes shows up on the board of directors of both a Rubicon subsidiary and one of the Agency's proprietary companies—Tasopé. The Lyon analyst caught it because he once had a neighbor in Philly by that name, so it jumped right out at him."

"So this confirms both the Agency and Rubicon are closely linked, but we pretty much knew that already. And we now know both are up to something secret in Uzbekistan, but we don't know they're working together on the same thing," Camille said. She felt bad he was carrying her bag, but the sun-baked sand of the compound was as hard as concrete and he could've rolled it. "But I'd bet anything they are cooperating. Rubicon has to be working under an Agency contract, otherwise there's no money in it."

"There's more. I was talking to some old Agency compadres about the black sites—you know, the prisons. Seems the heat's been on ever since that *Post* reporter broke the story that the Agency's running its own gulag system. The Poles and Romanians kicked them out. That Supreme Court ruling extending the Geneva Convention to detainees really mucked things up."

"Interesting, but what does that have to do with Hunter?"

"Hold on. The Agency's been scrambling to come up with a new way to keep control over prisoners and interrogations. Word is they've privatized." Iggy raised his voice, trying to be heard over the roar of the generators.

Camille stopped walking and looked at him. "You're kidding? You mean the Agency is using contractors to run their secret prisons?"

"Privately run prisons are a billion-dollar industry back home. Makes sense to me. They're a proven concept."

"Let me guess, another sole-source provider contract so they didn't have to open it up for competitive bids. Damn. I'd like to have had that one. We never get anything decent from them other than knuckle-dragger gigs from the SAD." She hated prisons, but knew they could be a good way to diversify her company if they could somehow land a contract. She could always hire someone else to run them.

"I heard that Fred Avocet gave Rubicon the contract right before he retired to work for them. Cofer was furious when Fred outmaneuvered him. He was sure Total Intel and Blackwater had it in the bag." Iggy stepped into the shade of a palm. Its fronds rustled in the light breeze which carried smoke and soot from the burn pit.

The sun burned Camille's face and she moved into the shade with Iggy. "Last I heard, the Agency only outsourced torture to shifty governments, not private companies."

"They use their own guys for the heart-to-hearts. It's the facility management they've outsourced, along with detainee transport. Remember the president's speech about how the CIA was no longer in the business of black sites? He was telling the truth, more or less. The CIA isn't doing it anymore—Rubicon is."

"Any idea what the money's like?"

"Margins are supposed to be terrific. I'll make some calls and get the specifics." Iggy's Gargoyles sunglasses slid down his nose and he pushed them back into place as he started walking toward the helicopters. "You know, it's brilliant. The Agency for once is actually looking ahead and positioning itself for the future. Bush isn't going to be around forever. If the next president's a bleeding-heart liberal, first day in office he'll repeal the presidential finding that allows black sites. Even Clinton let us outsource interrogations to the Third World, so I'm sure that'll still be an option, but so much of what they give you is self-serving shit. You need control of your own interrogations. That's the beauty of outsourcing: you can do whatever the fuck you want. You don't need a presidential finding because you're not the SOB doing it—the contractor is. Things go south, the contractor went too far. And god only knows if any laws apply to them. Geneva Conventions sure as hell don't. So much for that Supreme Court ruling. It's a beautiful workaround."

Pete pulled up beside them in the Gator as they approached the rows of helicopters. A Little Bird lifted into the air.

"News?" Camille shouted over the roar of engines.

"The spooks are buzzing that the spy our boys nabbed a few days ago in Syria led to the bust of some big French agent," Pete said as she turned the Gator off and pulled up the parking brake.

"I meant about GENGHIS."

"Not a trace. He must've split. Guys here do that sometimes—or maybe he was our mole and he couldn't take it."

Camille didn't believe for a second that GENGHIS would betray her, but she wouldn't put it past any of the guys to suddenly take off or shift over to another company. They did it all the time. "Guess I'm off to Ukraine alone." Especially after GENGHIS' disappearance, Camille wanted to keep the final destination as compart-mentalized as possible and tell only those who absolutely had a need to know. Rubicon had to keep believing she was after their wild Ukrainian goose so their Uzbek operations weren't put on the alert. She walked under the giant rotors of a Black Hawk and waved at Beach Dog, who was sitting in the pilot's seat. He pointed his thumb and little finger to the ground in the Hawaiian wave he always did.

"You need two shooters for your plan to have half a chance," Iggy said as he lifted Camille's suitcase into the crew area of the helicopter.

"You coming with me?" Camille looked over the top of her custom-made Oakley sunglasses.

"You asking? Thought you didn't want to risk taking along a tin man." He knocked on his artificial hand.

"Where we're headed, there's no chance of rust. I thought about what I said earlier. I was wrong. I need someone I can trust and right now, the three of us are the only ones I'm absolutely sure about."

"I'll go." Pete glanced at a Little Bird as it seemed to circle central Baghdad. "I'm a damn good shooter and you won't find anyone better at scrounging up whatever you need."

"I've got to grab my dumb leg and extra batteries for my combat arm. Like it or not, I'm going to snag a third opera-tor. We need someone for a third position to provide secu-rity. I'll be back in a flash." Iggy sprinted over to the Gator and drove off. Camille remembered that he'd had problems with the smart leg in loose sand before and she assumed he wanted to minimize the risk of electronic failures since the bendable ankle wasn't all that critical to the mission.

Camille took off her sunglasses and wiped the lenses on her shirt. Pete stood there, staring at her, waiting for something.

"Pete," Camille said. "I need someone I can trust back here just in case."

"We all know you can trust Virgil. He'd be the one you'd call anyway. I'm a good spotter, too, and you're going to need all the help you can get if Hunter's going to have half a chance. I've watched your back for years. Don't cut me out of the real action."

Camille squinted as she stared at Pete, trying to make up her mind. Pete had the expression of a little girl, begging to be taken along with the big kids. Camille preferred working alone and she had her father's old contacts to get the equipment they needed, but things always came up. Pete had more than once proven her loyalty and she felt bad about having been short with her lately. "Okay. You'll go as far as Tashkent, help us with the staging, then leave the country when we proceed to the target. You've got fifteen minutes to pack and tag someone to take care of the woman in my trailer and get her to the States." Camille patted the side of the Black Hawk. "This bird lifts off at eleven-hundred with or without you."

SIXTY-SEVEN

The airplane is a Gulfstream V turbojet, the sort favored by CEOs and celebrities. But since 2001 it has been seen at military airports from Pakistan to Indonesia to Jordan, sometimes being boarded by hooded and handcuffed passengers. . . . [T]he agency is flying captured terrorist suspects from one country to another for detention and interrogation. The CIA calls this activity "rendition."

—The Washington Post, Dec. 27, 2004, as reported by Dana Priest

Private American contractors who help the CIA capture terrorism suspects abroad and transfer them to secret jails are increasingly becoming the target of investigations in Europe and at home. . . . In some cases, inquiries focus on companies that appear to be thinly veiled CIA fronts. . . . But in other cases, scrutiny by European investigators and human rights advocates has focused on mainstream companies whose part-time work for the CIA now threatens to leave a permanent mark on their reputations.

—The Boston Globe, December 11, 2005, as reported by Farah Stockman

The Next Day

Hunter's arms ached from being cuffed behind his back for so long; he guessed they had been riding in the van for ten or twelve hours. A black hood covered his head and they wouldn't allow him to talk, but he could sense at least four other prisoners on the transfer with him. He figured they were either taking him overland to Syria or to an airstrip so remote there was no chance of Black Management noticing them. His bladder was full and it hurt when he shifted his weight. At least just before the trip they had given him an MRE to eat, the first food he'd had in days. It wasn't enough, but he could feel some strength returning. With little warning, the vehicle came to a stop. They opened the door and hot air rushed inside. It was heavy with the smell of jet fuel.

So it was going to be a rendition flight—a secret flight to a secret prison.

Someone pulled his arm and he tried to climb out, but his legs were shackled with plastic zip-ties. He fell onto the hard ground, smacking his right shoulder. Someone laughed.

He climbed to his feet, then a guard unhooked the hood and pulled it off. The bright morning sun hurt his eyes and it unnerved him that they were allowing the prisoners to see the guards' faces. Clearly they were on a one-way trip.

There were three other prisoners. Scott Miller, a fellow Bushman from Force Zulu, nodded recognition. Hunter recognized a man with a funky jawline beard as a retired Delta operator, GENGHIS, who worked for Black - Management. Suddenly things were looking up. He had no idea how Stella managed to infiltrate the group of prisoners, but he was confident she had something clever worked out.

A guard had trouble with the buckle of the last man's hood. When he finally got it open and took it off, Hunter couldn't believe what he was seeing. The hook nose, deep-set eyes and chin that was too short for the face Hunter could've recognized anywhere. In fact he had—among the Taliban in Afghanistan, in the insurgent safe house, in the Rubicon offices in the middle of the night. He was staring at the man who had started Hunter on this entire hellish journey when he accused him of selling arms to the tangos: Ashland.

Now absolutely nothing made sense as he stood with his accuser, both of them cuffed, wearing Day-Glo prison jumpsuits and about to board a one-way flight on the torture shuttle.

Hunter laughed for the first time in days.

One guard was close enough for Hunter to take out, but the other two stood at a distance with their AKs pointing at the prisoners as they shuffled toward an American-flagged Gulfstream V, registration number N379P. Hunter had always wanted a chance to fly the latest Gulfstream, but somehow he didn't think he was going to get his wish today. His arms cuffed behind his back made escape difficult, but not impossible. The Rubicon guards hardly knew what they were doing and most of them were foreign nationals imported from low-wage countries, no doubt a Rubicon cost-saving measure that padded its already fat margins.

Back when there was at least some limited cooperation between Force Zulu and the OGA, Hunter and his teammates had prepared dozens of suspected terrorists for rendition flights. They called the process "a twenty-minute takeout" because that's all the time it took to package a prisoner for a safe flight. In contrast to the Rubicon staff, Hunter and his teammates had takeouts down to a fine art. Dressed in black with their faces covered like ninjas, they communicated with one another through hand signals. He had always kind of enjoyed doing it because of the slick teamwork involved—and because he was convinced they were packaging another bad guy who wanted to harm America. The rendition team took a blindfolded tango into a small room, shoved him to the floor, cut off his clothes and conducted a full body cavity search. Afterwards, they removed the blindfold and snapped a photograph before what Hunter thought was the grossest part: they shoved a sedative up the tango's ass. Then they diapered him, stuck him in a prison jumpsuit, shackled him, and shoved an earplug headset on him. As soon as they had bagged the tango's head in a long, dark hood, the takeout was ready for pickup.

The thought of takeout made Hunter hungry. Chinese. Man, he'd love some cashew chicken right about now.

The poorly trained Rubicon guards hadn't thought of diapers, so he yelled at one he guessed was Filipino. "Dude, do me a favor and unzip my pants and hold my dick. I've got to go bad."

"Piss your pants," the guard said.

Hunter motioned toward the Gulfstream with his head. "That looks like one of those fancy executive jets. You really want me to whiz on the leather seats?"

"I not touch your dick."

"Up to you if you want to smell piss for the next few hours."

The American supervisor sighed. "Hold on. As soon as I cut you out, you have to immediately put your hands in front for me to cuff you again. You take as much as a second to think about it and you're full of lead."

Another guard kept his AK aimed at Hunter and he knew the time wasn't right, but he could work with arms zip-tied in front. The guard sliced through the cuffs and Hunter complied while he fastened him back up.

"Do it yourself now. Hurry."

"Thanks." As Hunter turned away from the group and fumbled with his zipper, he heard the other guys requesting the same accommodation. Peeing on the sand, he focused on the rush of relief, knowing he had to grab every little pleasure he could. Things were only going to get worse.

They were individually marched onto the plane and chained into their seats, but their hands were left fastened in front and the hoods were left off. Genghis was placed in the seat directly behind Hunter. He wanted to know Stella's plan immediately, but he couldn't risk the guards noticing any communication between him and GENGHIS. He would have to be patient and wait for GENGHIS to find the right opportunity to inform him.

When they hit cruising altitude, the guards passed out more MREs and threw them bottled water. Whatever they were going to do with him, they didn't intend to starve him into compliance. He ripped open the white plastic pouch. Just his luck—it was a frickin veggie burger in BBQ sauce. He devoured it and asked for seconds to try to regain his strength. They were stupid enough to give him another. This time he was luckier, he thought, as he read the outside of the pouch: meatloaf with gravy. Then he tore it open and a package of Charms fell out and onto the floor.

"Crap," he said to himself. Unlucky Charms, It seemed that whenever someone in the crew had eaten the Charms hard candy packed in an MRE, they had been ambushed or nearly had bit it from an IED. He had heard so many freaky stories about those cursed things, he couldn't understand why the Pentagon hadn't banned them. He kicked them under the seat in front of him.

The Gulfstream seats really were leather and Hunter felt comfortable for the first time in days—for the first time since he had been snuggled against Stella's soft body. She was all he could think of as he stared at the LCD view screen and watched the movement of an airplane icon along the projected flight path, south to the Persian Gulf, around Iran, then back north across the Pakistani air corridor. Stella had been so smooth, so wet.

Suddenly, it sunk in what he was looking at on the monitor. The flight plan overshot Afghanistan—they were headed deep into Uzbekistan.

"Okay, asswipes," the American guard said over the intercom. "We here at Air Rubicon know that you have a choice in your rendition flights and we're pleased you chose us. In a few minutes we'll be playing our *Halfway to Hell* game. The captain will be giving us important information on total miles flown, airspeed, headwinds and all that crap and whichever one of you can guess the closest time to our halfway mark, wins his very last cold beer. But before that, we're giving you your last shot at democracy and you get to choose the movie." He held up two DVDs. "We've got *Bourne Supremacy* with Matt Damon or the documentary *Manchurian Candidate* with Denzel Washington." He read the plot descriptions and the cover blurbs. "Okay, which flick will be the last one you ever see in your lives? Raise those cuffed paws if you want *Bourne*."

One of the guards snapped a picture with a digital camera of the prisoners with their cuffed hands in the air. They were far from professional and probably didn't have the training to handle any serious resistance, Hunter noted. He was pleased, too, that the dim lights for the movie would make it easier for GENGHIS to slip a message to him.

"Last call for *Bourne*," the guard said.

Hunter's choice was clear. One of the guys who had consulted on *Bourne* was a friend of his and even though they had some problems with their sniper weapons, some of the scenes were so realistic, they still gave him chills. He really didn't want to humor the guards by voting, but just in case it was his last movie, he raised his hands for *Bourne*.

A few minutes later, Hunter was getting into the chase scene in Goa, remembering one he had once had in Myanmar, when GENGHIS started kicking his seat. He was using Morse code.

Hunter couldn't figure out how the movie got to a crime scene in Berlin, but he didn't care while he concentrated on deciphering the message: "B-L-K—M-G-M-T."

Hunter moved his elbow back and forth between his body and the airframe where GENGHIS could see it, sometimes pulling it back quickly, other times leaving it there for a couple of seconds. "P-L-A-N?"

"N-O. C-A-P-T-U-R-E-D."

"F—"

SIXTY-EIGHT

> In Uzbekistan, he [Craig Murray, the former British Ambassador to Uzbekistan] said, "partial boiling of a hand or an arm is quite common." He also knew of two cases in which prisoners had been boiled to death.
> —THE NEW YORKER, February 14, 2005, as reported by Jane Mayer

Gora Muruntau, Kyzyl Kum Desert, Uzbekistan

The sun rose as Camille was lying on her belly in a ghillie suit in the saddle between two sand dunes, tasting dust, smelling of camel droppings and trying to become one with the desert. Every bug in the sun-baked wasteland seemed to have been waiting its entire existence for someone as sweet as she to come along, but she couldn't swat, she couldn't scratch. As a good sniper, she was the Kyzyl Kum and microterrain didn't claw at itself, no matter how badly it wanted to.

Iggy was positioned a good eight hundred meters away from her, across the runway at her twelve o'clock. The winds were still coming off the mountains as they did at night. In the day, when the desert floor heated up, the prevailing winds blew into the valleys and up the mountainsides. Since planes landed into the wind, Camille needed to make sure she and Iggy were positioned so that the main cabin door would be facing them. If it came in now, she would be the only shooter. As soon as the winds shifted, she would begin her slow creep to join Iggy's side of the runway so that they would both have a clear shot at the cabin door throughout the day.

Camille peered through the scope on the Dragunov sniper rifle, happy to be working with the gorgeous old girl again, particularly in such a grimy environment. As long as it wasn't over oiled, it could withstand a sandstorm without choking. The Dragunov was Soviet made—designed for abuse.

Gerbils scrambled across ripples of the red sand, but there was no sign of any larger life forms—or a jet for that matter. Hunter had better be on his way. If she had guessed wrong, she would never forgive herself, but this was the only airstrip within hundreds of kilometers aside from the commercial one at Zarafshan. The KGB had used this one to ferry prisoners to Gora Muruntau and if Rubicon was running the place now, they would do the same—she hoped.

She didn't like it that they were working without a net. The third operator that Iggy had brought along for overwatch was a longtime mercenary who had somehow caught the attention of Uzbek authorities. They had turned him away at the border. One man short, she and Iggy had decided to take Pete along to the target to provide some support, although they knew she couldn't handle being on her own in the third position.

Camille was a loner when it came to sniping. She didn't like doing it military style, working in teams of two, a sniper and a spotter, but Iggy had insisted that he could do it by himself and she wasn't about to challenge his abilities.

So Pete was working with her, lying prone off Camille's right calf, ready to help calculate distances and wind. Pete could drive her crazy with nonstop chatter, but today she was strangely quiet. She guessed Pete wasn't comfortable with the fact that she was about to help several people meet their deaths. Camille knew Pete hadn't seen much combat and she suspected she had never killed anyone. Camille didn't like killing either, but the mission required it and rescuing Hunter was worth ridding the world of a few more bad guys.

Camille scanned the skies for any sign of a plane, then studied a patch of dead weeds alongside the runway so she would be ready if one arrived. "Wind, south, southeast, twenty-two to twenty-five knots. Gusts at forty. Range me. Verify."

"Affirmative," Pete said.

"They've shifted." Camille slowly pulled a clunky Soviet-era walkie-talkie from her pack. "LIGHTNING SIX on the move."

Camille inched her body through the sand, beginning the long creep around the runway. Sand was pelting her, but at least her trail would be almost immediately covered.

An hour later Camille's forearms were burning from the coarse sand now embedded into her skin, but she and Pete were almost at the end of the runway—halfway.

Another hour later Camille and Pete had slithered the final inches to their new perch, some three hundred meters away from Iggy, with him at their three o'clock. The desert tasted saltier than in Iraq. Camille spat and slowly took a handful of peanut M&Ms from her pack and inched them to her mouth. The chocolate inside was liquid. She swirled it around in her mouth and chomped down on the peanuts as she set up the high powered rifle's bipod.

She studied tumbleweeds at the edge of the runway and recalculated the wind speed. The temperature had already climbed to one hundred and eleven and the humidity was so low she knew she had to take care not to overshoot the target; the round would easily tear through the hot, dry air. She could only guess where the plane would end its taxi and where her target would appear, so she calculated multiple ballistic scenarios, keenly aware that direct sun on the target could trick her into thinking it was farther away and any shadows combined with rising heat from the desert floor could jack her up just as easily.

Camille was lying in position on her belly, her weight supported by her left side and she was looking through her scope, studying plants for any change in the wind and distracting herself from worry about Hunter when Pete nudged her.

"Company," Pete said.

A small white van drove up the only access road, a dust trail blowing away from it in the strong wind. Only parts of the road were visible; the rest had returned to desert. The van crossed the runway and parked on the edge of the tarmac. The driver and passenger were both Caucasian, a Rubicon greeting party no doubt. Camille shoved in her earplugs.

"Watch the skies. They should be getting close." Camille double checked to make sure there were no unusual antennae mounted on the vehicle because she couldn't risk neutralizing them if they were in communication with the plane. There were none. "Hand me the radio." Camille called Iggy. "I count two."

"That's affirmative."

"I'm clear for both," Camille said.

"Same here. I'll take the passenger."

"Confirmed. Passenger is yours. Advise when target acquired. WILDCAT will countdown from three. Make contact on one." Camille turned her head slightly toward Pete. "Anything?"

"Negative." Pete searched the horizon.

Camille shoved the radio toward Pete, checked the wind, then the range to the van. The men sat inside with it running, probably enjoying the air conditioning. The crosswind of twenty-five knots would try to play games with the round. She adjusted the dope and confirmed her reading of five hundred seventy-five meters to the van.

The driver was a clean-cut blond, no older than thirty, wearing reflective sunglasses. Camille aimed just above them, at the middle of his forehead

Iggy's voice crackled over the radio. "Target acquired. Standing by."

"Start the count," Camille said to Pete.

"Three."

Camille took a deep breath.

"Two."

She held it.

"One."

She squeezed off.

Tariq was lying on a sand dune with his brother Habib, watching the abandoned Soviet-era airstrip through binoculars. He had seen the sleek private jets banking over the camp and more often than not, they came on Thursday afternoons and Monday mornings. It was time to practice his new reconnaissance skills on a real target. No one at al-Zahrani's midday teaching would miss him and his brother. He had shoved an al-Zahrani tract in his pocket to study so he didn't fall behind the others even though he didn't want to admit that he was growing weary of the lectures about purity within their ranks. He had left his family in Saudi Arabia to learn how to kill Westerners, not to purge their movement of other misguided Muslims. They were forbidden to leave the camp, but what good were skills at infiltration and evasion if they only tested them on each other? He'd had enough of the exercises with the other *mujahedin*. If he was going to succeed in New York, he needed real-world practice. Just as he had expected, he saw movement and followed it with his binoculars. Through a cloud of dust, he could see a white van approaching the runway.

Using binoculars, Tariq was studying the infidels in the van when he saw the driver's forehead explode in a spray of blood and flesh. As he refocused he saw the passenger's head fall forward, even though the body remained upright, the seat belt holding it in place. Tariq immediately scanned the dunes, but the sniper was invisible.

He whispered to his brother, "Go to the base. Inform Nasim the CIA plane is on its way. We will smite the infidels here, *masha'allah*—Allah's will."

"But we're not supposed to be here. We'll get lashings."

"Trust me. Nasim is the one who first pointed the plane out to me. He will understand. Go!"

His brother nodded and ran down the dune. Tariq remained on his belly, studying every weed, every pattern in the sand, dreaming of being that sniper, hidden like a scorpion in the dunes.

He watched and waited.

Camille reloaded, expecting to see the jet at any moment. No plane arrived. A half hour passed, then an hour, but still no plane. "Maybe they're not coming," Pete said, the first thought she had volunteered all day.

SIXTY-NINE

"I know that the Americans have brought people back to Uzbekistan from Bagram Airport in order to be interrogated and that those people have been brought back by the Americans, on American planes, with American personnel." Murray [former British Ambassador to Uzbekistan] says there's no doubt western intelligence knows the information it's getting is gained under torture, [and] as Ambassador he sent a [British] Embassy official to the US mission in Tashkent to make sure. "She reported back to me that the CIA Chief there said yes, you're right. I guess this material would have been obtained under torture."

—FOREIGN CORRESPONDENT, ABC-TV [AUSTRALIA], March 29, 2005, Ambassador Craig Murray, as interviewed by Evan Williams

Gora Muruntau, Kyzyl Kum Desert, Uzbekistan

Hunter looked outside the window as the Gulfstream descended. The landscape made him feel even farther away from home, farther away from Stella. The desolate valley looked like what was left long after the flames of hell had burned themselves out. The desert floor was scarred with the biggest quarries he'd ever seen, gashes in the earth stretching for miles and miles. The open pits themselves were terraced swirls of lifeless dirt, switchbacks into the depths. The sand and rock cleaved from the ground had been dumped in mounds of rubble that were collapsing back into the abandoned pits. The earth had been gutted and the innards left to rot.

Uzbekistan was where the Earth came to die.

Once they were inside a high security facility, he knew they would have little hope of escape and none of rescue.

Rubicon would never allow him to come out alive and he would much rather die fighting on a desolate runway than from torture or neglect. Taking over the Gulfstream was his only chance. He stretched as best he could, given the plastic cuffs on his wrists and ankles. His body had to be ready when they de-planed. If he and the other prisoners could find the right opportunity, maybe even one of them would survive. They were an even match with the guards—four prisoners, four guards. The flight crew seemed to stay huddled inside the cockpit, probably some well-paid flyboys who understood that the less they knew about their passengers, the safer they were. As long as the pilots weren't directly endangered, he doubted they would aid the guards in a rumble.

He knew he could trust the skills of Miller and GENGHIS and he was certain they would jump in if an opportunity presented itself, but he wasn't so sure about Ashland—or whoever he was. With Hunter's luck, the bastard would be the only one who came out alive.

As the plane banked, he spotted the landing strip and a vehicle waiting to meet the plane. He couldn't see how many were inside, but his clenched gut told him the odds had just gotten a little worse.

"Plane at eleven o'clock, turning into the wind to land," Pete said, kneeling in position a little behind Camille, to her right.

As Camille searched for the plane, she thought she saw Pete check her sidearm. The sparse desert terrain made it unlikely that someone could approach them without notice, but it never hurt to be vigilant. She reached to her right leg and made sure that her new Spetsnaz combat knife was in its thigh holster.

"Wind twenty-five to thirty knots. Verify," Camille said. The blowing sand felt like a hard rain, scratching at her face.

Pete looked through her scope. "Verified."

Camille added a click to the right to compensate for the wind.

The small jet taxied to a stop in a sand-covered part of the tarmac, on the edge of the range Camille had anticipated. Iggy had the better position. The additional meters would add several mils of inaccuracy to her shot, but that would be more than made up for because at that distance the bullet would be silent, friction from the air having slowed it enough to lose the crackling sound it made traveling at the speed of sound. She could get off multiple rounds before anyone noticed or could triangulate her position—not that she had any intention of breaking her perfect record: one shot, one kill.

"Range me to the airframe," Camille said.

"Eight-two-five."

"Negative. Eight-five-zero," Camille said. "Verify."

"Negative. Eight-two-five. Check your dope."

Camille checked the settings, but was sure they were correct.

The plane sat on the runway while the engines spooled down. After five minutes, the airstairs were lowered and a man appeared in the doorway, a mil dot above Camille's crosshairs. He was blond, average build and had what looked like a Russian version of an M4 at his side.

"Radio Iggy. First target acquired."

Tariq had learned a thing or two about stealth in the training camp, not that he really needed it. Whoever the sniper was, he was focused upon the runway, not Tariq approaching from behind. As he crept closer, he saw a white jet coming in for a landing.

The hot desert air took Hunter's breath away as he stepped through the jet's doorway, tactical scenarios running through his head. Whoever was picking them up was smart enough to keep a distance. A meter ahead of him, a guard stepped from the stairs onto the tarmac, looking around, his eyebrows knit.

Something was wrong.

Camille watched through her scope as the first prisoner stooped, exiting with the top of his head pointed at her. He looked up and she saw his face.

Hunter—thank god.

She caught sight of the second prisoner climbing down the stairs.

GENGHIS?

Pete took a long, deep breath, but it didn't clear her head. Her body dripped with sweat. Camille had been good to her, but Joe Chronister was not a man who bluffed. He would make sure the unsolved murder at Fort Bliss was reopened with new evidence that would send Pete to prison for life. She couldn't go through that.

Pete cocked the Makarov.

Hunter saw no cover, nowhere to run. The landing strip was between dunes with so little microterrain, the sand looked like it was in constant motion. He was actually surprised they hadn't swallowed the landing strip. The lead guard keyed his radio, calling for the absent greeting party. Something wasn't going according to plan which meant the guards were off-balance, even if for a few seconds. Hunter flashed a glance at GENGHIS, who seemed to already be inching into position behind one of the guards.

Camille saw GENGHIS edging closer to her objective, but the shot was still clear. She inhaled deeply to steady herself, then exhaled. The shot felt good, so she slowly squeezed the trigger and fired. The recoil jerked the sight. Without a breath, she acquired the next target.

"I'm sorry," she heard Pete say.

Camille fired again. As she did, her peripheral vision caught Pete getting up from her prone position.

What the hell?

Hunter inched toward the guard closest to him, ready to teach him why he should never zip-tie a prisoner's hands in front. Though if all went well, he wouldn't have the chance to use the lesson. Stella's man GENGHIS was almost in position behind his mark. Without warning, a bullet blew through GENGHIS' target and exited from the back. A pink mist splattered GENGHIS and both men crumpled to the ground. Another guard swung around and sprayed rounds into Hunter's fellow Force Zulu operator, then turned toward Hunter.

At the same time Hunter dropped, a sniper's bullet cratered the guard's chest.

Camille glanced away from the shot to see Pete kneeling beside her, pointing a pistol at her. She didn't pause to think. Her right hand reached for her knife as she rolled out of the line of fire, toward Pete. With a single stroke, she sliced through Pete's Achilles tendon. The calf muscles seized and Pete collapsed toward her, bringing her throat down where Camille needed it. She thrust her knife into her neck. An aerosol of blood spurted out.

"Why?" Camille whispered as she rolled over, using the knife as a handle to pull Pete's body over hers to hasten death as the blade ripped through her trachea and arteries, dousing her in a fountain of blood. Sickening steam rose from the sun-baked sand. She couldn't understand it, but she didn't have time to figure it out. Kicking free from Pete's body, she twisted around and righted the Dragunov.

Iggy was mad that his first target had moved at the wrong moment and it had taken him two rounds to make the kill.

And now he couldn't get a clear shot at the fourth guard. He was sure Camille had it. He had been in the field and on the range with her several times. Cam was lightning. What was taking her so damn long?

On the tarmac, Hunter saw a guard get up and scramble toward the stairs. Just as the guy lifted his left foot toward the first step, Hunter rushed up behind him and spun around, pushing his left hip against the right side of the man's body. Back-to-back with the guard, Hunter threw his zip-tied hands over his right shoulder and looped them around the man's chin. Hunter dropped to his knees, twisting the neck until he felt it give. He brought his hands back over his own head, flipping the dead guard over his shoulder and onto the ground.

Now the four guards were dead and there was no sign of the ground crew. He picked up the AK-102 with his cuffed hands and stuck his head through the strap.

At that moment he heard the Gulfstream's engines spooling up, preparing for takeoff.

Blood soaked Camille's sand-caked hair and she tasted copper as she peered through the Dragunov's sights. One Rubicon escort was down with an apparent broken neck and GENGHIS lay on the ground beside another one, pressing on his upper arm as blood spurted out. She counted bodies of three other guards and one prisoner. Then she focused on Hunter and saw his head jerk around as if startled. A second later, she heard the roar and understood why: the engines were starting up.

She shifted her sights to the cockpit. If bird strikes could sometimes shatter the reinforced windshield, she was certain her round could do it. It might even extend her the favor of slowing the bullet enough so that it didn't damage anything beyond the flight crew. An unpressurized ride out of there would be breezier, lower and chillier than she would have liked, but she didn't see a lot of options. She checked the wind and ranged the target.

The captain would be first; she always respected the chain of command. She took a long breath and exhaled. The shot felt right. But as she started to squeeze the trigger, the plane started rolling while the airstairs were still retracting.

Hunter was hanging underneath the stairs. He swung himself up onto them and climbed into the plane.

Camille had to do her best to make sure Hunter saw her and knew she was there before the plane took off. Otherwise he could head anywhere and she might not find him. But she didn't want to chance someone else seeing her too soon. She took off the restrictive ghillie suit, stripping down to the T-shirt and shorts underneath, snatched up the radio and called Iggy as she ran, carrying the Dragunov. "Hold your position and give me some cover fire."

Even though she had spent the entire morning watching the empty desert, she still didn't want to chance sky-lining at the top of the dune or casting shadows at its base. She ran along its military crest, halfway down it, but the soft sand gave way under her feet and she slid with each step. She couldn't get any traction. It went against her training, but she would have to risk casting a shadow if she wanted to reach Hunter in time.

Hunter rode the airstairs up and rolled onto the cabin floor of the moving plane. The plastic ties bound his wrists and ankles, but there was no time to search for something sharp enough to free himself. He lay on his back in front of the cockpit door, clutching the compact assault rifle, as he set it to single fire mode. After 9/11, commercial flight deck doors were always locked, but they still needed break-away panels in case of explosive decompression. Knowing Rubicon's thriftiness, he doubted that they had even installed the latest security door. He pulled his legs back until his knees were over his chest, then he kicked the panel at the bottom of the door. It separated and flew into the flight deck. Hunter flipped around as fast as he could, targeted the captain and fired a round into the back of his head while the copilot reached for the emergency axe. Hunter shot him, then wiggled through the hole.

The plane was picking up speed.

Camille felt the sand give way under her foot and she tumbled straight down the dune, surfing a small avalanche to the firm tarmac. Scrambling back up, she left the Dragunov on the ground and sprinted onto the runway to get Hunter's attention. Then she realized her mistake.

The plane was speeding toward her.

Hunter hooked his bound wrists over the back of the captain's seat and pulled himself up in time to see the plane hurtling toward the dunes at the end of the short runway. He glanced at the groundspeed: 131 knots. He had no idea what the rotation speed was, but he could feel the nose starting to lift—it was too late to stop.

Then he saw Stella directly in its path.

Using his elbows, he shoved the throttles forward, then sat on the captain's lap, grabbed the yoke and jerked the stick back as hard as he could, throwing it into a steep climb, twenty degrees nose high. The plane lurched violently as it zoomed into the sky. As long as he cleared her, he didn't care if he pulled the nose too steep and it stalled out, dropping him straight to the ground.

"Climb, dammit."

He wanted the gear up immediately to give her more clearance, but could only stare at the gear lever and his bound hands. The stick started to shake and a stall warning horn blared. Then he heard the electronic voice warning, "Stall! Stall!"

Camille saw the plane racing toward her, seconds away. It was beginning to lift into the air, but it wouldn't clear her, not with the gear hanging down. Just then the plane's nose seemed to lift high—too high. The tail scraped the tarmac as it barreled toward her. She dropped with a prayer, covering her head and face with her arms. There was a blast of blistering heat as the engines roared over her, then a small sandstorm scoured her.

Within seconds, she opened her eyes. The plane was already hundreds of feet in the air in a steep climb. Camille's spirits crashed as she watched Hunter fly away from her.

All Hunter could see was blue sky, but he didn't feel anything strike the plane. He tried to exhale, but the yoke was buried in his gut. The stall warning shrieked and he knew he had burned precious time. He slammed the throttles forward and shoved the nose over. He was still flying, just barely.

"Come on, punch it damn it," he shouted over the alarms.

The engines seemed to take forever to respond to firewalling the throttles. A few long seconds later he felt the thrust coming on line.

The alarm stopped.

He eased the nose back up a little and let up on the thrust, making sure he was still in controlled flight before he started a gentler climb. He had always wanted to learn how to fly a Glufstream, but had never had the chance beyond twenty hours of simulator time. It was all just roll, pitch and yaw, he reminded himself as sweat poured off his body. The glass cockpit that he had once admired was now pretty damn intimidating. The basics were displayed by default—artificial horizon, airspeed, fuel—and they all looked good, best he could tell. All of the engine gauges were running parallel.

The desert sky was cloudless and that would help him visually navigate back to Stella. The Gulfstream was a beautiful piece of engineering and most likely came standard with GPS mapping capabilities, but he couldn't take the time to fiddle with the monitors to figure it out. Right now he just needed to get it to a safe altitude, level out so he could pry the emergency axe from the copilot's fingers and free himself from the damn zip-ties. But more than anything at that moment, he wanted to quit giving the captain's corpse a lap dance.

SEVENTY

Gora Muruntau, Kyzyl Kum Desert, Uzbekistan

Camille ran back for the Dragunov, then sprinted down the runway toward GENGHIS. She now didn't care so much about being seen by an invisible enemy. She was more concerned about being shot by disoriented friendlies. She pulled her hat off and let her hair fall to her shoulders, aware that her gender might be what convinced him not to shoot her, in case he didn't recognize her at a distance. Now she couldn't see GENGHIS, but only several bodies. As she neared, she could sense someone watching her. She could always feel it when she was prey. She just hoped it was only Iggy following her with his scope.

"Friend! LIGHTNING SIX!" she shouted at the top of her lungs. She waved her hands in the air as she approached the bodies.

GENGHIS and a prisoner she didn't recognize lay behind corpses of the guards, using them for cover. Their hands were plastic cuffed, but they managed to point assault weapons at her. As soon as GENGHIS identified her, he lowered the gun and instructed the other guy to do the same.

"No offense, ma'am, but you're the prettiest thing I ever saw," GENGHIS said as she got closer. He pressed on the wound on his upper left arm.

Flies swarmed around her face, fighting the wind to get to the blood soaking her gritty hair. She was so thirsty she could barely swallow. Sand was a second skin. "You've lost a lot of blood. You're hallucinating." Camille turned to the prisoner. "Make absolutely sure they're dead." To GENGHIS she mouthed, "Who's he?"

GENGHIS shrugged.

Just because the guy had been a Rubicon prisoner didn't mean she trusted him around her with a weapon; she would have to disarm him. She handed GENGHIS her sidearm, a 9mm Makarov with a KGB emblem on the handle which she'd picked up in Tashkent. It would be easier for him than the AK. "Keep an eye on this for me, will you?" Camille kneeled beside GENGHIS and sliced through the plastic ties around his wrists and ankles, then cut away the blood-soaked sleeve.

"You got it," GENGHIS said. He held the gun as he used the palm of the same hand to press on the gunshot wound.

"They're all dead," the prisoner said as he shuffled toward Camille, carrying a shorty AK. His hands were bound, but that wouldn't stop him from pointing and spraying.

"Come over here and I'll cut you free," Camille said without taking the bloody knife from the holster.

As soon as he was near her, Camille rushed him, closing the distance. She pivoted her body from the line of fire right before she grabbed the butt of the weapon and twisted it away from his bound hands. At the same time she smacked her knee into his groin. He stumbled to the ground like a civilian. She turned the weapon around and pointed it at him.

"Bitch," he said, and doubled over.

"Get up and walk ten feet that way and sit up on your knees. If you so much as stand, one of us will shoot you. And I have a guardian angel on the dunes, so keep that in mind."

"We share the same enemy—Rubicon. I'll help you," he said as he struggled to his feet. "I'm no threat to you."

"But until I have time to figure out who the hell you are, you're our prisoner." Camille kept the AK-102 trained on him as she backed toward GENGHIS.

Camille grabbed the radio. "TIN MAN, break camp and join me. Bring your gear."

"Negative," Iggy said. "Will maintain overwatch."

She knew that Iggy was very worried they didn't have an overwatch position providing security, even though she didn't think there was any reason to believe that Rubicon would somehow approach them by surprise.

"We have a man down. I need your medic kit. Bring it."

"Negative."

"Dammit, GENGHIS will die. Bring it down, then you can reassume your position. We'll see a dust cloud well in advance of any approaching vehicles. Come on."

After a pause, Iggy said, "Affirmative."

Camille squatted beside GENGHIS, the AK slung around her shoulder. She pulled off her shooting glove. "Iggy has QuikClot, but I don't want to wait. You're losing too much blood."

"Don't bother with me. I'm fine." GENGHIS tried to stand, then sat back down again.

"Dizzy?" Camille said as she glanced at the prisoner, who seemed to be compliant.

"Yeah."

The hole was smaller than she expected for a second-hand steel-core cartridge. It must have hit a lot of bone, which slowed it down as it went through the guard. She had learned long ago not to second-guess gunshot wounds. Shots that should never kill often did and others that should've inflicted substantial damage sometimes barely slowed a target down. "Sorry. You moved a split-second after I squeezed off."

"If I'd moved a few more inches, you would've had one shot, two kills—doesn't get better than that in this business," GENGHIS said, his voice stressed. He kept the Makarov pointed at the prisoner, although his aim wasn't steady.

Sand was caked onto her fingers. She raked them across his pant leg, then she stuck them into her mouth and sucked as much sand and dirt off them as she could. She spat onto the ground, then pulled back on the edges of the wound. "This is going to hurt like hell. Brace yourself," she said as she thrust her fingers into the wound and pressed. It was warm, wet and soft. "How the hell did you get a ticket for that flight with Hunter?"

"Pete set me up. She's your traitor."

"I know. How you doing?"

"Alive," GENGHIS said in a whisper, his jaws clenched. "Just keep talking."

"You're in good hands. Daddy trained me well for combat wounds. You know he used to shoot my pet goats? It was up to me to save them or else they were Sunday dinner."

"Sounds like Charlie. The man understood motivation." GENGHIS smiled, but it was strained as he fought the pain. "You ever lose one?"

"Not many."

Camille looked up as Iggy approached, lugging his gear. Hers was still on the dune. He kept his AK aimed at the prisoner as he dropped his pack near GENGHIS. "What the hell are *you* doing here?"

"Pete sent me," GENGHIS said.

"What are you talking about? Where is Pete?" Iggy glanced around as he pulled the medic kit from his rucksack.

"Dead." Camille sighed. The bleeding was under control as long as she kept the pressure up. "She made a move on me."

"She's always making moves on you," Iggy said with a laugh as he used his teeth to tear open a foil packet of QuikClot. "I hope for once this shit lives up to its sales pitch. So where is Pete?"

"I'm serious. She tried to kill me. I didn't have a choice." Camille pulled her fingers from the wound and Iggy handed her the packet. She poured the grains directly into the hole. The substance turned dark. "This stuff always reminds me of kitty litter."

"Jesus. Pete's our mole?"

"Whoever she was working for must not want me comparing notes with Hunter. And I'm guessing that's the CIA." Camille stopped pouring the grains into the wound when the top layer quit soaking up fluid and remained light beige.

"Who the hell is our prisoner?" Iggy said as he gathered weapons from the dead guards, all the while looking around for any movement.

"Dammed if we know," Genghis said.

"You ask him?"

"We've been busy getting this bleeding under control. I can sew the artery up later." Camille took a piece of gauze and applied pressure. The QuikClot made the wound give off so much heat, she had to add an extra layer to insulate her hand. When she was convinced the coagulant had worked its wonders, she wrapped a dressing around his arm to maintain the pressure.

Iggy yelled to the prisoner. "You got a name?"

"Larry Ashland."

"I've heard of you." Iggy laughed. "You're the French spook the Agency nabbed yesterday, aren't you?"

"Yes, but I'm on your side in this. Cut me free," Ashland said, kneeling exactly as Camille had instructed him.

"I have a hard time imagining me being on the same side as the French," Iggy said.

Camille squinted. Even with her dark sunglasses, the sun was glaring. Her undershirt was completely drenched between her breasts and her skin was burning. "No way is the Agency going to nail some French mole, then hand him off to Rubicon, even if Rubicon is running some of their rendition flights. It doesn't add up."

"Nothing about Rubicon adds up," Ashland said.

"You got that right," Iggy said.

Camille pulled out an IV bag of saline from the medic kit. It was hot. Too hot. She broke open an instant ice pack and duct-taped it to the bag. "I'm going to get GENGHIS into the shadow of that dune, then start the IV as soon as it cools." Camille stood. "I want off this runway when Hunter makes it. If he's alive, he'll be back. I'm not sure if he saw me, but he'd never leave a man behind. He'll be back for GENGHIS and the others."

"My legs are good." GENGHIS stood slowly, then plopped back down.

An oily puddle had collected underneath him. *One down, four to go.* She was surprised he wasn't going into shock. GENGHIS was one tough mother.

"You grab the weapons and keep an eye on the prisoner." Camille reached under GENGHIS' arms, careful not to re-injure him and took a deep breath. He must have weighed over two hundred pounds—all muscle. She turned to Ashland. "Tell me something I don't know about Rubicon and we'll let you come into the shade with us. Otherwise, you're going to bake here until that plane comes back and runs you over."

"As I said, we're on the same side. I'll share all I know." Sweat rolled down Ashland's forehead.

"Start talking." Camille started walking away, supporting GENGHIS.

"Rubicon is working with al-Zahrani. I don't know exactly how or what, but the project's called SHANGRI-LA."

Camille stopped when she heard a code name Chronister had used in the intercepted conversation. "What do you know about SHANGRI-LA?"

"I've spent nearly two years at Rubicon trying to find out about SHANGRI-LA. It's highly compartmentalized. I only know the Iraqi side. Rubicon ships weapons seized from insurgents for use in the project."

"Where is SHANGRI-LA?"

"Uzbekistan."

"You're joking." Iggy chuckled. "SHANGRI-LA is in this hellhole? At least they have a sense of humor."

Camille walked GENGHIS to a strip of shade, a dune's thin shadow. Even without the direct sun, the temperature was agonizing. She eased him down, praying the QuikClot didn't pop out.

Iggy carried the scavenged weapons to the shady spot, piling them beside Camille. She knew the only reason he wasn't in a greater hurry to get back to the overwatch position had to be because he wanted to move out immediately. She wanted to give Hunter more time, though she couldn't imagine what could be taking him so long to circle around and land the damn plane unless the pilots had somehow taken him out first. But it was Hunter. He had to be fiddling around with some cool gadgets, making sure he mastered them before he set it down. He had to be.

She harvested a pair of cheap sunglasses from one of the guards and handed them to GENGHIS.

"Thanks," GENGHIS said as he put them on.

Iggy started checking the weapons one by one. "Get him mobile. I want to egress and get to that LZ. Someone from Rubicon is going to come looking for their buddies."

Camille tightened GENGHIS' belt and raised his feet onto a rucksack to slow down the onset of shock. Cutting back on circulation to the lower body was usually not a good idea, but in this case she was more worried about the vital organs. "I've got to pump fluids into him. And I don't want to move. Hunter will be back."

"Cam," Iggy said as he shoved a magazine back into an AK. "It's been twenty minutes. That's about two hundred miles in a Gulfstream."

"It's fifteen minutes and he'll be back." She was certain of it. Hunter had convinced her of his loyalty and that loyalty would extend to his fellow prisoners. She wasn't going to doubt him again.

"We need to send a burst to our contact in Zarafshan and get the hell out of here."

"He *will* be back."

"We can't wait."

"I'm not moving."

Iggy shook his head as he stared at her. "You've got fifteen minutes and that's it."

She scanned the area, ready to provide cover fire as Iggy climbed back to an overwatch position. Then she touched the IV bag and decided it was good enough. She tore open a needle packet and pushed the needle into GENGHIS' forearm to start the IV. She studied Ashland, unsure what to make of him.

Camille said to him, "What do you really think SHANGRI-LA's all about? You have to have a theory."

"I can't prove it, but I'd bet everything I own that Rubicon is helping al-Zahrani train terrorists." Ashland wiped sweat from his brow. His wrists were still bound.

"This al-Zahrani guy isn't exactly a politico who can be bought off. He's a true believer."

"I'm sure he doesn't know he has corporate sponsorship."

"You know, sometimes I even feel a little guilty the War on Terror has been so good to me, but there's nothing I'd like more than to see every tango wiped off the face of the earth. I can't imagine even Rubicon supporting the fuckers." Camille squeezed the bag, forcing the saline into GENGHIS' arm faster. She radioed Iggy. "He's going to need more than this. There's another one in Pete's ruck."

"I'll get it," Iggy said.

"No. I will. Maintain position."

"I'll go," Iggy said. "You don't need to see her again."

"Yeah, I do," Camille said. Her lips were cracked and her mouth parched. She sipped from a canteen and leaned her head back, looking at the deep blue sky.

No Hunter.

SEVENTY-ONE

Gora Muruntau, Kyzyl Kum Desert, Uzbekistan

A carpet of black flies and beetles already covered Pete's throat and face. Their constant movement made it harder for Camille to stare at the motionless body. She forced herself to reach for the butt of the Makarov in Pete's hand, but the muscles had already tightened so that she would have to break the fingers. Rigor mortis came fast in the desert heat. One 9mm pistol wouldn't make that much of a difference in their arsenal, so Camille decided to cut herself a break and let it go.

The dry desert wind wiped away her tears, but couldn't blow away the pain. Camille bowed her head and averted her eyes as she felt the hollowness that always follows a kill. She scooped up a handful of sand and let it flow out of her fist onto the body. She knew she had to hurry back with the IV solution, but she stood there, paralyzed by memories of the flesh giving way as she pulled the knife through Pete's trachea.

At first, Camille thought her guilt was haunting her when she felt a steel blade pressing against her throat.

"Don't move," a man said in Arabic.

Camille held her breath, hoping that Iggy was watching through his scope and could get a clear shot. The man's hand pressed against the back of her head and she couldn't move without slitting her throat.

The Arab slid her Makarov from the thigh holster, then the knife from her ankle holster. She looked around, searching for an opening. Pete's Makarov was less than two feet from her, but they couldn't help her. The tip of the blade pierced the skin under her chin and she could feel blood drip down her neck.

Come on, Iggy.

Then she saw the Gulfstream banking to align itself with the runway and she knew Iggy was distracted.

SEVENTY-TWO

Gora Muruntau, Kyzyl Kum Desert, Uzbekistan

The Gulfstream's airstairs couldn't go down fast enough for Hunter. He couldn't wait another moment to see Stella. When they were low enough for him to get a good look outside, he spotted two men in the shadow of a nearby dune and a pile of bodies on the runway, but no Stella.

Oh god. I hit her on takeoff.

As the stairs were being lowered to the ground, Hunter bounded down them, then dashed across the runway to the men. Thanks to the Day-Glo prison coveralls, he immediately recognized Ashland and GENGHIS. As he approached them, he could hear a voice coming over an oversized walkie-talkie.

"LIGHTNING SIX, come in. Report.,"

"Where is she?" Hunter shouted. "LIGHTNING SIX, where is she?"

"LIGHTNING SIX, come in."

"We just lost contact," GENGHIS said and pointed. "She went up there, Twelve o'clock, five hundred meters."

"Radio your overwatch and tell him I'm going there and not to shoot me." Hunter said as he scooped up an AK and checked it for ammo. "Get into the aircraft. Take what gear you can and make sure you load the body of the other prisoner. He's a Bushman. We don't leave men behind."

"Neither does Delta," GENGHIS said.

As Hunter ran up the dune, he could see a contorted life-less body lying in the sand. Everything in him screamed. She couldn't be dead. Not when he was this close. The sand crumbled away under his feet and he could hardly get any traction, as if the desert itself were struggling against him, trying to keep him from seeing her.

His feet finally found some packed sand and he was able to make some progress. He got close enough to see the body and forced himself to look.

Stella's alive!

Or at least the corpse wasn't hers.

"Looks like it happened a while ago," Hunter said as an operator with an artificial hand walked up. He knew him by reputation as Iggy, Stella's chief ops officer.

"Camille's work. I'll fill you in later." Iggy was breathing hard. He scanned the horizon with his binoculars, then lowered them. "She came back to grab the medic kit to help that worthless son of a bitch GENGHIS."

The heavy wind had wiped away traces of any footprints, but they could see indentures in the sand where someone had climbed down the back side of the dune. The trail stopped on the flat desert floor where the wind had erased it.

"Look at this," Hunter motioned for Iggy as he pointed to the ground beside Pete. "The blood preserved a footprint."

"Camille was wearing Merrell hikers," Iggy said as he squatted by the fly-covered body and studied the print. "That's from some kind of a sandal. No tread." Iggy stood. "We've got to get out of here. Keep an eye out for anything else unusual while you help me grab the stuff."

"We can't leave her," Hunter said as he wrestled the Makarov from Pete. The bones of the fingers snapped. His Day-Glo prison coveralls had no pockets for him to stick the gun in, so he held onto it.

Iggy reached for the rucksack and saw something that had blown against it. As he leaned over to pick up a small green booklet written in Arabic script, a bullet crackled nearby.

"Hit the deck!"

Both men dug into the sand and pointed their AKs in the direction the bullet had come from—the same direction someone had taken Stella.

"See a target?" Hunter said.

"Negative. So wherever they are, they're at an angle where they can't get a shot unless we stand up." Iggy slipped his arms into the pack's straps. "We're going to creep over there, then run down the dune and pray they can't get into a good firing position in time."

Several rounds flew over them. Hunter couldn't see anyone, but fired a burst anyway to discourage the shooter from moving to a better location.

Iggy reached for the walkie-talkie. "Genghis, this is Tin Man. We're taking fire. Do what you can to cover us. We're coming in."

"Understood," Ashland's voice crackled through the radio.

"We'll be vulnerable most of the way," Hunter said.

"You have any better ideas?"

"No, sir." Hunter fired more rounds, then began crawling as fast as he could.

The sun scorched Camille's skin and she regretted peeling down to shorts and a T-shirt, but she was sure she would be more modestly clothed soon enough, if the tangos didn't kill her first. She sat upright in the back of a pickup truck, surrounded by four young men with AKs. They all wore the telltale beards of the Muslim fundamentalists and spoke Arabic with one another. A cross-eyed one wore a T-shirt silk-screened with a picture she recognized from the wall of Omar's Electronics in Ramadi. Her translator had told her which one he was, but she couldn't remember now if he was Abdullah or al-Zahrani. Not that it really mattered which faction of al Qaeda had kidnapped her.

She could pick up only a word here and there, but pretended to understand nothing and wished she hadn't heard the mention of *jihad* so frequently. Her arms and feet were bound with a heavy, scratchy rope and she saw no immediate options for escape, but she kept reassessing.

A white Toyota truck passed them going the opposite way, toward the airstrip. She coughed from the dust that blew in its wake. It honked and some of the men in the back waved their AKs at them while others fired joy shots into the air. Well over a dozen tangos were squeezed into the truck bed and four or five more into the cab. This was the third pickup they had met and she hoped to god Hunter was getting them out of there and not coming after her. But she knew he would come. And she had little doubt that he would be too late.

She watched the sky for the Gulfstream.

Carrying his IV bag, GENGHIS wobbled toward the body of the dead Bushman. He grabbed the corpse by the arm and tugged. It barely moved. He plopped to the ground, light-headed, breathing hard. He raised his head toward Ashland. "Get your ass over here."

"I'm no harm to you. And none of us can get out of here alone, except Stone. Free me. You need me." He held out his bound hands.

"They didn't leave me with a knife. It'd be my pleasure to shoot the zip-cuff off you. Hold out your wrists." GENGHIS aimed his sidearm at Ashland's wrists.

"No, no, no. I saw Black using shears from the medic's bag. I'll retrieve them. And we might need every bullet."

"Suit yourself."

A few minutes later GENGHIS was lying in the aisle of

the Gulfstream hooked up to a second IV bag that Ashland had found onboard, when he heard Iggy call for backup. The bleeding was under control, but he was feeling light-headed. Ashland set down the walkie-talkie and picked up an AK-102.

"You're not going to be able to help them with that—too short range," GENGHIS said as he grabbed for the IV needle in his arm.

"Leave that in. You need it," Ashland said.

"Fine. But they need a long-range marksman. Help me to the door and hand me the one with the scope."

GENGHIS pulled himself up using the armrest and grabbed the IV bag from the leather seat. Ashland hurried to support him under his arm and helped him walk down the aisle. GENGHIS lowered himself onto the floor in front of the cabin door, dropping the plastic IV bag beside him. Ashland picked it up and hooked it on the bracket for the emergency flashlight instead, then handed him the Dragunov that Camille was carrying earlier.

"Check the rucksack for extra clips," GENGHIS said as he pulled off the magazine and checked the cartridges. Eight were left. Russian ammo was foreign to him, but he trusted that Camille always worked with the best equipment and had probably acquired match-grade rounds.

"Here." Ashland handed him three.

GENGHIS grabbed them and loaded two 7.62 rounds as fast as he could while he watched the distant dune. Iggy and Stone were skidding down it and no targets were in sight—yet. He set up the rifle's bipod and looked through the scope, estimating the wind and ranging to the top of the dune. He adjusted the dope.

Several seconds later, he was tweaking the settings when a man with an AK came into sight above Iggy and Stone. He moved him into his crosshairs and fired. The man dropped, but then two more replaced him. As quickly as he could, he acquired the mark, squeezed off a round

and without a breath, aimed and fired again just as the son
of a bitch hailed bullets at Iggy and Stone.

Bullets flew past Iggy and the sand was getting softer,
pouring in on top of his foot with each step, making it
harder for him to pull his leg up. Just as a round zoomed
too close to his head, his leg pulled out of its binding and
his stump waved in the air. Flapping his arms to catch his
balance, he tumbled to the ground and slid down the dune.
He looked back. His dumb leg was stuck in the sand, fifteen feet above him.

The tangos were appearing as fast as GENGHIS could take
them out and the growing collection of dead bodies
seemed to do little to discourage them. GENGHIS had seen
it before. The fuckers were determined to get to their
seventy-two virgins. He pulled off the magazine and
shoved more rounds into it.

Iggy saw Stone glance back, then turn around to help
him, but Iggy waved him on. Using his elbows to pull
himself along, Iggy dragged himself through the sand to
his leg. Bullets kicked up sand all around. When he got to
it, he took the knife from his ankle holster and sliced off
his pant leg above his knee, cursing himself for wearing
long pants. As he strapped it on, sand got into the sock
over his stump. With a good seven hundred yards to the
plane, it would rub blisters that would plague him for
days.

    He climbed to his feet and ran.

"Permission to come aboard." Hunter shouted from the
base of the Gulfstream's stairs, waiting so he didn't shake
the plane because it didn't take much to spoil a long-range
shot. Iggy hauled ass down the tarmac, a good four hundred meters away.

"Okay, now!" GENGHIS said as he refilled the mag. Hunter climbed up the stairs, taking two at a time.

GENGHIS fired off more rounds as Hunter stepped over him. GENGHIS said, "The fuckers keep coming. We've got to get out of here."

Ashland moved back so he could pass. He paused and said to Ashland, "As soon as Iggy's onboard, throw that switch to retract the airstairs, then turn the lever to secure the door."

Hunter hurried onto the flight deck. The dead first officer was still strapped in. Hunter flipped on the APU as he climbed over the captain's body into his seat.

As Iggy zigzagged down the runway, he could feel his stump rubbing raw against the sand that had come between him and his artificial leg. The stump had sweated so much, it felt like it was sloshing around in a bowl of water. The hot air seared his lungs, but the bullets skipping off the tarmac around him made him push harder.

It only took one, he reminded himself.

GENGHIS chambered a new round, retargeted and fired in less than five seconds—a personal record, but it wasn't enough. More and more tangos crested the saddle and he couldn't drop them all before they started heading down to the tarmac. He gave up on eliminating them as they came into sight and picked off the ones who were closest to Iggy. He was only a couple hundred meters out, but the hordes were gaining on him. They were running and shooting without aiming, but with enough rounds in the air, even a stray bullet could find a mark.

"Hand me an AK and keep 'em coming," GENGHIS said. They had salvaged four from the Rubicon guards.

The tangos were now within five hundred meters and Iggy was within one hundred. GENGHIS stood, the damn IV dangling from his arm. He saw bright flashes of light and became dizzy. He steadied himself on the bulkhead as he breathed deeply. He took the assault rifle and aimed as best he could, given the iron sights, the distance and the wind.

GENGHIS laid down a curtain of fire while Iggy dashed toward the airstairs. He emptied the weapon in his hands and Ashland passed him another one. Iggy ran up the stairs and GENGHIS extended his arm, grabbed Iggy's forearm, and pulled him inside.

"Go! Go!" Iggy yelled to Hunter.

GENGHIS threw the switch to raise the stairs and then he leaned outside and stepped onto the top stair while they were retracting. They were the type that the bottom part of the stairs folded over onto the top when they were halfway up and GENGHIS figured he could get off a couple more shots and jump back inside before they started to double over on themselves. Suddenly, the plane lurched and GENGHIS slipped.

The IV catheter ripped away from his arm and blood gushed from the vein. He grabbed for anything and latched onto a bar. Struggling to hold his legs up above the fast-moving ground, he reached for the bar on the opposite side. His muscles strained and blood was everywhere.

The bottom half of the airstairs was folding down on top of him, threatening to squeeze him to death. Bullets crackled through the air around him and he wished to god one of them would hit him. Dying in combat was supposed to be GENGHIS' fate, not being smashed in stairs. He became dizzier and dizzier as blood drained away and the ground streaked beneath him.

GENGHIS let out a scream and pulled as hard as he could just as everything faded to black.

Iggy climbed out on the airstairs, gripped the chrome with his artificial hand, trusting the microprocessors wouldn't fail him now because he couldn't feel if he had a good grip or if the contraption had let go. Only if the suction broke and the artificial limb pulled off his body would he feel anything and by then it would be too late.

The ground was a blur as he leaned out of the plane. He reached under GENGHIS' arm and pulled as hard as he could, leveraging the force of his own body weight, and yanked GENGHIS back inside. Blood smeared on him as the aircraft lifted into the sky.

SEVENTY-THREE

Kyzyl Kum Desert, Uzbekistan

Camille searched for landmarks along the route, but all she saw were endless sand dunes, mounds of tailings. After fifteen minutes, the ground opened up into the largest open mine pit she had seen in her life. All of Baghdad, Ramadi and Fallujah could've fit inside with room to spare. It dropped down four to five hundred feet in wide terraced steps. She couldn't see any equipment and some of the benches seemed to have collapsed down to the next level. When she thought they had finally passed it, it opened up again into a smaller pit, partially separated from the larger one by a high ridge of solid rock.

There was no mining equipment in the second pit and she thought it was completely abandoned until something flapping in the high winds caught her eye.

Camouflage netting.

The pickup turned down a switchback road and began its descent into the mine. A dozen structures were clustered along the north wall of the crater on the wide upper bench. Most of them were oversized tents being whipped by the high winds, but there were five buildings and more were under construction. They looked like they were made of plywood and had scrap metal for roofs. Beyond the building sites, a firing range was set up on the far side of the compound and she could see obstacle courses with coils of barbed wire.

She was being taken into a terrorist training camp—into SHANGRI-LA.

Paradise had never looked so hellish.

SEVENTY-FOUR

The boom in Iraq is just the tip of the iceberg for the $100-billion-a-year [private security] industry, which experts say has been the fastest-growing sector of the global economy during the past decade.

—THE SAN FRANCISCO CHRONICLE, March 28, 2004, as reported by Robert Collier

Above the Kyzyl Kum Desert, Uzbekistan

GENGHIS lay on the cabin floor, bleeding and breathing rapidly. He was barely conscious and slipping. Iggy dragged him partially into the galley so he'd have room to work. GENGHIS was covered with so much blood, it was impossible to be sure where it was all coming from. Using his combat knife, Iggy sliced open his prison coveralls to search for worst bleeders. He kept the knife close in case he needed to use it against Ashland.

GENGHIS seemed to be bleeding only from the earlier gunshot wound and from the vein where an IV had been. Chunks of QuikClot had popped out of the wound and the dressing was soaked with blood. Keeping Ashland in his sight at all times, he pressed against the wound with his bio-hand and used his mechanical one to stop the blood loss from where the IV catheter had been ripped out.

"Where the hell are we going?" Hunter yelled through the open cockpit door.

"Got a man down. Stand by," Iggy then made eye contact with Ashland. "Get me an IV now!"

Ashland plowed through a medic kit and held out the IV to Iggy.

"You know how to spike a vein?"

"In theory."

"Forget it. Press here and here."

Ashland wrinkled his face.

"Do it now you motherfucker or I'll kill you."

Ashland kneeled down and gingerly placed his fingers over Iggy's.

"Harder," Iggy said as he moved his bloody fingers away.

In seconds, Iggy inserted the IV into one of GENGHIS' veins and started the saline flowing. To hold it into place he slapped duct tape on it. He took over the bleeders from Ashland and ordered him to find blankets. Ashland had the bleeding from the vein under control, so Iggy quickly put a pressure bandage over it.

"Hey, it's your captain here. I'm taking destination requests," Hunter said from the flight deck. "I've got to head somewhere."

"Fuel status?" Iggy said, then spoke to GENGHIS, "Come on, come on, buddy. Hang with me."

"We're in good shape," Hunter said.

"Then circle the area and keep an eye out for anything that looks like a tango training camp. I couldn't get overheads so this is going to be the only look we get."

Ashland covered GENGHIS with several blankets, carefully tucking them under his legs.

Iggy took out scissors and a set of prepared sutures from the medic kit. He cut away the old soaked dressing, pulled out a big dark clump of QuikClot and several smaller ones and threw them onto the floor. He picked up a needle with his left hand and he stared at it. In the four years since he'd lost his right hand, his left had grown much more adept at everyday tasks, but the needle felt awkward. It was better than using his artificial one that lacked the fine motor coordination and the tactile feedback. He hated himself for not anticipating the need for one-handed sewing and practicing it along with the billion other simple tasks which he had to master all over again.

Asking for help wasn't something he did easily, but he wouldn't let his pride endanger a teammate. "Ashland, any chance you have experience tying off arteries?" He knew the answer before the question had left his mouth.

"A button pops off my shirt, I donate it to charity."

"Then get your ass up front and help Stone search for the tango camp." Iggy snarled at him. Stone could now take his turn babysitting him. "Find a camera. I want pictures."

"One of the guards was taking pictures on the flight over here," Ashland said as he ruffled through a bag stowed in an overhead bin. "Here."

"Great. We'll need all the shots you can get. Hurry it up," Iggy said in a normal voice, as he checked on his sidearm. He then turned toward the flight deck and shouted. "Stone, how are you at suturing? I can do it left-handed if I have to, but I'd rather not."

"Can you fly?" Hunter said.

"You don't want that," Iggy said. "Can't you put it on autopilot?"

"You don't get it," Hunter said. "I'm winging it here, trying to keep it between the ditches. This bird's light years beyond anything I've ever flown before. I haven't even figured out how to turn the autopilot on."

"Have a seat." Hunter glared at Ashland as he walked onto the flight deck. The first officer's body was pale, but it hadn't abandoned its post. "Think you better pile him in the back. Take the captain, too, while you're at it."

Hunter scanned the ground below while Ashland dragged the bodies away. He wanted to work him over, but knew he had to concentrate on keeping them in the air. Ashland returned with a blanket that he spread out over the bloody seat before he sat down on it.

"You're the son of a bitch who started this whole mess for me. Anything you want to say for yourself?" Hunter turned the yoke, awkardly coordinating the foot pedals. The plane banked to the left. He still didn't know what the important information about Rubicon was that he'd unearthed. He hoped to finally find out.

"You recognized me. I was afraid you were going to blow my cover. I've been investigating Rubicon for nearly two years and I didn't want to take any chances," Ashland craned his neck to look out the window. He held a digital camera.

"That's it?" Hunter turned toward him, his mouth agape. "You're saying I didn't come across some great Rubicon secret? Shit. That can't be all there is to this goat fuck."

"I'm sorry. I was the secret." Ashland shrugged his shoulders. "I set things in motion so that Rubicon and the CIA and even your Force Zulu all believed that you were a threat that had to be neutralized. It was the only way I could protect my cover."

"You son of a bitch."

"Nothing personal."

"Right. I'm just a pawn in the Agency's battle with the Pentagon. So the OGA's now willing to take out a Force Zulu operator to protect its agents."

"They're willing to do it. But I don't work for the CIA."

"Who the fuck do you work for then?"

"France."

"No fucking way. I got screwed by a goddamn French spy?"

Iggy yelled from the cabin. "Believe it, Stone. You got French kissed."

Hunter shook his head in disbelief. "So what the hell were you doing on the torture express?"

"My cover was blown." Ashland looked at Hunter and flashed a smile. "But not by you."

Hunter wanted to take him out, but he didn't dare let go of the controls for that long until he figured out the autopilot. He had thought of himself as a new breed of superspy/warrior, believing he had discovered one of the most important secrets of the War on Terror. That had made it worth risking his life. Now it seemed he was a minor player in an unremarkable skirmish. Then he thought of Stella and what she must be going through. He seethed with anger. "If anything happens to Camille Black, I will kill you."

"Stone! Enough!" Iggy shouted from the back. "No time to explain. Right now I need you to find that tango camp."

A few minutes earlier, Iggy had opened a clear plastic case of pre-threaded needles, then pulled on a pair of latex gloves. His head turned as he watched Ashland drag a corpse from the cockpit to the back of the plane. He said to GENGHIS, "You still with me, buddy?"

"You sure you can do it?" GENGHIS mumbled.

"Better than I can fly this plane. Hang on. It's going to hurt." Iggy stuck his fingers in the bullet hole and pushed around until he found something that felt like an earthworm. He grabbed it and held it while he used gauze to soak up blood until he could actually see what he was working with. He held his breath as he pinched it together with his real hand while his smart hand tied a loop around it, cutting off the wound. He repeated the procedure a couple of times for good measure, then sopped up the remaining blood to make sure he had stopped all the bleeding. In less than a minute he closed the wound with stitching his mother would've been proud of.

The Agency had been wrong not to take him back to the frontlines. Even with only one arm and one leg, Manuel Ignatius was still an operator.

"I think we've got something," Stone shouted from the flight deck as Iggy felt the plane descend. "A cluster of structures inside a quarry."

"On my way," Iggy said as he removed his leg and

brushed the sand off the stump. A couple of blisters were already forming. Whenever he was alone at home, he usually went without the prosthetic leg because it was a relief not to have it rubbing against the stump. Not since Walter Reed Hospital had he let anyone see him without it—until now. He grabbed a pair of binoculars from a pile of gear on a seat, then hopped into the cockpit. Gripping the back of the copilot's seat with his artificial hand, he steadied himself.

Stone changed the flap settings and pushed down on the yoke, then he banked the aircraft into a tight circle above the compound and pointed. "Look over there. This mine's abandoned. All the others all have buildings and equipment around them."

"Yeah, looks abandoned to me. So?" Iggy said.

"Right there. Along the north wall of the ridge between the two pits."

"Son of a bitch. That's a familiar footprint." Iggy studied the area through his binoculars. "I saw several of these in Afghanistan before the invasion. There's even camouflage netting flapping around. The high winds today must've ripped it."

"SHANGRI-LA," Ashland said.

"Yeah, SHANGRI-LA—right there in the pit of hell. Who would've thunk it?" Iggy pointed at the scattering of buildings nestled in the first level in the smaller of two adjoining terraced craters. Together the pits were some thirty kilometers long and between five and ten kilometers wide. Where the camp was situated on the upper level, the terraced benches were at least a football field wide. "Look at that. It's fucking brilliant to stick it in an old open pit mine in the middle of a desert wasteland—a fortress on a shoestring. They don't need to guard the perimeter—no one could rappelle down those walls because the sand would crumble into an avalanche. Looks like the main road is the only way in."

Iggy turned to Ashland. "Go in the back and get as many shots as you can—close ups and wide ones. Let us know when you've filled the camera and we'll get out of here."

Ashland exited the flight deck.

"You think Stella's down there?" Stone said while he played with the digital controls, apparently familiarizing himself.

"Stella?" Iggy chuckled. "Haven't heard her called that in a long time." He lowered himself into the copilot's seat. He reached into the pocket of his 5.11s and pulled out a booklet. Camille had told him that Stone was fluent in spoken Arabic and he hoped he could read it, too. "If this says what I think it does, I'd bet my good hand on it."

"What is it?" Stone reached for it.

"Someone dropped it when they nabbed Cam. I was picking it up when the shooting started."

Stone flipped through it. "It's a cleric ranting about returning to the roots of the true al Qaeda."

"Al-Zahrani?"

"How'd you know? What's all this got to do with Rubicon?"

"His name's come up a lot lately," Iggy said. "Can you take us a little lower? I need a good long look. Someone bought up all the commercial satellite pictures for the next several years."

"Rubicon?"

"You bet—one of their front companies." Iggy studied the compound, looking for the best avenues of approach. "I'd give one of my right arms for recon on the deck, but I'm afraid a bird's-eye view is all we're gonna get."

"I ran into some tangos outside of Ramadi who trained here in an al-Zahrani camp. They were the ones who kidnapped the geologist Jackie Nelson. I also know Rubicon has a lot of business here."

"Yeah, like supporting the frickin' terrorist camp. Obviously, they have a prison here, too. Camille said there's a former KGB facility built out of an old gold mine. She said there are underground mineshafts in the hills around here. Our guess is that's where they were taking you. Now I'm starting to think they're also using it to keep tabs on the al-Zahrani camp." Iggy lowered the binoculars and looked at the virtual gauges, but didn't really understand what he was seeing. "How's your fuel?"

"Twenty-nine thousand and two hundred-some pounds—enough to take us anywhere in Western Europe with leftovers."

"I only want to get to Bagram, to Black Management's Camp Obsidian. It's our nearest Afghan ops center."

"It'll take us about an hour to get there."

"Beautiful."

"Not really. It takes us too far away from Stella, uh, Camille. I'd rather find what we need locally and go back. And if you're thinking of returning with helicopters, you're asking for some extreme flying."

"We have to stage from where we have our assets and that's Bagram." Iggy scratched his face and felt a couple days' stubble.

"I think we should go somewhere here in-country, get gear on the black market and come back tonight."

"Would never work. I don't know how to contact Cam's local suppliers who outfitted us and it would be just you and me. Ashland's not an operator, GENGHIS is down and that airstrip we used is now out of the question."

"I don't want to leave Uzbekistan without her. I speak some Russian. You have to have some spooks on staff with old KGB ties who can set us up, wire us some money. The Uzbeks will sell anything for the right price. We can probably even pick up a few old Spetsnaz mercs in Tashkent."

"I'm not saying it can't be done, but it would take too much time to orchestrate. As it is, with all the assets we have in place in Afghanistan, it'll be all I can do to pull something together for tonight."

"As soon as he's done with the pictures, I'm heading to Tashkent," Stone said.

"No, you're not." Iggy pointed at him. He could feel his face and neck getting warm. "This is a Black Management op. We have a command structure. Let me introduce you to it—in our world, I'm a five-star and you get to keep your old rank—what's that, an E-6, E-7?" Iggy held his gaze. "Got that Devil Dog?"

Stone stared at him for several seconds, then said, "Yes, sir. Understood, sir."

"Good. What's the distance between SHANGRI-LA and Bagram?"

"You wouldn't know the station identifier code for Bagram, would you, sir?" Stone said. His voice was stiff with an underlying tone of controlled anger, but Iggy didn't care. Stone had accepted him as the alpha dog and that was all that mattered.

"Oscar–Alpha–India–X-ray."

Stone punched the code into the flight computer and a color chart of the Bagram airspace appeared on one of the LCD monitors. "Electronic *Jeppesens*. Cool. Says here the range is five hundred forty nautical miles—that's pushing it for helos, sir. And sir, I'm an E-8."

"Master Sergeant Stone, huh? You don't see a lot of Master Sergeants out doing fieldwork."

"I volunteered, sir."

"Good for you."

"And you can call me 'Top,' sir."

"We've got a rescue to plan, Top." Iggy reached into one of the pilot's salesman's cases and dug around until he found a pen, paper and a calculator. He sighed. "I hate this back-of-the-napkin math when roughing out a mission. Let's see, we can knock the back rows out of the Pave Hawks and stick in two one-hundred-eighty-five-gallon tanks and that will up our fuel to—three-sixty plus two times . . ." His voice trailed off, but he continued to move his lips and scribble on the notepad. "A gallon of JP8 weighs six point eight pounds . . . accounting for all the weight from the extra fuel coupled with the high altitude flying out of Bagram, I calculate a burn rate of nine hundred sixty pounds an hour, give or take twenty."

"Just listening to your calculus, I'd say you've got about five hours of flying time," Stone said as he tried to read Iggy's ciphers.

Iggy looked over at Stone. "You're good—four hours, fifty minutes plus the twenty-minute emergency reserve. Average of one-twenty knots is a safe bet, so we need four and a half hours to target. That means refueling twice which isn't easy."

"Ferry tanks?"

"Too much drag. We don't have that kind of time. We've got refueling arrangements with the big military for Combat Shadows and Combat Talons, but that's usually when we're working jobs across the border in Pakistan or Iran, and it's expensive."

"Air-to-air refueling is the way to go—Stella has Pave Hawks?"

"Afghan theater—right where we're headed."

"Too bad she doesn't have Pave Lows so we could take more troops in."

"We've got 'em, but they're all committed right now. When I left, it was very hot in Northern Pakistan, chasing down another lead on Abdullah. I might be able to move some around. I'll do what I can. We've also got a half-dozen Super Cobras with the latest upgrades." Iggy turned in his seat and shouted. "GENGHIS, you still with us?"

"Haven't got rid of me yet," GENGHIS yelled back.

"I'm not coming up with any good ideas about how to get into that camp," Stone said. "It'll be risky, but I'm thinking we're going to have to pass as tangos and try the main gate."

"Nah," Iggy shook his head and pointed to the larger

crater. "We'll fly a Pave Hawk right up to their backside. We'll come in at night, drop down into the pit at the far end—I'd say it's about twenty clicks from the camp—we fly inside the bowl right up to the rock ridge. It'll give us both audio and visual cover." Iggy motioned to the ridge between the two pits with his artificial finger. A narrow bench along the south tip of the ridge joined the two craters. "You fly. How tough is it to fly that in the dark?"

Stone laughed. "I can barely keep a helo in the air. You need real bus drivers—the best ones you've got."

Iggy pursed his lips and made a whistling noise as he exhaled through them. "My top flier is in Iraq. He's a cocky son of a bitch, but Beach Dog could pierce the eye of a needle in a sandstorm."

"I know the guy. Real friendly type." Stone banked the plane in another circle. "It's about fifteen hundred miles from Baghdad to Bagram—around three hours by jet if you're not exactly respectful of everyone's airspace. It'll be tight. What the hell is taking Ashland so long?"

"Cam's been wanting to buy a jet. We could sure use one of our own right now."

"Outsource it. Get Blackwater to fly Beach Dog up. They rent out."

"Great idea." Iggy swiveled in the seat, starting to get up. "I've got a secure satellite phone in one of the rucksacks. I'll start putting everything into place. We've got to get to Cam tonight before they fuck her up too bad."

Stone stopped him before he could leave. "You can't possibly trust Ashland," he said in a low voice.

"He's French," Iggy said, as if he had used his strongest swear word. "They ally with you only because they don't have the cajones to take you on, mano-a-mano. But we might need him."

Ashland cleared his throat. He stood in the doorway of the flight deck. "Camera's full."

"Get us out of here," Iggy said as he stood, ignoring Ashland.

He hopped to the door, but Ashland didn't move.

Ashland said. "Let's be clear. When it comes to stopping terrorists, we're allies—the War on Terror is where we have differences. I've risked my life for two years to infiltrate Rubicon—an American company funding terrorists to secure future business—and what's your CIA doing? Tell me who has cajones."

Iggy pursed his lips and took a deep breath. He wanted to punch him out on principle, but the son of a bitch was right.

Iggy pushed by him and hopped down the aisle to search for the sat phone and a laptop so he could rough out the SMEAC. If they were going to pull it off tonight, he needed his operation orders ready when they landed.

SEVENTY-FIVE

Shangri-la

The picture of the bearded leader was plastered everywhere in the camp—on banners, on murals painted on the sides of buildings and woven into tents. She had tried to listen in on several conversations to at least pick up which one he was, but she couldn't decipher anything. As the truck carrying Camille pulled into the terrorist training compound, the driver started honking his horn nonstop. Young men poured outside and circled around the pickup, glaring at her. Half of them wore white dishdashi, the others trousers and shirts. From the hatred in their eyes, she could only guess that some saw her as a Western whore, others as the devil herself. Their rage jabbed her from all directions. Any moment, they could mob her and she sure as hell was going to take as many with her as possible. Her hands were tied in front and she was confident she could at least spray an AK. She eyed the tango with the nearest assault rifle and prepared to ram herself into him and seize it for her big finale.

One of the men grabbed her by the arm and pulled her to her feet. He yelled something to the crowd and they started chanting. If she threw her body weight against the cross-eyed tango, she could probably get his weapon. The crowd was ready to rock any moment and she preferred to be the one on the offense.

Three. She took a deep breath.

Two. She leaned back to give herself a little more force.

One.

At that instant, she saw a man step from a tent and everyone looked toward him. He had a long peppery white beard and flowing white robe.

The Osama wannabe.

Abort.

The leader of al Qaeda, or at least one faction of al Qaeda, was less than ten meters from her. She could no longer grab an AK and spray.

She now had to aim.

The al Qaeda leader said something that quieted everyone down, then dispersed the crowd. He slipped back into a small white tent with stylized Arabic phrases over the doorway. She guessed they were verses from the Koran. It was the only tent without his image plastered on it. She had just located his lair.

A man in his midthirties, an elder in the crowd, directed the men in the pickup, pointing to a small building near one of the construction sites on the far side of the camp, deeper into the crater. The truck engine started and the driver honked for the leftover crowd to get out of his way. He didn't wait, just started moving, bumping into anyone in his way.

Haji was on a mission from god.

The pickup weaved through the center of the camp and she was starting to feel a little carsick. It was so hot the doors of the buildings, tent flaps and sides of tents were open. Most of the tents seemed to be dormitories and the fixed structures included a mosque, an open-air madressa and an office building crowned with satellite dishes and antennae.

The compound was perched on the upper level of the abandoned open pit mine's wide bench. On one side was a fifty-meter ridge of solid rock that ran for a couple kilometers beyond the camp, then seemed to open up into another pit; on the other side of the camp the ground suddenly dropped off a good fifteen meters to the next bench, leading to the lower depths of the mine. She could see half a dozen terraces and estimated that the mine was a hundred to a hundred fifty meters deep. The far side was several kilometers away and the south wall was a vertical cliff dropping to the crater's depths. Except for the rock ridge behind the main compound, the walls seemed to be crumbling. Large chunks of several benches had collapsed and were now sand piles on the next level.

They had no concertina wire, no fences to protect them. They didn't need it. There was one way in and one way out. Camille kept studying the terrain for alternate exits, but didn't discover any.

The truck stopped at a building site on the south perimeter of the main compound, two hundred meters from the nearest tent. Concrete pillars had been poured for something and one wall had been roughed out, but no tools were scattered about and she didn't get the feeling that any progress had been made there for a long time. Adjacent to the site was a small eight by ten shack made of scrap lumber. A padlock hung on the door, but it wasn't locked. No one had gotten around to painting the boss-man's likeness on its side. The tangos were slipping.

The truck stopped in front of the shed. Two tangos stayed in the back of the truck to guard Camille, but they didn't need to. She wasn't about to try to escape until she knew she could get the head of al Qaeda first.

Several men wheeled out a concrete mixer, then started throwing tools from the shed, emptying it as fast as they could. They clearly had not been expecting houseguests and she hated to impose.

SEVENTY-SIX

The private firms' role in the region continues today, with contractors now part of the CIA/military operation attempting to run down Osama bin Laden and his associates along the Pakistan-Afghanistan border.

—SALON.COM, April 15, 2004, as contributed by Peter W. Singer

Camp Obsidian, Bagram Airbase, Afghanistan

The Black Management war room was stuffy from the breath of over two dozen men. Nearly half wore flight jumpsuits, the rest combat fatigues. Hunter stood out with his Day-Glo orange prison uniform which he hadn't taken time to change out of because he wanted to be included in Iggy's planning before the mission briefing, not that he had been allowed any real input. Iggy didn't miss a chance to remind him who was in charge. The only break Hunter had taken was to make sure the body of his fellow Bushman was off-loaded from the Gulfstream, identified and transferred over to the big military. When he had ducked away the plan called for a minimum of four Super Cobras for close air support and Iggy was still hoping for six. He was curious if he had managed to round up the additional gunships.

Hunter looked around the room for a place to sit. There was an empty chair by the helo pilot Beach Dog. The last time he'd seen him was in Baghdad when he had knocked him out and duct-taped him to a steering wheel. He decided it was better to grab the seat beside GENGHIS.

Standing at the head of the conference table, Iggy introduced his staff—adjutant, intel, operations and logistics officers. Hunter looked back to the doorway to see if the others were coming in, then he realized Iggy must only have included the flight crews and the team leaders. The commanders would brief their men en route, he guessed.

Each of Iggy's officers briefed his area of responsibility in the op orders, then Iggy spoke, outlining his commander's intent. So far so good, Hunter thought when he heard that the extraction of Stella was the primary objective and destruction of the tango training facility was secondary.

A giant LCD screen displayed one of Ashland's long-range photos of the terrorist training camp, marked up with arrows and symbols showing each chalk, aircraft, and the surface danger zone. Iggy used it to describe the fire-plan sketch.

"Each Pave Hawk will insert a team of three operators. CHALK ONE provides recon, security and support by fire." He gave the grid where the main force was going. "CHALK ONE will locate the objective while CHALK TWO sets up a kill box around the tangos' barracks using Claymores to cover our egress." He explained that Camille—Stella—was being extracted, so that everyone knew that one extra body would be reentering friendly lines. The entire operation was expected to take forty minutes. Iggy continued, "If everyone's taken out, the Cobras will destroy the target. Now I anticipate a successful mission and upon completion, the Cobras will go in hot and neutralize the camp. When we're finished, not one of those *muj* is ever going to threaten America."

Hunter opened his mouth, then forced it closed. He caught himself shaking his head and tightened his neck muscles. This was definitely not the plan they had roughed out. He flipped to the second page of the op orders to be sure. Without saying a word to him, Iggy had slashed the number of troops to a fraction of the originally planned size.

When they last left off, Iggy was going to shuffle things

around so they would have Pave Lows, helicopters that could carry over thirty troops. Without consulting him the operation had gone from fifty tier-one operators to six. Stella had the men and the equipment, but Iggy had obviously decided against it, if that had ever really been his intent. Hunter could've accepted the decision from regular military, but this was Stella's company and her life was the one on the line. He remembered Stella once telling him that she had to give Iggy a minority stake in the company to lure him on board and Hunter was starting to wonder if this didn't give him a motive to want her out of the picture. He took a deep breath as he tried to hold his military bearing together, listening intently to the rest of the briefing on the mission's execution, then the administration and logistics. He knew there was no need to hear the command and control section of the briefing because it was far too clear who was in control of Stella's army.

"Two Cobras will be running forward reconnaissance and providing route security and CAS."

Hunter wrinkled his brow and felt himself get warm.

"We are expecting soft targets only, so the Cobras are carrying full complements of Hydras and fully loaded turrets with HE and SLAP rounds. The Pave Hawks are each outfitted with rocket pods. The intent is to level the camp after the extraction. We're taking along AIM-9 Sidewinders in case the Uzbek air force manages to get its MIG off the ground. When inside Uzbek airspace, if anyone lights you up, you're authorized to neutralize the threat. They've allowed al-Zahrani to train terrorists in their country and they'll have to face the consequences."

Beach Dog leaned back in his chair and stretched. He was in the requisite olive green flight suit, but wore a bright red, yellow and blue Hawaiian shirt over it like a smock. He held one finger in the air and started speaking before Iggy called on him. "You expecting hostile locals?"

"Negative. We don't anticipate letting them know we're

there. The only tricky part is crossing the border. The Russians are still helping them keep up their radar equipment there. We'll fly nap-of-the-earth and through known radar gaps. Intel says that everywhere outside of the border zone, the old Soviet radar net hasn't been working for years. They have some localized radar at their major airports, but they don't even have radar contact to control commercial flights over their territory and rely exclusively on position-reports by pilots. Their airspace is up for grabs and tonight Black Management's going to own it. As for their forces, they have less than two dozen operational Fishbeds and Fulcrums— for you post-cold warriors, I'm talking about MIG-21s and MIG-29s. Their pilots get very little training time in them because Uzbekistan is too cash-strapped."

Iggy continued, "Two Pave Hawks will transport two teams of three operators each." Iggy tapped his computer and an old satellite photo of Uzbekistan appeared on the monitor. He gave a six-digit grid for the refueling points. "At zero-one-thirty hours the Hawks will rendezvous at the second refueling point, designation STARLIGHT with a Combat Talon for air-to-air refueling." He waved his hand in the air for emphasis. "If ever de-briefed, you are to claim that we landed twice each leg in the desert and you believe it was the Russian mob that met us with two Soviet-era fuel trucks. Do I make myself clear?"

GENGHIS carried an IV bag with him and sipped on a Gatorade. He whispered to Hunter. "I'd guess some general's putting a star on the line for Camille by loaning us that tanker."

"I'd put my money on the OGA doing it to wipe out the tango base. After we grab her, the tangos will bug out and scatter." Hunter leaned over to GENGHIS and spoke out of the corner of his mouth.

Iggy slapped the table with his artificial hand. "Gentlemen. There is to be no speculation—no discussion—not a whisper."

"Yes, sir," Hunter said and GENGHIS echoed him.

"Each Pave Hawk will top off, then land at STAR-BRIGHT to refuel the Cobras that do not have air-to-air refueling capabilities. You'll find the grid in your orders. The Pave Hawks will be carrying hoses and portable pumps. The Hawks will then return to the MC-130 and refuel themselves."

The briefing ended twenty minutes later and Hunter waited for the men to leave before he approached Iggy, who was sitting down while he turned off the laptop.

"Permission to speak freely, sir," Hunter said.

"Close the door."

"Two Cobras and two Pave Hawks—what's that all about? Where the hell are the Pave Lows and all the troops?"

"Three of our Cobras are in for heavy maintenance. I'm still waiting on the green light from the mechanics for one of the two we're taking and it has to launch in twenty minutes if everything's going to run on time."

"We can't do this with six operators."

"It just has to be a little more surgical than originally planned."

"Doesn't Black Management have additional air support in theater?"

"It's committed. There's a major sweep going on in Northern Pakistan against al Qaeda and the Taliban. Everyone's stretched so thin, I've even got the big Army screaming for more. You're a Marine. Do the math."

"I have. You lied to me." Hunter clenched his jaws and gritted his teeth. He felt a jab of pain from the empty tooth socket, but ignored it. "You said you would redeploy whatever it took to save her. This is Stella's company for god's sake. This isn't the real military. Pull the fucking resources."

"Get with the 21st century, Stone. We *are* the real military and we're in the middle of WWIII right now. Camille understands that. She would never forgive me if I yanked resources in the middle of an op. You don't do that and you know it." Iggy closed the laptop. "And I said I would try and I sure as hell did."

"I'm starting to think you don't want to save her."

"Enough, Stone." Iggy stood and took a step toward Hunter. His face was bright red. "You are not the only one who loves Cam. You're just the only one who can have her. It's not fucking fair, but I still saved your ass when that was what she wanted. And you can bet your life I'm going to do everything I can to get her back safely."

"I didn't know."

"Well now you do. And I appreciate you not telling her. Dismissed."

The rotors of the Pave Hawks were starting to move when Hunter walked with Iggy to the lead bird. The operators were standing around on the ramp. The Super Cobras had already left. Hunter patted the side of the Hawk for good luck as he climbed into the back. Beach Dog had stuck a small cat figure with a raised paw onto the dashboard. Hunter had seen them all over Okinawa and was pretty sure they were some kind of a Japanese good luck charm, but he couldn't figure out how it fit into the guy's usual Hawaiian motif.

Hunter stuck his head into the front and put his hand on Beach Dog's shoulder.

"Sorry about what happened back in Baghdad," Hunter said. "I want you to know I have nothing against your kind of people."

"Surfers?" Beach Dog looked up from his checklist and smiled. "I think you misunderstood me. All's cool, dude. Let's just go save the lady."

Hunter watched as GENGHIS positioned himself on the outside seat of the four-man NOMEX bench so that he didn't risk anyone bumping against his arm.

"Sure you're up to it, buddy?" Hunter said as he sat beside him, not happy that he was about to spend nearly five hours cramped in a middle seat. GENGHIS' quick rebound surprised him, but he'd known other snake eaters like him. The more bunged up, the more hard-assed they became.

Just then Iggy boarded the helicopter and pointed at GENGHIS. "What are you doing here? You're supposed to be in the infirmary."

"Waste of time. The nurse was a dude."

"Get out. Raab here is my second shooter." He motioned to a stocky guy standing several feet away on the ramp who looked like he could drive fence posts with his bare hands. He and Ashland were hurrying to smoke the last of their cigarettes.

"With all due respect, sir," GENGHIS said and continued, "Ms. Black is there because she tried to get an IV to save my life. I owe her and I don't like debts."

"I can't risk others by asking them to count on a teammate who's already wounded."

GENGHIS glared at him, then stared at his artificial arm. Hunter started to say something, but Iggy could take care of himself. He'd sure proven that.

"Sir," GENGHIS said. "Ms. Black has earned my loyalty and my respect. I'll give my last breath to save her. Besides I'm all knitted up and ready to tango."

Iggy pursed his lips and held his breath for several seconds as he stared at GENGHIS. "If you show any signs of disorientation along the way, you're staying in the helo."

Ashland and Raab approached the Pave Hawk and Hunter could smell the cigarette smoke even over the jet fumes.

Iggy motioned to Raab. "You're bumped to CHALK TWO. Take Callaghan's place and tell him to go home for the night."

"Yes, sir."

Iggy radioed the replacement orders to the CHALK

Two team leader while Ashland climbed onto the empty backwards-facing seats. The extra internal fuel tanks were a plastic wall within twelve inches of the seats. He wedged himself in and sat sideways with his legs facing the door.

"Hey, hey, hey. What are you doing?" Iggy tapped his artificial hand on Ashland's leg.

"I left you the last seat. I didn't think you'd want to sit back here," Ashland said.

Hunter could tell from the bulges that Ashland had body armor on even though he wore civilian clothes—brown trousers and a white shirt. With his curly jet black hair and swarthy complexion, he could easily pass as one of the tangos like he had when Hunter and Stella had discovered him in the insurgent safe house back in Anbar.

"You don't have the right skill set for this," Iggy said.

"But I do. My Arabic is flawless. I might be French, but my mother is Algerian. My father was pied-noir."

"I don't give a flip about your pedigree. Get out." Iggy glanced at his watch.

"You need another Arabic speaker if you want to find her. I know you have enough margin with the fuel to cover my weight."

"Can you shoot?"

"Definitely."

"I can use you for recon. Finding her is going to be a bitch. But fuck with me and I'll draw and quarter you myself." Iggy stifled a yawn as he climbed into the Pave Hawk and strapped himself in. He was ready to blow, so he took a deep breath to calm himself down. He was getting fed up with constantly being challenged and argued with every step of the way. Private military had its drawbacks and one of them was the lack of a stockade.

SEVENTY-SEVEN

Shangri-la

The toolshed was a blast-furnace and Camille was breathing hard. The shed was single-wall construction—thick plywood on a frame of scrap lumber. She was confident that she could kick through the walls and felt a little insulted that they thought so little of a female prisoner that they would stick her in such a minimum security shack. Light came in through a knot in one of the boards and she used it to search the ground for anything that she could use as a weapon. It wasn't likely, but they might have missed something when hastily clearing it for use as makeshift guest quarters.

The call to prayer sounded tinny. She laughed that even al Qaeda used canned calls to prayer over loudspeakers and didn't even bother with a real live muezzin. It was the second one that she'd heard since her arrival and it was still daylight out so it had to be late afternoon. She couldn't wait for the sun to go down, she thought, as she ran her fingers through the sandy floor, systematically searching for a tool. About a half inch below the loose top layer, the sand was as hard as concrete. Sand and dirt were wedged under her fingernails and she reeked of sweat, which wasn't strong enough to mask the smell of Pete's blood.

Her finger hit something sharp. A nail. Her spirits soared when she realized it was between four and five inches long. Finally, she had something serious to work with. In case they searched her quarters, she reburied it and then continued her treasure hunt, raking her fingers through the sand, wondering where Hunter was and trying to convince herself that he had gotten safely far away.

If she only could've seen him, smelled him, tasted him

one last time. They had been within a few feet of each other when the airplane had zoomed over her and now she'd never see him again. She tried to come up with rescue scenarios, but she didn't want to deceive herself into false hopes that could distract her from what she had to do.

She was confident she could break out of the shack at night, but she doubted she could survive the desert if she ever made it out of the camp. It was a moot point anyway. As soon as she saw the head of one of the two al Qaeda factions, she knew she had to do whatever it took to assassinate him. Taking him out would be a blow the terrorist organization might never recover from, particularly now that it seemed to be splintering in a bitter succession struggle. It didn't know it, but al Qaeda had brought a suicide bomber into its midst. All she needed now was a bomb.

"*Marhaba,*" a voice said as someone fumbled with the padlock on the shed door.

She immediately sat down and leaned against the wall and drew her legs up close to her body. It was time to paint the picture of a compliant, fearful female. The Muslim fundamentalists had such a low opinion of women, she was determined to give them what they wanted.

Fresh air rushed inside as the door opened.

"Stay against back wall, please," a young man said in heavily accented English as he set a large bucket full of water inside the shed. A guard stood outside the door with an AK pointing in at her.

"Don't hurt me," Camille said, making her voice crack as if she had been crying.

"Water to clean. Prepare yourself." He tossed Camille a light gray jilbab and a head scarf.

"Prepare myself for what?"

"Tonight—marriage. The *mut'a, insh'allah.*"

Camille wanted to laugh and toss the clothes back into

his face, but instead she said, "I'll do whatever you want. Please don't hurt me."

"Tonight, you marry or you die."

"No!" She pretended to cry and raised her bound wrists in front of her face and put her hands together as if praying. "I don't want to die. Help me, please."

He looked away.

"Who is the groom?" Camille said.

"Al-Zahrani, may peace and blessings of Allah be upon him," the messenger said as he closed the door.

"And may al-Zahrani fuck off and die," Camille whispered as she got back on her hands and knees and continued her search for more nails.

SEVENTY-EIGHT

39° 45' 10.02 N, 65° 09' 15.12 E (Uzbekistan)

Three hours into the operation, Hunter was still awake, unable to snooze like he usually did during insertions, and his body had grown stiff and achy. The seats were nylon stretched over an aluminum frame and they were only marginally better than the alternative, which was the metal floor. More than once he'd sat on the floor for entire missions when the seats had been removed so more troops could be crammed inside. Usually the troop doors of the helicopter were also removed for easy access, but given the sandstorm that they had already gone through, he was happy Iggy had decided against it, probably to reduce drag and conserve fuel. Hunter stretched as much as he could, but with Iggy and GENGHIS sandwiching him, he could move only enough to keep some circulation going in his lymph systems so his muscles didn't get worse. At least his legs had room to stretch out toward the pilots.

The only light in the Pave Hawk was the glow from the partial glass cockpit. Hunter watched the line of the color weather radar sweep the area, then glanced over to the Doppler navigation system and the LCD map of their location. The Pave Hawk was an older model that seemed to have been retrofitted with the latest in glass cockpit avionics.

An orange light to the left of the pilot flickered, indicating a warning light had gone off. Hunter turned his head to read the caution message on the middle display, but before he could see what the problem was about, it went off. He prayed it was an anomaly. They were pushing the equipment to its limits because Stella couldn't wait. Right after the sandstorm one of the Cobras had had to turn back because of fluctuating turbine gas temperature. They didn't need any more problems that might force them back. Iggy had established liberal go/no parameters of one Hawk and one Cobra, but Hunter had his own: as long as one bird would stay in the air long enough to get him within walking distance, it was a green light. Hell, as long as he was still breathing, it was a go.

Beach Dog's ass was numb and his mind wasn't far behind. Extended range missions had a way of grinding him down with boredom. Top Guns who retired to long hauls in civilian aircraft must go out of their minds, he thought as he relieved himself in his pee bag.

As usual with a black mission, radio contact was minimal. Today the Pave Hawks were using the call signs JACKAL ONE and TWO and the remaining Super Cobra was DRAGON ONE. He laughed when he heard that the MC-130's designation was COWBIRD. Those gas station attendants either had a self-image problem or they didn't get what the game was all about.

Finally they were approaching the point STARLIGHT and some action. He knew it was too early to start searching for the tanker, but he couldn't help but watch the radar screen as if it were a video game. Any minute the race with his wingman would begin to see who would be the first one to make radar contact with the tanker.

The radar swept around and around on the screen. He saw a blip, then it faded. A few sweeps later, it reappeared. He was trying to get a fix on it when he heard the voice of the second Pave Hawk's pilot. "JACKAL TWO, contact five right for forty, beaming south at 120 knots."

"Damn," Beach Dog whispered to himself. The first round of drinks after the mission was completed was now on him. He confirmed that the MC-130 was five degrees to their right at a range of forty nautical miles. "Contact," Beach Dog said over the radio.

"JACKAL ONE is channel 50, looking for gas," Beach Dog said.

"JACKAL ONE, COWBIRD is holding at STARLIGHT, three thousand feet."

Beach Dog picked him up on the situation display. He punched the data into the flight computer and it confirmed his rendezvous heading. Pulling up on the collective, he pushed the Pave Hawk to match the plane's airspeed and worked the cyclic so that the helicopter began to climb up to meet the MC-130. He searched the dark skies for the turboprop aircraft. He had lost the beer in the first bet, but he could still win the second round of drinks from his wingman if he could be the first now to make visual contact.

Several minutes passed and he couldn't spot it, although the radar told him he was getting close. He hated to roll over and ask for an assist, but he squeezed his mike and did it anyway. "COWBIRD, JACKAL ONE. No joy. Request Christmas tree."

A flash of red and green caught Beach Dog's eye as the Combat Talon briefly turned on its exterior lights. "Tally the tanker, one-thirty, high, seven miles," Beach Dog said to his copilot as he spotted it. He leveled his helo out at two thousand feet, a thousand feet below the tanker and a mere three hundred above the highest terrain. Keying the mike, he said, "COWBIRD, JACKAL ONE, you're seven-thirty, low for seven."

JACKAL TWO also called in its position relative to the tanker, indicating that it was also below it and seven nautical miles away.

"JACKAL FLIGHT, you are also cleared into the right observation position," the commander of the tanker said, giving permission for both helicopters to approach.

Beach Dog climbed five hundred feet above the tanker and positioned himself a thousand feet abeam its wing line so that the MC-130's commander could see him. Then he heard, "JACKAL FLIGHT. COWBIRD has a tally.

Cleared into the stabilized position, left hose. Check nose is cold, switches safe."

Beach Dog turned off his radar and glanced at the panel to confirm that all weapons switches were off. "COWBIRD, JACKAL ONE's nose cold, switches safe."

"COWBIRD, JACKAL TWO's nose is cold, switches safe," the second Pave Hawk pilot said.

"JACKAL FLIGHT ready," Beach Dog said as he had hundreds of times before.

"Cleared to plug," the MC-130 commander said as he banked the aircraft into a tight circle with the helos on the inside so that they could close on the tanker using their smaller turn radius since they didn't have excess speed to narrow the gap.

Beach Dog and his wingman were about to pull within feet of the airplane, out of sight of its commander who was relying upon intercom reports from observers watching from the aft side doors. The slightest error could cause a collision in the pitch-black night.

Pucker time.

Beach Dog lived for these moments.

Holding his breath, he studied the small yellow light on the pod hydraulic system. It was ready to plug and play. He tapped the controls, coaxing a little more speed out of the craft.

"Forward three, down two," the commander said as Beach Dog moved toward the basket at the end of the long invisible hose trailing from the aircraft. He fought the airplane's wake as he stabilized the helicopter just below and behind the tanker. The basket was at his one o'clock. He caressed the controls and flew the fixed probe on the front of the Pave Hawk into the basket. It mated and the gas pump started.

Now Beach Dog had to keep it steady for the next seven or eight minutes. At least the air was smooth tonight. This was his most vulnerable time and he trusted the Cobra was somewhere out there, covering his back. He lowered his seat and ducked down so he could keep an eye on the green refueling light. The world faded away as he focused on the slow dance with the tanker. As much as he wanted to use his feet, he forced himself not to touch the pedals and risk overcompensating. When necessary, he lightly tapped the controls, adjusting his position.

Several minutes later, the red light came on and the transfer was complete. He reduced power and drifted aft for disengagement from the basket and to position the helo on the outer edge of the airplane's wake.

Time for the Beach Dog to surf the wave.

Banzai!

Expecting to come free of the aircraft, he felt a small vibration, then a tug, so he looked outside. The Pave Hawk was still connected to the tanker. Working the controls, he tried to gently move away from the basket. The MC-130's take-up reel was supposed to retract the hose. Nothing happened. They were stuck together in midair. The basket needed a little more convincing to let go. He cut back on the throttle and lifted the nose higher to cause drag to slow down his helo so the damn hose was jerked away by the faster plane.

He felt a jolt. The helicopter shuddered and he saw the guide lights under the plane move away. The Hawk yawed to the right, then dropped. Something smacked the windshield with a loud clap and he jumped. It whacked again and again.

Beach Dog worked the controls as if they were an extension of his own body. The Pave Hawk stabilized, but something kept whipping the helo, pounding the glass like an out of control dominatrix.

The hose.

With each whack, Beach Dog was sure the window was going to give and send daggers into them. As the helicop-

ter was thrown around and beaten, he suddenly pictured
the steel hose flipping into the path of the rotors. If that
happened, that would be it. The forward motion had to
stop fast. His airspeed was still over one hundred knots.
He shoved down the collective and tipped the nose right
up to the edge, daring the craft to flip while he used the
airframe to brake. His stomach did a somersault, but the
Hawk slowed and the thumping stopped. A caution light
flashed on the console to his left. He glanced at the center
panel and a gearbox chip light winked at him. The controls
were responsive, but the light was now glowing steadily.
The detector screened for ferrous particles in the system
and if it was telling the truth, the tail rotor's gearbox was
chewing itself up.

"JACKAL ONE, declaring an emergency and setting
down."

Beach Dog slowly looked around below him for suitable
landing terrain.

Iggy grabbed the extra headset and gave orders as they
were losing altitude. That guy was a true operator, never
giving up, giving orders even when Beach Dog wasn't
completely sure they were going to make it.

"JACKAL TWO this is TIN MAN. Activate bump plan.
DRAGON ONE, hold position and stand by."

The helicopter descended straight down. Hunter had
thought Beach Dog had it back under control, but they
were going straight down so fast, he wasn't sure anymore.
Suddenly, the descent slowed and a few seconds later it
kissed the ground. Everyone clapped and whistled and
Beach Dog reached over and petted his lucky cat attached
to the dash.

"Sierra Hotel," Hunter congratulated him with insider
lingo for shit hot.

Hunter and GENGHIS made eye contact with each other
and GENGHIS shook his head, closing his eyes as he said,

"Dodged another one. You know my big fear is I'm not going to go in combat. I just know it's going to be some dumb-ass accident like this because somebody packed the fucking apricots and ate the goddamn Charms."

Hunter smiled. He had never really believed the old WWII myth among mechanized infantry that every time a tank had been blown up, it had been found to have had a can of apricots inside. He told himself that the modern version about the Charms candy was equally untrue and it couldn't possibly have been the cause of the difficulties earlier. Urban combat legend or not, he wasn't about to admit that when he'd downed a MRE in Bagram, he did eat a handful of Charms before he realized what he had done. Bad juju was not something he wanted to mess with.

Everyone sat inside the helo waiting for the dust and sand to settle before getting out. The second Pave Hawk would be there any minute and they would swap aircraft according to Iggy's bump plan. If this helo could be fixed, it would follow with the second chalk as soon as it was airworthy. The delay shouldn't cost them more than five minutes, Hunter told himself while he tried not to think about how they were down to one Hawk, one Cobra and one team. Thinking about how bad things were could only jinx them further.

At least the weather was good, Hunter was thinking, when he saw a bright flash of white lightning, then a firestorm of arching electricity. A blue fireball ballooned about thirty meters away from them in the air, to their three o'clock, then he felt their Pave Hawk shake as the blast wave passed through them.

Oh god. JACKAL TWO. Power lines.

An electrical line had snagged another bird.

The helo smacked into the ground and an orange fireball shot a hundred feet into the air, turning night into day. Within seconds, ammunition started to cook off and began popping and shooting out in all directions. Bullets rained on them, pinging against their Hawk while rockets screamed overhead, flames streaming behind them as they launched themselves from the crashed Hawk. *Damn Charms.*

Hunter ducked, then felt stupid for doing it.

A few moments later, more rocket trails spewed wildly as their motors detonated. Hunter felt for the seven men aboard, then he realized he had just witnessed the rescue mission going up in flames.

Stella.

"Beach Dog," Iggy said as he released the safety restraints. "You think you can pry that cage off the fuel intake?"

"NSDQ."

"Night Stalkers don't quit, I know—but did the Hawk quit us?"

"The coupling didn't disengage. We were stuck to the end of the fuel hose until the hose finally broke. Without the fuel and air pressure to hold the basket on, you should be able to pull it straight off—don't even need a hammer." Beach Dog was already pulling out a toolkit.

"So what's that for? Something you failed to tell me?"

"The gearbox chip light came on."

"Serious?"

"Could ground us. You get a lot of false readings in desert conditions, but it can also mean the tail rotor's gearbox is ready to go. I need to check it out."

"Do that first. I need to know if she's airworthy." Iggy turned to the rest of the crew. "Wilson, get that piece of crap off the probe. Monroe, Ashland, secure the perimeter. Stone, GENGHIS, check if anyone was thrown clear. Look out for the electrical wires and the unexploded ordnance that's still cooking off."

"If the aircraft checks out, is the mission a go, sir?" Hunter said, fully aware they were dancing on the edge of the go/no go parameters. He felt to make sure his sidearm was still in place.

"If there are survivors, we have to scrub and work out something else for tomorrow night." Iggy shook his head. "This is going to hell fast and I can't leave men here to die."

"Then call in the Cobra, bump the gunner and let me take the front seat. You can insert me tonight and I'll gather intel for a second shot tomorrow night. You know Stella might not have until then. Hell, she might not have until morning."

Iggy ignored him as he put his hand on the fuel probe. The metal arm extended from the right front of the helicopter and was half the length of the crew cabin, but didn't go out as far as the rotors. The tip was mated with the metal basket and a couple meters of hose dangled from its end. Most of the rubber sheath had been stripped away from the steel hose.

Hunter stood staring at Iggy, waiting for a response. Iggy looked up at him.

"You go in there, Rambo, without support, you'll get yourself and Cam killed. I'm not going to let that happen. I'm going to get her."

"Sending me in tonight might be her only hope."

"We're not there yet." Iggy reached for the metal basket and tugged. It slid off. He threw it as far into the desert as he could, then a transmission from the Cobra came over the headsets.

"TIN MAN this is DRAGON ONE. Be advised we are at joker."

The Cobra had reached the fuel state where it needed to start thinking about getting onto the ground so the Hawk could refuel it. The Cobras were killer machines, but they had one critical flaw: they couldn't refuel in the air.

The burning wreckage continued to send out sporadic rocket fire and bullets. Iggy wanted to wait as long as he could to let the fireworks die down before bringing the Cobra in. They would have to stay in the air until their fuel situation reached critical—bingo. At that moment it didn't look like the mission would proceed and there was no need to risk another bird if he didn't have to. He keyed his mike, "DRAGON ONE, TIN MAN. Land at bingo. Caution high-voltage lines."

The Pave Hawk lay on its side, its tail rotor broken off. Hunter could see bodies burning inside the airframe and he could feel the heat increasing. He and GENGHIS walked around it, giving it a wide berth due to the popping ordnance. The fire crackled with gunshots as bullets aboard the downed craft heated up, but the electric lines troubled him more. When they were near the line, both he and GENGHIS shuffled along, keeping their feet close together and in contact with the ground at all times to avoid electricity arcing through them. The flames were so bright they made his night vision goggles useless.

Beach Dog hurried to the tail and opened a panel so he could get to the intermediate gearbox. Holding a penlight in his mouth, he pulled out the chip detector screen, hoping he wouldn't find metal slivers. The dipstick looked as if it had been rolled in glitter. Beach Dog smiled as it sparkled at him—sand. Sand had gotten into the system and magnetic particles in it were causing the false readings. The gearbox was fine.

"Iggy," he called back, "she's good."

Iggy spoke into his microphone to bring in the Cobra and hurry up with the fuel transfer so they could get moving. "DRAGON ONE, this is TIN MAN. Cleared to land at our eight o'clock. Caution high-voltage lines."

Hunter and GENGHIS had canvassed the area near the burning helicopter, then methodically expanded their search grid. Hunter heard the Cobra come in for the fuel transfer and knew he had to get back in the next five minutes to have a chance at persuading Iggy to send him on it. He was ready to break off from the search and return to the Hawk.

"You hear that?" GENGHIS said.

The Cobra's engines stopped and Hunter could hear a faint moan that seemed to come from the desert, beyond where he could see with the light of the flames. He turned away from the wreckage, put on the goggles and cupped his hands over the sides to block out as much light as he could. As he scanned the desert floor, he was sure he heard someone.

"My ten o'clock, twenty meters out," GENGHIS said.

Hunter spotted the body and shuffled in that direction. When he was confident that he was far enough away from the power line, he sprinted. He smelled burnt flesh as he approached the man. Shining an infrared beam on him, he could see black crispy flesh and raw meat. The face was a grotesque Halloween mask, unrecognizable. His clothes had burned away along with most of his skin. The legs and arms were twisted and obviously broken from the fall. The moan grew fainter.

Hunter squatted down beside him and started to feel for a pulse in his neck, then decided it was better not to touch him and risk further injury. "Can you talk to me? What's your name?"

The guy groaned softly, giving no sign he comprehended anything. Hunter looked at GENGHIS and shook his head. "You know even if we get the bird in the air, Iggy's gonna scrub the mission because of this guy."

"I heard. You fly. Do you think they can fix it?"

Hunter took a deep breath. "We've been through quite a bit of sand and dust. I'd bet on a false read."

Iggy's voice came over Hunter's earpiece. "SABER TOOTH this is TIN MAN. Return to base. Any survivors?"

Hunter didn't respond, but stared at the charred casualty. If he allowed a dying man to keep him away from Stella, he would never forgive himself. He also knew he couldn't live with himself if he left a teammate behind.

Iggy's voice came over their earpieces again. "Repeat, any survivors?"

Hunter stared at the man and knew what he had to do. He squatted down to pick him up. "Give me a hand with him."

"Sure thing." GENGHIS pulled out his sidearm and fired.

Hunter and GENGHIS returned to the Pave Hawk to see the flight engineer retracting the hose. The refueling was complete. "She airworthy?" Hunter said to Beach Dog, dreading the confrontation with Iggy if she wasn't.

"Itching to go back up there and visit her tanker friend for more juice," Beach Dog said. "She's a go."

As GENGHIS climbed into the helicopter, Iggy grabbed his arm. His face was stormy. "You pulled the same thing you did in Libya, didn't you?"

GENGHIS stared at him for a few moments without saying anything, then twisted his body away from Iggy and climbed into the helicopter. Iggy gripped Hunter's shoulder as he got in. "The truth, Stone. Any survivors?"

Hunter strapped himself into his seat before speaking. He despised GENGHIS for what he'd done, and at the same time felt enormously grateful to the son of a bitch. He looked straight ahead and said, "There are no survivors."

"I thought so," Iggy said with a grunt as he slid the door shut. "Beach Dog, get us the hell out of here. We've got to get to that tango camp before Camille kicks all their asses without us."

SEVENTY-NINE

Shangri-la

Al-Zahrani was taller and thinner than Camille had expected; he had mysterious brown eyes, peaceful eyes which at the same time had glints of mercy and flashes of vengeance. A cleric in a white skullcap read from a Koran while two guards pointed AKs at her. Back home in the Ozarks, they called this a shotgun wedding, except she wasn't pregnant and the groom wasn't the one with the guns pointed at him.

Al-Zahrani held her gaze. For a moment she thought he was trying to tell her something.

The young man who had earlier brought her the water and clothes translated the cleric's words, cheating whenever he could read the same verse from an English translation of the Koran. "And among His signs in this, that He created for you mates, from among yourselves, that ye may dwell . . ."

She didn't have much tolerance for religious writings in any language and quit listening while she assessed the tactical situation. Two guards pointed AKs at her. It was a poor choice of weapon for the circumstances and she considered baiting them to shoot her just as she maneuvered in front of al-Zahrani so they hit him as well. It wasn't her best option since she couldn't guarantee that he'd be killed, but it might be the best she could do.

Her wrists were tied in front of her, but her legs were now free since they intended for her to spread them soon. No one had bothered to search her since they'd thrown her into the shed. The long nail concealed in her sleeve was an awkward weapon, but it was the best she had found. She figured her best chance was to spike it into the soft spot behind his ear just before he tried to enter her. The thought was so disgusting. What a way to die, shot by bodyguards while being raped by the world's most wanted terrorist. At least Muslims seemed to bathe a lot.

"The Holy Prophet, may the peace and blessings of Allah be upon him, made the *mut'a* marriage *halal*." The interpreter stumbled through the translation. She couldn't figure out why the hell they were bothering, but she guessed it was part of their screwy ethics.

On the way over she had heard a generator, but al-Zahrani's tent was lit by several oil lamps. They seemed to reserve the power to run their phones and communications and the few lights outside. She hoped al-Zahrani liked to do it in the dark. Like her Night Stalker buddies always said, "Death waits in the dark."

She hoped the damn thing would get a move on. At least they had fed her before the ceremony and she guessed that was her dowry. They could at least have given her the whole goat. She made a mental note not to serve boiled goat if she survived this and ever married.

After stifling several mini-yawns she managed to get her eyes to tear up, then she caught al-Zahrani's gaze and made herself smile at him.

He smiled back.

Dumb fuck.

Soon the peace and blessings of Camille Black would be upon him—god help his soul.

EIGHTY

Despite the snafu with the last air-to-air refueling, the next one didn't make Beach Dog nearly as nervous as Iggy did, whipping out his laptop and revising the mission plan on the fly. He'd seen it happen many times and he had learned long ago that when things started sliding south the next thing he knew he was waking up in an alley in Tijuana with no wallet and no pants, smelling of booze and puke.

Beach Dog descended and began to hug the ground as closely as he could in case the tangos had some kind of radar warning system, even though he guessed it probably consisted of pie tins tied to a clothesline. He was using FLIR the entire mission, but only through the Afghan-Uzbek border region did he fly close enough to the ground to really need the navigational system. Now it was time to show off why Night Stalkers ruled the darkness. He flew five feet above the dunes, too fast to kick up a trail of sand.

"Five minutes to the LZ. Wax up them boards, dudes," Beach Dog said as he passed over the south rim of the open pit mine, pointed the nose down and plunged two hundred and fifty feet in seconds. He pushed the speed to one hundred sixty knots and boomed through the man-made canyon, a few feet above the floor. "And hang on. We're going to be flying the Pipeline."

For the next several minutes the helicopter lurched sharp to port, then to starboard, up, down, sudden drops and immediate climbs. *Man, this is flying.*

Beach Dog saw a mound directly in front of them and threw the Hawk hard right, but the canyon wall was dead ahead. Beach Dog spun the Hawk in a Bat-turn, rotating one hundred eighty degrees. He slalomed around the hills, throwing the crew left, then tumbling their stomachs to the right.

"You know what Night Stalkers say," Beach Dog yelled to anyone listening.

" 'Night Stalkers don't quit,' " several men said in unison.

A vertical cliff popped up out of nowhere. Beach Dog yanked back on the cyclic and shot straight up and onward at warp speed. "NSDQ is so true, but I was thinking, 'Death waits in the dark.' "

EIGHTY-ONE

Shangri-la

The cleric, interpreter and one of the two guards left the tent, extinguishing all the lights except a single candle. Al-Zahrani put his arm around Camille's waist and pulled her close. His breath smelled, even from a few feet away. She met his lips and kissed him violently, channeling her anger into passion, seducing him into lowering his defenses. His mouth tasted like an old tennis shoe and his beard and moustache were steel wool, scratching her face. When she couldn't stand it any longer, she leaned her head back, inviting him to kiss her neck. She giggled, visualizing the soft sounds of bubbles rising to the surface in her witch's cauldron.

Keeping her bound hands pressed together so he couldn't see the nail, she touched his face with the sides of her little fingers and rippled her hands down his body as if she were a belly dancer. She stopped short of his hard-on.

Gross.

Al-Zahrani shouted something to the guard as he shoved her down onto his sleeping mat and tore off the 5.11s she had left on underneath the jilbab. The guard blew out the candle.

His vigilance was waning.

Good.

Just before the guard left the tent, al-Zahrani pinned her down. He groped at her breasts, shoving the jilbab up around her neck. Camille's hate was acid burning in her belly. She wanted to fight back, but she knew she had to force herself to play it out until the opportune moment. As soon as he got bored with her breasts, she would work her hands up into position. She prayed he wasn't a breast man who would linger forever. There was an artery in the stomach, but she doubted she could find it.

Playing with his chest hairs totally disgusted her, so she gave herself a break and worked her hands up to his beard, but when she got there it still had food in it and she didn't want to touch it. Just as she started to doubt if she could pull it off, he let her slip her arms over the top of his head and move her wrists right where she wanted them— behind his occipital bone at the lower back of his skull. She would've preferred to snap his neck, but it was impossible from that angle.

His cock pressed against her, trying to enter her. She wasn't in position yet and she had to get this right because she couldn't stomach this again. Wiggling her hips away, she evaded it while she put her right leg on his hipbone. Her foot there kept him stabilized so she could scoot slightly to the left and maneuver her arms into position.

Her forearms rubbed against his neck, underneath his ears and he laughed. She bent her right arm, bringing it down to her chest and pulling his head closer. As hard as she could, she thrust the nail at the sweet spot behind his left ear.

Al-Zahrani moved his head. She missed and the nail flew from her sweaty hands. He didn't notice. He shoved her foot off his hip bone and pushed hard into her. She was as dry as the Kyzyl Kum and it hurt like hell. The fucker had her pinned down like a pro wrestler.

She turned her head to the side and waited.

In less than two minutes, he pulled out and called for the guards and the interpreter. They were inside his tent within seconds. Al-Zahrani said something to her as he stroked her hair. She jerked her head away from him and turned her back to him and she pushed down the jilbab. The interpreter said it meant that she pleased him and they would stay married for the next three days.

At least they weren't going to kill her tonight, though the way she felt, it would've been welcome. She would have at least two more chances to take him out and thoroughly disgust herself in the process.

She could do just about anything, but not this again. She had to find a way to take out the fucker tonight.

Two of the guards escorted her from al-Zahrani's quarters. She forced herself to focus on situational awareness and not how utterly miserable she was feeling because she had to remain in control of her emotions if she was going to succeed.

They passed two huge tents with men sleeping on the ground inside. Nearly as many bedded down on mats outside to get away from the heat. She had seen another barracks on the other side of al-Zahrani's tent and estimated that the camp held three to four hundred tangos.

The last tent before the dark void between her shack and the compound was more of a canopy like the ones used in big weddings back home. Weddings—she couldn't let herself think about weddings. And they were *not* married.

Under the canopy, three dozen men sat on oriental carpets in four different groups. Each of them had an AK within arm's length and several wore belts with short daggers hanging off them. Some had Korans open in front of them, though she couldn't imagine that they could see to read from the few kerosene lamps scattered about. They stopped their debates long enough to watch her march by. She could feel their hate.

It was mutual.

One guard walked ahead of her, the other behind. Even after she had passed the last tent, she found no openings to escape.

They arrived at the shed and shoved her inside without

tying her feet back up—her first lucky break of the day, she consoled herself, even though all she wanted to do was collapse on the ground and cry.

The shed was pitch-black, but gradually she sensed someone else in with her.

EIGHTY-TWO

Hunter was feeling queasy when the Pave Hawk deposited him, Genghis and Ashland at the release point on the other side of the rock ridge from the tango camp. Expecting to feel amped since he was only a three-and-a-half kilometer hike from Stella, instead he fought away a nagging concern for her. He had done scores of extractions and he always went into them convinced that they could handle whatever came at them, but this one worried him. These stakes were too personal. As he humped the three kilometers around the ridge to the camp, he fought to get Stella off his mind and think of her only as their mission objective, code name Grackle. It didn't do much good. However he reframed it, he was still on his way to rescue the woman he loved.

The passage between the two open pits was a mound of soft sand that slowed them down. As they rounded the base of the ridge, Hunter could see the compound in the distance through the night vision device. It was a new moon and Hunter was happy he didn't have too much ambient light messing with the night vision goggles. The PVS-14 helmet-mounted monocle was far superior to the old PVS-7 head-mounted goggles that Rubicon had supplied him with. Camille didn't cut corners with her equipment. Tonight he hoped her investment would pay off.

Hunter carried a rucksack with a half-dozen Claymores. Despite his injuries, Genghis wore a pack with the blasting cap assemblies. The spools were light, but the hundreds of feet of wire made them bulky. Ashland was traveling light, looking like a tango with a knock-off Adidas duffle bag. They were two kilometers from the far edge of the camp and Ashland had fallen behind. At least it was easy running. The ground was hard and level, packed down by tons of earthmoving equipment.

"How you doing?" Hunter ran alongside GENGHIS. He didn't show any signs that his earlier injuries were affecting him, but he was the type who would never show it until he keeled over.

"Better than Ashland," GENGHIS said. "You trust him?"

Hunter laughed. "He's the fucker who started this mess. Burned me bad. Was afraid I'd blow his cover because I recognized him."

"You think there's a chance he's working with the tangos?"

"Even with what you did back at the crash site, you're still the one I want watching my back." Hunter jogged past him.

The Pave Hawk flew out of the crater and dropped Iggy off on the desert floor, upwind and a kilometer from the start of the ridge above the compound. He was relieved that the desert floor there was hard like in Iraq and he supposed that had to do with the way the winds whipped up from the crater, sweeping the rim clean. Whatever the reason, he was grateful. The M240G medium machine gun weighed enough on its own and the ammo cans were like carrying car batteries: dense, concentrated weight that didn't help the blisters on his stump. But Iggy knew it wasn't really the heavy, awkward gear that was irritating him as he jogged to his position. He had lost seven men in a stupid accident that had cut his team in half. The team was smaller than he knew he should be working with, but for Camille, he was willing to take the risk. He hoped to god those bastards hadn't messed her up too much yet, but he knew what they did to women—and to men.

Several minutes later, Iggy set down his gear and looked

over the ridge at the terrorist camp. Through his night vision monocle, he found the reflection of the square inch of glint tape attached to the top of Hunter and GENGHIS' helmets. It would be invisible to the tangos without night vision equipment, which he hoped they wouldn't be using. He could see they were approaching the training grounds on the edge of the camp.

Aside from the drop-off one hundred meters behind him, the spot was ideal: He was in range and sight of the entire compound. The tangos seemed to be slumbering away or at least they weren't loitering about. He took out his binoculars for a quick scan of the perimeter. Their only sentry post with four men was set up at the entry to the pit, but that was over a kilometer away from the camp.

The tangos were a trusting bunch.

Working as fast as he could, he set up the 240-Golf's tripod and boresighted the AN/PVS-17 night vision scope so that the crosshairs were aligned with the barrel. He fed the first rounds of the ammo belt into the machine gun.

"CHALK ONE this is TIN MAN. In position and standing by," he said over the encrypted radio.

"Copy that," Stone said.

With everything ready, he took out his thermal binoculars to confirm that they were targeting the right tents with the Claymores. The desert landscape held onto the summer heat as if it remembered the chill of the Uzbek winter and it made most things look shades of yellow and orange, but the dark red of body heat couldn't be mistaken. He guessed he was looking at three to four hundred tangos, snoozing away in three tents.

Now Iggy could start searching for Camille. Prisoners tended to be kept separated from others and he hoped to find a structure with only a few heat signatures inside. A terrorist training facility was not the type of place that usually held prisoners, so that made it even more likely they'd lock her up somewhere alone—if they hadn't already killed her. He shoved that thought from his mind as fast as he could.

He started with the structures closest to the entrance of the mine and worked his way toward the raiding party. In each structure he picked up several bodies and assumed they were tangos sleeping wherever they could find a good spot. The body density was far greater than he was looking for, so he kept scanning.

In the middle of the camp, he found something. The pattern appeared to be a single individual with two others positioned less than three meters away. He swapped the thermal imaging binoculars for standard night vision ones. The structure appeared to be a small tent, but it was difficult to see much more because of the camouflage netting blowing in the wind. The pattern was consistent with a prisoner being held by two guards, but he couldn't imagine anyone stupid enough to hold a prisoner in a tent. It was more likely the camp's head honcho. He radioed Stone instructions for one of them to check it out after they had infiltrated the camp. Switching back to the thermal binoculars, he kept searching.

Please be alive.

EIGHTY-THREE

The CIA program's original scope was to hide and interrogate the two dozen or so al Qaeda leaders believed to be directly responsible for the Sept. 11 attacks, or who posed an imminent threat, or had knowledge of the larger al Qaeda network. But as the volume of leads pouring into the CTC from abroad increased, and the capacity of its paramilitary group to seize suspects grew, the CIA began apprehending more people whose intelligence value and links to terrorism were less certain, according to four current and former officials.

The original standard for consigning suspects to the invisible universe was lowered or ignored, they said. "They've got many, many more who don't reach any threshold," one intelligence official said.

—THE WASHINGTON POST, November 2, 2005, as reported by
Dana Priest

Shangri-la

"Hunter?" Camille said in an intentionally weak voice, just in case it wasn't him. Then fell to the ground, pretending to whimper as she moved toward her cache of buried nails. No one answered, but she heard breathing and kept herself turned toward it while she ran her fingers along the exposed wooden frame, searching until she found the knot that marked where she had buried the nails.

"Cut the bullshit, Camille."

Joe Chronister.

"Joe? Thank god you're here." She lied. She had no illusion that he was there to rescue her. If he was in the heart of the terrorist camp, it could only mean that he was somehow working with the tangos. The only question was, was he working on his own or with the CIA? At that moment, it didn't matter much. All she really cared about was surviving to wreak revenge on al-Zahrani. Her fingers sifted through the sand until she found the nail. "He raped me."

"Stay where you are. I've got a Glock trained on you in case you can't see it."

He shined a flashlight on her. She squatted, so he couldn't easily see that her legs weren't tied and she contorted her face before she looked up. He had a false beard and was dressed like a *muj* in a dishdashah. As a smart operative, it was a safe assumption that he was wearing a bulletproof vest. She would have to plan her attack accordingly. She shielded her eyes with her forearm, holding up her bound hands to help paint the picture of a distraught female prisoner. It wouldn't take much acting.

"You shouldn't have come here, Camille. You fucked things really good. I set you up for a nice little excursion to Ukraine. You would've kept your pretty ass safe."

"He violated me, Joe." Her voice cracked and she whimpered. She forced herself to flashback to al-Zahrani rooting around on top of her and let herself feel the pain until she started crying.

"Pretty impressive operation, we've got here, isn't it? You're one of the few people who can really appreciate the brilliance of what I've got going on here. Everything you see here—Rubicon is pulling the strings."

Camille cried harder, then started sobbing. She fell into the part far too easily. She knew she was in danger of believing herself a victim and losing her edge. She pulled herself back and began moaning, breathing through her mouth as if she couldn't stop crying.

"Enough of the fucking theatrics. You listening to me?" Joe stepped closer.

Camille rocked herself as she whimpered. Joe Chronister

was not someone she had ever thought of as needy, but she realized then that he had a strong need for her to appreciate his work. The more she ignored him, the more he talked.

"I told al-Zahrani he could keep you a couple of nights so it didn't look bad in front of the boys, then you're coming over to us at BALI HAI. It's our duck blind that we use to keep an eye on this goddamn place. It's also a prison—and a well-built one I might add, thank you KGB. It's a hundred feet down inside an old gold mine that dates back to tsarist times. BALI HAI is the jewel in our newly privatized little gulag chain. With Congress and that *Post* reporter Dana Priest breathing down our neck about Agency-run black sites, we're putting them under new management—privately-run prisons, just like stateside. You don't even need presidential approval when the other motherfucker is the one who's doing it. That's the beauty of outsourcing—plausible deniability. Gotta love it."

She looked up, counting on her puffy eyes. "He raped me. They had AKs. They pinned me down and held me," Camille said in a near-whisper. "They held me while he . . ." She gasped for air and then continued "raped me."

"What the fuck are you talking about? Is this for real? You're sniveling like my goddamn wife, for christssake. Pull it together, Camille. What the hell happened to fuck you up like this so fast?"

"Al-Zahrani," she whispered as quietly as she could. "He, he . . . raped me."

"I can't hear you. What'd you say?"

Chronister bent down toward her and Camille sprang.

She shoved the nail deep into his left eye as she twisted her body at a forty-five-degree angle so she would be clear in case he managed to discharge the weapon. He screamed and the flashlight fell to the ground as he raised his hands up to his eye. Camille put her hands over the hand that was holding the gun. She guided his right hand across his chest underneath his left armpit to avoid any bulletproof vest, then she twisted his wrist into a downward angle. She pulled the trigger, sending a round through his heart and lung.

"That's for Jackie and the others, you asshole," Camille whispered before letting him drop.

EIGHTY-FOUR

Shangri-la

Hunter was a kilometer away from the camp's perimeter when he heard a single gunshot from somewhere directly between him and the compound. He stopped and held his closed fist in the air and GENGHIS halted. Neither man could see anything, so Hunter radioed Iggy.

"TIN MAN this is SABER TOOTH. Request IR recon. One click, my twelve o'clock."

"SABER TOOTH, TIN MAN. Two heat signatures inside a small fixed structure at your twelve o'clock."

Hunter started running as fast as he could toward the shack. If Stella was wounded, he might still be able to save her.

Camille didn't want to touch Chronister, but forced herself to run her hands over his body in search of a knife or other weapons. He was traveling light with only a smashed roll of Mentos in his pocket. She devoured them. Al-Zahrani's tennis-shoe taste wouldn't leave her mouth.

Using the water bucket as a bidet, she washed herself although she knew it would take a while until she felt clean again. She took longer than she should have, but less time than she wanted. The polyester jilbab made a lousy towel and she hated wearing it, but her pants were left in al-Zahrani's tent. The bastard probably kept her panties under his pillow. She spat, but it didn't help.

She stripped Chronister of his Glock and Kevlar vest, put it on, then pulled up the jilbab so she could run. Lying on her back near a wall, she kicked as hard as she could with both bare feet. The plywood splintered.

The cooler night air felt good as she sprinted toward the camp and al-Zahrani's tent.

Iggy's voice came over Hunter's earpiece. "SABER TOOTH this is TIN MAN. I'm tracking a runner three hundred meters and twelve o'clock from your position, leaving the structure."

Hunter scanned the area, but was too far away. The lights of the tango camp extended his NVG's range, but he couldn't see out more than two hundred meters. The thought of Stella, lying only a few hundred meters from him, bleeding out, made him push harder.

Fifteen seconds later, he could see a shack. He ordered GENGHIS to continue into the camp and take out the generators. If the runner really was Stella at the edge of the compound, he could always call GENGHIS back, but if it wasn't, he wanted the advantage of total darkness as soon as he could get it.

GENGHIS sprinted ahead past the concrete pillars of the construction site while Hunter circled to the front of the shed. Tools were thrown into a pile just outside the door as if someone had hastily emptied it. His experience told him that's where they had held Stella. He slipped inside, fanning his weapon from side to side in case someone was there. Then he saw the body and dropped to his knees.

"Oh, my god. Stella."

Then he saw a bearded face and an under-the-arm gunshot wound, angled to avoid body armor and pierce vital organs. A dead tango and an operator's signature.

Stella's alive.

Hunter heard Ashland's voice over the earpiece. The guy sounded out of breath. "SABER TOOTH. Ashland here. Don't shoot me. Can I come in?"

"Cleared to enter," Hunter said, then keyed his mike.

"SABER TOOTH to CHALK ONE. Confirmed one dead tango. Suspect GRACKLE is the runner. GENGHIS, attempt intercept."

GENGHIS confirmed the order as Ashland came into the shed and bent down beside the corpse. "Jesus. That's Joe Chronister."

Hunter looked more closely at the tango, then he recognized him. He'd seen the man before, clean-cut and dressed as a Westerner—the interrogator he knew as Zorro. "Who the hell is Joe Chronister?"

"The CIA SOB who put both of us on that flight to hell." Ashland tried to catch his breath.

"What the hell is the CIA doing working with Rubicon? Oh, forget it. Until we get the lights out, you're the only one of us who can walk into that place after her without alerting them. You better haul ass right now or I'm shooting you right here."

It was a new moon and Camille could barely see where she was going. At least her feet were untied so she could run, but her bound hands threw her off balance. She could see the flicker of the lamps of the debating circles in the mess hall.

She moved into the deeper shadows along the base of the cliff rising above the compound, but the ground was a giant mound of loose debris that had fallen from the rock face. The study groups' lamps were dim, but bright enough to reach the rubble. Rather than double back and move along the edge between the tent and the drop-off to the next lower level of the mine, she lay flat on her belly and crept like a sniper. Even though the jilbab was partially tied around her waist, her knees kept catching on the cloth, tripping her and pulling it loose.

A minute earlier, GENGHIS had been able to see someone running ahead of him at the edge of his sight, then the figure disappeared. The closer he got to the first tent, the

more the light from the tangos' lamps increased the range
of his night vision, but he still couldn't see her. That girl
was sure slippery and if he wasn't running toward a few
hundred tangos, he would've enjoyed the chase a lot more.
He keyed his mike, "SABER TOOTH, GENGHIS here.
Contact with the runner has been broken. Proceeding on to
generators."

There was a rock pile blocking Hunter's passage between
the tent and the ridge. He didn't like to risk sky-lining by
walking along the drop-off on the other side, but it was so
dark, only a stargazer would notice someone moving between the camp and Orion's belt. He decided to veer around
the tent and hug the edge of the cliff that dropped to the
lower level.

He tapped Ashland on the arm and whispered. "This
way."

Ashland pulled off his NVGs and his comm set and
stuck them into his duffle bag. Then he walked straight
ahead into the light of the camp.

Hunter ran as far as he dared, then dropped to his knees
to lower his profile and crawled along the edge. He heard
Ashland speak to the men in Arabic as he walked on into
the heart of the camp.

Camille was shocked at the tangos' lack of internal security, but she wasn't about to complain. They were sleeping
everywhere and they all had AKs at their fingertips, but
there were no lookouts, no sentries anywhere. As she
crawled past the second row of barracks, she was starting
to think she might be able to escape or at least die trying.
Al-Zahrani was in a tent, not a fortress. If she took him out
quietly, she might be able to steal one of their trucks and
get away. She just needed a knife to free her hands and slit
his throat.

The half-dozen electric lights hanging outside were

dim, but enough for her to see and be seen. Camille searched for one of the snoozing terrorists who was separated from the herd. Along the outside of the group, a teenager wearing a knife attached to his belt was curled up on his right side on a rug that was too small for him. She crept over to him and held her breath while she slowly slipped his knife from its sheath.

Suddenly he rolled over on his back and opened his eyes. Stella shoved her right forearm down on his mouth to mute any screams. The knife was in her right hand, positioned behind his left ear. She raked her forearm across his mouth, thrusting the knife into the soft spot behind his left ear. She kept her arm pressed against his mouth for a few seconds in case he used his dying breath to scream.

Back in the shadows, she cut off the rope and rubbed her sore wrists, then moved them in a luxurious range of motion. But if she was going to pull this off, she needed full movement and not only in her wrists. She crept back to the dead tango, grabbed his ankles and dragged him into the darkness where she undressed him.

His stinky clothes were liberating, even if they weren't the best fit. She rolled up the pant legs and tried on his sandals. They were several sizes too big. The hard sandy ground wasn't too punishing and her bare feet were quieter anyway, so she pushed them aside. Slinking back to his sleeping mat, she kept her body out of the light and stretched her arm as far as she could as she reached for his AK. Violating every safety rule she knew about firearms, she grabbed it by the barrel and pulled it toward her.

Careful to stay away from light, she worked her way over to al-Zahrani's tent. For the home of the leader of the world's most sophisticated and most wanted terrorist organization, al-Zahrani's tent was modest. It was also poorly guarded like everything else. Earlier in the evening she had noticed the two guards at its entrance, but security on the other sides seemed to have been ignored, aside from one small light illuminating the back. She followed the shadows as far as they would conceal her and she was about to dash into the lit area when she noticed the adjacent plywood structure with the satellite dishes and antennae—the al Qaeda home office. A few meters away from her was enough intelligence to roll up the organization's entire network—or at least severely damage al-Zahrani's faction.

She couldn't live with herself if she managed to escape from the tangos and didn't take a few extra minutes to pull off an intelligence coup—one that would make her a legend. Since they were on generator, they had to be using laptops. It wouldn't take her that long to grab a computer or two.

Ashland wasn't about to waste his time looking for the girl when he was so close to the mother lode of intelligence on SHANGRI-LA and al Qaeda. Since he looked like one of them, he was able to move quickly past the tents toward the fixed structure with the satellite dishes that they had seen in blow-ups of his photos.

If Paris only knew their agent that the CIA captured yesterday was now walking through the front door of al Qaeda's central administration. Soon enough the president of the republic himself would be hanging the National Order of Merit around his neck, Ashland was certain. He went inside, pulled on his night vision goggles and switched them on. The office was empty and he speculated that the terrorists were prohibited from sleeping in the headquarters, all the better for him.

He ignored the outer office since those areas were usually confined to low-level support staff and he ducked into the first private office he found to begin his collection. Binders filled one wall and he wished he could haul away a truckload, but instead he settled for yanking out every hard drive he could find. He flipped over a laptop and realized that even with a small screwdriver, he was looking at several minutes to remove the drive. He ripped the computer from its power cable and shoved it into his duffle bag along with his communications headset, then he went on to the next office.

In the al Qaeda offices Camille was reaching under a desk for a bag in which to carry the laptops when she heard the door open. Rolling under the desk, she aimed the Glock at the intruder. If he turned the lights on, she would have little choice but to shoot him, then run over to al-Zahrani's tent and give the bastard what he deserved before the whole camp swarmed her. She should've stuck with her primary mission objective like her father had tried so often to drum into her.

A rectangular hole was cut into the plywood wall, a makeshift window for ventilation. Enough light from al-Zahrani's security lamp came through it so that she could see the silhouette of a bearded male figure carrying a bulky bag. The interloper made little noise, moved over to the desk and set his bag on the floor beside her, but didn't seem to notice her. She heard him pull a binder from a shelf and flip it open. He could take hours studying the damn thing and she had to move on to her primary target. Camille shoved the Glock into her waistband and slid the knife from its sheath, preferring to eliminate him silently. Just as she reached out to slice his Achilles tendon, she heard Iggy's voice coming from the guy's bag. She had never heard such a welcome sound. She stopped and reached into the duffle bag. Her hand bumped into the headset's mouthpiece. In less than a second, her fingers oriented themselves and she put her thumb over the ear speaker in case there was more comm traffic while she was removing it. The intruder was probably part of a rescue team, but he could also be a tango who had killed an operator and stolen the comm set. He grabbed for the bag just as she jerked her hand back along with her prize. He stuck a laptop and some papers inside and hurried from the room, shutting the door behind him.

The moment she donned the headset, the compound went black. Camille smiled. She knew what the blackout meant:

Black Management has arrived.

Hunter hugged the shadows, searching the areas between the buildings for anyone moving quickly as he worked his way to the second generator. GENGHIS had already knocked out lights to the south portion of the camp. As he cut the generator's fuel intake line, he heard Iggy trying to get a response from Ashland, who was refusing to answer. The goddamn French spook had gone feral. He had known better than to trust the fucker. Within seconds of cutting the line, the generator fell silent and the lights went out.

Then Hunter heard over his comm set. "TIN MAN this is LIGHTNING SIX. Reporting for duty, sir."

Hunter's eyes teared up.

"Copy that, LIGHTNING SIX. Good to hear your voice," Iggy said smoothly. The man was a true professional. "What is your status and position?"

"Acquired comm from someone who appeared to be a tango. Is he yours?"

"One asset confirmed. Not responding to comm," Iggy said. "Repeat, what is your status and position?"

"Good. I'm in the office building. Fixed structure in the center of the compound with the satellite dishes."

Upon hearing that, Hunter spun around and rushed toward the building, all the while continuing to monitor the radio traffic.

"LIGHTNING SIX, egress building and proceed to your twelve o'clock to the edge. CHALK ONE will link up with you and escort to the LZ."

"Negative on the escort. Will link up with CHALK ONE, then proceed to neutralize HVT."

Hunter wondered what *High Value Target* Stella had discovered.

"Request identity HVT and location," Iggy said.

"JOURNEYMAN."

JOURNEYMAN—al-Zahrani's code name. Hunter was nearly as excited as he was that they had found Stella. They'd finally located the terror mastermind.

"Location, small tent in center of compound," Stella said.

"CHALK ONE this is TIN MAN. Link up with LIGHTNING SIX twenty meters to the twelve o'clock of the office structure. Proceed with LIGHTNING SIX to extract JOURNEYMAN."

"CHALK ONE this is LIGHTNING SIX. Belay that order. Link up, then proceed to neutralize JOURNEYMAN."

"CHALK ONE, this is TIN MAN. Order stands."

"TIN MAN, sorry, but I'm taking him out with or without help," Stella said.

"CHALK ONE, this is TIN MAN. Intercept LIGHTNING SIX and extract HVT. Dammit, LIGHTNING SIX. Standing orders are to take him alive. He's got invaluable intel. What's gotten into you?"

Hunter ran up to the building and raced inside, but didn't immediately see Stella. He kicked open an office door and Ashland whirled around, pointing a pistol at him; his other hand held a computer.

"Where is she?" Hunter said.

"Who?"

"GRACKLE—Camille Black, you idiot."

"How would I know?" Ashland said, shoving a laptop into his bag.

"She's using your comm."

"Impossible. It's here." Ashland reached into bag stuffed with laptops and rooted around.

Hunter looked around to check out his surroundings, and through a hole cut out for a window, he saw Stella. She was moving toward the smaller tent, the one she had described as al-Zahrani's. Without thinking, he vaulted the desk and sprung through the hole toward her. He landed hard because of the weight from the Claymore mines in his rucksack.

Camille thought she heard someone and jerked her head around, but it was so dark she could barely see. She had always been clear with Iggy whenever she was along on a mission, he was the commander. Technically, she wasn't on the mission, so she excused her insubordination as she moved ahead, treading lightly, trying not to step on a sleeping tango. Iggy was right that they should capture al-Zahrani, but she didn't care. All she wanted was to feel that knife pushing into his throat and ripping through the cartilage.

She heard footsteps, stopped and aimed the AK in that direction. Suddenly someone slapped his hand across her mouth. Reaching for her knife, she heard Hunter whisper into her ear.

"I love you. Walk with me."

He took her arm and led her away from the tent, toward the rim where the bench dropped off to the next one. She didn't resist. Tears of relief and joy rolled down her face. Hunter whispered into his mouthpiece. "TIN MAN, SABER TOOTH here. LIGHTNING SIX intercepted. Falling back to regroup."

Hunter said in a low voice, "Did you hear me? I said, I love you."

"Someone's behind us," Camille whispered back. "And I love you, too."

Hunter glanced around. "It's Ashland."

"Who?"

"A French spy. Long story."

Hunter stopped sixty meters away from the nearest structure and squatted down. He held her with one hand

and kept the other on his XM8. She wanted to kiss him more than anything, but she knew they couldn't let their guard down even for a moment. The French piece of *merde* had already proven he couldn't be trusted for security.

"You know we have to take al-Zahrani alive if we can. It's been a standing order with Force Zulu. Iggy's right."

"I know, I want the fucker dead anyway."

"What'd he do to you?"

Camille turned her head away while she fought back tears.

Hunter squeezed her close. "If he did anything to hurt you, I promise you, he'll suffer more if we take him back. Guaranteed. Slitting his throat is giving him the easy way out."

GENGHIS jogged up to them. Hunter continued to focus on her. "Are you with us or do I have to zip-tie you?"

Camille laughed.

"GENGHIS, stand guard for a minute," Hunter said, then he pushed up his NVG and rotated the mike away from his mouth. He pulled her to his lips.

For the brief moment while they kissed, she really did feel like she was in Shangri-la.

Iggy was going crazy, waiting. Even though they had Camille and the tangos hadn't yet figured out they had visitors, the op was taking too damn long. The helicopters were in holding positions and burning up several pounds of fuel every minute and now he was watching Stone and Camille lip-lock. Too much. He gave them five seconds, then keyed his radio. "CHALK ONE this is TIN MAN. Nautical twilight isn't far off. Get a move on."

Hunter heard Iggy's voice, but wanted to stretch the kiss, aware it might be their last. He forced himself to stop and pull away, unhooking from his belt webbing the extra

NVGs he'd carried. Without losing a moment, he pressed the NVGs into her hands.

"What's this?" Stella said, then laughed softly. "NVGs? You always knew how to give a girl what she needs." She pulled them on over her head.

"GENGHIS, Ashland. Get over here," Hunter said, just loud enough for them to hear.

They came over and squatted down.

"Approximately thirty to forty minutes ago, al-Zahrani was in that tent," Stella said. She pointed to where Hunter had grabbed her. "I have every reason to believe that he was getting ready to go to sleep there."

Stella spoke before Hunter could say anything. It was his team and she wasn't briefed on their capabilities. He was going to have a hard time keeping her from taking over. The woman loved to be on top.

"Any other intel we need to know before I distribute the orders?" Hunter said in his most professional voice.

"He had two guards in front of the tent. I saw no patrol. However, he has three barracks within thirty meters—two to the south at our two o'clock, one north at our ten o'clock. Everyone here is carrying an AK and tangos are sleeping on the ground everywhere."

"Thanks, Stella. Snake the tent." He removed a PAQ-4C infrared laser pointer from his belt and handed it to her. Hunter keyed his mike. "TIN MAN this is SABER TOOTH. Snaking the HVT's suspected location. Confirm IR signature of a single individual inside."

Stella turned on the infrared beam and shined it on al-Zahrani's tent, moving it in a figure eight. It was very bright to anyone wearing night vision equipment, but invisible to everyone else.

"SABER TOOTH this is TIN MAN. I see it. Steady."

She quit moving the pointer and held a constant beam on the target.

"SABER TOOTH, TIN MAN. Terminate snake."

She turned off the pointer.

A few seconds later, Iggy continued, "Confirmed. One body inside. Two outside at your twelve o'clock."

Taking off his pack, Hunter turned toward the group and said, "It's a go, then. GENGHIS, set up a line of Claymores in front of the barracks here, as planned." Hunter ran his finger through the sand, sketching a rough diagram of the camp so Stella could visualize it. "I figure GENGHIS will have two to three minutes while Stella and I grab al-Zahrani. Make certain that range fan is pointing south to the camp's six o'clock, our current three o'clock." The last thing they needed was for the danger zone to be inadvertently pointed toward them. "If there's noise and some unhappy campers come running out, I want to be ready to even the odds as fast as we can with the Claymores. If things go hot, Iggy will call in close air support and use his 240-Golf."

Hunter outlined how he and Stella would take out the guards, then snatch al-Zahrani and meet up. "If we use the Claymores, we'll go south through the weakened force to LZ-two. If everything stays quiet, it's LZ-one." He drew Xs in the sand to indicate the pick-up zones.

"What do you need me to do?" Ashland said.

"Find a weapon and if we start firing, don't hit us," Hunter said in a low voice. "And you better hang close and not go off on any more of your own missions if you want out of here. I won't leave a man behind, but you've made it clear you're not one of my men."

"Tell me what you need and I'll do it," Ashland said.

"Baby-sit al-Zahrani after we get him."

"Head's up," GENGHIS whispered. "Company."

A tango was walking toward them. He called out something. Before Hunter could do anything, Ashland responded in Arabic. "My brother's lost his wedding band. Come help us."

GENGHIS rose slowly and circled around behind the man, who didn't have their night-vision advantage. Hunter called out in Arabic. "I must find it, insh'allah. Izdihar will never forgive me."

GENGHIS flanked the tango. Stone and Ashland kept the man talking while he moved into position, slinking up behind him with his knife drawn. Placing his left hand on one side of the tango's head, he struck his temple with the grip of his knife as hard as he could, shocking the temporal artery into a quick death. The body fell limp in his hands and he let it drop to the ground.

One tango down, four hundred ninety-nine to go.

Against his better judgment, GENGHIS picked up the man's AK to give to Ashland.

A few minutes later, Camille crept up behind the guard she was assigned to neutralize. He was squatting on the ground, chewing something, probably qat to keep himself awake. She jabbed the knife in between the occipital bone and the first vertebrae, turned it, then pulled it out. Just as she was sticking it back into the sheath, she heard an AK fire, then another and another.

She heard GENGHIS say over the radio, "Taking fire."

GENGHIS didn't want to fire off and give away his position to the whole goddamn camp, but the shooters were getting close. Bullets were crackling on all sides of him. It was hard to hit someone on the ground, so he lay on his belly while he twisted the wires to the detonators, then inserted them into the Claymore and hooked up the firing device. Reaching around the mine, he ran his fingers across the metal face plate to make sure he could feel the raised letters, FRONT TOWARD ENEMY. His arm was starting to throb from the morning's bullet wound as he crawled on to the next position, dragging the combat packs with him and stringing wire to daisy chain as many mines together as he could.

More shooters joined in.

One more mine and he was out of there.

The gunfire was picking up and it was now coming from two sides. Hunter signaled Stella that he was going into the tent with a flash-bang grenade and he rolled it into the tent. He looked away until he heard the loud clap and saw the reflection of the bright burst, designed to stun and blind anyone inside. Then they rushed inside.

Al-Zahrani was on the ground in his bed reaching for a gun, but Stella knocked it away with her bare foot, then kicked him in the face. He shrieked like a girl.

Hunter rolled him over, shouting at him in Arabic as he smacked his combat boot down onto his back, pinning him down. He handed her a plastic tie and pulled al-Zahrani's arms together. She zip-tied his wrists as tightly as she could and restrained herself from breaking a thumb.

Bullets were ripping through the tent. They had to get out of there fast. Hunter took out a swath of duct tape and slapped it over al-Zahrani's mouth and pulled him to his feet. He didn't resist as they led him away. He thought it was strange not to offer resistance, but bin Laden had been the same way.

Ashland was waiting outside, lying on the ground. Hunter transferred al-Zahrani to his custody. Ashland pulled him down to the ground and gave him orders in Arabic.

Through the night vision equipment, Hunter could see dozens of tangos running toward their leader's tent, holding AKs at their sides. Their muzzle bursts flashed white and green tracers crisscrossed the raiding party. The morons were firing into the dark, risking friendly fire hitting al-Zahrani. They hit the ground and began firing in opposite directions.

Hundreds of tangos were swarming toward their position and GENGHIS was split off from them.

"TIN MAN this is SABER TOOTH. Request suppressive fire, your two o'clock. GENGHIS, SABER TOOTH. Fire whatever's ready and move to link up. Now!"

GENGHIS twisted the last wires together and crawled as fast as he could to the north, toward Stone's last known position. As soon as he felt resistance from the wires attached to the firing devices he was carrying, he stopped and keyed his mike. "CHALK ONE, GENGHIS. Fire in the hole."

Scores of tangos were about to overrun the Claymore line. GENGHIS dropped to his belly and pumped the firing device several times for good measure. The C-4 in the mines flashed, then sent fireballs into the air and a thousand steel balls hurtling toward the tangos. His ears were still ringing, but he could hear a crossfire of screams. He took his XM8 and pelted the tangos who'd overrun his line. Staying low, he searched for his teammates.

God, I love this job.

Through the machine gun's night vision scope Iggy could see tangos pouring from the barracks on all sides of his chalk's last known position, but he couldn't see them now that they needed him to take out the tangos. He had to get them to signal their location. "SABER TOOTH this is TIN MAN. Rope your position."

The tangos were coming as fast as Hunter could shoot. They'd be overrun if he paused to signal his position. "SABER TOOTH to TIN MAN. Busy here. Stand by."

"I got it. Slowing down on my side," Camille said as she removed the IR laser pointer from the soft case on Hunter's belt. Pointing it into the air, she turned it on and moved it in circles, until the lasso formed a cone of invisible light.

"SABER TOOTH this is TIN MAN. Contact. Terminate rope." Iggy aimed the machine gun and it roared. His NVGs refocused so fast that the glare of the muzzle burst hardly bothered him. He took out the tangos nearest his chalk, then moved his line away from them, sweeping toward the north. But the area was too wide and some were getting through.

GENGHIS heard the rapid chatter of the machine gun just as he spotted the cone of light and started to run toward it. The Claymores had knocked out dozens of tangos, but more were coming at them, shouting something about Allah as they ran and fired.

Crazy Mofos.

The rope stopped, but he could see the team. "CHALK ONE, GENGHIS. Approaching from your six o'clock. Hold fire."

GENGHIS slid in beside the boss lady and began firing. He yelled at Stone. "SABER TOOTH, they're pouring in from our six o'clock. You better call in the CAS."

"TIN MAN, SABER TOOTH here. Request CAS, our six o'clock. Stand by for position rope." Then Stone shouted. "Stella, rope, now!"

Iggy would've given anything for someone to work the machine gun. They were all stretched too thin. No commander should be gunning, playing forward air controller for close air support all the while commanding the battle. He had pushed ahead with no intel and with too few of resources because it was Camille and now the situation was going to hell fast. He keyed his mike as he continued to shoot, stopping only to speak.

"DRAGON ONE, TIN MAN. Cleared hot." Iggy approved

the helo to come in with guns blazing. He reached for his commander's pointer, turned it on and moved it in a figure eight on the target area. "Snaking target now."

"TIN MAN this is DRAGON ONE. CAS on station. Contact the mark. Steady. Coming in hot, fangs out."

"DRAGON ONE, TIN MAN here. Caution CHALK ONE roping on deck."

"Roger that."

Camille heard the whop, whop of the Cobra and saw it rise from the pit, its guns spitting fire. Hundreds of small explosions flashed and it sounded as if an entire minefield were exploding at once.

High Explosive Rounds.

The machine-gun fire started up again north of their position. She knew she should cover her head with her arms, but she couldn't resist watching. Then she saw a large figure run toward the firestorm.

Al-Zahrani. He'd escaped from Ashland.

Camille leapt up and dashed after him, keying her mike. "DRAGON ONE, LIGHTNING SIX. Break, break, break."

The Cobras continued firing, not recognizing her orders since she wasn't officially attached to the mission. Al-Zahrani was almost in their line of fire, which was moving toward them.

"DRAGON ONE, TIN MAN here. Break, break, break." Iggy's voice was as rapid-fire as the rounds coming at them.

She tackled al-Zahrani just as the explosions stopped, only meters away.

In seconds, her teammates joined her. "I'm not sure we can punch through to the pick-up zone," Camille said as she sat on al-Zahrani. Every time he started to wiggle, she pulled his head up by his hair and smacked it down into the sand.

Green and red tracers were flying everywhere in search of targets. Some of the tents were starting to burn from the Cobra attack, throwing off deadly light, leveling the playing field in the tangos' favor.

"We'll never make it," Camille said, shaking her head. "The tangos keep coming and they're going to see us any moment. It's too bright. Who's your pilot?"

"An Night Stalker named Beach Dog," Hunter said.

"You made my day." Camille keyed her radio. "BEACH DOG this is LIGHTNING SIX. Request extraction. Dude, come straight up the Pali and meet us at the top. Stand by for rope."

"LIGHTNING SIX, Beach Dog. Coming up the Pali, warp nine. I've got an extra package with me."

"What the hell was that?" Hunter said.

"An Hawaii thing. I'll take you there if we make it out of here." Camille rolled off al-Zahrani and jerked him to his feet. "Move out. Head to the edge."

They ran to the drop-off at the next level of the mine with GENGHIS and Hunter leapfrogging one another's positions, firing back at the tangos. The burning tents exposed their position and Camille hoped the IR pointer would be bright enough against the flames as she roped the beam.

The chop of rotors came from the pit in front of her and the Hawk rose from the depths, then hung directly off the ledge, nearly flush with the bench floor, but with a three-foot cleft between the crew door and the edge. Running toward the open door as fast as she could force al-Zahrani to move, she wasn't sure how she was going to get him to jump the gap. She kept running and leaped, giving him a fast choice: jump or plummet.

He jumped.

They landed on the metal floor. She immediately smacked him on the back of the head, knocking him out.

The Hawk's gunner mowed down the approaching tangos. Green tracers hit the fuel tank and sparks flew. She hoped the damn thing really was self-sealing. Ashland came out of nowhere and sprang aboard next, but Hunter and GENGHIS were still twenty meters away, providing cover for one another.

"TIN MAN this is LIGHTNING SIX. Recommend take the Cobra in hot after we egress."

"Copy that. Call it in at your discretion. Got that DRAGON ONE?"

"DRAGON ONE here. That's affirmative and welcome back LIGHTNING SIX."

Hunter reached the helicopter first and jumped inside, landing on al-Zahrani. He got up, reached out his hand and helped GENGHIS aboard.

"Beach Dog, pick up Iggy and get us the hell out of here." Camille keyed the mike. "DRAGON ONE, LIGHTNING SIX. Light up the fuckers."

EIGHTY-FIVE

In the United States, for instance, the executive branch hires contractors. Although the U.S. Congress approves the military budget, its access to information about contracts is often limited. The president can use this advantage to evade restrictions on U.S. actions, effectively limiting congressional checks on foreign policy. . . . Furthermore, contractors can facilitate foreign policy by proxy, allowing the government (or parts of it) to change events on the ground, but at a distance that allows for plausible deniability.

—FOREIGN POLICY, July/August 2004, as contributed by Professor Deborah Avant

41° 34' 34.96 N, 63° 07' 25.32 E (Uzbekistan)

Camille had heard the detailed account of the harrowing basket separation and she held her breath along with everyone else while Beach Dog pulled the Pave Hawk straight back, away from the MC-130. The basket released. She let out a sigh of relief and held onto Hunter while Beach Dog hot-dogged, surfing the wake, tossing the Hawk in sharp turns that knocked the passengers into one another. They were wedged in tightly, but Camille didn't mind sitting on Hunter's lap even though she knew she really shouldn't in front of GENGHIS, Beach Dog and Iggy. They would just have to deal with it. She wanted the safety and reassurance of the closeness. Her body was still revved from the constant adrenaline bombardment and as exhausted as she felt, she still couldn't relax. The happiness and relief of being with Hunter kept getting interrupted with flashbacks to the horror of al-Zahrani each time he groaned from the back row.

Al-Zahrani was lying on his side with his arms bound behind his back and shackled to his feet. Part of her wanted to take a blade to him, but she was so repulsed by him, she didn't want close contact. A couple of bullets through his forehead would have been cleaner. And she still felt dirty. She could hardly wait to get his smell and touch off her. Whenever they touched down in the Uzbek desert to refuel the Cobra, she planned on taking a dirt bath in the sand.

Memory of the rape smoldered inside. But she knew she couldn't tell Hunter. Iggy, maybe, but not Hunter. It would absolutely kill him to know what al-Zahrani had done to her. It would be even worse because he had gotten there only an hour too late to save her from him.

Packed in with everything else was a creeping sense of guilt from having killed her former mentor Joe Chronister. At the same time, part of her was glad she'd done it because of what he had done to Jackie and because of how he had sabotaged her dream.

Al-Zahrani cleared his throat loudly and everyone looked around. He and Ashland were crammed together onto the stretched nylon bench with no leg room due to the internal fuel tanks. Ashland looked miserable, hugging the door to put as much space as possible between them.

"That was quite the cluster fuck," al-Zahrani said with a perfect American accent.

Camille was shocked to hear him speaking English, let alone American English. He had given no indication of it earlier and the intel reports she had read on both him and Abdullah had been clear that neither of them spoke English.

"Depends on whose side you're on," Iggy said.

"I meant for our side. For the US," al-Zahrani said, craning his neck.

"What the fuck are you talking about?"

"You have to have a secure satellite uplink onboard,

don't you? Contact the DDO or the Director. Inform him you have NOC BARKER in your custody and you just compromised GOLD DRIFT."

"Holy mother of god," Iggy said, unbuckling his harness so he could turn around completely and get a good look at the guy.

"You can't believe this piece of shit," Camille said as she felt the helicopter descending to land and refuel.

Al-Zahrani smiled. "Maybe you know it as SHANGRI-LA. That's only the designation for the Rubicon op running us. The Agency program is called GOLD DRIFT."

"No one's calling anyone. We're handing him over to Force Zulu," Camille said. As far as she was concerned, he was Hunter's trophy. He had already been on the team that captured bin Laden and taking in al-Zahrani would make him a legend in the spec ops community. She could really get into the idea of dating a legend, almost as much as creating one.

"You can't do that," al-Zahrani said, his voice becoming alarmed. "The Pentagon will fuck it up even more than they already have."

"Ashland, shut the fucker up," Camille said, turning back toward the front of the helicopter.

"You do it. I'm not touching him."

"I got it," Iggy said as he took out his knife and sliced off the lower part of his 5.11s that covered up his dumb leg. Camille watched as he squeezed into the back and had to lean part of his weight on Ashland's lap.

Al-Zahrani jerked his head away as Iggy tried to gag him. "You dumb fucks. You destroyed the CIA's most successful counterterrorism operation against al Qaeda." Iggy stopped. "We might be able to salvage some of it, but not if you give it over to the wannabe spies at the Pentagon. They have the finesse of a rhino."

"Ah, I understand now. You're an *agent provocateur*,"

Ashland said with the arrogance of a professor. "Don't you see? It's not only Rubicon ensuring that the War-on-Terror industry doesn't extinguish itself by mopping up all the terrorists. The CIA's in with them, just like I suspected."

Al-Zahrani laughed. "You sound like some dumb-ass conspiracy theorist, like that Frenchman who claimed the US was behind 9/11. How in the world did bozos like you find us and manage to do so much damage?" Al-Zahrani shifted his weight and tried to get upright again. "We're running a false-flag op. Rubicon is the contractor running SHANGRI-LA. By outsourcing it, the president didn't have to inform Congress. There's also plausible deniability. A greedy company running a terrorist training camp would be a huge scandal, but not a White House scandal."

"Clever, but the Americans didn't invent that tactic," Ashland said, sounding more and more to her like a Frenchman. "The tsarist secret police used to set up fake Russian dissident groups among the émigrés in Paris."

Al-Zahrani cleared his throat. "We've succeeded in splitting al Qaeda between my faction and Abdullah's. I've recreated the succession problem after Mohammad's death that split Islam between the Shi'a and Sunni. I keep my followers focused on purity of the movement and that means the foremost duty of the faithful is wiping out Abdullah's heretics."

"Can someone please shut him up?" Camille said.

"Cam, I think he's got something," Iggy said as he moved back to his seat.

Al-Zahrani continued. "Training the tangos also allows us to keep tabs on who's who, where everyone is and to preempt any serious plots against the West. Not to mention the lousy training we gave them. Any time the Agency wants to send another mole into al Qaeda, all it has to do is have Rubicon drop them off at our doorstep and we take care of the rest. And then there are all the homegrown al

Qaeda-wannabe groups who turn to us for official endorsement and support."

"You've turned al Qaeda on itself. That's genius. It sure beats the Whack-A-Mole game we've been playing, taking out individual terrorists when they pop up," Iggy said, taking a deep breath.

Hunter chimed in. "I've seen it in action. Some of your followers in Iraq were trying to truck bomb a wedding of Abdullah's followers. Crazy SOBs, eating their young."

"It's working brilliantly—or it was until you fucked it up," al-Zahrani said.

"What was Chronister's role?" Iggy said.

"Joe? He's my inside officer and he was the project case officer for SHANGRI-LA and BALI HAI. He's also the contracting officer's technical rep for both contracts."

"What the hell's all that?" Hunter said.

Iggy turned toward Hunter. "It means he was this SOB's main contact and he ran the shows and controlled the purse strings on behalf of The Agency. Then Joe wasn't selling out the Agency for a retirement package with Rubicon?" Iggy said. "That was a hard one for me to believe."

"Are you kidding? The man's incorruptible—prickly, but clean. He kept Rubicon in line. Those bastards were cutting costs every chance they got. Joe was the only one who could break their balls and even then they got caught shipping us arms they seized from al Qaeda in Iraq. Stupid, greedy bastards."

"Oh my god," Camille whispered. Camille suddenly felt alarmed. She remembered her father telling her about the old Cold War days when the CIA used to run its own Marxist organizations so it would know which activists to keep an eye on. The Agency also kept the left constantly infighting this way. The FBI used to do it to anti-Vietnam groups and she vaguely recalled the British doing something similar in Kenya when they couldn't defeat the Mau

Mau tribesmen through conventional means. If the CIA were really running the al Qaeda faction and they had just destroyed the operation, Black Management was finished. They all were. It couldn't be the truth. "Are we really supposed to believe you would give your life to do this? This is bullshit, I tell you. This is bullshit."

"I was with the Bureau, getting ready to go undercover with a fundamentalist Islamic group in New Jersey because I was one of their few native Arabic speakers. My wife and kid had just flown in from Dearborn and we were celebrating my kid's birthday with brunch at the Windows on the World restaurant that day at the top of the Twin Towers. I got delayed."

"That's no excuse." Camille swung around and shouted, surprising herself.

"For what I did back there?" Al-Zahrani licked his lips. "Honey, you were the best lay I've had in years."

"You son of a bitch," Hunter shouted and nearly knocked Camille off his lap as he tried to get up.

"Later, Top." Iggy grabbed his arm as he blocked him. "GENGHIS, Cam, help me out."

Hunter pulled away from Iggy and swung around to get to al-Zahrani the other way. Fucking middle seat. He couldn't wait to tear into the bastard. GENGHIS jumped into his way and Stella grabbed his arm.

"Sit down. Now." The force in Stella's voice caught him off guard. "He's mine."

Hunter stood there for a moment, then without saying a word, sat back down and strapped in.

As he waited for the helicopter to land, all he could think about was what he had done to Jackie Nelson.

The Pave Hawk bounced slightly as it landed and the Cobra came in beside them, kicking up more desert. They waited in silence for the rotors to die down and for the sandstorm to settle. Camille sat there, trying to decide what to do. Everything she had worked for was collapsing in on itself. She wanted to pop al-Zahrani and leave the body in the desert for vermin to devour, but she knew if what he was claiming was true, he was too important to national security for that. With the Agency running an al Qaeda faction, she wasn't even so sure what national security meant anymore.

She wanted the fucker dead.

GENGHIS slid the door open. He held his hand out to help Camille from the bird.

They stood beside the Hawk stretching while the flight engineer ran a hose between the two helicopters for the fuel transfer.

"Stone, GENGHIS, I've got to make a call to the seventh floor at Langley and confirm that motherfucker's story," Iggy said as he punched a number into a satellite phone. "The refueling is going to take about ten minutes. Why don't you two take our passenger for a walk? Be careful. I want him alive and I don't want to get any hospitals involved; doctors, but not hospitals."

"No." Camille moved in front of Hunter, grabbing his sidearm and pointing it at al-Zahrani's head. "I said he's mine."

"Cam, don't do it. The boys will take care of him," Iggy said, as he lowered the phone. "He's too valuable. And you've got too much to lose."

"Not anymore." She flicked off the safety.

Hunter grabbed for the gun just as she fired.

Al-Zahrani dropped to the ground. Hunter put his hand on the gun and guided it so that it pointed away from them as he drew her close. She released it without resistance and collapsed into his arms.

GENGHIS walked over to al-Zahrani and kicked him in

the kidneys. "You pantywaist. It hardly grazed you. On your feet. We're going for a walk."

Several minutes later, GENGHIS and Hunter dragged al-Zahrani back, bloody and moaning. Camille wasn't surprised he was still conscious because they probably had wanted him to be aware of his pain. "Boys, why don't we let him relax his hands a bit?" Camille picked up a pair of bolt cutters from the engineer's toolbox.

She approached al-Zahrani from behind and moved the bolt cutters close to the zip-cuff binding his wrists. Then she whispered into al-Zahrani's ear. "An eye for an eye, you piece of shit." She shifted the bolt cutters and snapped off his right thumb. It snapped off with much less pressure than she had expected.

Al-Zahrani shrieked.

Without a word, she walked back to the toolbox, wiped off the blood with a rag and dropped the bolt cutters back inside the engineer's toolbox. "Thanks, chief."

They shoved al-Zahrani back into the helo, this time stuffing a gag over his mouth and a duffle bag over his head.

Everyone stood around while they waited for the engineer to finish the fuel transfer. Ashland smoked a cigarette closer to the aircraft than he should have.

"I made the call to Langley, said the magic words and they couldn't patch me through to the Director fast enough." Iggy shook his head. "The story checks out. The fucker's who he says he is. He's CIA. We just screwed the pooch. Black Management's going to be history. We had a good run, guys. It was fun."

"Hold on." Camille held up her hand. "I was thinking while they were on that walk. The camp's gone, but if the world believes al-Zahrani escaped, that would only add to his legend. I've got plenty to work with to save us. Black Management will come out on top. Trust me."

"I love it," Ashland said, holding the glowing cigarette at his side. "The Americans are running al Qaeda for a profit. Let me guess, now you're going to try to get a piece of the action. Wait until Paris learns about this."

"GENGHIS," Iggy said, inching closer to Ashland. "Why don't you take Monsieur Ashland for a walk?"

Ashland reached for his gun, but Iggy's artificial hand grabbed his forearm. Ashland yelped in pain. Camille knew his hydraulics could squeeze harder than his other hand ever could.

EIGHTY-SIX

"The CIA has the right to break any law, just not American. . . ."
—DIE ZEIT [HAMBURG], December 29, 2005, interview with Michael
    Scheuer, former CIA intelligence analyst

To Mr. Clarridge [a 33 year CIA operations veteran], "intelligence ethics" is "an oxymoron," he said. "It's not an issue. It never was and never will be, not if you want a real spy service." Spies operate under false names, lie about their jobs, and bribe or blackmail foreigners to betray their countries, he said. "If you don't want to do that," he added, "just have a State Department."
    —THE NEW YORK TIMES, January 28, 2006, as reported by Scott Shane

Black Management World Headquarters, McLean, Virginia
One Day Later

Camille had considered going to CIA headquarters in Langley for the meeting, but she preferred the subtle message it sent for the CIA's Director to come onto her turf, to the headquarters of Black Management. After a brief stopover at Black Management's Camp Obsidian in Afghanistan, Hunter had flown her and Iggy back to the States aboard the Rubicon Gulfstream, now outfitted with new livery and a fake registration number, the handiwork of Black Management mechanics. GENGHIS had stayed behind at Camp Obsidian to look after al-Zahrani. They had arrived only an hour ago and Camille was dying to be alone with Hunter, but circumstances had yet to permit it. Time was critical if she was going to save her company from the wrath of the Agency. After what felt like over seventy-two hours of constant motion, they sat at the black glass conference table with the panther design etched into it, waiting on CIA Director Doherty. Iggy was squarely on board with the plan, but Hunter had reservations. She knew he wouldn't cross her intentionally, but she doubted he would contribute much.

Her executive assistant showed Director Doherty in and Iggy started to introduce everyone when Doherty interrupted.

"Black, I'm shutting you down." He pointed at her, wagging his finger. The Irishman's face turned redder with each word. "This is the biggest setback in the War on Terror since the Pentagon botched our intel on Tora Bora. Maybe bigger."

"A lot of us have a very different take on Tora Bora, but we won't go there." Camille held her hand up, nervous as hell because so much was at stake, but appearing the cool and calm operator that she was. "It seems to me that without a presidential finding authorizing GOLD DRIFT, it's an illegal op. No way do I believe that you guys played by the book on this one and ran a presidential finding by Congressional leaders."

"Don't quote the Bible to me."

"What would happen if Congressional leaders found out the Agency's running an al Qaeda training camp? Or the media?" Camille said as she watched his face.

"You mean what would happen if they found out a subsidiary of Rubicon was running the camp. Don't you think we've already war-gamed media plans? Try this headline: HALLIBURTON'S EVIL TWIN RUNS TERROR, INC."

"We have a full confession from al-Zahrani. He seems to think the whole thing was hatched in the Vice President's office," Camille said, bluffing. The last time she had talked to GENGHIS, al-Zahrani was only semiconscious from a bad concussion.

"Al-Zahrani's confession is so easy to spin, we won't even need Fox News for that one. It would go something like, 'al-Zahrani's last desperate move against the US, trying to turn the American people against its government.' We've got them chasing their tails and killing each other off. Al-Zahrani is the ultimate counterterrorist weapon."

"And he's mine now," Camille said, pushing to the edge as she relied on instinct. She was too tired to think several steps ahead, as she usually did, and had to rely on the plan she and Iggy had come up with beforehand.

"Look, Black, this is the single most successful program we've ever had against al Qaeda. It's stopped dozens of attacks. How do you think we caught those London bombers who wanted to take out the planes over the Atlantic? They were a homegrown group of British Muslims, but eventually they reached out for al Qaeda's blessings—they all do. That's when we give them a little money, a slap on the back and take over operational control until we can be sure we've got everyone, then we roll it up. Christ, we're not fighting an organization anymore. Al Qaeda's a social movement and this is just about the only weapon we've got. We're all on the same side on this one. We've got to figure out how to pick up the pieces. Turn him over to us."

"Right, then you shut me down like you threatened. No deal."

Iggy smiled and leaned back in his chair as they had planned. "You know, Cam, I know you'd never run to the media or Congress. But what I was thinking, we hand al-Zahrani over to General Smillie at the Pentagon's SSB—you know, home of the super-spies of Force Zulu." Iggy chuckled. "I'm sure Smillie will know what to do with him. Like Director Doherty said, 'we're all on the same side.' "

Camille would never endanger a successful ongoing antiterrorist operation, but she also had to save herself and Black Management. She smiled as she sensed the shift in dynamics and felt their plan working. "The CIA's been battling the Pentagon for its very existence and the mili-

tary's winning. My guess is that first thing he'd do is run to
the President." She paused for a moment to let the implica-
tions sink in. "Mr. Doherty, how fast do you think you can
close up shop at the CIA and fold your operations and resources into the Pentagon?"

"Could never happen." The Director fidgeted in his
chair.

"Oh, yeah?" Iggy said. "What happened to the last two
CIA directors that crossed the Pentagon? Seems like
there's a word for those guys—*former* directors. Hate to
say it, but in the War on Terror, the Pentagon's the eight-
hundred-pound gorilla and at best you guys at Langley are
Lancelot Link: Secret Chimp."

Director Doherty rubbed his fingers together, swiveled
his seat around and stared out the window. Camille knew
she needed to keep cool, but it drove her crazy to wait on a
response. The man's face was impossible to read. The
back of his bald head was even worse.

Then Hunter opened his mouth to speak and Camille
cringed inside. Hunter was a warrior who liked to remain
above politics and he had made it clear that he didn't approve of playing one part of the government off against
another. "Sir." The Director kept looking out the window.
"You should know that I'm a member of the SSB's Force
Zulu—"

"I know."

"Sir, part of my orders when Zulu sent me to infiltrate
Rubicon were to report back any signs of CIA involvement with them. And you should also know, sir, we have
standing orders to report back any intel on any OGA black
ops we come across. Zulu is definitely keeping an eye on
the Agency."

"Keeping it in its crosshairs is more like it," Iggy said
with a grin.

"I'm aware of the SSB's unilateral operations." Director
Doherty swiveled his chair back toward the conference

table. Camille was almost trembling from fatigue and nerves. The Director cleared his throat and said, "I think we would all like to see this successful program continue. It seems our current contractor, Rubicon Solutions, has had some recent security lapses. Everyone at the Agency thinks very highly of Black Management. Is there any chance you would be interested in assuming Rubicon's training and recruitment contract?"

"It better be a sole source contract—I don't want to write another RFP ever again in my life," Camille said as she exchanged triumphant glances with Iggy. The outcome was looking better than they had imagined.

"We can run it through an existing Black Management training contract," Director Doherty said. "Seems you've got secret contracts channeled throughout several government agencies. I think Department of Education would be a fitting cover for this one."

Iggy scribbled figures on a legal pad, then looked up at the Director. "So what do you guys pay Rubicon to run the al-Zahrani organization? My back-of-the-napkin math says al-Zahrani's whole global operation probably has an annual operating budget of $70-80 million."

"Half that. Al Qaeda is a shoestring operation run out of caves and Web sites. And keep in mind thirty to forty percent of its operating budget is subsidized through Sunni Islamic charities. The Rubicon budget is only $10-15 million."

"Sweet," Iggy said. "Forty million dollars of influence for a $10 mil investment. I bet that keeps your budget guys happy. Though I have one question: would we be responsible for fund-raising and what happens if we raise surplus funds? Do we get to keep them?"

"A percentage. We can make it worth your while to divert anything you can from the real bad guys. Islamic charities throw around $200 million every year at terrorist groups. You won't have to run any telethons, that's for sure."

Camille turned her head and stifled a yawn before she

spoke. "We'll need additional start-up costs budgeted for the first year. And those numbers seem too low. I'm not sure you're factoring in the risk of not having a presidential finding. She felt the addictive rush of success waking her up. "I also want that prison contract—BALI HAI."

"That's a little more complicated."

"I'll develop the expertise. We'll buy up a corrections company stateside and cherry-pick their executives to run it."

"I'll look into it."

"Good, I'll get with my fiscal people to cost everything out and we can meet again tomorrow." Camille nodded, secretly hoping she hadn't overreached. She hated prisons, but she loved taking business away from Rubicon.

Hunter made eye contact with Camille. "Ms. Black, I need a word with you—in private." His voice was forceful, but not enough so to embarrass her in front of the Director. "Now."

"Gentlemen, I'll be back in a moment. In the meantime, you two can sketch out an understanding so we can get something worked out as fast as we can before anyone realizes al-Zahrani's AWOL. Contract transitions can be rough and I don't expect any assistance from your previous contractor." Camille followed Hunter outside the conference room and shut the door.

"Have you lost your mind? You can't run an al Qaeda terrorist camp," Hunter said, his voice tense, controlling anger she sensed underneath.

"It's all about hiring the right staff to pull it off. I have some old East German Stasi contacts who've run tango camps in Yemen. I'll bring them in for technical assist."

"That's not what I was talking about. We're becoming the terrorists in order to save ourselves from terrorism. That's not right. It wasn't right when Rubicon did it, it's not right if you do it."

"Maybe not, but so far it's effective. I love my country and I want to keep it safe."

"So do I. But not by becoming like them."

"Give me a break. We already torture, kidnap and kill in the name of national security and you know as well as I do, a lot of innocent civilians have been caught up in that system—because it is a system, it has to be fed and sometimes there aren't enough really bad guys to keep it going. And you know, I think it's worth it. It's kept the Homeland safe." She watched the tension in his face grow and his gaze become more distant. That scared her.

"You know, it's all starting to sound like one big, sick scam."

She slipped her arm around his waist. "Why don't you come help me? I need someone I can trust who's fluent in Arabic and who can keep an eye on things on the ground. We've got the Agency by the balls right now. I'll broker a deal that forces them to straighten things out for you with Force Zulu. They wouldn't like it, but they could do it. We could throw in an honorable discharge or maybe even another staged death. You could become Mr. White to my Ms. Black and we could—"

"I love you, but I can't. I live to track down and kill the bad guys, not train them."

"Are you sure you can still do that with the same gusto? From now on, every time you've got a tango in your sights, you'll be wondering if he's one of ours, if he's the guy who's going to take out the next set of hijackers because he's convinced they're al Qaeda dissidents." She could see the trouble in his face. She pulled him close and kissed him, taking her time, playing with his lower lip. "Join me."

Hunter pushed her away. "For god's sake, al-Zahrani raped you. How can you suddenly forget everything and become his puppet-master?"

"Believe me, I'll take him out and replace him as soon as we can. Doherty is low-balling me, but even so, with the prison contract thrown in, we're looking at over $100 million a year by the time I get through with it. That would sure pay for a lot of victim therapy, if that's what it takes to keep me sane until we can pop him. I can live with that. And I love it that we can skim off the top from Islamic charity terror tithes. That could really expand the margins."

"I love you. I really do."

"Honey, understand I have to start positioning the company for post-Iraq. We've been trying to break into serious Agency contracting, but so far we've only gotten scraps. Cofer is pulling in everything to Blackwater. Finally, I'm getting a plum."

"You're selling your soul. I can't," Hunter said as he turned and walked away.

"Wait! We've still got Rubicon's Gulfstream. What do you say we fly to the Ozarks for a few days together while you think about it?"

"There's nothing to think about," Hunter said and kept walking.

"That Gulfstream's got the range to take us to Hawaii. I did promise you. We could go swimming with sharks."

"You already are," he said without stopping.

"Stop! Please." She ran up to him and blocked him from getting on the elevator. "I love you. More than anyone or anything. I can't lose you now after all we've been through."

"Well, maybe you ought to get your priorities straight." His voice was cold and it hurt.

They looked each other in the eyes for several seconds without speaking. The worst part was that she knew he was right about the immorality of the contract. And deep down she also knew she couldn't lose him. Not again.

Camille blinked.

"I've boxed myself into a corner," Camille said, reaching out to his hand. "I guess I could sell my part of the company to Iggy."

"You can't do that. Just walk away from the deal."

"I can't screw Iggy over. Without some kind of an understanding with the Agency, Black Management is finished."

The elevator arrived with three men inside. They stared at them in silence as they waited for it to leave. It gave Camille a chance to try to figure out a solution. Several seconds later the elevator doors closed.

"You know, I just thought of something," Camille said as she let go of Hunter's hand and started to move back toward the conference room to see if he would follow. "There might be a problem with that contract."

"There are a lot of problems."

"Yeah, but this one could be a deal-breaker, one that could let me save face if I back out." She flashed him a conspiratorial smile. "I know you were one of the guys who caught bin Laden. I need you to tell me what you know about the joint CIA-Pentagon operation running him."

He took a deep breath and pursed his lips. "Stella."

"I'm pretty sure you're not read into the project, so you wouldn't be divulging any secrets you were officially entrusted with. Just tell me rumors."

"I don't believe the rumors. It's just wrong. The Agency bastards would kiss the devil's balls if that's what it took, but I can't imagine soldiers, stroking that fucker's ass, even if it meant neutralizing al Qaeda. You know it's the civilians in the Pentagon that brought us to this. Just watch. Some operator is going to blow him away; it's the only honorable thing to do. Hell, if I'd known what they were going to do with OBL, I would've taken him out myself when I had the chance."

"The rumors." Camille tugged his arm.

A few minutes later, Hunter returned to the conference room with Stella. He felt like a war was raging inside him;

the casualties were serious and the outcome still undetermined. Part of him wanted to get the hell out of there before things got more screwed up between them, but he was a warrior. And this time with Stella, he had to fight to the end.

Stella sat down with Hunter on her right side, Iggy on her left. Director Doherty was directly across from them. She looked him in the eyes and said, "I have one condition before I commit to the project."

Come on, Stella. Stick to the plan. Don't get greedy.

She continued, "Now I know that the Agency and the Pentagon have been holding bin Laden for years, running a joint covert op that put you two in control of al Qaeda, keeping its followers busy, constantly sending them on fool's errands—"

The Director raised his hand and interrupted. "Ms. Black, do you want the contract or not?"

Iggy shot her a quizzical look. She gave him a quick reassuring nod, then turned back to the CIA Director. "Hear me out. Al-Zahrani and Abdullah popped onto the scene a little over two years ago, fighting each other for control of al Qaeda. I can't help but notice that's around the same time that things really started heating up between the CIA and the Pentagon."

"Jesus," Iggy muttered under his breath. Hunter sat there, proud of her.

Stella took a deep breath and paused for an agonizing moment. "Before I take on the contract, I need to know that your joint bin Laden operation didn't break down. I want absolute assurance that Abdullah isn't the Pentagon's man."

The Director's face suddenly turned ashen and his jaw clenched. He paused for a few moments, then said, "I'll have to get back to you on that."

Hunter smiled as he listened to her and thought of

swimming together in Hawaii. Then she glanced at him with a familiar twinkle in her eye that made his gut clench.

"Don't misunderstand me." She continued speaking to Director Doherty, calculating inflated costs in her head. "The prison contract is a totally separate issue. I'm ready to move forward on that immediately. Just a rough estimate, but I figure you're running a surge capacity of one hundred, so with a three to one staffing ratio, each detainee will cost around fourteen-hundred dollars a day, plus transportation and—what's your term for the cost of bribing the local officials?"

"Host country fees," Iggy said. "A simple cost plus fixed-fee work order contract."

"And without start-up costs, we're realistically looking at around ninety-five million for a firm fixed-price contract. Interrogation costs would be extra, of course, unless you want to provide the service yourselves."

"Stella, what are you doing?" Hunter whispered.

She turned to him, her eyes glistening with excitement. He really did love watching her in action.

"You didn't say a word about secret prisons," she said. "And besides, we've got to have some way to pay for our Hawaii trip and your tooth implant. Not to mention your new Gulfstream."

Through selfless commitment and compassion for all people, Blackwater works to make a difference in the world and provide hope to those who still live in desperate times.

—Blackwater USA, LLC

THE FACTS BEHIND THE FICTION

During the Cold War, the battle lines were clear: soldiers were soldiers and spies were spies—and they all took home paychecks from one government or another. On the American side, the spies who gathered human intelligence were civilian employees of the CIA, lurking in the shadows of history, secretly breaking foreign laws to quietly manipulate international affairs to the American advantage. At the same time, the Pentagon controlled all soldiers who did the obvious things soldiers (and marines) do: they fought wars for their country. In only a few short years, the global War on Terror changed all of this: soldiers are now spies; spies are now soldiers and tens of thousands of both soldiers and spies work for private corporations, accountable only to their shareholders. Wars, both conventional and covert, have been outsourced.

In the aftermath of 9/11, a frightened nation dumped cash into the CIA, but Congress did not expand the number of full-time positions allotted to the Agency to keep pace with the funding increases, so the CIA turned to the private sector to swell its ranks. Companies were eager to pick up the new business and to meet the demand for intelligence professionals with requisite training and security clearances; after tapping into the pool of CIA retirees, they then turned to existing CIA personnel and used higher pay to lure away experienced midcareer officers into their ranks. These former CIA employees are frequently leased back to the CIA to perform their old jobs, with a higher salary for the individual and a large profit for the company. Recruitment within the Agency became so common that former CIA Director Goss intervened to stop companies from recruiting within the Agency's own cafeteria; new CIA contracts usually carry a clause prohibiting this practice. As a direct result of outsourcing, the Agency now faces a critical personnel shortage and it can no longer function without contracted personnel. *The number of contractors working for the CIA now outnumbers the Agency's own workforce.*

Positions that were formerly reserved for government personnel are regularly filled with private sector employees. Traditionally, tasks performed by contractors were for technical support, but increasingly critical functions in the CIA are now being handled by employees of private corporations. Outsourced jobs include "regional desk officers who control clandestine operations around the world; watch officers at the 24-hour crisis center; analysts who sift through reams of intelligence data; counterintelligence officers who oversee clandestine meetings between agency officers and their recruited spies; and reports officers who act as liaisons between officers in the field and analysts back at headquarters."[1] Up to 75 percent of the personnel at the CIA's Islamabad station work for private companies and contractors are often in the majority at the CIA's Baghdad station, where they regularly perform such traditional spy activities as recruiting and handling agents.[2] The outsourcing of the management of the black sites or secret CIA prisons is but the next progression. The intelligence industry has succeeded where few foreign governments have: private agents have infiltrated the CIA.

The highly secretive National Security Agency outsources over $2 billion of services annually.[3] Private

1. James Bramford, "This Spy for Rent," *The New York Times*, June 13, 2004; see also Walter Pincus, "Increase in Contracting Intelligence Jobs Raises Concerns," *The Washington Post*, March 20, 2006; and Tim Shorrock, "The Spy Who Billed Me," *Mother Jones*, January/February 2005.

2. Greg Miller, "Spy Agencies Outsourcing to Fill Key Jobs," *The Los Angeles Times*, September 17, 2006.

3. Robert Little, "Outsourcing at NSA boots Md., security," *The Baltimore Sun*, March 31, 2004.

industry provides the NSA with the equivalent of 5,000 additional full-time employees, boosting its civilian staffing by 30 percent. Contractors often work side by side with NSA staff, inside high security facilities.[4] Not only does the US government monitor some domestic calls and most domestic calling patterns, but so do private for-profit companies. Big Brother, Inc. is listening.

All US government intelligence agencies are now highly dependent upon the staff of private companies for critical national security positions, including the National Counterterrorism Center (NCTC). The NCTC was created in 2004 to serve as a hub for all government intelligence collection relating to terrorism and counterterrorism. It is one of the most influential government agencies because NCTC analysts are responsible for aggregating intelligence produced by sixteen government agencies and using this to prepare the daily National Terrorism Brief (NTB), a document that is appended to the Presidential Daily Brief.[5] The Presidential Daily Brief is a summary and analysis of national security issues warranting the President's immediate attention that the National Intelligence Director presents to the President each morning. According to a twenty-four-year CIA veteran who is a current intelligence contractor, "When I left the Hill over a year ago, a significant majority of the analysts assigned to the NCTC . . . were contractors."[6] Thanks to

4. Little, "Outsourcing at NSA."
5. Alfred Cumming, Specialist in Intelligence and National Security, Foreign Affairs, Defense and Trade Division of the Congressional Research Service, Memorandum to Senator Dianne Feinstein, "Congress as Consumer of Intelligence Information," December 14, 2005, http://feinstein.senate.gov/crs-intel.htm.
6. Dr. John Gannon, testimony before the United States Senate Committee on the Judiciary, May 2, 2006, http://judiciary.senate.gov/testimony.cfm?id=1858&wit_id=5282.

outsourcing, private, for-profit companies have the American president's ear on a daily basis and their words carry the weight of the combined intelligence agencies of the United States.

The extensive use of private, for-profit companies in critical intelligence positions raises a host of national security concerns and *The Washington Post* reported in March 2006 that the office of the Director of National Intelligence was reportedly studying the issue.[7] But in 2000 the Army was already concerned with potential dangers arising from the use of private contractors performing sensitive intelligence functions. That year the Assistant Secretary of the Army for Manpower and Reserve Affairs attempted to bar private contractors from performing intelligence functions, citing a risk to national security. He noted with caution, "Private contractors may be acquired by foreign interests, acquire and maintain interests in foreign countries, and provide support to foreign customers."[8] He also requested that the Army modify its field manual, *Contractors on the Battlefield*, to reflect this determination. Such requests by secretaries of the Army are usually honored, but in this case, when the new version of the manual was issued in 2003, the ban on private contractors performing intelligence functions was omitted. Ironically enough, the Army did not revise its own field manual for contractors, but rather outsourced the project to Military Professional Resources, Inc. (MPRI), a private military corporation that states on its own Web site that it serves the national security interests of "selected foreign

7. Walter Pincus, "Increase in Contracting Intelligence," *The Washington Post*, March 20, 2006.
8. Patrick T. Henry, Assistant Secretary of the Army (Manpower and Reserve Affairs), Memorandum to the Assistant Deputy Chief of Staff for Intelligence, through the Secretary of the Army and Director of Army Staff, "Intelligence Exemption," December 26, 2000.

governments."[9] In the Pentagon, private contractors write their own rules.

The Pentagon is the government's biggest fan of outsourcing, although actual figures of the true extent of private contracting are unknown, even to the Department of Defense.[10] Everything ranging from aircraft maintenance and prisoner interrogations to background checks for security clearances and ROTC programs at over 200 universities is handled by private firms. Also, 28 percent of all weapons systems are maintained by the private sector.[11] Even key aspects of the preparation of the defense budget itself are outsourced to a major defense contractor, Booz, Allen, Hamilton, as well as others.[12] With the Pentagon as its largest consumer, the private military business has grown into a $100 billion global industry.[13]

The Pentagon's use of private companies for intelligence functions has exploded in recent years. Private contractors make up 70 percent of the staff of the Pentagon's newest intelligence entity, the Counterintelligence Field Activity

9. The primary author of the new manual claims to have received little guidance from the Army other than initial basic guidelines. See Jonathan Were, "Contractors Write the Rules," Center for Public Integrity, June 30, 2004, http://www.publicintegrity.org/wow/report.aspx?aid=334. MPRI is now owned by Level-3 Communications, a publicly traded company listed on the New York Stock Exchange.

10. See Jason Peckenpaugh, "Army Contractor Count Stymied by Red Tape," *GovExec.com*, June 3, 2004, http://www.govexec.com/dailyfed/0604/060304p1.htm.

11. Barry Yeoman, "Soldiers of Good Fortune," *Mother Jones*, May/June 2003.

12. Ellen McCarthy, "Contractors' Budget Work Criticized," *The Washington Post*, June 30, 2004.

13. The size of the private intelligence industry is unknown. However, private companies reportedly receive one half of the $40 billion US intelligence budget. See Congressman David Price, "Intelligence Authorization Act of 2007," *Congressional Record*, April 26, 2006.

(CIFA).[14] CENTCOM, the military's unified command responsible for the Iraq and Afghan wars, now contracts out to Lockheed Martin's Information Technology-Professional Services division for human intelligence collection and analysis. At the time of this writing in June 2006, Lockheed Martin is advertising on an intel community job board for four intelligence support positions for CENTCOM. Three of the positions are seeking "HUMINT Collectors" with "strategic debriefing" training to work in Afghanistan. Translation: SPIES WANTED. [15]

Not only has spying been outsourced, but so has soldiering. Thanks to the Iraq war, the private military industry is booming. No one—not the Pentagon, not the CIA, not the Iraqi government—knows the exact number of contract soldiers in Iraq.[16] In 2005 many experts believed the figure to be around 25,000, but in April 2006 the Director of the Private Security Company Association in Iraq estimated that the number was somewhere over 48,000 heavily armed men and women.[17] One reporter who studied the issue in-depth

14. Walter Pincus, "Lawmakers Want More Data on Contracting Out Intelligence," *The Washington Post*, May 7, 2006.

15. See Intelligencecareers.com, Job Number 282513 IC Job ID: 49033; and Job Number 300220 IC Job ID: 118587. The "HUMINT Collector" positions in Afghanistan require a minimum education of a high school diploma, five years' experience and training as a "strategic debriefer" and it pays $70,000 to $90,000 per year with benefits.

16. Jenny Mandel, "Military Seeks Head Count of Contractors in Iraq," GovExec.com, May 19, 2006, http://www.govexec.com/dailyfed/0506/051906m1.htm; and Robert A. Burton, Associate Administrator, Office of Management and Budget, Office of Federal Procurement Policy, Memorandum for Chief Acquisitions Officers, Senior Procurement Executives, "Request Contracting Information on Contractors Operating in Iraq," May 16, 2006.

17. Statement of William Solis, *Rebuilding Iraq. Actions Still Needed to Improve the Use of Private Security Providers.* (Washington: GAO, June 2006).

wrote, "no one is really keeping track of all the businesses that provide squads of soldiers equipped with assault rifles and belt-fed light machine guns."[18] More than one in four Coalition soldiers in Iraq now works for a private company.[19] Private industry is the single largest coalition partner in the conflict, with private soldiers outnumbering all international coalition troops combined.

These contract soldiers guard VIPs, airports, pipelines, government buildings and even US military facilities. They regularly engage insurgents in firefights. They are often referred to as private security, but as one expert on private military wrote, "These are not private guards who stroll at the local shopping mall. They involve personnel with military skills and weapons who carry out military functions, within a war zone, against military-level threats."[20] They operate in a legal vacuum, outside of Iraqi and American law, the military's own Rules of Engagement as well as the Uniform Code of Military Justice.[21] However, they do have one clear rule: they are to provide defensive security only; they are not to engage in direct action or participate in offensive missions. Many question whether this rule is often ignored.[22]

Among these contract soldiers are former members of

18. Daniel Berger, "The Other Army," *The New York Times*, August 14, 2005.
19. In the summer of 2006, the US military had some 133,000 troops in Iraq.
20. Peter W. Singer, "Warriors for Hire in Iraq," Salon.com, April 15, 2004.
21. Peter W. Singer, "War, Profits and the Vacuum of Law: Privatized Military Firms and International Law," *Columbia Journal of Transnational Law*, Spring 2004.
22. T. Christian Miller, "The Torment of Col. Westhusing," *The Los Angeles Times*, November 27, 2005; see also "Military Ethicist's Suicide in Iraq Raises Questions," *All Things Considered*. NPR, November 28, 2006.

America's most highly trained counterterrorism units. Two companies in particular, Blackwater USA and Triple Canopy, were early specialists in providing tier-one operators—former SEALs, Delta Force and Recon Marines. These are the elite warriors who have carried out some of the most challenging and secretive military operations. They are the best of the best, the most highly trained soldiers in the world and collectively they are one of the most sophisticated and lethal weapons in the US arsenal. And they are now for rent.

In 2003 Triple Canopy explained its mission on its Web site, writing, "Triple Canopy provides legal, moral and ethical Special Operations services consistent with US National Security interests."[23] These private military corporations have secret contracts with multiple government agencies, reportedly with the Departments of Energy, State, and Defense as well as the CIA. Blackwater also has secret contracts with the Department of Homeland Security.[24] The president of Blackwater, who openly aspires to create the world's largest private army, once boasted that he has contracts that are so secret "he can't tell one federal agency about the business he's doing with another."[25] Private military corporations have privatized the fog of war, conveniently obscuring questionable activities from the light of public scrutiny.

23. The company has now replaced this with a more sanitized version, omitting mention of special operations and also excluding any mention of alignment with US interests. The version quoted can be found in the Internet archive at: http://web.archive.org/web/20040914020610/www.triplecanopy.com/company/mission.php.

24. In the aftermath of Hurricane Katrina, Blackwater sent 150 heavily armed soldiers to patrol the disaster area under contract with the Department of Homeland Security. Many were fresh from Iraq and others waiting for security clearance to go to Iraq. See Jeremy Scahill, "Blackwater Down," *The Nation*, October 10, 2005.

25. Yeoman, "Soldiers of Good Fortune."

* * *

Blackwater claims to be ready for any type of mission. At a conference in Amman, Jordan in early 2006, Cofer Black, the former director of the CIA's Counterterrorism Center and now the Vice Chairman of Blackwater, offered Blackwater's for-hire army to police global hotspots. "Black said, Blackwater could have a small, nimble, brigade-size force ready to move into a troubled region on short notice."[26] Blackwater recently announced plans to open jungle training facilities at Subic Bay in the Philippines and desert training facilities at an undisclosed site in Southern California. It's positioning itself for United Nations peacekeeping missions, and, according to its Web site, "Blackwater Mobile Security Teams stand ready to deploy around the world with little notice in support of US national security objectives, *private or foreign* interests [emphasis mine]."[27]

The Pentagon's most secretive and controversial spy unit has not been outsourced.[28] As part of Defense Secretary Rumsfeld's desire to stop "near total dependence on the CIA," he created a new espionage organization, planting military boots firmly in CIA turf.[29] Title 10 of the United States Code has traditionally been interpreted in such a way as to limit the collection of human intelligence in foreign countries to times of hostilities or when the threat of hostilities is imminent, but Pentagon lawyers have recently found a creative work-around for these restrictions

26. Bill Sizemore, "Blackwater USA Says It Can Supply Forces for Conflicts," *The Virginian-Pilot*, March 30, 2006.
27. http://www.blackwaterusa.com/securityconsulting/services.asp, June 7, 2006.
28. Seymour Hersh, "The Coming Wars. What the Pentagon Can Now Do in Secret," *The New Yorker*, January 24, 2005.
29. Barton Gellman, "Controversial Pentagon Espionage Unit Loses Its Leader," *The Washington Post*, February 13, 2005.

by defining the War on Terror as global and ongoing.[30] This cleared the way for military spies, GI Joe's 21st Century replacement: Bond. Master Sergeant Bond.

The new Pentagon spy agency, the Strategic Support Branch (SSB, portrayed as Force Zulu in this novel), is staffed with linguists, case officers, signals intelligence specialists, interrogators and, most strikingly, Special Forces operators, reportedly drawn from the military's most elite special units—Delta Force, former Gray Fox, and DEVGRU/SEAL Team 6.[31] The unit frequently changes its name and it fields spies throughout the world to gather human intelligence and to recruit foreign assets, functions that are the mainstay of CIA clandestine operations. It is active in both friendly and unfriendly countries,

30. Barton Gellman, "Secret Unit Expands Rumsfeld's Domain," *The Washington Post*, January 23, 2005. From the 1980s until the creation of the SSB, the Pentagon has maintained a small spy unit, sometimes known as Gray Fox, that worked within the confines of traditional legal interpretations of Title 10.

31. Gellman, "Secret Unit;" Thom Shanker and Scott Shane, "Elite Troops Get Expanded Role on Intelligence," *The New York Times*, March 8, 2006; and Barton Gellman, "Controversial Pentagon Espionage Unit Loses Its Leader," *The Washington Post*, February 13, 2005.

These espionage units are distinct from the equally highly classified teams of Special Forces operators that were created shortly after 9/11 to track down and eliminate high-level al Qaeda leaders. These hunter-killer teams, similar to the CIA's Phoenix program during the Vietnam War, frequently change their designations, but have been known as Task Force 20, 121, 5-25, 6-26 and 145 and have been implicated in abuse of prisoners. See Barton Gellman and R. Jeffery Smith, "Report to Defense Alleged Abuse by Prison Interrogation Teams," *The Washington Post*, December 8, 2004; Eric Schmitt and Carolyn Marshall, "Before and After Abu Ghraib, a US Unit Abused Detainees," *The New York Times*, March 19, 2006; and Brian Ross, "Secret US Task Force 145 Changes Its Name, Again," *The Blotter—ABC News*, June 12, 2006, http://blogs.abcnews.com/theblotter/2006/06/secret_us_task_.html.

operating outside of Congressional oversight, largely due to the diversion of funds approved for other programs and because of its claims that its activities do not strictly meet its own definition of covert actions. However, the new CIA Director General Hayden has noted the problem of overlapping missions between the CIA and the SSB. According to *The New York Times*, "General Hayden said it had become more difficult to distinguish between traditional secret intelligence missions carried out by the military and those by the CIA. 'There's a blurring of functions here.' "[32]

The Department of Defense running spy networks around the world signals a major shift toward the militarization of intelligence and challenges the very existence of the CIA. It's very probable that the shift in leadership at the Pentagon is a reprieve for the Agency and may even signal the end of unilateral covert actions by the Department of Defense.

With very little strategic planning, public debate, or Congressional oversight, American national security has been handed over to the private sector—to small loyal companies run by longtime US government veterans as well as to large multinational firms—corporations with international clientele, foreign ownership and with primary allegiance to their shareholders. With proper oversight, the private sector has consistently demonstrated its ability to deliver government services more effectively and more efficiently than the state, but we may be approaching the limits of government privatization as national security is put in question.

32. Eric Schmitt, "Clash Foreseen Between CIA and Pentagon," *The New York Times*, May 10, 2006. See also Alfred Cumming, Specialist in Intelligence and National Security, Foreign Affairs, Defense and Trade Division of the Congressional Research Service, *CRS Report for Congress. Covert Action: Legislative Background and Possible Policy Questions*, November 2, 2006.

War and espionage have been transformed in the twenty-first century as the government has scrambled to respond to an unconventional enemy. Soldiers are spies. Spies are soldiers. And the War on Terror has been outsourced.

GLOSSARY

240-Golf or 240G	a medium, belt-fed machine gun
4th Generation Warfare	conflict involving stateless ideologically-based actors using unconventional warfare techniques such as terrorism; the classic example is the global War on Terror
5.11s	reinforced tactical shirt and pants made by Royal Robbins, originally for mountain climbers, that feature many cargo pockets; the pants, an Under Armour T-shirt and a photographer's vest is the preferred uniform of most contract soldiers in Iraq
Abraxas	a private intelligence corporation that, among other services, creates and maintains nonofficial cover alias identities for case officers
adhan	call to prayer (Arabic)
the Agency	slang for the CIA
AK	AK-47; Soviet-designed assault rifle
AK-102	Russian-built short assault rifle; shorty AK
Allahu akbar	Allah is great (Arabic)
Anbar	province in western Iraq
Babylon	Iraq
backstop	to provide backup evidence for a cover identity
bingo	fuel state of an aircraft at which return-to-base must be initiated
black	secret, off-the-books; as in black ops, black units; opposite of white or unclassified
Black Hawk	UH-60 utility helicopter widely used for a variety of missions by US military
black site	a secret CIA prison outside US legal jurisdiction; see also rendition
Bushmen	nickname for members of Force Zulu
CAS	Close Air Support

case officer	CIA personnel responsible for recruiting and handling agents
chalk	designation for the troops making up an aircraft load for a specific mission
Christians In Action	slang for the CIA
Christmas tree	an airplane flying on a secret mission without lights flashes its red and green lights on and off for quick identification
Claymore	directional antipersonnel mine
click	one kilometer
collective	one of the primary helicopter controls that governs the pitch of the main rotors
Combat Talon	MC-130 special operations aircraft used by the CIA and military Special Forces for helicopter air-to-air refueling on deep penetration missions over hostile territory
comm	communications
Cougar	state-of-the-art blast-resistant troop transport
crawl, walk, run	mission rehearsal, usually using a sand table; a small terrain mock-up
cyclic	one of the primary helicopter controls that governs direction; similar in appearance to a large joystick
Delta Force	popular name for the Army's elite counter-terrorism unit (SFO-D)
Dragunov	Soviet-designed semiautomatic sniper rifle
ECM	Electronic Counter Measures
egress	exit, escape; opposite of ingress
EOD	Explosive Ordnance Disposal—bomb experts
flash-bang	grenade that emits a bright flash of light intended to temporarily blind and distract
FLIR	Forward Looking Infrared
Force Zulu	a deep-cover espionage and covert action unit that combines elements of espionage along with commando tactics; part of the

Pentagon's Strategic Support Branch (SSB); the real-life designation of the unit is highly classified and changes frequently; also referred to as Task Force Zulu

frag-o fragmented operations order; an on-the-fly order that answers the basic questions about the operation—who, what, where, when and how and sometimes why

ghillie suit sniper's camouflage outfit

green badger private contractor working for the CIA

Green Zone government district of downtown Baghdad protected from the rest of the city by eight miles of blast walls, razor wire, and armed guards

grid GPS coordinates

haji military slang for terrorist/insurgent; a Muslim who has made the pilgrimage to Mecca

halal permitted (Arabic)

haram forbidden (Arabic)

HE High Explosive

helo helicopter

hootch sleeping quarters

HVT High Value Target

IED Improvised Explosive Device

ingress entrance, approach; opposite of egress

insh'allah Allah willing (Arabic)

inside the bubble inside the Green Zone

inside the wire inside the camp

IR infrared

joker fuel state above "bingo" at which event termination must begin

JSOC Joint Special Operations Command, a branch of SOCOM specializing in counterterrorism that commands all Special Mission (SMU) or black units, including Delta Force, DEVGRU (former SEAL Team 6), the various incarnations of Task Force(s) 11, 20, 121, 5-25, 6-26, 145, etc.

KIA	Killed in Action
Langley	slang for the CIA because of its headquarters in Langley, Virginia
legend	cover identity
LIGHTNING SIX	Stella/Camille Black's call sign
Little Bird	AH-6 helicopter; a light, high-performance assault helicopter often used by Special Forces
LZ	Landing Zone
M4	short assault rifle
mag	magazine; a container with multiple rounds of ammunition to be fed into a gun
masha'allah	Allah's will (Arabic)
MC-130	Combat Talon, a C-130 variant operated by the Air Force and rented by the CIA and Special Forces for air-to-air refueling as well as infiltration, exfiltration and resupply of Special Forces troops
merc	mercenary
MI6	British foreign intelligence service; also known as SIS
Mi-8	Soviet-designed, Russian-built helicopter, NATO code-named Hip
MRE	Meals, Ready-to-Eat—combat rations
muj	slang for mujahedin/terrorists
mut'a	temporary marriage (Arabic)
Night Stalker	Army Special Operations helicopter regiment specializing in nighttime and adverse conditions in support of Army Special Operations
NOC	Nonofficial cover; the most secretive type of CIA case officer operating without the protection of an official cover
NVG	Night Vision Goggles
OBL	Osama bin Laden; CIA usage is UBL
OGA	Other Government Agency—military slang for the CIA

on deck	on the ground; on site
operative	a clandestine agent, spy
operator	a highly trained, Special Forces counter-terrorism soldier
opsec	operational security
overheads	satellite images
overwatch	security; a position responsible for providing operational security and keeping track of the key players; also called tertiary position or guardian angel
Pave Hawk	medium-sized utility helicopter; Special Forces variant of a Black Hawk
Pave Low	large-sized utility helicopter; Special Forces variant of a Super Jolly Green Giant
quasi-personal	something that is issued to a cover operative as an accessory to an alias to make it seem more realistic
plastic tie	plastic electricians' ties used as handcuffs
PT	physical training; exercises
rack	slang for bed
read into	to have official knowledge of a secret project
recon	reconnaissance
rendition	the CIA system of kidnapping suspected terrorists anywhere outside the US and taking them on secret flights for interrogation and torture in either a select Third World country or a secret CIA prison ("black site") outside US legal jurisdiction
ROE	Rules of Engagement
RPG	rocket propelled grenade
Saber Tooth	Hunter Stone's call sign
Semper Fi	short for "Semper Fidelis" (Always Faithful), the motto of the Marine Corps
SERE training	Survival, Evasion, Resistance and Escape training
sigint	signals intelligence—electronic intercepts
SIS	Secret Intelligence Service; British foreign intelligence, also known as MI6

sitrep	situation report
SMEAC	Situation, Mission, Execution, Admin & logistic, Command & signal
SOCOM	Special Operations Command, oversees Special Operations commands of all branches of the military
SOCOM pistol	Heckler & Koch Mark .23 offensive pistol developed for US Special Operations forces; many operators prefer the slightly smaller and less awkward civilian version, the USP Tactical
SOP	Standard Operating Procedure
souk	market, bazaar (Arabic)
spec ops	Special Operations
SSB	Strategic Support Branch, the Pentagon's new spy organization responsible for black units of Special Forces operators specially trained to collect human intelligence and run covert actions; the agency responsible for Force Zulu
tango	slang for terrorist
tier-one operator	the military's most highly trained combatants; DEVGRU SEALs, Delta Force and Recon Marines
TIN MAN	Manuel "Iggy" Ignatius' call sign (Black Management's Chief of Operations)
USP Tactical	Heckler & Koch offensive sidearm, smaller version of the SOCOM USP
webbing	a lacing system on vests, belts and body armor that allows attachment of pockets and pouches for ammunition, grenades, first aid kit, radio, canteen, etc.
wet job	assassination, hit
wingman	pilot who flies beside and behind the lead aircraft, providing support and protection
XM8	experimental Heckler & Koch assault rifle, designed to replace the M4 and M16
zip-tie	flex-cuff; plastic restraints similar to electricians' ties

ABOUT THE AUTHOR

R J Hillhouse has run Cuban rum between East and West Berlin, smuggled jewels from the Soviet Union, and slipped through some of the world's tightest borders. From Uzbekistan to Romania, she's been followed, held at gunpoint and interrogated. Foreign governments have solicited her for recruitment as a spy. (They failed.) The *St. Louis Post-Dispatch* wrote that "she's truly like James Bond and Indiana Jones all rolled into one."

A former professor and Fulbright fellow, she earned her Ph.D. in political science at the University of Michigan. She is fluent in several languages. An expert on international affairs and national security, she has published in major academic journals and has lectured at such diverse institutions as Harvard, the Smithsonian, and the Soviet Academy of Sciences. Her work on outsourcing has appeared in *The New York Times*, *The Washington Post*, *The Nation*, and others.

She lives in Hawaii, on the slopes of Mauna Loa volcano. She blogs about the outsourcing of national security at www.TheSpyWhoBilledMe.com.